I0555590

Johnny Ludlow by Mrs Henry Wood

The Fifth Series

Ellen Price was born on 17th January 1814 in Worcester.

In 1836 she married Henry Wood, whose career in banking and shipping meant living in Dauphiné, in the South of France, for two decades. During their time there they had four children.

Henry's business collapsed and he and Ellen together with their four children returned to England and settled in Upper Norwood near London.

Ellen now turned to writing and with her second book 'East Lynne' enjoyed remarkable popularity. This enabled her to support her family and to maintain a literary career.

It was a career in which she would write over 30 novels including 'Danesbury House', 'Oswald Cray', 'Mrs. Halliburton's Troubles', 'The Channings' and 'The Shadow of Ashlydyat'.

Sadly, her husband, Henry died in 1866.

Ellen though continued to strive on. In 1867, she purchased the magazine 'Argosy', founded two years previously by Alexander Strahan. She was a prolific writer and wrote much of the magazine herself although she had some very respected contributors, amongst them Hesba Stretton and Christina Rossetti. Although she would gradually pare down writing for the magazine she continued to write novel after novel. Such was her talent that for a time she was, in Australia, more popular than Charles Dickens.

Apart from novels she was an excellent translator and a writer of short stories. 'Reality or Delusion?' is a staple of supernatural anthologies to this day.

Ellen Wood died of bronchitis on 10th February 1887. He estate was valued at a very considerable £36,000.

She is buried in Highgate Cemetery, London.

A monument to her in Worcester Cathedral was unveiled in 1916.

Index of Contents

FEATHERSTON'S STORY

I

I have called this Featherston's story, because it was through him that I heard about it—and, indeed, saw a little of it towards the end.

Buttermead, the wide straggling district to which Featherston enjoyed the honour of being doctor-in-ordinary, was as rural as any that can be found in Worcestershire. Featherston's house stood at the end of the village. Whitney Hall lay close by; as did our school, Dr. Frost's. In the neighbourhood were scattered a few other substantial residences, some farmers' homesteads and labourers' cottages. Featherston was a slim man, with long thin legs and a face grey and careworn. His patients (like the soldier's steam arm) gave him no rest day or night.

There is no need to go into details here about Featherston's people. His sister, Mary Ann, lived in his house at one time, and for everyday ailments was almost as good a doctor as he. She was not at all like him: a merry, talkative, sociable little woman, with black hair and quick, kindly dark eyes.

Our resident French master in those days at Dr. Frost's was one Monsieur Jules Carimon: a small man with honest blue eyes in his clean-shaven face, and light brown hair cropped close to his head. He was an awful martinet at study, but a genial little gentleman out of it. To the surprise of Buttermead, he and Mary Featherston set up a courtship. It was carried on in sober fashion, as befitted a sober couple who had both left thirty years, and the rest, behind them; and after a summer or two of it they laid plans for their marriage and for living in France.

"I'm sure I don't know what on earth I shall do amongst the French, Johnny Ludlow," Mary said to me in her laughing way, when I and Bill Whitney were having tea at Featherston's one half-holiday, the week before the wedding. "Jules protests they are easier to get on with than the English; not so stiff and formal; but I don't pay attention to all he says, you know."

Monsieur Jules Carimon was going to settle down at his native place, Sainteville—a town on the opposite coast, which had a service of English steamers running to it two or three times a-week. He had obtained the post of first classical master at the college there, and meant to eke out his salary (never large in French colleges) by teaching French and mathematics to as many English pupils as he could obtain out of hours. Like other northern French seaport towns, Sainteville had its small colony of British residents.

"We shall get on; I am not afraid," answered Mary Featherston to a doubting remark made to her by old Mrs. Selby of the Court. "Neither I nor Jules have been accustomed to luxury, and we don't care for it. We would as soon make our dinner of bread-and-butter and radishes, as of chicken and apple-tart."

So the wedding took place, and they departed the same day for Sainteville. And of the first two or three years after that there's nothing good or bad to record.

Selby Court lay just outside Buttermead. Its mistress, an ancient lady now, was related to the Preen family, of whom I spoke in that story which told of the tragic death of Oliver. Lavinia Preen, sister to

Oliver's father, Gervase Preen, but younger, lived with Mrs. Selby as a sort of adopted daughter; and when the death of the father, old Mr. Preen, left nearly all his large family with scarcely any cheese to their bread, Mrs. Selby told Ann Preen, the youngest of them all, that she might come to her also. So Lavinia and Ann Preen lived at the Court, and had no other home.

These two ladies were intimate with Mary Featherston, all three being much attached to one another. When Mary married and left her country for France, the Miss Preens openly resented it, saying she ought to have had more consideration. Did some premonitory instinct prompt that unreasonable resentment? I cannot say. No one can say. But it is certain that had Mary Featherston not gone to live abroad, the ominous chain of events fated to engulf the sisters could not have touched them, and this account, which is a perfectly true one, would never have been written.

For a short time after the marriage they and Mary Carimon exchanged a letter now and then; not often, for foreign postage was expensive; and then it dropped altogether.

Mrs. Selby became an invalid, and died. She left each of the two sisters seventy pounds a-year for life; if the one died, the other was to enjoy the whole; when both were dead, it would lapse back to the Selby estate.

"Seventy pounds a-year!" remarked Ann Preen to her sister. "It does not seem very much, does it, Lavinia? Shall we be able to live upon it?"

They were seated in the wainscoted parlour at Selby Court, talking of the future. The funeral was over, and they must soon leave; for the house was waiting to be done up for the reception of its new master, Mr. Paul Selby, an old bachelor full of nervous fancies.

"We must live upon it, Nancy," said Lavinia in answer to her.

She was the stronger-minded of the two, and she looked it. A keen, practical woman, of rather more than middle height, with smooth brown hair, pleasant, dark hazel eyes, and a bright glow in her cheeks. Ann (or Nancy, as she was more often called) was smaller and lighter, with a pretty face, a shower of fair ringlets, and mild, light-blue eyes; altogether not unlike a pink-and-white wax doll.

"We should have been worse off, Nancy, had she not left us anything; and sometimes I have feared she might not," remarked Lavinia cheerfully. "It will be a hundred and forty pounds between us, dear; we can live upon that."

"Of course we can, if you think so, Lavinia," said the other, who deemed her elder sister wiser than any one in the world, and revered her accordingly.

"But we should live cheaper abroad than here, I expect," continued Lavinia. "It's said money goes twice as far in France as in England. Suppose we were to go over, Nancy, and try? We could come back if we did not like it."

Nancy's eyes sparkled. "I think it would be delightful," she said. "Money go further in France—why, to be sure it does! Aunt Emily is able to live like a princess at Tours, by all accounts. Yes, yes, Lavinia, let us try France!"

One fine spring morning the Miss Preens packed up their bag and baggage and started for the Continent. They went direct to Tours, intending to make that place their pied-à-terre, as the French phrase it; at any rate, for a time. It was not, perhaps, the wisest thing they could have done.

For Mrs. Magnus, formerly Emily Preen, and their late father's sister, did not welcome them warmly. She lived in style herself, one of the leading stars in the society of Tours; and she did not at all like that two middle-aged nieces, of straitened means, should take up their abode in the next street. So Mrs. Magnus met her nieces with the assurance that Tours would not do for them; it was too expensive a place; they would be swamped in it. Mrs. Magnus was drawing near to the close of her life then; had she known it, she might have been kinder, and let them remain; but she was not able to foresee the hour of that great event which must happen to us all any more than other people are. Oliver Preen was with her then, revelling in the sunny days which were flitting away on gossamer wings.

"Lavinia, do you think we can stay at Tours?"

The Miss Preens had descended at a fourth-rate hotel, picked out of the guide-book. When Ann asked this question, they were sitting after dinner in the table d'hôte room, their feet on the sanded floor. Sanded floors were quite usual at that time in many parts of France.

"Stay here to put up with Aunt Emily's pride and insolence!" quickly answered Miss Preen. "No. I will tell you what I have done, Ann. I wrote yesterday to Mary Carimon, asking her about Sainteville; whether she thinks it will suit us, and so on. As soon as her answer comes—she's certain to say yes—we will go, dear, and leave Mrs. Magnus to her grandeur. And, once we are safe away, I shall write her a letter," added Lavinia, in decisive tones; "a letter which she won't like."

Madame Carimon's answer came by return of post. It was as cordial as herself. Sainteville would be the very place for them, she said, and she should count the hours until they were there.

The Miss Preens turned their backs upon Tours, shaking its dust off their shoes. Lavinia had a little nest of accumulated money, so was at ease in that respect. And when the evening of the following day the railway terminus at Sainteville was reached, the pleasant, smiling face of Mary Carimon was the first they saw outside the barrière. She must have been nearly forty now, but she did not look a day older than when she had left Buttermead. Miss Lavinia was a year or two older than Mary; Miss Ann a year or two younger.

"You must put up at the Hôtel des Princes," remarked Madame Carimon. "It is the only really good one in the town. They won't charge you too much; my husband has spoken to the landlady. And you must spend to-morrow with me."

The hotel omnibus was waiting for them and other passengers, the luggage was piled on the roof, and Madame Carimon accompanied them to the hotel. A handsome hotel, the sisters thought; quite another thing from the one at Tours. Mary Carimon introduced them to the landlady, Madame Podevin, saw them seated down to tea and a cold fowl, and then left for the night.

With Sainteville the Miss Preens were simply charmed. It was a fresh, clean town, with wide streets, and good houses and old families, and some bright shops. The harbour was large, and the pier extended out to the open sea.

"I should like to live here!" exclaimed Miss Lavinia, sitting down at Madame Carimon's, in a state of rapture. "I never saw such a nice town, or such a lovely market."

They had been about all the morning with Madame Carimon. It was market-day, Wednesday. The market was held on the Grande Place; and the delicious butter, the eggs, the fresh vegetables, the flowers and the poultry, took Miss Lavinia's heart by storm. Nancy was more taken with the picturesque market-women, in their white caps and long gold ear-rings. Other ladies were doing their marketing as well as Madame Carimon. She spoke to most of them, in French or in English, as the case might be. Under the able tuition of her husband, she talked French fluently now.

Madame Carimon's habitation—very nice, small and compact—was in the Rue Pomme Cuite. The streets have queer names in some of these old French towns. It was near the college, which was convenient for Monsieur Carimon. Here they lived, with their elderly servant, Pauline. The same routine went on daily in the steady little domicile from year's end to year's end.

"Jules goes to the college at eight o'clock every week-day, after a cup of coffee and a petit pain," said madame to her guests, "and he returns at five to dinner. He takes his déjeûner in the college at twelve, and I take mine alone at home. On Sundays he has no duty: we attend the French Protestant Church in a morning, dine at one o'clock, and go for a walk in the afternoon."

"You have no children, Mary?"

Mary Carimon's lively face turned sad as she answered: "There was one little one; she stayed with us six months, and then God took her. I wrote to you of it, you know, Lavinia. No, we have not any children. Best not, Jules says; and I agree with him. They might only leave us when we have learnt to love them; and that's a trial hard to bear. Best as it is."

"I'm sure I should never learn to speak French, though we lived here for a century," exclaimed Miss Lavinia. "Only to hear you jabbering to your servant, Mary, quite distracts one's ears."

"Yes, you would. You would soon pick up enough to be understood in the shops and at market."

At five o'clock, home came Monsieur Carimon. He welcomed the Miss Preens with honest, genuine pleasure, interspersed with a little French ceremony; making them about a dozen bows apiece before he met the hands held out to him.

They had quite a gala dinner. Soup to begin with—broth, the English ladies inwardly pronounced it—and then fish. A small cod, bought by Madame Carimon at the fish-market in the morning, with oyster sauce. Ten sous she had given for the cod, for she knew how to bargain now, and six sous for a dozen oysters, as large as a five-franc piece. This was followed by a delicious little fricandeau of veal, and that by a tarte à la crême from the pastrycook's. She told her guests unreservedly what all the dishes cost, to show them how reasonably people might live at Sainteville.

Over the coffee, after dinner, the question of their settling in the place was fully gone into, for the benefit of Monsieur Carimon's opinions, who gave them in good English.

"Depend upon it, Lavinia, you could not do better," remarked Mary Carimon. "If you cannot make your income do here, you cannot anywhere."

"We want to make it do well; not to betray our poverty, but to be able to maintain a fairly good appearance," said Lavinia. "You understand me, I am sure, monsieur."

"But certainly, mademoiselle," he answered; "it is what we all like to do at Sainteville, I reckon."

"And can do, if we are provident," added madame. "French ways are not English ways. Our own income is small, Lavinia, yet we put by out of it."

"A fact that goes without saying," confirmed the pleasant little man. "If we did not put by, where would my wife be when I am no longer able to work?"

"Provisions being so cheap— What did you say, Nancy?" asked Madame Carimon, interrupting herself.

"I was going to say that I could live upon oysters, and should like to," replied Nancy, shaking back her flaxen curls with a laugh. "Half-a-dozen of those great big oysters would make me a lovely dinner any day—and the cost would be only three halfpence."

"And only fivepence the cost of that beautiful fish," put in her sister. "In Sainteville our income would amply suffice."

"It seems to me that it would, mesdemoiselles," observed Monsieur Carimon. "Three thousand five hundred francs yearly! We French should think it a sufficient sum. Doubtless much would depend upon the way in which you laid it out."

"What should we have to pay for lodgings, Mary?" inquired Lavinia. "Just a nice sitting-room and two small bedrooms; or a large room with two beds in it; and to be waited on?"

"Oh, you won't find that at Sainteville," was the unexpected answer. "Nobody lets lodgings English fashion: it's not the custom over here. You can find a furnished apartment, but the people will not wait upon you. There is always a little kitchen let with the rooms, and you must have your own servant."

It was the first check the ladies had received. They sat thinking. "Dear me!" exclaimed Nancy. "No lodgings!"

"Would the apartments you speak of be very dear?" asked Lavinia.

"That depends upon the number of rooms and the situation," replied Madame Carimon. "I cannot call to mind just now any small apartment that is vacant. If you like, we will go to-morrow and look about."

It was so arranged. And little Monsieur Carimon attended the ladies back to the Hôtel des Princes at the sober hour of nine, and bowed them into the porte cochère with two sweeps of his hat, wishing them the good-evening and the very good-night.

Thursday morning. Nancy Preen awoke with a sick headache, and could not get up. But in the afternoon, when she was better, they went to Mary Carimon's, and all three set out to look for an apartment—not meeting with great success.

All they saw were too large, and priced accordingly. There was one, indeed, in the Rue Lamartine, which suited as to size, but the rooms were inconvenient and stuffy; and there was another small one on the Grande Place, dainty and desirable, but the rent was very high. Madame Carimon at once offered the landlord half-price, French custom: she dealt at his shop for her groceries. No, no, he answered; his apartment was the nicest in the town for its size, as mesdames saw, and it was in the best situation—and not a single sou would the worthy grocer abate.

They were growing tired, then; and five o'clock, the universal hour at Sainteville for dinner, was approaching.

"Come round to me after dinner, and we will talk it over," said Mary Carimon, when they parted. "I will give you a cup of tea."

They dined at the table d'hôte, which both of them thought charming, and then proceeded to the Rue Pomme Cuite. Monsieur Carimon was on the point of going out, to spend an hour at the Café Pillaud, but he put down his hat to wait awhile, out of respect to the ladies. They told him about not having found an apartment to suit them.

"Of course we have not searched all parts of the town, only the most likely ones," said Madame Carimon. "There are large apartments to be had, but no small ones. We can search again to-morrow."

"I suppose there's not a little house to be had cheap, if we cannot find an apartment?" cried Miss Nancy, who was in love with Sainteville, and had set her heart upon remaining there.

"Tiens," quickly spoke Monsieur Carimon in French to his wife, "there's the Petite Maison Rouge belonging to Madame Veuve Sauvage, in the Place Ronde. It is still to let: I saw the affiche in the shop window to-day. What do you think of it, Marie?"

Madame Carimon did not seem to know quite what to think. She looked at her husband, then at the eager faces of her two friends; but she did not speak.

About half-way down the Rue Tessin, a busy street leading to the port, was a wide opening, giving on to the Place Ronde. The Place Ronde agreed with its name, for it was somewhat in form of a horseshoe. Some fifteen or sixteen substantial houses were built round it, each having a shop for its basement; and trees, green and feathery, were scattered about, affording a slight though pleasant shelter from the hot sun in summer weather.

The middle house at the bottom of the Place Ronde, exactly facing the opening from the Rue Tessin, was a very conspicuous house indeed, inasmuch as it was painted red, whilst the other houses were white. All of them had green persienne shutters to the upper windows. The shop, a large one, belonging to this red house was that of the late Monsieur Jean Sauvage, "Marchand de Vin en gros et en détail," as the announcement over his door used to run in the later years of his life. But when Jean Sauvage commenced business, in that same shop, it was only as a retail vendor. Casting about in his mind one day for some means by which his shop might be distinguished from other wine-shops and attract customers, he hit upon the plan of painting the house red. No sooner thought of than done. A painter was called, who converted the white walls into a fiery vermilion, and stretched a board across the upper part, between the windows of the first and second floors, on which appeared in large letters "A la Maison Rouge."

Whether this sort of advertisement drew the public, or whether it might have been the sterling respectability and devotion to business of Monsieur Sauvage, he got on most successfully. The Marchand en détail became also Marchand en gros, and in course of time he added liqueurs to his wines. No citizen of Sainteville was more highly esteemed than he, both as a man and a tradesman. Since his death the business had been carried on by his widow, aided by the two sons, Gustave and Emile. Latterly Madame Veuve Sauvage had given up all work to them; she was now in years, and had well earned her rest. They lived in the rooms over the shop, which were large and handsome. In former days, when the energies of herself and her husband were chiefly devoted to acquiring and saving money, they had let these upper rooms for a good sum yearly. Old Madame Sauvage might be seen any day now sitting at a front-window, looking out upon the world between her embroidered white curtains.

The door of this prosperous shop was between the two windows. The one window displayed a few bottles of wine, most of them in straw cases; in the other window were clear flacons of liqueurs: chartreuse, green and yellow; curaçoa, warm and ruby; eau de vie de Danzick, with its fluttering gold leaf; and many other sorts.

However, it is not with the goods of Madame Veuve Sauvage that we have to do, but with her premises. Standing in front of the shop, as if coveting a bottle of that choice wine for to-day's dinner, or an immediate glass of delicious liqueur, you may see on your right hand, but to the left of the shop, the private door of the house. On the other side the shop is also a door which opens to a narrow entry. The entry looks dark, even in the mid-day sun, for it is pretty long, extending down a portion of the side of the Maison Rouge, which is a deep house, and terminating in a paved yard surrounded by high buildings. At the end of the yard is a small dwelling, with two modern windows, one above the other. Near the under window is the entrance-door, painted oak colour, with a brass knob, a bell-wire with a curious handle, and a knocker. This little house the late Monsieur Sauvage had also caused to be converted into a red one, the same as the larger.

In earlier days, when Jean Sauvage and his wife were putting their shoulders to the wheel, they had lived in the little house with their children; the two sons and the daughter, Jeanne. Jeanne Sauvage married early and very well, an avocat. But since they had left it, the house in the yard seemed to have been, as the Widow Sauvage herself expressed it, unlucky. The first of the tenants had died there; the second had disappeared—decamped in fact, to avoid paying rent and other debts; the third had moved into a better house; and the fourth, an old widow lady, had also died, owing a year's rent to Madame Sauvage, and leaving no money to pay it.

It was of this small dwelling, lying under the shadow of the Maison Rouge, that Monsieur Carimon had thought. Turning to the Miss Preens, he gave them briefly a few particulars, and said he believed the house was to be had on very reasonable terms.

"What do you call it?" exclaimed Lavinia. "The little red house?"

"Yes, we call it so," said Monsieur Carimon. "Emile Sauvage was talking of it to me the other evening at the café, saying they would be glad to have it tenanted."

"I fear our good friends here would find it dull," remarked Madame Carimon to him. "It is in so gloomy a situation, you know, Jules."

"Mon amie, I do not myself see how that signifies," said he in reply. "If your house is comfortable inside, does it matter what it looks out upon?"

"Very true," assented Miss Lavinia, whose hopes had gone up again. "But this house may not be furnished, Mary."

"It is partly furnished," said Madame Carimon. "When the old lady who was last in it died, they had to take her furniture for the rent. It was not much, I have heard."

"We should not want much, only two of us," cried Miss Ann eagerly. "Do let us go to look at it to-morrow!"

On the following day, Friday, the Miss Preens went to the Place Ronde, piloted by Mary Carimon. They were struck with admiration at the Maison Rouge, all a fiery glow in the morning sun, and a novelty to English eyes. Whilst Madame Carimon went into the shop to explain and ask for the key, the sisters gazed in at the windows. Lying on the wine-bottles was a small black board on which was written in white letters, "Petite Maison à louer."

Monsieur Gustave Sauvage, key in hand, saluted the ladies in English, which he spoke fairly well, and accompanied them to view the house. The sun was very bright that day, and the confined yard did not look so dull as at a less favourable time; and perhaps the brilliant red of the little house, at which Nancy laughed, imparted a cheerfulness to it. Monsieur Gustave opened the door with a latch-key, drew back, and waited for them to enter.

The first to do so, or to attempt to do so, was Miss Preen. But no sooner had she put one foot over the threshold than she drew back with a start, somewhat discomposing the others by the movement.

"What is it, Lavinia?" inquired Ann.

"Something seemed to startle me, and throw me backward!" exclaimed Lavinia Preen, regaining her breath. "Perhaps it was the gloom of the passage: it is very dark."

"Pardon, mesdames," spoke Monsieur Gustave politely. "If the ladies will forgive my entering before them, I will open the salon door."

The passage was narrow. The broad shoulders of Monsieur Gustave almost touched the wall on either side as he walked along. Almost at the other end of it, on his left hand, was the salon door; he threw it open, and a little light shone forth. The passage terminated in a small square recess. At the back of this was fixed a shallow marble slab for holding things, above which was a cupboard let into the wall. On the right of the recess was the staircase; and opposite the staircase the kitchen-door, the kitchen being behind the salon.

The salon was nice when they were in it; the paint was fresh, the paper light and handsome. It was of good size, and its large window looked to the front. The kitchen opened upon a small back-yard, furnished with a pump and a shed for wood or coal. On the floor above were two very good chambers, one behind the other. Opposite these, on the other side of the passage, was another room, not so large, but of fair size. It was apparently built out over some part of the next-door premises, and was lighted by a skylight. All the rooms were fresh and good, and the passage had a window at the end.

Altogether it was not an inconvenient abode for people who did not go in for show. The furniture was plain, clean and useful, but it would have to be added to. There were no grates, not even a cooking-stove in the kitchen. It was very much the Sainteville custom at that period for tenants to provide grates for themselves, plenty of which could be bought or hired for a small sum. An easy-chair or two would be needed; tea-cups and saucers and wine-glasses; and though, there were washing-stands, these contained no jugs or basins; and there were no sheets or tablecloths or towels, no knives or forks, no brooms or brushes, and so on.

"There is only this one sitting-room, you perceive," remarked Madame Carimon, as they turned about, looking at the salon again, after coming downstairs.

"Yes, that's a pity, on account of dining," replied Miss Nancy.

"One of our tenants made a pretty salon of the room above this, and this the salle à manger," replied Monsieur Gustave. "Mesdames might like to do the same, possibly?"

He had pointedly addressed Miss Lavinia, near whom he stood. She did not answer. In fact—it was a very curious thing, but a fact—Miss Lavinia had not spoken a word since she entered. She had gone through the house taking in its features in complete silence, just as if that shock at the door had scared away her speech.

The rent asked by Monsieur Gustave, acting for his mother, was very moderate indeed—twenty pounds a-year, including the use of the furniture. There would be no taxes to pay, he said; absolutely none; the taxes of this little house, being upon their premises, were included in their own. But to ensure this low rental, the house must be taken for five years.

"Of course we will take it—won't we, Lavinia?" cried Miss Ann in a loud whisper. "Only twenty pounds a-year! Just think of it!"

"Sir," Miss Lavinia said to Monsieur Gustave, speaking at last, "the house would suit us in some respects, especially as regards rent. But we might find it too lonely: and I should hardly like to be bound for five years."

All that was of course for mesdames' consideration, he frankly responded. But he thought that if the ladies were established in it with their ménage about them, they would not find it lonely.

"We will give you an answer to-morrow or Monday," decided Miss Lavinia.

They went about the town all that day with Madame Carimon; but nothing in the shape of an apartment could be found to suit them. Madame invited them again to tea in the evening. And by that time they had decided to take the house. Nancy was wild about it. What with the change from the monotony of their country house to the bright and busy streets, the gay outdoor life, the delights of the table d'hôte, Ann Preen looked upon Sainteville as an earthly paradise.

"The house is certainly more suited to you than anything else we have seen," observed Madame Carimon. "I have nothing to say against the Petite Maison Rouge, except its dull situation."

"Did it strike you, Mary, apart from its situation, as being gloomy?" asked Lavinia.

"No. Once you are in the rooms they are cheerful enough."

"It did me. Gloomy, with a peculiar gloom, you understand. I'm sure the passage was dark as night. It must have been its darkness that startled me as we were going in."

"By the way, Lavinia, what was the matter with you then?" interrupted her sister.

"I don't know, Nancy; I said at the time I did not know. With my first step into the passage, some horror seemed to meet me and drive me backward."

"Some horror!" repeated Nancy.

"I seemed to feel it so. I had still the glare of the streets and the fiery red walls in my eyes, which must have caused the house passage to look darker than it ought. That was all, I suppose—but it turned me sick with a sort of fear; sick and shivery."

"That salon may be made as pretty a room as any in Sainteville," remarked Madame Carimon. "Many of the English residents here have only one salon in their apartments. You see, we don't go in for ceremony; France is not like England."

On the morrow the little house under the wing of the Maison Rouge was secured by the Miss Preens. They took it in their joint names for five years. To complete the transaction they were ushered upstairs to the salon and presence of Madame Veuve Sauvage—a rather stately looking old lady, attired in a voluminous black silk robe and a mourning cap of fine muslin. Madame, who could not speak a syllable of English, conversed graciously with her future tenants through the interpretation of Mary Carimon, offering to be useful to them in any way she could. Lavinia and Ann Preen both signed the bail, or agreement, and Madame Veuve Sauvage likewise signed it; by virtue of which she became their landlady, and they her tenants of the little house for five years. Madame Carimon, and a shopman who came upstairs for the purpose, signed as witnesses.

Wine and the little cakes called pistolets were then introduced; and so the bargain was complete.

Oh if some kindly spirit from the all-seeing world above could only have whispered a hint to those ill-fated sisters of what they were doing!—had only whispered a warning in time to prevent it! Might not that horror, which fell upon Lavinia as she was about to pass over the door-sill, have served her as such? But who regards these warnings when they come to us? Who personally applies them? None.

Having purchased or hired the additional things required, the Miss Preens took possession of their house. Nancy had the front bed-chamber, which Lavinia thought rather the best, and so gave it up to her; Lavinia took the back one. The one opposite, with the skylight, remained unoccupied, as their servant did not sleep in the house. Not at all an uncommon custom at Sainteville.

An excellent servant had been found for them in the person of Flore Pamart, a widow, who was honest, cooked well, and could talk away in English; all recommendations that the ladies liked. Flore let herself in with a latch-key before breakfast, and left as soon after five o'clock in the evening as she could get the dinner things removed. Madame Flore Pamart had one little boy named Dion, who went to school by day, but was at home night and morning; for which reason his mother could only take a daily service.

Thus the Miss Preens became part of the small colony of English at Sainteville. They took sittings in the English Protestant Church, which was not much more than a room; and they subscribed to the casino on the port when it opened for the summer season, spending many an evening there, listening to the music, watching the dancing when there was any, and chattering with the acquaintances they met. They were well regarded, these new-comers, and they began to speak French after a fashion. Now and then they went out to a soirée; once in a way gave one in return. Very sober soirées indeed were those of Sainteville; consisting (as Sam Weller might inform us) of tea at seven o'clock with, hot galette, conversation, cake at ten (gâteau Suisse or gâteau au rhum), and a glass of Picardin wine.

They were pleased with the house, once they had settled down in it, and never a shadow of regret crossed either of them for having taken the Petite Maison Rouge.

In this way about a twelvemonth wore on.

III

It was a fine morning at the beginning of April; the sun being particularly welcome, as Sainteville had latterly been favoured with a spell of ill-natured, bitter east winds. About eleven o'clock, Miss Preen and her sister turned out of their house to take a walk on the pier—which they liked to do most days, wind and weather permitting. In going down the Rue des Arbres, they were met by a fresh-looking little elderly gentleman, with rather long white hair, and wearing a white necktie. He stopped to salute the ladies, bowing ceremoniously low to each of them. It was Monsieur le Docteur Dupuis, a kindly man of skilful reputation, who had now mostly, though not altogether, given up practice to his son, Monsieur Henri Dupuis. Miss Lavinia had a little acquaintance with the doctor, and took occasion to ask him news of the public welfare; for there was raging in the town the malady called "la grippe," which, being interpreted, means influenza.

It was not much better at present, Monsieur Dupuis answered; but this genial sunshine he hoped would begin to drive it away; and, with another bow, he passed onward.

The pier was soon reached, and they enjoyed their walk upon it. The sunlight glinted on the rather turbulent waves of the sea in the distance, but there was not much breeze to be felt on land. When nearing the end of the pier their attention was attracted to a fishing-boat, which was tumbling about rather unaccountably in its efforts to make the harbour.

"It almost looks from here as though it had lost its rudder, Nancy," remarked Miss Lavinia.

They halted, and stood looking over the side at the object of interest; not particularly noticing that a gentleman stood near them, also looking at the same through an opera-glass. He was spare, of middle height and middle age; his hair was grey, his face pale and impassive; the light over-coat he wore was of fashionable English cut.

"Oh, Lavinia, look, look! It is coming right on to the end of the pier," cried Ann Preen.

"Hush, Nancy, don't excite yourself," said Miss Lavinia, in lowered tones. "It will take care not to do that."

The gentleman gave a wary glance at them. He saw two ladies dressed alike, in handsome black velvet mantles, and bonnets with violet feathers; by which he judged them to be sisters, though there was no resemblance in face. The elder had clear-cut features, a healthy colour, dark brown hair, worn plain, and a keen, sensible expression. The other was fair, with blue eyes and light ringlets.

"Pardon me," he said, turning to them, and his accent was that of a gentleman. "May I offer you the use of my glasses?"

"Oh, thank you!" exclaimed Nancy, in a light tone bordering on a giggle; and she accepted the glasses. She was evidently pleased with the offer and with the stranger.

Lavinia, on the contrary, was not. The moment she saw his full face she shrank from it—shrank from him. The feeling might have been as unaccountable as that which came over her when she had been first entering the Petite Maison Rouge; but it was there. However, she put it from her, and thanked him.

"I don't think I see so well with the glasses as without them; it seems all a mist," remarked Nancy, who was standing next the stranger.

"They are not properly focused for you. Allow me," said he, as he took the glasses from her to alter them. "Young eyes need a less powerful focus than elderly ones like mine."

He spoke in a laughing tone; Nancy, fond of compliments, giggled outright this time. She was approaching forty; he might have been ten years older. They continued standing there, watching the fishing-boat, and exchanging remarks at intervals. When it had made the harbour without accident, the Miss Preens wished him good-morning, and went back down the pier; he took off his hat to them, and walked the other way.

"What a charming man!" exclaimed Nancy, when they were at a safe distance.

"I don't like him," dissented Lavinia.

"Not like him!" echoed the other in surprise. "Why, Lavinia, his manners are delightful. I wonder who he is?"

When nearly home, in turning into the Place Ronde, they met an English lady of their acquaintance, the wife of Major Smith. She had been ordering a dozen of vin Picardin from the Maison Rouge. As they stood talking together, the gentleman of the pier passed up the Rue de Tessin. He lifted his hat, and they all, including Mrs. Smith, bowed.

"Do you know him?" quickly asked Nancy, in a whisper.

"Hardly that," answered Mrs. Smith. "When we were passing the Hôtel des Princes this morning, a gentleman turned out of the courtyard, and he and my husband spoke to one another. The major said to me afterwards that he had formerly been in the—I forget which—regiment. He called him Mr. Fennel."

Now, as ill-fortune had it, Miss Preen found herself very poorly after she got home. She began to sneeze and cough, and thought she must have taken cold through standing on the pier to watch the vagaries of the fishing-smack.

"I hope you are not going to have the influenza!" cried Nancy, her blue eyes wide with concern.

But the influenza it proved to be. Miss Preen seemed about to have it badly, and lay in bed the next day. Nancy proposed to send Flore for Monsieur Dupuis, but Lavinia said she knew how to treat herself as well as he could treat her.

The next day she was no better. Poor Nancy had to go out alone, or to stay indoors. She did not like doing the latter at all; it was too dull; her own inclination would have led her abroad all day long and every day.

"I saw Captain Fennel on the pier again," said she to her sister that afternoon, when she was making the tea at Lavinia's bedside, Flore having carried up the tray.

"I hope you did not talk to him, Ann," spoke the invalid, as well as she could articulate.

"I talked a little," said Nancy, turning hot, conscious that she had gossiped with him for three-quarters-of-an-hour. "He stopped to speak to me; I could not walk on rudely."

"Any way, don't talk to him again, my dear. I do not like that man."

"What is there to dislike in him, Lavinia?"

"That I can't say. His countenance is not a good one; it is shifty and deceitful. He is a man you could never trust."

"I'm sure I've heard you say the same of other people."

"Because I can read faces," returned Lavinia.

"Oh—well—I consider Captain Fennel's is a handsome face," debated Nancy.

"Why do you call him 'Captain'?"

"He calls himself so," answered Nancy. "I suppose it was his rank in the army when he retired. They retain it afterwards by courtesy, don't they, Lavinia?"

"I am not sure. It depends upon whether they retire in rotation or sell out, I fancy. Mrs. Smith said the major called him Mr. Fennel, and he ought to know. There, I can't talk any more, Nancy, and the man is nothing to us, that we need discuss him."

La grippe had taken rather sharp hold of Lavinia Preen, and she was upstairs for ten days. On the first afternoon she went down to the salon, Captain Fennel called, very much to her surprise; and, also to her surprise, he and Nancy appeared to be pretty intimate.

In point of fact, they had met every day, generally upon the pier. Nancy had said nothing about it at home. She was neither sly nor deceitful in disposition; rather notably simple and unsophisticated; but, after Lavinia's reproof the first time she told about meeting him, she would not tell again.

Miss Preen behaved coolly to him; which he would not appear to see. She sat over the fire, wrapped in a shawl, for it was a cold afternoon. He stayed only a little time, and put his card down on the slab near the stairs when he left. Lavinia had it brought to her.

"Mr. Edwin Fennel."

"Then he is not Captain Fennel," she observed. "But, Nancy, what in the world could have induced the man to call here? And how is it you seem to be familiar with him?"

"I have met him out-of-doors, sometimes, while you were ill," said Nancy. "As to his calling here—he came, I suppose, out of politeness. There's no harm in it, Lavinia."

Miss Lavinia did not say there was. But she disliked the man too much to favour his acquaintanceship. Instinct warned her against him.

How little was she prepared for what was to follow! Before she was well out-of-doors again, before she had been anywhere except to church, Nancy gave her a shock. With no end of simperings and blushings, she confessed that she had been asked to marry Captain Fennel.

Had Miss Lavinia Preen been herself politely asked to marry a certain gentleman popularly supposed to reside underground, she would not have been much more indignantly startled. Perhaps "frightened" would be the better word for it.

"But—you would not, Nancy!" she gasped, when she found her voice.

"I don't know," simpered foolish Nancy. "I—I—think him very nice and gentlemanly, Lavinia."

Lavinia came out of her fright sufficiently to reason. She strove to show Nancy how utterly unwise such a step would be. They knew nothing of Captain Fennel or his antecedents; to become his wife might just be courting misery and destruction. Nancy ceased to argue; and Lavinia hoped she had yielded.

Both sisters kept a diary. But for that fact, and also that the diaries were preserved, Featherston could not have arrived at the details of the story so perfectly. About this time, a trifle earlier or later, Ann Preen wrote as follows in hers:

"April 16th.—I met Captain Fennel on the pier again this morning. I do think he goes there because he knows he may meet me. Lavinia is not out yet; she has not quite got rid of that Grip, as they stupidly call it here. I'm sure it has gripped her. We walked quite to the end of the pier, and then I sat down on the edge for a little while, and he stood talking to me. I do wish I could tell Lavinia of these meetings; but she was so cross the first day I met him, and told her of it, that I don't like to. Captain Fennel lent me his glasses as usual, and I looked at the London steamer, which was coming in. Somehow we fell to talking of the Smiths; he said they were poor, had not much more than the major's half-pay. 'Not like you rich people, Miss Nancy,' he said—he thinks that's my right name. 'Your income is different from theirs.' 'Oh,' I screamed out, 'why, it's only a hundred and forty pounds a-year!' 'Well,' he answered, smiling, 'that's a comfortable sum for a place like this; five francs will buy as much at Sainteville as half-a-sovereign will in England.' Which is pretty nearly true."

Skipping a few entries of little importance, we come to another:

"May 1st, and such a lovely day!—It reminds me of one May-day at home, when the Jacks-in-the-green were dancing on the grass-plot before the Court windows at Buttermead, and Mrs. Selby sat watching them, as pleased as they were, saying she should like to dance, too, if she could only go first to the mill to be ground young again. Jane and Edith Peckham were spending the day with us. It was just such a day as this, warm and bright; light, fleecy clouds flitting across the blue sky. I wish Lavinia were out to enjoy it! but she is hardly strong enough for long walks yet, and only potters about, when she does get out, in the Rue des Arbres or the Grande Place, or perhaps over to see Mary Carimon.

"I don't know what to do. I lay awake all last night, and sat moping yesterday, thinking what I could do. Edwin wants me to marry him; I told Lavinia, and she absolutely forbids it, saying I should rush upon misery. He says I should be happy as the day's long. I feel like a distracted lunatic, not knowing which of them is right, or which opinion I ought to yield to. I have obeyed Lavinia all my life; we have never had a difference before; her wishes have been mine, and mine have been hers. But I can't see why she need have taken up this prejudice against him, for I'm sure he's more like an angel than a man; and, as he whispers to me, Nancy Fennel would be a prettier name than Nancy Preen. I said to him to-day, 'My name is Ann, not really Nancy.' 'My dear,' he answered, 'I shall always call you Nancy; I love the simple name.'

"I no longer talk about him to Lavinia, or let her suspect that we still meet on the pier. It would make her angry, and I can't bear that. I dare not hint to her what Edwin said to-day—that he should take matters into his own hands. He means to go over to Dover, viâ Calais; stay at Dover a fortnight, as the marriage law requires, and then come back to fetch me; and after the marriage has taken place we shall return here to live.

"Oh dear, what am I to do? It will be a dreadful thing to deceive Lavinia; and it will be equally dreadful to lose him. He declares that if I do not agree to this he shall set sail for India (where he used to be with his regiment), and never, never see me again. Good gracious! never to see me again!

"The worst is, he wants to go off to Dover at once, giving one no time for consideration! Must I say Yes, or No? The uncertainty shakes me to pieces. He laughed to-day when I said something of this, assuring me Lavinia's anger would pass away like a summer cloud when I was his wife; that sisters had no authority over one another, and that Lavinia's opposition arose from selfishness only, because she did not want to lose me. 'Risk it, Nancy,' said he; 'she will receive you with open arms when I bring you back from Dover.' If I could only think so! Now and then I feel inclined to confide my dilemma to Mary Carimon, and ask her opinion, only that I fear she might tell Lavinia."

Mr. Edwin Fennel quitted Sainteville. When he was missed people thought he might have gone for good. But one Saturday morning some time onwards, when the month of May was drawing towards its close, Miss Lavinia, out with Nancy at market, came full upon Captain Fennel in the crowd on the Grande Place. He held out his hand.

"I thought you had left Sainteville, Mr. Fennel," she remarked, meeting his hand and the sinister look in his face unwillingly.

"Got back this morning," he said; "travelled by night. Shall be leaving again to-day or to-morrow. How are you, Miss Nancy?"

Lavinia pushed her way to the nearest poultry stall. "Will you come here, Ann?" she said. "I want to choose a fowl."

She began to bargain, half in French, half in English, with the poultry man, all to get rid of that other man, and she looked round, expecting Nancy had followed her. Nancy had not stirred from the spot near the butter-baskets: she and Captain Fennel had their heads together, he talking hard and fast.

They saw Lavinia looking at them; looking angry, too. "Remember," impressively whispered Captain Fennel to Nancy: and, lifting his hat to Lavinia, over the white caps of the market-women, he disappeared across the Place.

"I wonder what that man has come back for?" cried Miss Preen, as Nancy reached her—not that she had any suspicion. "And I wonder you should stay talking with him, Nancy!"

Nancy did not answer.

Sending Flore—who had attended them with her market-basket—home with the fowl and eggs and vegetables, they called at the butcher's and the grocer's, and then went home themselves. Miss Preen then remembered that she had forgotten one or two things, and must go out again. Nancy remained at home. When Lavinia returned, which was not for an hour, for she had met various friends and stayed to gossip, her sister was in her room. Flore thought Mademoiselle Nancy was setting her drawers to rights: she had heard her opening and shutting them.

Time went on until the afternoon. Just before five o'clock, when Flore came into lay the cloth for dinner, Lavinia, sitting at the window, saw her sister leave the house and cross the yard, a good-sized paper parcel in her hand.

"Why, that is Miss Nancy," she exclaimed, in much surprise. "Where can she be going to now?"

"Miss Nancy came down the stairs as I was coming in here," replied Flore. "She said to me that she had just time to run to Madame Carimon's before dinner."

"Hardly," dissented Miss Lavinia. "What can she be going for?"

As five o'clock struck, Flore (always punctual, from self-interest) came in to ask if she should serve the fish; but was told to wait until Miss Nancy returned. When half-past five was at hand, and Nancy had not appeared, Miss Preen ordered the fish in, remarking that Madame Carimon must be keeping her sister to dinner.

Afterwards Miss Preen set out for the casino, expecting she should meet them both there; for Lavinia and Nancy had intended to go. Madame Carimon was not a subscriber, but she sometimes paid her ten sous and went in. It would be quite a pretty sight to-night—a children's dance. Lavinia soon joined some friends there, but the others did not come.

At eight o'clock she was in the Rue Pomme Cuite, approaching Madame Carimon's. Pauline, in her short woollen petticoats, and shoeless feet thrust into wooden sabots, was splashing buckets of water before the door to scrub the pavement, and keeping up a screaming chatter with the other servants in the street, who were doing the same, Saturday-night fashion.

Madame Carimon was in the salon, sitting idle in the fading light; her sewing lay on the table. Lavinia's eyes went round the room, but she saw no one else in it.

"Mary, where is Nancy?" she asked, as Madame Carimon rose to greet her with outstretched hands.

"I'm sure I don't know," answered Madame Carimon lightly. "She has not been here. Did you think she had?"

"She dined here—did she not?"

"What, Nancy? Oh no! I and Jules dined alone. He is out now, giving a French lesson. I have not seen Nancy since—let me see—since Thursday, I think; the day before yesterday."

Lavinia Preen sat down, half-bewildered. She related the history of the evening.

"It is elsewhere that Nancy is gone," remarked Madame Carimon. "Flore must have misunderstood her."

Concluding that to be the case, and that Nancy might already be at home, Lavinia returned at once to the Petite Maison Rouge, Mary Carimon bearing her company in the sweet summer twilight. Lavinia opened the door with her latch-key. Flore had departed long before. There were three latch-keys to the house, Nancy possessing one of them.

They looked into every room, and called out "Nancy! Nancy!" But she was not there.

Nancy Preen had gone off with Captain Fennel by the six-o'clock train, en route for Dover, there to be converted into Mrs. Fennel.

And had Nancy foreseen the terrible events and final crime which this most disastrous step would bring about, she might have chosen, rather than take it, to run away to the Protestant cemetery outside the gates of Sainteville, there to lay herself down to die.

IV

"Where can Nancy be?"

Miss Preen spoke these words to Mary Carimon in a sort of flurry. After letting themselves into the house, the Petite Maison Rouge, and calling up and down it in vain for Nancy, the question as to where she could be naturally arose.

"She must be spending the evening with the friends she stayed to dine with," said Madame Carimon.

"I don't know where she would be likely to stay. Unless—yes—perhaps at Mrs. Hardy's."

"That must be it, Lavinia," pronounced Madame Carimon.

It was then getting towards nine o'clock. They set out again for Mrs. Hardy's to escort Nancy home. She lived in the Rue Lothaire; a long street, leading to the railway-station.

Mrs. Hardy was an elderly lady. When near her door they saw her grand-nephew, Charles Palliser, turn out of it. Charley was a good-hearted young fellow, the son of a rich merchant in London. He was staying at Sainteville for the purpose of acquiring the art of speaking French as a native.

"Looking for Miss Ann Preen!" cried he, as they explained in a word or two. "No, she is not at our house; has not been there. I saw her going off this evening by the six-o'clock train."

"Going off by the six-o'clock train!" echoed Miss Lavinia, staring at him. "Why, what do you mean, Mr. Charles? My sister has not gone off by any train."

"It was in this way," answered the young man, too polite to flatly contradict a lady. "Mrs. Hardy's cousin, Louise Soubitez, came to town this morning; she spent the day with us, and after dinner I went to see her off by the train. And there, at the station, was Miss Ann Preen."

"But not going away by train," returned Miss Lavinia.

"Why, yes, she was. I watched the train out of the station. She and Louise Soubitez sat in the same compartment."

A smile stole to Charles Palliser's face. In truth, he was amused at Miss Lavinia's consternation. It suddenly struck her that the young man was joking.

"Did you speak to Ann, Mr. Charles?"

"Oh yes; just a few words. There was not time for much conversation; Louise was late."

Miss Preen felt a little shaken.

"Was Ann alone?"

"No; she was with Captain Fennel."

And, with that, a suspicion of the truth, and the full horror of it, dawned upon Lavinia Preen. She grasped Madame Carimon's arm and turned white as death.

"It never can be," she whispered, her lips trembling: "it never can be! She cannot have—have—run away—with that man!"

Unconsciously perhaps to herself, her eyes were fixed on Charles. He thought the question was put to him, and answered it.

"Well—I—I'm afraid it looks like it, as she seems to have said nothing to you," he slowly said. "But I give you my word, Miss Preen, that until this moment that aspect of the matter never suggested itself to me. I supposed they were just going up the line together for some purpose or other; though, in fact, I hardly thought about it at all."

"And perhaps that is all the mystery!" interposed Madame Carimon briskly. "He may have taken Ann to Drecques for a little jaunt, and they will be back again by the last train. It must be almost due, Lavinia."

With one impulse they turned to the station, which was near at hand. Drecques, a village, was the first place the trains stopped at on the up-line. The passengers were already issuing from the gate. Standing aside until all had passed, and not seeing Nancy anywhere, Charley Palliser looked into the omnibuses. But she was not there.

"They may have intended to come back and missed the train, Miss Preen; it's very easy to miss a train," said he in his good nature.

"I think it must be so, Lavinia," spoke up Madame Carimon. "Any way, we will assume it until we hear to the contrary. And, Charley, we had better not talk of this to-night."

"I won't," answered Charley earnestly. "You may be sure of me."

Unless Captain Fennel and Miss Ann Preen chartered a balloon, there was little probability of their reaching Sainteville that evening, for this had been the last train. Lavinia Preen passed a night of discomfort, striving to hope against hope, as the saying runs. Not a very wise saying; it might run better, striving to hope against despair.

When Sunday did not bring back the truants, or any news of them, the three in the secret—Mary Carimon, Lavinia, and Charley Palliser—had little doubt that the disappearance meant an elopement. Monsieur Jules Carimon, not easily understanding such an escapade, so little in accordance with the customs and manners of his own country, said in his wife's ear he hoped it would turn out that there was a marriage in the case.

Miss Preen received a letter from Dover pretty early in the week, written by Ann. She had been married that day to Captain Fennel.

Altogether, the matter was the most bitter blow ever yet dealt to Lavinia Preen. No living being knew, or ever would know, how cruelly her heart was wrung by it. But, being a kindly woman of good sound sense, she saw that the best must be made of it, not the worst; and this she set herself out to do. She began by hoping that her own instinct, warning her against Captain Fennel, might be a mistaken one, and that he had a good home to offer his wife and would make her happy in it.

She knew no more about him—his family, his fortune, his former life, his antecedents—than she knew of the man in the moon. Major Smith perhaps did; he had been acquainted with him in the past. Nancy's letter, though written the previous day, had been delivered by the afternoon post. As soon as she could get dinner over, Lavinia went to Major Smith's. He lived at the top of the Rue Lambeau, a street turning out of the Grande Place. He and his wife, their own dinner just removed, were sitting together, the major indulging in a steaming glass of schiedam and water, flavoured with a slice of lemon. He was a very jolly little man, with rosy cheeks and a bald head. They welcomed Miss Lavinia warmly. She, not quite as composed as usual, opened her business without preamble; her sister Ann had married Captain Fennel, and she had come to ask Major Smith what he knew of him.

"Not very much," answered the major.

There was something behind his tone, and Lavinia burst into tears. Compassionating her distress, the major offered her a comforting glass, similar to his own. Lavinia declined it.

"You will tell me what you know," she said; and he proceeded to do so.

Edwin Fennel, the son of Colonel Fennel, was stationed in India with his regiment for several years. He got on well enough, but was not much liked by his brother officers: they thought him unscrupulous and deceitful. All at once, something very disagreeable occurred, which obliged Captain Fennel to quit her Majesty's service. The affair was hushed up, out of consideration to his family and his father's long term of service. "In fact, I believe he was allowed to retire, instead of being cashiered," added the major, "but I am not quite sure which it was."

"What was it that occurred—that Captain Fennel did, to necessitate his dismissal?" questioned Lavinia.

"I don't much like to mention it," said the major, shaking his head. "It might get about, you see, Miss Preen, which would make it awkward for him. I have no wish, or right either, to do the man a gratuitous injury."

"I promise you it shall not get about through me," returned Lavinia; "my sister's being his wife will be the best guarantee for that. You must please tell me, Major Smith."

"Well, Fennel was suspected—detected, in short—of cheating at cards."

Lavinia drew a deep breath. "Do you know," she said presently, in an undertone, "that when I first met the man I shrank from his face."

"Oh my! And it has such nice features!" put in Mrs. Smith, who was but a silly little woman.

"There was something in its shifty look which spoke to me as a warning," continued Lavinia. "It did, indeed. All my life I have been able to read faces, and my first instinct has rarely, if ever, deceived me. Each time I have seen this man since, that instinct against him has become stronger."

Major Smith took a sip at his schiedam. "I believe—between ourselves—he is just a mauvais sujet," said he. "He has a brother who is one, out and out; as I chance to know."

"What is Edwin Fennel's income, major?"

"I can't tell at all. I should not be surprised to hear that he has none."

"How does he live then?" asked Lavinia, her heart going at a gallop.

"Don't know that either," said the major. "His father is dead now and can't help him. A very respectable man, the old colonel, but always poor."

"He cannot live upon air; he must have some means," debated Lavinia.

"Lives upon his wits, perhaps; some men do. He wanted to borrow ten pounds from me a short time ago," added the major, taking another sip at his tumbler; "but I told him I had no money to lend—which was a fact. I have an idea that he got it out of Charley Palliser."

The more Lavinia Preen heard of this unhappy case, the worse it seemed to be. Declining to stay for tea, as Mrs. Smith wished, she betook her miserable steps home again, rather wishing that the sea would swallow up Captain Fennel.

The next day she saw Charles Palliser. Pouncing upon him as he was airing his long legs in the Grande Place, she put the question to him in so determined a way that Charley had no chance against her. He turned red.

"I don't know who can have set that about," said he. "But it's true, Miss Preen. Fennel pressed me to lend him ten pounds for a month; and I—well, I did it. I happened to have it in my pocket, you see, having just cashed a remittance from my father."

"Has he repaid you, Mr. Charles?"

"Oh, the month's not quite up yet," cried Charley. "Please don't talk of it, Miss Preen; he wouldn't like it, you know. How on earth it has slipped out I can't imagine."

"No, I shall not talk of it," said Lavinia, as she wished him good-day and walked onwards, wondering what sort of a home Captain Fennel meant to provide for Ann.

Lavinia Preen's cup of sorrow was not yet full. A morning or two after this she was seated at breakfast with the window open, when she saw the postman come striding across the yard with a letter. It was from the bride; a very short letter, and one that Miss Lavinia did not at once understand. She read it again.

"MY DEAR LAVINIA,

"All being well, we shall be home to-morrow; that is, on the day you   receive this letter; reaching Sainteville by the last train in the   evening. Please get something nice and substantial for tea, Edwin says, and please see that Flore has the bedroom in good order.

"Your affectionate sister,
"ANN FENNEL."

The thing that Miss Lavinia did, when comprehension came to her, was to fly into a passion.

"Come home here—he!—is that what she means?" cried she. "Never. Have that man in my house? Never, never."

"But what has mademoiselle received?" exclaimed Flore, appearing just then with a boiled egg. "Is it bad news?"

"It is news that I will not put up with—will not tolerate," cried Miss Lavinia. And, in the moment's dismay, she told the woman what it was.

"Tiens!" commented Flore, taking a common-sense view of matters: "they must be coming just to show themselves to mademoiselle on their marriage. Likely enough they will not stay more than a night or two, while looking out for an apartment."

Lavinia did not believe it; but the very suggestion somewhat soothed her. To receive that man even for a night or two, as Flore put it, would be to her most repugnant, cruel pain, and she resolved not to do it. Breakfast over, she carried the letter and her trouble to the Rue Pomme Cuite.

"But I am afraid, Lavinia, you cannot refuse to receive them," spoke Madame Carimon, after considering the problem.

"Not refuse to receive them!" echoed Lavinia. "Why do you say that?"

"Well," replied Mary Carimon uneasily, for she disliked to add to trouble, "you see the house is as much Ann's as yours. It was taken in your joint names. Ann has the right to return to it; and also, I suppose"—more dubiously—"to introduce her husband into it."

"Is that French law?"

"I think so. I'll ask Jules when he comes home to dinner. Would it not be English law also, Lavinia?"

Lavinia was feeling wretchedly uncomfortable. With all her plain common-sense, this phase of the matter had not struck her.

"Mary," said she—and there stopped, for she was seized with a violent shivering, which seemed difficult to be accounted for. "Mary, if that man has to take up his abode in the house, I can never remain in it. I would rather die."

"Look here, dear friend," whispered Mary: "life is full of trouble—as Job tells us in the Holy Scriptures—none of us are exempt from it. It attacks us all in turn. The only one thing we can do is to strive to make the best of it, under God; to ask Him to help us. I am afraid there is a severe cross before you, Lavinia; better bear it than fight against it."

"I will never bear that," retorted Lavinia, turning a deaf ear in her anger. "You ought not to wish me to do so."

"And I would not if I saw anything better for you."

Madame Veuve Sauvage, sitting as usual at her front-window that same morning, was surprised at receiving an early call from her tenant, Miss Preen. Madame handed her into her best crimson velvet fauteuil, and they began talking.

Not to much purpose, however; for neither very well understood what the other said. Lavinia tried to explain the object of her visit, but found her French was not equal to it. Madame called her maid, Mariette, and sent her into the shop below to ask Monsieur Gustave to be good enough to step up.

Lavinia had gone to beg of them to cancel the agreement for the little house, so far as her sister was concerned, and to place it in her name only.

Monsieur Gustave, when he had mastered the request, politely answered that such a thing was not practicable; Miss Ann's name could not be struck out of the lease without her consent, or, as he expressed it, breaking the bail. His mother and himself had every disposition to oblige Miss Preen in any way, as indeed she must know, but they had no power to act against the law.

So poor Miss Lavinia went into her home wringing her hands in despair. She was perfectly helpless.

V

The summer days went on. Mr. Edwin Fennel, with all the impudence in the world, had taken up his abode in the Petite Maison Rouge, without saying with your leave or by your leave.

"How could you think of bringing him here, Ann?" Lavinia demanded of her sister in the first days.

"I did not think of it; it was he thought of it," returned Mrs. Fennel in her simple way. "I feared you would not like it, Lavinia; but what could I do? He seemed to look upon it as a matter of course that he should come."

Yes, there he was; "a matter of course;" making one in the home. Lavinia could not show fight; he was Ann's husband, and the place was as much Ann's as hers. The more Lavinia saw of him the more she disliked him; which was perhaps unreasonable, since he made himself agreeable to her in social intercourse, though he took care to have things his own way. If Lavinia's will went one way in the house and his the other, she found herself smilingly set at naught. Ann was his willing slave; and when opinions differed she sided with her husband.

It was no light charge, having a third person in the house to live upon their small income, especially one who studied his appetite. For a very short time Lavinia, in her indignation at affairs generally, turned the housekeeping over to Mrs. Fennel. But she had to take to it again. Ann was naturally an incautious manager; she ordered in delicacies to please her husband's palate without regard to cost, and nothing could have come of that but debt and disaster.

That the gallant ex-Captain Fennel had married Ann Preen just to have a roof over his head, Lavinia felt as sure of as that the moon occasionally shone in the heavens. She did not suppose he had any other refuge in the wide world. And through something told her by Ann she judged that he had believed he was doing better for himself in marrying than he had done.

The day after the marriage Mr. and Mrs. Fennel were sitting on a bench at Dover, romantically gazing at the sea, honeymoon fashion, and talking of course of hearts and darts. Suddenly the bridegroom turned his thoughts to more practical things.

"Nancy, how do you receive your money—half-yearly or quarterly?" asked he.

"Oh, quarterly," said Nancy. "It is paid punctually to us by the acting-trustee, Colonel Selby."

"Ah, yes. Then you have thirty-five pounds every quarter?"

"Between us, we do," assented Nancy. "Lavinia has seventeen pounds ten, and I have the same; and the colonel makes us each give a receipt for our own share."

Captain Fennel turned his head and gazed at her with a hard stare.

"You told me your income was a hundred and forty pounds a-year."

"Yes, it is that exactly," said she quietly; "mine and Lavinia's together. We do not each have that, Edwin; I never meant to imply—"

Mrs. Fennel broke off, frightened. On the captain's face, cruel enough just then, there sat an expression which she might have thought diabolical had it been any one else's face. Any way, it scared her.

"What is it?" she gasped.

Rising rapidly, Captain Fennel walked forward, caught up some pebbles, flung them from him and waited, apparently watching to see where they fell. Then he strolled back again.

"Were you angry with me?" faltered Nancy. "Had I done anything?"

"My dear, what should you have done? Angry?" repeated he, in a light tone, as if intensely amused. "You must not take up fancies, Mrs. Fennel."

"I suppose Mrs. Selby thought it would be sufficient income for us, both living together," remarked Nancy. "If either of us should die it all lapses to the other. We found it quite enough last year, I assure you, Edwin; Sainteville is so cheap a place."

"Oh, delightfully cheap!" agreed the captain.

It was this conversation that Nancy repeated to Lavinia; but she did not speak of the queer look which had frightened her. Lavinia saw that Mr. Edwin Fennel had taken up a wrong idea of their income. Of course the disappointment angered him.

An aspect of semi-courtesy was outwardly maintained in the intercourse of home life. Lavinia was a gentlewoman; she had not spoken unpleasant things to the captain's face, or hinted that he was a weight upon the housekeeping pocket; whilst he, as yet, was quite officiously civil to her. But there was no love lost between them; and Lavinia could not divest her mind of an undercurrent of conviction that he was, in some way or other, a man to be dreaded.

Thus Captain Fennel (as he was mostly called), being domiciled with the estimable ladies in the Petite Maison Rouge, grew to be considered one of the English colony of Sainteville, and was received as such. As nobody knew aught against him, nobody thought anything. Major Smith had not spoken of antecedents, neither had Miss Preen; the Carimons, who were in the secret, never spoke ill of any one: and as the captain could assume pleasing manners at will, he became fairly well liked by his country-people in a passing sort of way.

Lavinia Preen sat one day upon the low edge of the pier, her back to the sun and the sea. She had called in at the little shoe-shop on the port, just as you turn out of the Rue Tessin, and had left her parasol there. The sun was not then out in the grey sky, and she did not miss it. Now that the sun was shining, and the grey canopy above had become blue, she said to herself that she had been stupid. It was September weather, so the sun was not unbearable.

Lavinia Preen was thinner; the thraldom of the past three months had made her so. Now and then it would cross her mind to leave the Petite Maison Rouge to its married inmates; but for Nancy's sake she hesitated. Nancy had made the one love of her life, and Nancy had loved her in return. Now, the love was chiefly given to the new tie she had formed; Lavinia was second in every respect.

"They go their way now, and I have to go mine," sighed Lavinia, as she sat this morning on the pier. "Even my walks have to be solitary."

A cloud came sailing up and the sun went in again. Lavinia rose; she walked onwards till she came to the end of the pier, where she again sat down. The next moment, chancing to look the way she had come, she saw a lady and gentleman advancing arm-in-arm.

"Oh, they are on the pier, are they!" mentally spoke Lavinia. For it was Mr. and Mrs. Edwin Fennel.

Nancy sat down beside her. "It is a long walk!" cried she, drawing a quick breath or two. "Lavinia, what do you think we have just heard?"

"How can I tell?" returned the elder sister.

"You know those queer people, an old English aunt and three nieces, who took Madame Gibon's rooms in the Rue Ménar? They have all disappeared and have paid nobody," continued Nancy. "Charley Palliser told us just how; he was laughing like anything over it."

"I never thought they looked like people to be trusted," remarked Lavinia. "Dear me! here's the sun coming out again."

"Where is your parasol?"

Lavinia recounted her negligence in having left it at the shoe-mart. Captain Fennel had brought out a small silk umbrella; he turned from the end of the pier, where he stood looking out to sea, opened the umbrella, and offered it.

"It is not much larger than a good-sized parasol," remarked he. "Pray take it, Miss Lavinia."

Lavinia did so after a moment's imperceptible hesitation, and thanked him. She hated to be under the slightest obligation to him, but the sun was now full in her eyes, and might make her head ache.

The pleasant smell of a cigar caused them to look up. A youngish man, rather remarkably tall, with a shepherd's plaid across his broad shoulders, was striding up the pier. He sat down near Miss Preen, and she glanced round at him. Appearing to think that she looked at his cigar, he immediately threw it into the sea behind him.

"Oh, I am sorry you did that," said Lavinia, speaking impulsively. "I like the smell of a cigar."

"Oh, thank you; thank you very much," he answered. "I had nearly smoked it out."

Voice and manner were alike pleasant and easy, and Lavinia spoke again—some trivial remark about the fine expanse of sea; upon which they drifted into conversation. We are reserved enough with strangers at home, we Islanders, as the world knows, but most of us are less ungracious abroad.

"Sainteville seems a clean, healthy place," remarked the new-comer.

"Very," said Miss Lavinia. "Do you know it well?"

"I never saw it before to-day," he replied. "I have come here from Douai to meet a friend, having two or three days to spare."

"Douai is a fine town," remarked Captain Fennel, turning to speak, for he was still looking out over the sea, and had his opera-glasses in his hand. "I spent a week there not long ago."

"Douai!" exclaimed Nancy. "That's the place where the great Law Courts are, is it not? Don't you remember the man last year, Lavinia, who committed some dreadful crime, and was taken up to Douai to be tried at the Assizes there?"

"We have a great case coming on there as soon as the Courts meet," said the stranger, who seemed a talkative man; "and that's what I am at Douai for. A case of extensive swindling."

"You are a lawyer, I presume?" said Miss Preen.

The stranger nodded. "Being the only one of our London firm who can speak French readily, and we are four of us in it, I had to come over and watch this affair and wait for the trial. For the young fellow is an Englishman, I am sorry to say, and his people, worthy and well-to-do merchants, are nearly mad over it."

"But did he commit it in England?" cried Miss Preen.

"Oh no; in France, within the arrondissement of the Douai Courts. He is in prison there. I dare say you get some swindling in a petty way even at Sainteville," added the speaker.

"That we do," put in Nancy. "An English family of ladies ran away only yesterday, owing twenty pounds at least, it is said."

"Ah," said the stranger, with a smile. "I think the ladies are sometimes more clever at that game than the men. By the way," he went on briskly, "do you know a Mr. Dangerfield at Sainteville?"

"No," replied Lavinia.

"He is staying here, I believe, or has been."

"Not that I know of," said Lavinia. "I never heard his name."

"Changed it again, probably," carelessly observed the young man.

"Is Dangerfield not his true name, then?"

"Just as much as it is mine, madam. His real name is Fennel; but he has found it convenient to drop that on occasion."

Now it was a curious fact that Nancy did not hear the name which the stranger had given as the true one. Her attention was diverted by some men who were working at the mud in the harbour, for it was low water, and who were loudly disputing together. Nancy had moved to the side of the pier to look down at them.

"Is he a swindler, that Mr. Dangerfield?" asked she, half-turning her head to speak. But the stranger did not answer.

As to Lavinia, the avowal had struck her speechless. She glanced at Captain Fennel. He had his back to them, and stood immovable, apparently unconcerned, possibly not having heard. A thought struck her— and frightened her.

"Do you know that Mr. Dangerfield yourself?" she asked the stranger, in a tone of indifference.

"No, I do not," he said; "but there's a man coming over in yonder boat who does."

He pointed over his shoulder at the sea as he spoke. Lavinia glanced quickly in the same direction.

"In yonder boat?" she repeated vaguely.

"I mean the London boat, which is on its way here, and will get in this evening," he explained.

"Oh, of course," said Lavinia, as if her wits had been wool-gathering.

The young man took out his watch and looked at it. Then he rose, lifted his hat, and, with a general good-morning, walked quickly down the pier.

Nancy was still at the side of the pier, looking down at the men. Captain Fennel put up his glasses and sat down beside Lavinia, his impassive face still as usual.

"I wonder who that man is?" he cried, watching the footsteps of the retreating stranger.

"Did you hear what he said?" asked Lavinia, dropping her voice.

"Yes. Had Nancy not been here, I should have given him a taste of my mind; but she hates even the semblance of a quarrel. He had no right to say what he did."

"What could it have meant?" murmured Lavinia.

"It meant my brother, I expect," said Captain Fennel savagely, and, as Lavinia thought, with every appearance of truth. "But he has never been at Sainteville, so far as I know; the fellow is mistaken in that."

"Does he pass under the name of Dangerfield?"

"Possibly. This is the first I've heard of it. He is an extravagant man, often in embarrassment from debt. There's nothing worse against him."

He did not say more; neither did Lavinia. They sat on in silence. The tall figure in the Scotch plaid disappeared from sight; the men in the harbour kept on disputing.

"How long are you going to stay here?" asked Nancy, turning towards her husband.

"I'm ready to go now," he answered. And giving his arm to Nancy, they walked down the pier together.

Never a word to Lavinia; never a question put by him or by Nancy, if only to say, "Are you not coming with us?" It was ever so now. Nancy, absorbed in her husband, neglected her sister.

Lavinia sighed. She sat on a little while longer, and then took her departure.

The shoe-shop on the port was opposite the place in the harbour where the London steamers were generally moored. The one now there was taking in cargo. As Lavinia was turning into the shop for her parasol, she heard a stentorian English voice call out to a man who was superintending the work in his shirt-sleeves: "At what hour does this boat leave to-night?"

"At eight o'clock, sir," was the answer. "Eight sharp; we want to get away with the first o' the tide."

From Miss Lavinia Preen's Diary.

September 22nd.—The town clocks have just struck eight, and I could almost fancy that I hear the faint sound of the boat steaming down the harbour in the dark night, carrying Nancy away with it, and carrying him. However, that is fancy and nothing else, for the sound could not penetrate to me here.

Perhaps it surprised me, perhaps it did not, when Nancy came to me this afternoon as I was sitting in my bedroom reading Scott's "Legend of Montrose," which Mary Carimon had lent me from her little stock of English books, and said she and Captain Fennel were going to London that night by the boat. He had received a letter, he told her, calling him thither. He might tell Nancy that if he liked, but it would not do for me. He is going, I can only believe, in consequence of what that gentleman in the shepherd's plaid said on the pier to-day. Can it be that the "Mr. Dangerfield" spoken of applies to Edwin Fennel himself and not to his brother? Is he finding himself in some dangerous strait, and is running away from the individual coming over in the approaching boat, who personally knows Mr. Dangerfield? "Can you lend me a five-pound note, Lavinia?" Nancy went on, when she had told me the news; "lend it to myself, I mean. I will repay you when I receive my next quarter's income, which is due, you know, in a few days." I chanced to have a five-pound note by me in my own private store, and I gave it her, reminding her that unless she did let me have it again, it would be so much less in hand to meet expenses with, and that I had found difficulty enough in the past quarter. "On the other hand," said Nancy, "if I and Edwin stay away a week or two, you will be spared our housekeeping; and when our money comes, Lavinia, you can open my letter and repay yourself if I am not here. I don't at all know where we are going to stay," she said, in answer to my question. "I was beginning to ask Edwin just now in the other room, but he was busy packing his portmanteau, and told me not to bother him."

And so, there it is: they are gone, and I am left here all alone.

I wonder whether any Mr. Dangerfield has been at Sainteville? I think we should have heard the name. Why, that is the door-bell! I must go and answer it.

It was Charley Palliser. He had come with a message from Major and Mrs. Smith. They are going to Drecques to-morrow morning by the eleven-o'clock train with a few friends and a basket of provisions, and had sent Charley to say they would be glad of my company. "Do come, Miss Preen," urged Charley as I hesitated; "you are all alone now, and I'm sure it must be dreadfully dull."

"How do you know I am alone?" I asked.

"Because," said Charley, "I have been watching the London boat out, and I saw Captain Fennel and your sister go by it. Major and Mrs. Smith were with me. It is a lovely night."

"Wait a moment," I said, as Charley was about to depart when I had accepted the invitation. "Do you know whether an Englishman named Dangerfield is living here?"

"Don't think there is; I have not met with him," said Charley. "Why, Miss Preen?"

"Oh, only that I was asked to-day whether I knew any one of that name," I returned carelessly. "Good-night, Mr. Charles. Thank you for coming."

They have invited me, finding I was left alone, and I think it very kind of them. But the Smiths are both kind-hearted people.

September 23rd.—Half-past nine o'clock, p.m. Have just returned from Drecques by the last train after spending a pleasant day. Quiet, of course, for there is not much to do at Drecques except stroll over the ruins of the old castle, or saunter about the quaint little ancient town, and go into the grand old church. It was so fine and warm that we had dinner on the grass, the people at the cottage bringing our plates and knives and forks. Later in the day we took tea indoors. In the afternoon, when all the rest were scattered about and the major sat smoking his cigar on the bench under the trees, I sat down by him to tell him what happened yesterday, and I begged him to give me his opinion. It was no betrayal of confidence, for Major Smith is better acquainted with the shady side of the Fennels than I am.

"I heard there was an English lawyer staying at the Hôtel des Princes, and that he had come here from Douai," observed the major. "His name's Lockett. It must have been he who spoke to you on the pier."

"Yes, of course. Do you know, major, whether any one has stayed at Sainteville passing as Mr. Dangerfield?"

"I don't think so," replied the major. "Unless he has kept himself remarkably quiet."

"Could it apply to Captain Fennel?"

"I never knew that he had gone under an assumed name. The accusation is one more likely to apply to his brother than to himself. James Fennel is unscrupulous, very incautious: notwithstanding that, I like him better than I like the other. There's something about Edwin Fennel that repels you; at least, it does me; but one can hardly help liking James, mauvais sujet though he is," added the speaker, pausing to flirt off the ashes of his cigar.

"The doubt pointing to Edwin Fennel in the affair is his suddenly decamping," continued Major Smith. "It was quite impromptu, you say, Miss Preen?"

"Quite so. I feel sure he had no thought of going away in the morning; and he did not receive any letter from England later, which was the excuse he gave Nancy for departing. Rely upon it that what he heard about the Mr. Dangerfield on the pier drove him away."

"Well, that looks suspicious, you see."

"Oh yes, I do see it," I answered, unable to conceal the pain I felt. "It was a bitter calamity, Major Smith, when Nancy married him."

"I'll make a few cautious inquiries in the town, and try to find out if there's anything against him in secret, or if any man named Dangerfield has been in the place and got into a mess. But, indeed, I don't altogether see that it could apply to him," concluded the major after a pause. "One can't well go under two names in the same town; and every one knows him as Edwin Fennel.—Here they are, some of them, coming back!" And when the wanderers were close up, they found Major Smith arguing with me about the architecture of the castle.

Ten o'clock. Time for bed. I am in no haste to go, for I don't sleep as well as I used to.

A thought has lately sometimes crossed me that this miserable trouble worries me more than it ought to do. "Accept it as your cross, and yield to it, Lavinia," says Mary Carimon to me. But I cannot yield to it; that is, I cannot in the least diminish the anxiety which always clings to me, or forget the distress and dread that lie upon me like a shadow. I know that my life has been on the whole an easy life—that during all the years I spent at Selby Court I never had any trouble; I know that crosses do come to us all, earlier or later, and that I ought not to be surprised that "no new thing has happened to me," the world being full of such experiences. I suppose it is because I have been so exempt from care, that I feel this the more.

Half-past ten! just half-an-hour writing these last few lines and thinking! Time I put up. I wonder when I shall hear from Nancy?

VI

A curious phase, taken in conjunction with what was to follow, now occurred in the history. Miss Preen began to experience a nervous dread at going into the Petite Maison Rouge at night.

She could go into the house ten times a-day when it was empty; she could stay in the house alone in the evening after Flore took her departure; she could be its only inmate all night long; and never at these times have the slightest sense of fear. But if she went out to spend the evening, she felt an unaccountable dread, amounting to horror, at entering it when she arrived home.

It came on suddenly. One evening when Lavinia had been at Mrs. Hardy's, Charley Palliser having run over to London, she returned home a little before ten o'clock. Opening the door with her latch-key, she was stepping into the passage when a sharp horror of entering it seized her. A dread, as it seemed to her, of going into the empty house, up the long, dark, narrow passage. It was the same sort of sensation that had struck her the first time she attempted to enter it under the escort of Monsieur Gustave Sauvage, and it came on now with as little reason as it had come on then. For Lavinia this night had not a thought in her mind of fear or loneliness, or anything else unpleasant. Mrs. Hardy had been relating a laughable adventure that Charley Palliser met with on board the boat when going over, the account of which he had written to her, and Lavinia was thinking brightly of it all the way home. She was smiling to herself as she unlatched the door and opened it. And then, without warning, arose the horrible fear.

How she conquered it sufficiently to enter the passage and reach the slab, where her candle and matches were always placed, she did not know. It had to be done, for Lavinia Preen could not remain in the dark yard all night, or patrol the streets; but her face had turned moist, and her hands trembled.

That was the beginning of it. Never since had she come home in the same way at night but the same terror assailed her; and I must beg the reader to understand that this is no invention. Devoid of reason and unaccountable though the terror was, Lavinia Preen experienced it.

She went out often—two or three times a-week, perhaps—either to dine or to spend the evening. Captain Fennel and Nancy were still away, and friends, remembering Miss Preen's solitary position, invited her.

October had passed, November was passing, and as yet no news came to Lavinia of the return of the travellers. At first they did not write to her at all, leaving her to infer that as the boat reached London safely they had done the same. After the lapse of a fortnight she received a short letter from Nancy telling her really nothing, and not giving any address. The next letter came towards the end of November, and was as follows:

"MY DEAR LAVINIA,

"I have not written to you, for, truly, there is nothing to write   about, and almost every day I expect Edwin to tell me we are going   home. Will you kindly lend me a ten-pound note? Please send it in   a letter. We are staying at Camberwell, and I enclose you the   address in strict confidence. Do not repeat it to any one—not even   to Mary Carimon. It is a relation of Edwin's we are staying with,   but he is not well off. I like his wife. Edwin desires his best   regards.

"Your loving sister,
"NANCY."

Miss Preen did not send the ten-pound note. She wrote to tell Nancy that she could not do it, and was uncomfortably pressed for money herself in consequence of Nancy's own action.

The five-pound note borrowed from Lavinia by Nancy on her departure had not been repaid; neither had Nancy's share of the previous quarter's money been remitted. On the usual day of payment at the end of September, Lavinia's quarterly income came to her at Sainteville, as was customary; not Nancy's. For Nancy there came neither money nor letter. The fact was, Nancy, escorted by her husband, had presented herself at Colonel Selby's bank—he was junior partner and manager of a small private bank in the City—the day before the dividends were due, and personally claimed the quarterly payment, which was paid to her.

But now, the summary docking of just half their income was a matter of embarrassment to Miss Preen, as may readily be imagined. The house expenses had to go on, with only half the money to meet them. Lavinia had a little nest-egg of her own, it has been said before, saved in earlier years; and this she drew upon, and so kept debt down. But it was very inconvenient, as well as vexatious. Lavinia told the whole truth now to Mary Carimon and her husband, with Nancy's recent application for a ten-pound note, and her refusal. Little Monsieur Carimon muttered a word between his closed lips which sounded like "Rat," and was no doubt applied to Edwin Fennel.

Pretty close upon this, Lavinia received a blowing-up letter from Colonel Selby. Having known Lavinia when she was in pinafores, the colonel, a peppery man, considered he had a right to take her to task at will. He was brother to Paul Selby, of Selby Court, and heir presumptive to it. The colonel had a wife and children, and much ado at times to keep them, for his income was not large at present, and growing-up sons are expensive.

"DEAR LAVINIA,

"What in the name of common sense could have induced you to imagine   that I should pay the two quarterly incomes some weeks before they   were due, and to send Ann and that man Fennel here with your orders   that I should do so? Pretty ideas of trusteeship you must have! If   you are over head and ears in debt, as they tell me, and for that   reason wish to forestall the time for payment, I can't help it. It is no reason with me. Your money will be forwarded to Sainteville,   at the proper period, to yourself. Do not ask me again to pay it   into Ann's hands, and to accept her receipt for it. I can do nothing   of the kind. Ann's share will be sent at the same time. She tells me   she is returning to you. She must give me her own receipt for it,   and you must give me yours.

"Your affectionate kinsman,
"WILLIAM SELBY."

Just for a few minutes Lavinia Preen did not understand this letter. What could it mean? Why had Colonel Selby written it to her? Then the truth flashed into her mind.

Nancy (induced, of course, by Edwin Fennel) had gone with him to Colonel Selby, purporting to have been sent by Lavinia, to ask him to pay them the quarter's money not due until the end of December, and not only Nancy's share but Lavinia's as well.

"Why, it would have been nothing short of swindling!" cried Lavinia, as she gazed in dismay at the colonel's letter.

In the indignation of the moment, she took pen and ink and wrote an answer to William Selby. Partly enlightening him—not quite—but telling him that her money must never be paid to any one but herself, and that the present matter had better be hushed up for Ann's sake, who was as a reed in the hands of the man she had married.

Colonel Selby exploded a little when he received this answer. Down he sat in his turn, and wrote a short, sharp note to Edwin Fennel, giving that estimable man a little of his mind, and warning him that he must not be surprised if the police were advised to look after him.

When Edward Fennel received this decisive note through an address he had given to Colonel Selby, but not the one at Camberwell, he called Miss Lavinia Preen all the laudatory names in the thieves' dictionary.

And on the feast of St. Andrew, which as every one knows is the last day of November, the letters came to an end with the following one from Nancy:

"All being well, my dear Lavinia, we propose to return home by next Sunday's boat, which ought to get in before three o'clock in the afternoon. On Wednesday, Edwin met Charley Palliser in the Strand, and had a chat with him, and heard all the Sainteville news; not that there seemed much to hear. Charley says he runs over to London pretty often now, his mother being ill. Of course you will not mind waiting dinner for us on Sunday.

"Ever your loving sister,
"ANN."

So at length they were coming! Either that threat of being looked after by the police had been too much for Captain Fennel, or the failure to obtain funds was cutting short his stay in London. Any way, they were coming. Lavinia laid the letter beside her breakfast-plate and fell into thought. She resolved to welcome them graciously, and to say nothing about bygones.

Flore was told the news, and warned that instead of dining at half-past one on the morrow, the usual Sunday hour, it would be delayed until three. Flore did not much like the prospect of her afternoon's holiday being shortened, but there was no help for it. Lavinia provided a couple of ducks for dinner, going into the market after breakfast to buy them; the dish was an especial favourite of the captain's. She invited Mary Carimon to partake of it, for Monsieur Carimon was going to spend Sunday at Lille with an old friend of his, who was now master of the college there.

On this evening, Saturday, Lavinia dined out herself. Some ladies named Bosanquet, three sisters, with whom she had become pretty intimate, called at the Petite Maison Rouge, and carried her off to their home in the Rue Lamartine, where they had lived for years. After a very pleasant evening with them, Lavinia left at ten o'clock.

And when she reached her own door, and was putting the latch-key into the lock, the old fear came over her. Dropping her hands, she stood there trembling. She looked round at the silent, deserted yard, she looked up at the high encircling walls; she glanced at the frosty sky and the bright stars; and she stood there shivering.

But she must go in. Throwing the door back with an effort of will, she turned sick and faint: to enter that dark, lonely, empty house seemed beyond her strength and courage. What could this strange feeling portend?—why should it thus attack her? It was just as if some fatality were in the house waiting to destroy her, and a subtle power would keep her from entering it.

Her heart beating wildly, her breath laboured, Lavinia went in; she shut the door behind her and sped up the passage. Feeling for the match-box on the slab, put ready to her hand, she struck a match and lighted the candle. At that moment, when turning round, she saw, or thought she saw, Captain Fennel. He was standing just within the front-door, which she had now come in at, staring at her with a fixed gaze, and with the most malignant expression on his usually impassive face. Lavinia's terror partly gave place to astonishment. Was it he himself? How had he come in?

Turning to take the candle from the slab in her bewilderment, when she looked again he was gone. What had become of him? Lavinia called to him by name, but he did not answer. She took the candle into the salon, though feeling sure he could not have come up the passage; but he was not there. Had he slipped out again? Had she left the door open when thinking she closed it, and had he followed her in, and was now gone again? Lavinia carried her lighted candle to the door, and found it was fastened. She had not left it open.

Then, as she undressed in her room, trying all the while to solve the problem, an idea crept into her mind that the appearance might have been supernatural. Yet—supernatural visitants of the living do not appear to us, but of the dead. Was Edwin Fennel dead?

So disturbed was the brain of Lavinia Preen that she could not get to sleep; but tossed and turned about the bed almost until daybreak. At six o'clock she fell into an uneasy slumber, and into a most distressing dream.

It was a confused dream; nothing in it was clear. All she knew when she awoke, was that she had appeared to be in a state of inexplicable terror, of most intense apprehension throughout it, arising from some evil threatened her by Captain Fennel.

VII

It was a fine, frosty day, and the first of December. The sun shone on the fair streets of Sainteville and on the small congregation turning out of the English Protestant Church after morning service.

Lavinia Preen went straight home. There she found that Madame Carimon, who was to spend the rest of the day with her—monsieur having gone to Lille—had not yet arrived, though the French Church Evangélique was always over before the English. After glancing at Flore in the kitchen, busy over the fine ducks, Lavinia set off for the Rue Pomme Cuite.

She met Mary Carimon turning out of it. "Let us go and sit under the wall in the sun," said Mary. "It is too early yet for the boat."

This was a high wall belonging to the strong north gates of the town, near Madame Carimon's. The sun shone full upon the benches beneath it, which it sheltered from the bleak winds; in front was a patch of green grass, on which the children ran about amidst the straight poplar trees. It was very pleasant sitting there, even on this December day—bright and cheerful; the wall behind them was quite warm, the sunshine rested upon all.

Sitting there, Lavinia Preen told Madame Carimon of the curious dread of entering her house at night, which had pursued her for the past two months that she had been alone in it, and which she had never spoken of to any one before. She went on to speak of the belief that she had seen Captain Fennel the previous night in the passage, and of the dream which had visited her when at length she fell asleep.

Madame Carimon turned her kindly, sensible face and her quiet, dark, surprised eyes upon Lavinia. "I cannot understand you," she said.

"You mean, I suppose, that you cannot understand the facts, Mary. Neither can I. Why this fear of going into the house should lie upon me is most strange. I never was nervous before."

"I don't know that that is so very strange," dissented Mary Carimon, after a pause. "It must seem lonely to let one's self into a dark, empty house in the middle of the night; and your house is in what may be called an isolated situation; I should not much like it myself. That's nothing. What I cannot understand, Lavinia, is the fancy that you saw Captain Fennel."

"He appeared to be standing there, and was quite visible to me. The expression on his face, which seemed to be looking straight into mine, was most malicious. I never saw such an expression upon it in reality."

Mary Carimon laughed a little, saying she had never been troubled with nervous fears herself; she was too practical for anything of the sort.

"And I have been practical hitherto," returned Lavinia. "When the first surprise of seeing him there, or fancying I saw him there, was over, I began to think, Mary, that he might be dead; that it was his apparition which had stood there looking at me."

Mary Carimon shook her head. "Had anything of that sort happened, Nancy would have telegraphed to you. Rely upon it, Lavinia, it was pure fancy. You have been disagreeably exercised in mind lately, you know, about that man; hearing he was coming home, your brain was somewhat thrown off its balance."

"It may be so. The dream followed on it; and I did not like the dream."

"We all have bad dreams now and then. You say you do not remember much of this one."

"I think I did not know much of it when dreaming it," quaintly spoke Lavinia. "I was in a sea of trouble, throughout which I seemed to be striving to escape some evil menaced me by Captain Fennel, and could not do so. Whichever way I turned, there he was at a distance, scowling at me with a threatening, evil countenance. Mary," she added in impassioned tones, "I am sure some ill awaits me from that man."

"I am sure, were I you, I would put these foolish notions from me," calmly spoke Madame Carimon. "If Nancy set up a vocation for seeing ghosts and dreaming dreams, one would not so much wonder at it. You have always been reasonable, Lavinia; be so now."

Miss Preen took out her watch and looked at it. "We may as well be walking towards the port, Mary," she remarked. "It is past two. The boat ought to be in sight."

Not only in sight was the steamer, but rapidly nearing the port. She had made a calm and quick passage. When at length she was in and about to swing round, and the two ladies were looking down at it, with a small crowd of other assembled spectators, the first passengers they saw on board were Nancy and Captain Fennel, who began to wave their hands in greeting and to nod their heads.

"Any way, Lavinia, it could not have been his ghost last night," whispered Mary Carimon.

Far from presenting an evil countenance to Lavinia, as the days passed on, Captain Fennel appeared to wish to please her, and was all suavity. So at present nothing disturbed the peace of the Petite Maison Rouge.

"What people were they that you stayed with in London, Nancy?" Lavinia inquired of her sister on the first favourable opportunity.

Nancy glanced round the salon before answering, as if to make sure they were alone; but Captain Fennel had gone out for a stroll.

"We were at James Fennel's, Lavinia."

"What—the brother's! And has he a wife?"

"Yes; a wife, but no children. Mrs. James Fennel has money of her own, which she receives weekly."

"Receives weekly!" echoed Lavinia.

"She owns some little houses which are let out in weekly tenements; an agent collects the rents, and brings her the money every Tuesday morning. She dresses in the shabbiest things sometimes, and does her own housework, and altogether is not what I should call quite a lady, but she is very good-hearted. She did her best to make us comfortable, and never grumbled at our staying so long. I expect Edwin paid her something. James only came home by fits and starts. I think he was in some embarrassment—debt, you know. He used to dash into the house like a whirlwind when he did come, and steal out of it when he left, peering about on all sides."

"Have they a nice house?" asked Lavinia.

"Oh, good gracious, no! It's not a house at all, only small lodgings. And Mrs. James changed them twice over whilst we were there. When we first went they were at a place called Ball's Pond."

"Why did you remain all that time?"

Mrs. Edwin Fennel shook her head helplessly; she could not answer the question. "I should have liked to come back before," she said; "it was very wearisome, knowing nobody and having nothing to do. Did you find it dull here, Lavinia, all by yourself?"

"'Dull' is not the right word for it," answered Lavinia, catching her breath with a sigh. "I felt more lonely, Ann, than I shall ever care to feel again. Especially when I had to come home at night from some soirée, or from spending the evening quietly with Mary Carimon or any other friend." And she went on to tell of the feeling of terror which had so tried her.

"I never heard of such a thing!" exclaimed Ann. "How silly you must be, Lavinia! What could there have been in the house to frighten you?"

"I don't know; I wish I did know," sighed Lavinia, just as she had said more than once before.

Nancy, who was attired in a bright ruby cashmere robe, with a gold chain and locket, some blue ribbons adorning her light ringlets, for she had made a point of dressing more youthfully than ever since her marriage, leaned back in her chair, as she sat staring at her sister and thinking.

"Lavinia," she said huskily, "you remember the feeling you had the day we were about to look at the house with Mary Carimon, and which you thought was through the darkness of the passage striking you unpleasantly? Well, my opinion is that it must have given you a scare."

"Why, of course it did."

"Ah, but I mean a scare which lasts," said Ann; "one of those scares which affect the mind and take very long to get rid of. You recollect poor Mrs. Hunt, at Buttermead? She was frightened at a violent thunderstorm, though she never had been before; and for years afterwards, whenever it thundered, she became so alarmingly ill and agitated that Mr. Featherston had to be run for. He called it a scare. I think the fear you felt that past day must have left that sort of scare upon you. How else can you account for what you tell me?"

Truth to say, the same idea had more than once struck Lavinia. She knew how devoid of reason some of these "scares" are, and yet how terribly they disturb the mind on which they fasten.

"But I had quite forgotten that fear, Ann," she urged in reply. "We had lived in the house eighteen months when you went away, and I had never recalled it."

"All the same, I think you received the scare; it had only lain dormant," persisted Ann.

"Well, well; you are back again now, and it is over," said Lavinia. "Let us forget it. Do not speak of it again at all to any one, Nancy love."

Winter that year had quite set in when Sainteville found itself honoured with rather a remarkable visitor; one Signor Talcke, who descended, one morning at the beginning of December, at the Hôtel des Princes. Though he called himself "Signor," it seemed uncertain to what country he owed his birth. He spoke five or six languages as a native, including Hindustani. Signor Talcke was a professor of occult sciences; he was a great astronomer; astrology he had at his fingers' ends. He was a powerful mesmerist; he would foretell the events of your life by your hands, or your fortune by the cards.

For a fee of twenty-five francs, he would attend an evening party, and exhibit some of his powers. Amidst others who engaged him were the Miss Bosanquets, in the Rue Lamartine. A relative of theirs, Sir George Bosanquet, K.C.B., had come over with his wife to spend Christmas with them. Sir George laughed at what he heard of Signor Talcke's powers of reading the future, and said he should much like to witness a specimen of it. So Miss Bosanquet and her sisters hastily arranged an evening entertainment, engaged the mystical man, and invited their friends and acquaintances, those of the Petite Maison Rouge included.

It took place on the Friday after Christmas-Day. Something that occurred during the evening was rather remarkable. Miss Preen's diary gives a full account of it, and that shall be transcribed here. And I, Johnny Ludlow, take this opportunity of assuring the reader that what she wrote was in faithful accordance with the facts of the case.

From Miss Preen's Diary.

Saturday morning.—I feel very tired; fit for nothing. Nancy has undertaken to do the marketing, and is gone out for that purpose with her husband. It is to be hoped she will be moderate, and not attempt to buy up half the market.

I lay awake all night, after the evening at Miss Bosanquet's, thinking how foolish Ann was to have had her "future cast," as that Italian (if he is Italian) called it, and how worse than foolish I was to let what he said worry me. "As if there could be anything in it!" laughed Ann, as we were coming home; fortunately she is not as I am in temperament—nervously anxious. "It is only nonsense," said Miss Anna Bosanquet to me when the signor's predictions were at an end; "he will tell some one else just the same next time." But I did not think so. Of course, one is at a loss how to trust this kind of man. Take him for all in all, I rather like him; and he appears to believe implicitly in what he says: or, rather, in what he tell us the cards say.

They are charming women, these three sisters—Grace, Rose, and Anna Bosanquet; good, considerate, high-bred ladies. I wonder how it is they have lived to middle life without any one of them marrying? And I often wonder how they came to take up their residence at Sainteville, for they are very well off, and have great connections. I remember, though, Anna once said to me that the dry, pure air of the place suited her sister Rose, who has bad health, better than any other they had tried.

When seven o'clock struck, the hour named, Nancy and I appeared together in the sitting-room, ready to start, for we observe punctuality at Sainteville. I wore my black satin, handsome yet, trimmed with the rich white lace that Mrs. Selby gave me. Nancy looked very nice and young in her lilac silk. She wore a white rose in her hair, and her gold chain and locket round her neck. Captain Fennel surprised us by saying he was not going—his neuralgia had come on. I fancied it was an excuse—that he did not wish to meet Sir George Bosanquet. He had complained of the same thing on Christmas-Day, so it might be true. Ann and I set off together, leaving him nursing his cheek at the table.

It was a large gathering for Sainteville—forty guests, I should think; but the rooms are large. Professor Talcke exhibited some wonderful feats in—what shall I call it?—necromancy?—as good a word, perhaps, as any other. He mesmerized some people, and put one of them into a state of clairvoyance, and her revelations took my breath away. Signor Talcke assured us that what she said would be found minutely true. I think he has the strangest eyes I ever saw: grey eyes, with a sort of light in their depths. His features are fair and delicate, his voice is gentle as a woman's, his manner retiring; Sir George seemed much taken with him.

Later, when the evening was passing, he asked if any one present would like to have their future cast, for he had cards which would do it. Three of his listeners pressed forward at once; two of them with gay laughter, the other pale and awestruck. The signor went into the recess in the small room, and sat down behind the little table there, and as many as could crowd round to look on, did so. I don't know what passed; there was no room for me; or whether the "Futures" he disclosed were good or bad. I had sat on the sofa at a distance, talking with Anna Bosanquet and Madame Carimon.

Suddenly, as we were for a moment silent, Ann's voice was heard, eager and laughing:

"Will you tell my fortune, Signor Talcke? I should like to have mine revealed."

"With pleasure, madame," he answered.

We got up and drew near. I felt vexed that Ann should put herself forward in any such matter, and whispered to her; but she only shook her curls, laughed at me, and persisted. Signor Talcke put the cards in her hands, telling her to shuffle them.

"It is all fun, Lavinia," she whispered to me. "Did you hear him tell Miss Peet she was going to have money left her?"

After Ann had shuffled the cards, he made her cut them into three divisions, and he then turned them up on the table himself, faces upwards, and laid them out in three rows. They were not like the cards we play with; quite different from those; nearly all were picture-cards, and the plain ones bore cabalistic characters. We stood looking on with two or three other people; the rest had dispersed, and had gone into the next room to listen to the singing.

At first Signor Talcke never spoke a word. He looked at the cards, and looked at Nancy; looked, and looked again. "They are not propitious," he said in low tones, and picked them up, and asked Nancy to shuffle and cut them again. Then he laid them as before, and we stood waiting in silence.

Chancing at that moment to look at Signor Talcke, his face startled me. He was frowning at the cards in so painful a manner as to quite alter its expression. But he did not speak. He still only gazed at the cards with bent eyes, and glanced up at Ann occasionally. Then, with an impatient sweep of the hand, he pushed the cards together.

"I must trouble you to shuffle and cut them once more, madame," he said. "Shuffle them well."

"Are they still unpropitious?" asked a jesting voice at my elbow. Turning, I saw Charley Palliser's smiling face. He must have been standing there, and heard Signor Talcke's previous remark.

"Yes, sir, they are," replied the signor, with marked emphasis. "I never saw the cards so unpropitious in my life."

Nancy took up the cards, shuffled them well, and cut them three times. Signor Talcke laid them out as before, bent his head, and looked attentively at them. He did not speak, but there was no mistaking the vexed, pained, and puzzled look on his face.

I do not think he knew Nancy, even by name. I do not think he knew me, or had the least notion that we were related. Neither of us had ever met him before. He put his hand to his brow, still gazing at the cards.

"But when are you going to begin my fortune, sir?" broke in Nancy.

"I would rather not tell it at all, madame," he answered.

"Cannot you tell it?—have your powers of forecasting inconveniently run away?" said she incautiously, her tone mocking in her disappointment.

"I could tell it, all too surely; but you might not like to hear it," returned he.

"Our magician has lost his divining-rod just when he needed it," observed a gentleman with a grey beard, a stranger to me, who was standing opposite, speaking in a tone of ill-natured satire; and a laugh went round.

"It is not that," said the signor, keeping his temper perfectly. "I could tell what the cards say, all too certainly; but it would not give satisfaction."

"Oh yes, it would," returned Nancy. "I should like to hear it, every bit of it. Please do begin."

"The cards are dark, very dark indeed," he said; "I don't remember ever to have seen them like it. Each time they have been turned the darkness has increased. Nothing can show worse than they do now."

"Never mind that," gaily returned Ann. "You undertook to tell my fortune, sir; and you ought not to make excuses in the middle of it. Let the cards be as dark as night, we must hear what they say."

He drew in his thin lips for a moment, and then spoke, his tone quiet, calm, unemotional.

"Some great evil threatens you," he began; "you seem to be living in the midst of it. It is not only you that it threatens; there is another also—"

"Oh, my goodness!" interrupted Nancy, in her childish way. "I hope it does not threaten Edwin. What is the evil?—sickness?"

"Worse than that. It—is—" Signor Talcke's attention was so absorbed by the aspect of the cards that, as it struck me, he appeared hardly to heed what he was saying. He had a long, thin black pencil in his long, thin fingers, and kept pointing to different cards as if in accordance with his thoughts, but not touching them. "There is some peculiar form of terror here," he went on. "I cannot make it out; it is very unusual. It does not come close to you; not yet, at any rate; and it seems to surround you. It seems to be in the house. May I ask"—quickly lifting his eyes to Ann—"whether you are given to superstitious fears?"

"Do you mean ghosts?" cried Ann, and Charley Palliser burst out laughing. "Not at all, sir; I don't believe in ghosts. I'm sure there are none in our house."

Remembering my own terror in regard to the house, and the nervous fancy of having seen Captain Fennel in it when he was miles away, a curious impression came over me that he must surely be reading my fortune as well as Nancy's. But I was not prepared for her next words. Truly she has no more reticence than a child.

"My sister has a feeling that the house is lonely. She shivers when she has to go into it after night-fall."

Signor Talcke let his hands fall on the table, and lifted his face. Apparently, he was digesting this revelation. I do not think he knew the "sister" was present. For my part, disliking publicity, I slipped behind Anna Bosanquet, and stood by Charley Palliser.

"Shivers?" repeated the Italian.

"Shivers and trembles, and turns sick at having to go in," affirmed Nancy. "So she told me when I arrived home from England."

"If a feeling of that sort assailed me, I should never go into the house again," said the signor.

"But how could you help it, if it were your home?" she argued.

"All the same. I should regard that feeling as a warning against the house, and never enter it. Then you are not yourself troubled with superstitious fears?" he broke off, returning to the business in hand, and looking at the cards. "Well—at present—it does not seem to touch you, this curious terror which is assuredly in the house—"

"I beg your pardon," interrupted Ann. "Why do you say 'at present'? Is it to touch me later?"

"I cannot say. Each time that the cards have been spread it has shown itself nearer to you. It is not yet very near. Apart from that terror—or perhaps remotely connected with it—I see evil threatening you— great evil."

"Is it in the house?"

"Yes; hovering about it. It is not only yourself it seems to threaten. There is some one else. And it is nearer to that person than it is to you."

"But who is that person?—man or woman?"

"It is a woman. See this ugly card," continued he, pointing with his pencil; "it will not be got rid of, shuffle as you will; it has come nearer to that woman each time."

The card he pointed to was more curious-looking than any other in the pack. It was not unlike the nine of spades, but crowded with devices. The gentleman opposite, whom I did not know, leaned forward and touched the card with the tip of his forefinger.

"Le cercueil, n'est-ce-pas?" said he.

"My!" whispered an English lad's voice behind me. "Cercueil? that means coffin."

"How did you know?" asked Signor Talcke of the grey-bearded man.

"I was at the Sous-Préfect's soirée on Sunday evening when you were exhibiting. I heard you tell him in French that that was the ugliest card in the pack: indicating death."

"Well, it is not this lady the card is pursuing," said the signor, smiling at Ann to reassure her. "Not yet awhile, at least. And we must all be pursued by it in our turn, whenever that shall come," he added, bending over the cards again. "Pardon me, madame—may I ask whether there has not been some unpleasantness in the house concerning money?"

Nancy's face turned red. "Not—exactly," she answered with hesitation. "We are like a great many more people—not as rich as we should wish to be."

"It does not appear to lie precisely in the want of money: but certainly money is in some way connected with the evil," he was beginning to say, his eyes fixed dreamily on the cards, when Ann interrupted him.

"That is too strong a word—evil. Why do you use it?"

"I use it because the evil is there. No lighter word would be appropriate. There is some evil element pervading your house, very grave and formidable; it is most threatening; likely to go on to—to—darkness. I mean that it looks as if there would be some great break-up," he corrected swiftly, as if to soften the other word.

"That the house would be broken up?" questioned Ann.

He stole a glance at her. "Something of that sort," he said carelessly.

"Do you mean that the evil comes from an enemy?" she went on.

"Assuredly."

"But we have no enemy. I'm sure we have not one in all the world."

He slightly shook his head. "You may not suspect it yet, though I should have said"—waving the pencil thoughtfully over some of the cards—"that he was already suspected—doubted."

Nancy took up the personal pronoun briskly. "He!—then the evil enemy must be a man? I assure you we do not know any man likely to be our enemy or to wish us harm. No, nor woman either. Perhaps your cards don't tell true to-night, Signor Talcke?"

"Perhaps not, madame; we will let it be so if you will," he quietly said, and shuffled all the cards together.

That ended the séance. As if determined not to tell any more fortunes, the signor hurriedly put up the cards and disappeared from the recess. Nancy did not appear to be in the least impressed.

"What a curious 'future' it was!" she exclaimed lightly to Mary Carimon. "I might as well not have had it cast. He told me nothing."

They walked away together. I went back to the sofa and Anna Bosanquet followed me.

"Mrs. Fennel calls it 'curious,'" I said to her. "I call it more than that—strange; ominous. I wish I had not heard it."

"Dear Miss Preen, it is only nonsense," she answered. "He will tell some one else the same next time." But she only so spoke to console me.

A wild wish flashed into my mind—that I should ask the man to tell my future. But had I not heard enough? Mine was blended with this of Ann's. I was the other woman whom the dark fate was more relentlessly pursuing. There could be no doubt of that. There could be as little doubt that it was I who already suspected the author of the "evil." What can the "dark fate" be that we are threatened with? Debt? Will his debts spring upon us and break up our home, and turn us out of it? Or will it be something worse? That card which followed me meant a coffin, they said. Ah me! Perhaps I am foolish to dwell upon such ideas. Certainly they are more fitting for the world's dark ages than for this enlightened nineteenth century of it.

Charley Palliser gallantly offered to see us home. I said no; as if we were not old enough to go by ourselves; but he would come with us. As we went along Ann began talking of the party, criticizing the dresses, and so on. Charley seemed to be unusually silent.

"Was not mine a grand fortune?" she presently said with a laugh, as we crossed the Place Ronde.

"Stunning," said he.

"As if there could be anything in it, you know! Does the man think we believe him, I wonder?"

"Oh, these conjurers like to fancy they impose on us," remarked Charley, shaking hands as we halted before the house of Madame Sauvage.

And I have had a wretched night, for somehow the thing has frightened me. I never was superstitious; never; and I'm sure I never believed in conjurers, as Charles had it. If I should come across Signor Talcke again while he stays here, I would ask him— Here comes Nancy! and Flore behind her with the marketings. I'll put up my diary.

"I've bought such a lovely capon," began Nancy, as Lavinia went into the kitchen. "Show it to madame, Flore."

It was one that even Lavinia could praise; they both understood poultry. "It really is a beauty," said Lavinia. "And did you remember the salsifis? And, Ann, where have you left your husband?"

"Oh, we met old Mr. Griffin, and Edwin has gone up to Drecques with him. My opinion is, Lavinia, that that poor old Griffin dare not go about far by himself since his attack. He had to see his landlord at Drecques to-day, and he asked Edwin to accompany him. They went by the eleven-o'clock train."

Lavinia felt it a relief. Even that little absence, part of a day, she felt thankful for, so much had she grown to dislike the presence in the house of Edwin Fennel.

"Did you tell your husband about your 'fortune' Nancy?"

"No; I was too sleepy last night to talk, and I was late in getting up this morning. I'm not sure that I shall tell him," added Mrs. Fennel thoughtfully; "he might be angry with me for having had it done."

"That is more than likely," replied Lavinia.

Late in the afternoon, as they were sitting together in the salon, they saw the postman come marching up the yard. He brought two letters—one for Miss Preen, the other for her sister.

"It is the remittance from William Selby," said Lavinia as she opened hers. "He has sent it a day or two earlier than usual; it is not really due until Monday or Tuesday."

Seventeen pounds ten shillings each. Nancy, in a hasty sort of manner, put her cheque into the hands of Lavinia, almost as if she feared it would burn her own fingers. "You had better take it from me whilst you can," she said in low tones.

"Yes; for I must have it, Ann," was the answer. "We are in debt—as you may readily conceive—with only half the usual amount to spend last quarter."

"It was not my fault; I was very sorry," said Ann humbly; and she rose hastily to go to the kitchen, saying she was thirsty, and wanted a glass of water. But Lavinia thought she went to avoid being questioned.

Lavinia carried the two cheques to her room and locked them up. After their five-o'clock dinner, each sister wrote a note to Colonel Selby, enclosing her receipt. Flore took them out to post when she left. The evening passed on. Lavinia worked; Nancy nodded over the fire: she was very sleepy, and went to bed early.

It was past eleven o'clock when Captain Fennel came in, a little the worse for something or other. After returning from Drecques by the last train, he had gone home with Mr. Griffin to supper. He told Lavinia, in words running into one another, that the jolting train had made him giddy. Of course she believed as much of that as she liked, but did not contradict it. He went to the cupboard in the recess, unlocked it to get out the cognac, and then sat down with his pipe by the embers of the dying fire. Lavinia, unasked, brought in a decanter of water, put it on the table with a glass, and wished him good-night.

All next day Captain Fennel lay in bed with a racking headache. His wife carried up a choice bit of the capon when they were dining after morning service, but he could not so much as look at it. Being a fairly cautious man as a rule, he had to pay for—for the jolting of the train.

He was better on Monday morning, but not well, still shaky, and did not come down to breakfast. It was bitterly cold—a sort of black frost; but Lavinia, wrapping herself up warmly, went out as soon as breakfast was over.

Her first errand was to the bank, where she paid in the cheques and received French money for them. Then she visited sundry shops; the butcher's, the grocer's, and others, settling the accounts due. Last of all, she made a call upon Madame Veuve Sauvage, and paid the rent for the past quarter. All this left her with exactly nineteen pounds, which was all the money she had to go on with for every purpose until the end of March—three whole months.

Lunch was ready when she returned. Taking off her things upstairs and locking up her cash, she went down to it. Flore had made some delicious soupe maigre. Only those who have tried it know how good it is on a sharp winter's day. Captain Fennel seemed to relish it much, though his appetite had not quite come back to him, and he turned from the dish of scrambled eggs which supplemented the soup. In the evening they went, by appointment, to dine at Madame Carimon's, the other guests being Monsieur Henri Dupuis with his recently married wife, and Charles Palliser.

After dinner, over the coffee, Monsieur Henri Dupuis suddenly spoke of the soirée at Miss Bosanquet's the previous Friday, regretting that he and his wife had been unable to attend it. He was engaged the whole evening with a patient dangerously ill, and his wife did not like to appear at it without him. Nancy—Nancy!—then began to tell about the "fortune" which had been forecast for her by Signor Talcke, thinking possibly that her husband could not reproach her for it before company. She was very gay over it; a proof that it had left no bad impression on her mind.

"What's that, Nancy?" cried Captain Fennel, who had listened as if he disbelieved his ears. "The fellow told you we had something evil in our house?"

"Yes, he did," assented Nancy. "An evil influence, he said, which was destined to bring forth something dark and dreadful."

"I am sorry you did not tell this before," returned the captain stiffly. "I should have requested you not again to allude to such folly. It was downright insolence."

"I—you—you were out on Saturday, you know, Edwin, and in bed with your headache all Sunday; and to-day I forgot it," said Nancy in less brave tones.

"Suppose we have a game at wholesome card-playing," interposed Mary Carimon, bringing forth a new pack. "Open them, will you, Jules? Do you remember, mon ami, having your fortune told once by a gipsy woman when we were in Sir John Whitney's coppice with the two Peckham girls? She told you you would fall into a rich inheritance and marry a Frenchwoman."

"Neither of which agreeable promises is yet fulfilled," said little Monsieur Carimon with his happy smile. Monsieur Carimon had heard the account of Nancy's "forecast" from his wife; he was not himself present, but taking a hand at whist in the card-room.

They sat down to a round game—spin. Monsieur Henri Dupuis and his pretty young wife had never played it before, but they soon learned it and liked it much. Both of them spoke English well; she with the prettiest accent imaginable. Thus the evening passed, and no more allusion was made to the fortune-telling at Miss Bosanquet's.

That was Monday. On Tuesday, Miss Preen was dispensing the coffee at breakfast in the Petite Maison Rouge to her sister and Mr. Fennel, when Flore came bustling in with a letter in her hand.

"Tenez, madame," she said, putting it beside Mrs. Fennel. "I laid it down in the kitchen when the facteur brought it, whilst I was preparing the déjeûner, and forgot it afterwards."

Before Nancy could touch the letter, her husband caught it up. He gazed at the address, at the postmark, and turned it about to look at the seal. The letters of gentlefolk were generally fastened with a seal in those days: this had one in transparent bronze wax.

Mr. Fennel put the letter down with a remark peevishly uttered. "It is not from London; it is from Buttermead."

"And from your old friend, Jane Peckham, Nancy," struck in Lavinia. "I recognize her handwriting."

"I am glad," exclaimed Nancy. "I have not heard from them for ages. Why now—is it not odd?—that Madame Carimon should mention the Peckhams last night, and I receive a letter from them this morning?"

"I supposed it might be from London, with your remittance," said Mr. Fennel to his wife. "It is due, is it not?"

"Oh, that came on Saturday, Edwin," she said, as she opened her letter.

"Came on Saturday!" echoed Captain Fennel ungraciously, as if disputing the assertion.

"By the afternoon post; you were at Drecques, you know."

"The money came? Your money?"

"Yes," said Nancy, who had stepped to the window to read her letter, for it was a dark day, and stood there with her back to the room.

"And where is it?" demanded he.

"I gave it to Lavinia. I always give it to her."

Captain Fennel glared at his wife for a moment, then smoothed his face to its ordinary placidity, and turned to Lavinia.

"Will you be good enough to hand over to me my wife's money, Miss Preen?"

"No," she answered quietly.

"I must trouble you to do so, when breakfast shall be finished."

"I cannot," pursued Lavinia. "I have paid it away."

"That I do not believe. I claim it from you in right of my wife; and I shall enforce the claim."

"The money is Nancy's, not yours," said Lavinia. "In consequence of your having stopped her share last quarter in London, I was plunged here into debt and great inconvenience. Yesterday morning I went out to settle the debts—and it has taken the whole of her money to do it. That is the state of things, Captain Fennel."

"I am in debt here myself," retorted he, but not angrily. "I owe money to my tailor and bootmaker; I owe an account at the chemist's; I want money in my pockets—and I must indeed have it."

"Not from me," returned Lavinia.

Edwin Fennel broke into a little access of temper. He dashed his serviette on the table, strode to the window, and roughly caught his wife by the arm. She cried out.

"How dared you hand your money to any one but me?" he asked in a low voice of passion.

"But how are we to live if I don't give it to Lavinia for the housekeeping?" returned Nancy, bursting into tears. "It takes all we have; her share and mine; every farthing of it."

"Let my sister alone, Mr. Fennel," spoke up Lavinia with authority. "She is responsible for the debts we contract in this house, just as much as I am, and she must contribute her part to pay them. You ought to be aware that the expenses are now increased by nearly a third; I assure you I hardly like to face the difficulties I see before me."

"Do you suppose I can stop in the place without some loose cash to keep me going?" he asked calmly. "Is that reasonable, Miss Lavinia?"

"And do you suppose I can keep you and Ann here without her money to help me to do it?" she rejoined. "Perhaps the better plan will be for me to take up my abode elsewhere, and leave the house to you and Ann to do as you please in it."

Captain Fennel dropped his argument, returned to the table, and went on with his breakfast. The last words had startled him. Without Lavinia, which meant without her money, they could not live in the house at all.

Matters were partly patched up in the course of the day. Nancy came upstairs to Lavinia, begging and praying, as if she were praying for her life, for a little ready money for her husband—just a hundred francs. Trembling and sobbing, she confessed that she dared not return to him without it; she should be too frightened at his anger.

And Lavinia gave it to her.

Matters went on to the spring. There were no outward differences in the Petite Maison Rouge, but it was full of an undercurrent of discomfort. At least for Lavinia. Captain Fennel was simply to her an incubus; and now and again petty accounts of his would be brought to the door by tradespeople who wanted them settled. As to keeping up the legitimate payments, she could not do it.

March was drawing to an end, when a surprise came to them. Lavinia received a letter from Paris, written by Colonel Selby. He had been there for two days on business, he said, and purposed returning viâ Sainteville, to take a passing glimpse at herself and her sister. He hoped to be down that afternoon by the three-o'clock train, and he asked them to meet him at the Hôtel des Princes afterwards, and to stay and dine with him. He proposed crossing to London by the night boat.

Lavinia read the letter aloud. Nancy went into ecstasies, for a wonder; she had been curiously subdued in manner lately. Edwin Fennel made no remark, but his pale face wore a look of thought.

During the morning he betook himself to the Rue Lothaire to call upon Mr. Griffin; and he persuaded that easy-natured old gentleman to take advantage of the sunny day and make an excursion en voiture to the nearest town, a place called Pontipette. Of course the captain went also, as his companion.

Colonel Selby arrived at three. Lavinia and Nancy met him at the station, and went with him in the omnibus to the hotel. They then showed him about Sainteville, to which he was a stranger, took him to see their domicile, the little red house (which he did not seem to admire), and thence to Madame Carimon's. In the Buttermead days, the colonel and Mary Featherston had been great friends. He invited her and her husband to join them at the table d'hôte dinner at five o'clock.

Lavinia and Nancy went home again to change their dresses for it. Nancy put on a pretty light green silk, which had been recently modernized. Mrs. Selby had kept up an extensive wardrobe, and had left it between the two sisters.

"You should wear your gold chain and locket," remarked Lavinia, who always took pride in her sister's appearance. "It will look very nice upon that dress."

She alluded to a short, thick chain of gold, the gold locket attached to it being set round with pearls, Nancy's best ornament; nay, the only one she had of any value; it was the one she had worn at Miss Bosanquet's celebrated party. Nancy made no answer. She was turning red and white.

"What's the matter?" cried Lavinia.

The matter was, that Mr. Edwin Fennel had obtained possession of the chain and locket more than a month ago. Silly Nancy confessed with trembling lips that she feared he had pledged it.

Or sold it, thought Lavinia. She felt terribly vexed and indignant. "I suppose, Ann, it will end in his grasping everything," she said, "and starving us out of house and home: myself, at any rate."

"He expects money from his brother James, and then he will get it back for me," twittered Nancy.

Monsieur Jules Carimon was not able to come to the table d'hôte; his duties that night would detain him at the college until seven o'clock. It happened so on occasion. Colonel Selby sat at one end of their party, Lavinia at the other; Mary Carimon and Nancy between them. A gentleman was on the other side of Lavinia whom she did not particularly notice; and, upon his asking the waiter for something, his voice seemed to strike upon her memory. Turning, she saw that it was the tall Englishman they had seen on the pier some months before in the shepherd's plaid, the lawyer named Lockett. He recognized her face at the same moment, and they entered into conversation.

"Are you making any stay at Sainteville?" she inquired.

"For a few days. I must be back in London on Monday morning."

Colonel Selby's attention was attracted to the speakers. "What, is it you, Lockett?" he exclaimed.

Mr. Lockett bent forward to look beyond Lavinia and Madame Carimon. "Why, colonel, are you here?" he cried. So it was evident that they knew one another.

But you can't talk very much across people at a table d'hôte; and Lavinia and Mr. Lockett were, so to say, left together again. She put a question to him, dropping her voice to a whisper.

"Did you ever find that person you were looking for?"

"The person I was looking for?" repeated the lawyer, not remembering. "What person was that?"

"The one you spoke of on the pier that day—a Mr. Dangerfield."

"Oh, ay; but I was not looking for him myself. No; I believe he is not dropped upon yet. He is keeping quiet, I expect."

"Is he still being looked for?"

"Little doubt of that. My friend here, on my left, could tell you more about him than I can, if you want to know."

"No, thank you," said Lavinia hastily, in a sort of fear. And she then observed that next to Mr. Lockett another Englishman was sitting, who looked very much like a lawyer also.

After dinner Colonel Selby took his guests, the three ladies, into the little salon, which opened to Madame Podevin's bureau; for it was she who, French fashion, kept the bureau and all its accounts, not her husband. Whilst the coffee which the colonel ordered was preparing, he took from his pocket-book two cheques, and gave one each to Lavinia and Mrs. Fennel. It was their quarterly income, due about a week hence.

"I thought I might as well give it you now, as I am here, and save the trouble of sending," he remarked. "You can write me a receipt for it; here's pen, ink and paper."

Each wrote her receipt, and gave it him. Nancy held the cheque in her hand, looking at her sister in a vacillating manner. "I suppose I ought to give it you, Lavinia," she said. "Must I do so?"

"What do you think about it yourself?" coldly rejoined Lavinia.

"He was so very angry with me the last time," sighed Nancy, still withholding the cheque. "He said I ought to keep possession of my own, and he ordered me to do so in future."

"That he may have the pleasure of spending it," said Mary Carimon in a sharp tone, though she laughed at the same time. "Lavinia has to pay for the bread-and-cheese that you and he eat, Nancy; how can she do that unless she receives your money?"

"Yes, I know; it is very difficult," said poor Nancy. "Take the cheque, Lavinia; I shall tell him that you and Mary Carimon both said I must give it up."

"Oh, tell him I said so, and welcome," spoke Madame Carimon. "I will tell him so myself, if you like."

As Colonel Selby returned to the room—he had been seeing to his luggage—the coffee was brought in, and close upon it came Monsieur Carimon.

The boat for London was leaving early that night—eight o'clock; they all went down to it to see William Selby off. It was a calm night, warm for the time of year, the moon beautifully bright. After the boat's departure, Lavinia and Ann went home, and found Captain Fennel there. He had just got in, he said, and wanted some supper.

Whilst he was taking it, his wife told him of Mr. Lockett's having sat by them at the table d'hôte, and that he and Colonel Selby were acquainted with one another. Captain Fennel drew a grim face at the information, and asked whether the lawyer had also "cleared out" for London.

"I don't think so; I did not see him go on board," said Nancy. "Lavinia knows; she was talking with Mr. Lockett all dinner-time."

Captain Fennel turned his impassive face to Lavinia, as if demanding an answer to his question.

"Mr. Lockett intends to remain here until Sunday, I fancy; he said he had to be in London on Monday morning. He has some friend with him here. I inquired whether they had found the Mr. Dangerfield he spoke of last autumn," added Lavinia slowly and distinctly. "'Not yet,' he answered, 'but he is still being looked for.'"

Whether Lavinia said this with a little spice of malice, or whether she really meant to warn him, she best knew. Captain Fennel finished his supper in silence.

"I presume the colonel did not hand you over your quarter's money?" he next said to his wife in a mocking sort of way. "It is not due for a week yet; he is not one to pay beforehand."

Upon which Nancy began to tremble and looked imploringly at her sister, who was putting the plates together upon the tray. After Flore went home they had to wait upon themselves.

"Colonel Selby did hand us the money," said Lavinia. "I hold both cheques for it."

Well, there ensued a mild disturbance; what schoolboys might call a genteel row. Mr. Edwin Fennel insisted upon his wife's cheque being given to him. Lavinia decisively refused. She went into a bit of a temper, and told him some home truths. He said he had a right to hold his wife's money, and should appeal to the law on the morrow to enforce it. He might do that, Lavinia retorted; no French law would make her give it up. Nancy began to cry.

Probably he knew his threats were futile. Instead of appealing to the law on the morrow, he went off by an early train, carrying Nancy with him. Lavinia's private opinion was that he thought it safer to take her, though it did increase the expense, than to leave her; she might get talking with Mr. Lockett. Ann's eyes were red, as if she had spent the night in crying.

"Has he beaten you?" Lavinia inquired, snatching the opportunity of a private moment.

"Oh, Lavinia, don't, don't! I shall never dare to let you have the cheque again," she wailed.

"Where is it that you are going?"

"He has not told me," Nancy whispered back again. "To Calais, I think, or else up to Lille. We are to be away all the week."

"Until Mr. Lockett and his friend are gone," thought Lavinia. "Nancy, how can he find money for it?"

"He has some napoleons in his pocket—borrowed yesterday, I think, from old Griffin."

Lavinia understood. Old Griffin, as Nancy styled him, had been careless of his money since his very slight attack of paralysis; he would freely lend to any one who asked him. She had not the slightest doubt that Captain Fennel had borrowed of him—and not for the first time.

It was on Wednesday morning that they went away, and for the rest of the week Lavinia was at peace. She changed the cheques at the bank as before, and paid the outstanding debts. But it left her so little to go on with, that she really knew not how she should get through the months until midsummer.

On Friday two of the Miss Bosanquets called. Hearing she was alone, they came to ask her to dine with them in the evening. Lavinia did so. But upon returning home at night, the old horror of going into the house came on again. Lavinia was in despair; she had hoped it had passed away for good.

On Saturday morning at market she met Madame Carimon, who invited her for the following day, Sunday. Lavinia hesitated. Glad enough indeed she was at the prospect of being taken out of her solitary home for a happy day at Mary Carimon's; but she shrank from again risking the dreadful feeling which would be sure to attack her when going into the house at night.

"You must come, Lavinia," cheerily urged Madame Carimon. "I have invited the English teacher at Madame Deauville's school; she has no friends here, poor thing."

"Well, I will come, Mary; thank you," said Lavinia slowly.

"To be sure you will. Why do you hesitate at all?"

Lavinia could not say why in the midst of the jostling market-place; perhaps would not had they been alone. "For one thing, they may be coming home before to-morrow," observed Lavinia, alluding to Mr. and Mrs. Fennel.

"Let them come. You are not obliged to stay at home with them," laughed Mary.

From the Diary of Miss Preen.

Monday morning.—Well, it is over. The horror of last night is over, and I have not died of it. That will be considered a strong expression, should any eye save my own see this diary: but I truly believe the horror would kill me if I were subjected many more times to it.

I went to Mary Carimon's after our service was over in the morning, and we had a pleasant day there. The more I see of Monsieur Jules the more I esteem and respect him. He is so genuine, so good at heart, so simple in manner. Miss Perry is very agreeable; not so young as I had thought—thirty last birthday, she says. Her English is good and refined, and that is not always the case with the English teachers who come over to France—the French ladies who engage them cannot judge of our accent.

Miss Perry and I left together a little before ten. She wished me good-night in the Rue Tessin, Madame Deauville's house lying one way, mine another. The horror began to come over me as I crossed the Place Ronde, which had never happened before. Stay; not the horror itself, but the dread of it. An impulse actually crossed me to ring at Madame Sauvage's, and ask Mariette to accompany me up the entry, and stand at my open door whilst I went in to light the candle. But I could see no light in the house, not even in madame's salon, and supposed she and Mariette might be gone to bed. They are early people on Sundays, and the two young men have their latch-keys.

I will try to overcome it this time, I bravely said to myself, and not allow the fear to keep me halting outside the door as it has done before. So I took out my latch-key, put it straight into the door, opened it, went in, and closed it again. Before I had well reached the top of the passage and felt for the match-box on the slab, I was in a paroxysm of horror. Something, like an icy wind coming up the passage, seemed to flutter the candle as I lighted it. Can I have left the door open? I thought, and turned to look. There stood Edwin Fennel. He stood just inside the door, which appeared to be shut, and he was looking straight at me with a threatening, malignant expression on his pale face.

"Oh! have you come home to-night?" I exclaimed aloud. For I really thought it was so.

The candle continued to flicker quickly as if it meant to go out, causing me to glance at it. When I looked up again Mr. Fennel was gone. It was not himself who had been there; it was only an illusion.

Exactly as he had seemed to appear to me the night before he and Nancy returned from London in December, so he had appeared again, his back to the door, and the evil menace on his countenance. Did the appearance come to me as a warning? or was the thing nothing but a delusion of my own optic nerves?

I dragged my shaking limbs upstairs, on the verge of screaming at each step with the fear of what might be behind me, and undressed and went to bed. For nearly the whole night I could not sleep, and when I did get to sleep in the morning I was tormented by a distressing dream. All, all as it had been that other night from three to four months ago.

A confused dream, no method in it. Several people were about—Nancy for one; I saw her fair curls. We all seemed to be in grievous discomfort and distress; whilst I, in worse fear than this world can know, was ever striving to hide myself from Edwin Fennel, to escape some dreadful fate which he held in store for me. And I knew I should not escape it.

X

Like many another active housewife, Madame Carimon was always busy on Monday mornings. On the one about to be referred to, she had finished her household duties by eleven o'clock, and then sat down in her little salle-à-manger, which she also made her workroom, to mend some of Monsieur Carimon's cotton socks. By her side, on the small work-table, lay a silver brooch which Miss Perry had inadvertently left behind her the previous evening. Mary Carimon was considering at what hour she could most conveniently go out to leave it at Madame Deauville's when she heard Pauline answer a ring at the door-bell, and Miss Preen came in.

"Oh, Lavinia, I am glad to see you. You are an early visitor. Are you not well?" continued Madame Carimon, noticing the pale, sad face. "Is anything the matter?"

"I am in great trouble, Mary; I cannot rest; and I have come to talk to you about it," said Lavinia, taking the sable boa from her neck and untying her bonnet-strings. "If things were to continue as they are now, I should die of it."

Drawing a chair near to Mary Carimon, Lavinia entered upon her narrative. She spoke first of general matters. The home discomfort, the trouble with Captain Fennel regarding Nancy's money, and the difficulty she had to keep up the indispensable payments to the tradespeople, expressing her firm belief that in future he would inevitably seize upon Nancy's portion when it came and confiscate it. Next, she went on to tell the story of the past night—Sunday: how the old terrible horror had come upon her of entering the house, of a fancied appearance of Edwin Fennel in the passage, and of the dream that followed. All this latter part was but a repetition of what she had told Madame Carimon three or four months ago. Hearing it for the second time, it impressed Mary Carimon's imagination. But she did not speak at once.

"I never in my life saw anything plainer or that looked more life-like than Captain Fennel, as he stood and gazed at me from the end of the passage with the evil look on his countenance," resumed Lavinia. "And I hardly know why I tell you about it again, Mary, except that I have no one else to speak to. You rather laughed at me the first time, if you remember; perhaps you will laugh again now."

"No, no," dissented Mary Carimon. "I did not put faith in it before, believing you were deceived by the uncertain light in the passage, and were, perhaps, thinking of him, and that the dream afterwards was merely the result of your fright; nothing else. But now that you have had a second experience of it, I don't doubt that you do see this spectre, and that the dream follows as a sequence to it. And I think," she added, slowly and emphatically, "that it has come to warn you of some threatened harm."

"I seem to see that it has," murmured Lavinia. "Why else should it come at all? I wish I could picture it to you half vividly enough: the reality of it and the horror. Mary, I am growing seriously afraid."

"Were I you, I should get away from the house," said Madame Carimon. "Leave them to themselves."

"It is what I mean to do, Mary. I cannot remain in it, apart from this undefined fear—which of course may be only superstitious fancy," hastily acknowledged Lavinia. "If things continue in the present state—and there is no prospect of their changing—"

"I should leave at once—as soon as they arrive home," rather sharply interrupted Mary Carimon, who seemed to like the aspect of what she had heard less and less.

"As soon as I can make arrangements. They come home to-night; I received a letter from Nancy this morning. They have been only at Pontipette all the time."

"Only at Pontipette!"

"Nancy says so. It did as well as any other place. Captain Fennel's motive was to hide away from the lawyers we met at the table d'hôte."

"Have they left Sainteville, I wonder, those lawyers?"

"Yes," said Lavinia. "On Friday I met Mr. Lockett when I was going to the Rue Lamartine, and he told me he was leaving for Calais with his friend on Saturday morning. It is rather remarkable," she added, after a pause, "that the first time I saw that appearance in the passage and dreamed the dream, should have been the eve of Mr. Fennel's return here, and that it is the same again now."

"You must leave the house, Lavinia," reiterated Madame Carimon.

"Let me see," considered Lavinia. "April comes in this week. Next week will be Passion Week, preceding Easter. I will stay with them over Easter, and then leave."

Monsieur Jules Carimon's sock, in process of renovation, had been allowed to fall upon the mender's lap. She slowly took it up again, speaking thoughtfully.

"I should leave at once; before Easter. But you will see how he behaves, Lavinia. If not well; if he gives you any cause of annoyance, come away there and then. We will take you in, mind, if you have not found a place to go to."

Lavinia thanked her, and rearranged her bonnet preparatory to returning home. She went out with a heavy heart. Only one poor twelvemonth to have brought about all this change!

At the door of the Petite Maison Rouge, when she reached it, stood Flore, parleying with a slim youth, who held an open paper in his outstretched hand. Flore was refusing to touch the paper, which was both printed and written on, and looked official.

"I tell him that Monsieur le Capitaine is not at home; he can bring it when he is," explained Flore to her mistress in English.

Lavinia turned to the young man. "Captain Fennel has been away from Sainteville for a few days; he probably will be here to-morrow," she said. "Do you wish to leave this paper for him?"

"Yes," said the messenger, evidently understanding English but speaking in French, as he contrived to slip the paper into Miss Preen's unconscious hand. "You will have the politeness to give it to him, madame."

And, with that, he went off down the entry, whistling.

"Do you know what the paper is, Flore?" asked Lavinia.

"I think so," said Flore. "I've seen these papers before to-day. It's just a sort of order from the law court on Captain Fennel, to pay up some debt that he owes; and, if he does not pay, the court will issue a procès against him. That's what it is, madame."

Lavinia carried the paper into the salon, and sat studying it. As far as she could make it out, Mr. Edwin Fennel was called upon to pay to some creditor the sum of one hundred and eighty-three francs, without delay.

"Over seven pounds! And if he does not pay, the law expenses, to enforce it, will increase the debt perhaps by one-half," sighed Lavinia. "There may be, and no doubt are, other things at the back of this. Will he turn us out of house and home?"

Propping the paper against the wall over the mantelpiece, she left it there, that it might meet the captain's eye on his return.

Not until quite late that evening did Madame Carimon get her husband to herself, for he brought in one of the young under-masters at the college to dine with them. But as soon as they were sitting cosily alone, he smoking his pipe before bed-time, she told him all she had heard from Lavinia Preen.

"I don't like it, Jules; I don't indeed," she said. "It has made a strangely disagreeable impression on me. What is your opinion?"

Placid Monsieur Jules did not seem to have much opinion one way or the other. Upon the superstitious portion of the tale he, being a practical Frenchman, totally declined to have any at all. He was very sorry for the uncomfortable position Miss Preen found herself in, and he certainly was not surprised she should wish to quit the Petite Maison Rouge if affairs could not be made more agreeable there. As to the Capitaine Fennel, he felt free to confess there was something about him which he did not like: and he was sure no man of honour ought to have run away clandestinely, as he did, with Miss Nancy.

"You see, Jules, what the man aims at is to get hold of Nancy's income and apply it to his own uses—and for Lavinia to keep them upon hers."

"I see," said Jules.

"And Lavinia cannot do it; she has not half enough. It troubles me very much," flashed Madame Carimon. "She says she shall stay with them until Easter is over. I should not; I should leave them to it to-morrow."

"Yes, my dear, that's all very well," nodded Monsieur Jules; "but we cannot always do precisely what we would. Miss Preen is responsible for the rent of that house, and if Fennel and his wife do not pay it, she would have to. She must have a thorough understanding upon that point before she leaves it."

By the nine-o'clock train that night they came home, Lavinia, pleading a bad headache and feeling altogether out of sorts, got Flore to remain for once, and went herself to bed. She dreaded the very sight of Captain Fennel.

In the morning she saw that the paper had disappeared from the mantelpiece. He was quite jaunty at breakfast, talking to her and Nancy about Pontipette; and things passed pleasantly. About eleven o'clock he began brushing his hat to go out.

"I'm going to have a look at Griffin, and see how he's getting on," he remarked. "Perhaps the old man would enjoy a drive this fine day; if so, you may not see me back till dinner-time."

But just as Captain Fennel turned out of the Place Ronde to the Rue Tessin, he came upon Charles Palliser, strolling along.

"Fine day, Mr. Charles," he remarked graciously.

"Capital," assented Charles, "and I'm glad of it; the old gentleman will have a good passage. I've just seen him off by the eleven train."

"Seems to me you spend your time in seeing people off by trains. Which old gentleman is it now?—him from below?"

Charley laughed. "It's Griffin this time," said he. "Being feeble, I thought I might be of use in starting him, and went up."

"Griffin!" exclaimed Captain Fennel. "Why, where's he gone to?"

"To Calais. En route for Dover and—"

"What's he gone for? When's he coming back?" interrupted the captain, speaking like a man in great amazement.

"He is not coming back at all; he has gone for good," said Charley. "His daughter came to fetch him."

"Why on earth should she do that?"

"It seems that her husband, a clergyman at Kensington, fell across Major Smith last week in London, and put some pretty close questions to him about the old man, for they had been made uneasy by his letters of late. The major—"

"What business had the major in London?" questioned Captain Fennel impatiently.

"You can ask him," said Charles equably, "I didn't. He is back again. Well, Major Smith, being questioned, made no bones about it at all; said Griffin and Griffin's money both wanted looking after. Upon that, the daughter came straight off, arriving here on Sunday morning; she settled things yesterday, and has carried her father away to-day. He was as pleased as Punch, poor childish old fellow, at the prospect of a voyage in the boat."

Whether this information put a check upon any little plan Captain Fennel may have been entertaining, Charles Palliser could not positively know; but he thought he had never seen so evil an eye as the one glaring upon him. Only for a moment; just a flash; and then the face was smoothed again. Charley had his ideas—and all his wits about him; and old Griffin had babbled publicly.

Captain Fennel strolled by his side towards the port, talking of Pontipette and other matters of indifference. When in sight of the harbour, he halted.

"I must wish you good-day now, Palliser; I have letters to write," said he; and walked briskly back again.

Lavinia and Nancy were sitting together in the salon when he reached home. Nancy was looking scared.

"Edwin," she said, leaving her chair to meet him—"Edwin, what do you think Lavinia has been saying? That she is going to leave us."

"Oh, indeed," he carelessly answered.

"But it is true, Edwin; she means it."

"Yes, I mean it," interposed Lavinia very quietly. "You and Nancy will be better without me; perhaps happier."

He looked at her for a full minute in silence, then laughed a little. "Like Darby and Joan," he remarked, as he put his writing-case on the table and sat down to it.

Mrs. Fennel returned to her chair by Lavinia, who was sitting close to the window mending a lace collar which had been torn in the ironing. As usual Nancy was doing nothing.

"You couldn't leave me, Lavinia, you know," she said in coaxing tones.

"I know that I never thought to do so, Ann, but circumstances alter cases," answered the elder sister. Both of them had dropped their voices to a low key, not to disturb the letter-writer. But he could hear if he chose to listen. "I began putting my things together yesterday, and shall finish doing it at leisure. I will stay over Easter with you; but go then I shall."

"You must be cruel to think of such a thing, Lavinia."

"Not cruel," corrected Lavinia. "I am sorry, Ann, but the step is forced upon me. The anxieties in regard to money matters are wearing me out; they would wear me out altogether if I did not end them. And there are other things which urge upon me the expediency of departure from this house."

"What things?"

"I cannot speak of them. Never mind what they are, Ann. They concern myself; not you."

Ann Fennel sat twirling one of her fair silken ringlets between her thumb and finger; a habit of hers when thinking.

"Where shall you live, Lavinia, if you do leave? Take another apartment at Sainteville?"

"I think not. It is a puzzling question. Possibly I may go back to Buttermead, and get some family to take me in as a boarder," dreamily answered Lavinia. "Seventy pounds a-year will not keep me luxuriously."

Captain Fennel lifted his face. "If it will not keep one, how is it to keep two?" he demanded, in rather defiant tones.

"I don't know anything about that," said Lavinia civilly. "I have not two to keep; only one."

Nancy chanced to catch a glimpse of his face just then, and its look frightened her. Lavinia had her back to him, and did not see it. Nancy began to cry quietly.

"Oh, Lavinia, you will think better of this; you will not leave us!" she implored. "We could not do at all without you and your half of the money."

Lavinia had finished her collar, and rose to take it upstairs. "Don't be distressed, Nancy," she paused to say; "it is a thing that must be. I am very sorry; but it is not my fault. As you—"

"You can stay in the house if you choose!" flashed Nancy, growing feebly angry.

"No, I cannot. I cannot," repeated Lavinia. "I begin to foresee that I might—might die of it."

XI

Sainteville felt surprised and sorry to hear that Miss Preen was going to leave it to its own devices, for the town had grown to like her. Lavinia did not herself talk about going, but the news somehow got wind. People wondered why she went. Matters, as connected with the financial department of the Petite Maison Rouge, were known but imperfectly—to most people not known at all; so that reason was not thought of. It was quite understood that Ann Preen's stolen marriage, capped by the bringing home of her husband to the Petite Maison Rouge, had been a sharp blow to Miss Preen: perhaps, said Sainteville now, she had tried living with them and found it did not answer. Or perhaps she was only going away for a change, and would return after a while.

Passion week passed, and Easter week came in, and Lavinia made her arrangements for the succeeding one. On the Tuesday in that next week, all being well, she would quit Sainteville. Her preparations were made; her larger box was already packed and corded. Nancy, of shallow temperament and elastic spirits, seemed quite to have recovered from the sting of the proposed parting; she helped Lavinia to put up her laces and other little fine things, prattling all the time. Captain Fennel maintained his suavity. Beyond the words he had spoken—as to how she expected the income to keep two if it would not keep one—he had said nothing. It might be that he hardly yet believed Lavinia would positively go.

But she was going. At first only to Boulogne-sur-Mer. Monsieur Jules Carimon had a cousin, Madame Degravier, who kept a superior boarding-house there, much patronized by the English; he had written to her to introduce Miss Preen, and to intimate that it would oblige him if the terms were made très facile. Madame had written back to Lavinia most satisfactorily, and, so far, that was arranged.

Once at Boulogne in peace and quietness, Lavinia would have leisure to decide upon her future plans. She hoped to pay a visit to Buttermead in the summer-time, for she had begun to yearn for a sight of the old place and its people. After that—well, she should see. If things went on pleasantly at Sainteville— that is, if Captain Fennel and Nancy were still in the Petite Maison Rouge, and he was enabled to find means to continue in it—then, perhaps, she might return to the town. Not to make one of the household—never again that; but she might find a little pied-à-terre in some other home.

Meanwhile, Lavinia heard no more of the procès, and she wondered how the captain was meeting it. During the Easter week she made her farewell calls. That week she was not very much at home; one or other of her old acquaintances wanted her. Major and Mrs. Smith had her to spend a day with them; the Miss Bosanquets invited her also; and so on.

One call, involving also private business, she made upon old Madame Sauvage, Mary Carimon accompanying her. Monsieur Gustave was called up to the salon to assist at the conference. Lavinia partly explained her position to them in strict confidence, and the motive, as touching pecuniary affairs, which was taking her away: she said nothing of that other and greater motive, her superstitious fear.

"I have come to speak of the rent," she said to Monsieur Gustave, and Mary Carimon repeated the words in French to old Madame Sauvage. "You must in future look to Captain Fennel for it; you must make him pay it if possible. At the same time, I admit my own responsibility," added Lavinia, "and if it be found totally impracticable to get it from Captain Fennel or my sister, I shall pay it to you. This must, of course, be kept strictly between ourselves, Monsieur Gustave; you and madame understand that. If Captain Fennel gained any intimation of it, he would take care not to pay it."

Monsieur Gustave and madame his mother assured her that they fully understood, and that she might rely upon their honour. They were grieved to lose so excellent a tenant and neighbour as Miss Preen, and wished circumstances had been more kindly. One thing she might rest assured of—that they should feel at least as mortified at having to apply to her for the rent as she herself would be, and they would not leave a stone unturned to extract it from the hands of Captain Fennel.

"It has altogether been a most bitter trial to me," sighed Lavinia, as she stood up to say farewell to madame.

The old lady understood, and the tears came into her compassionate eyes as she held Lavinia's hands between her own. "Ay, for certain," she replied in French. "She and her sons had said so privately to one another ever since the abrupt coming home of the strange captain to the petite maison à côté."

On Sunday, Lavinia, accompanied by Nancy and Captain Fennel, attended morning service for the last time. She spoke to several acquaintances coming out, wishing them good-bye, and was hastening to overtake her sister, when she heard rapid steps behind her, and a voice speaking. Turning, she saw Charley Palliser.

"Miss Preen," cried he, "my aunt wants you to come home and dine with us. See, she is waiting for you. You could not come any one day last week, you know."

"I was not able to come to you last week, Mr. Charles; I had so much to do, and so many engagements," said Lavinia, as she walked back to Mrs. Hardy, who stood smiling.

"But you will come to-day, dear Miss Preen," said old Mrs. Hardy, who had caught the words. "We have a lovely fricandeau of veal, and—"

"Why, that is just our own dinner," interrupted Lavinia gaily. "I should like to come to you, Mrs. Hardy, but I cannot. It is my last Sunday at home, and I could not well go out and leave them."

They saw the force of the objection. Mrs. Hardy asked whether she should be at church in the evening. Lavinia replied that she intended to be, and they agreed to bid each other farewell then.

"You don't know what you've lost, Miss Preen," said Charley comically. "There's a huge cream tart— lovely."

Captain Fennel was quite lively at the dinner-table. He related a rather laughable story which had been told him by Major Smith, with whom he had walked for ten minutes after church, and was otherwise gracious.

After dinner, while Flore was taking away the things, he left the room, and came back with three glasses of liqueur, on a small waiter, handing one to Lavinia, another to his wife, and keeping the third himself. It was the yellow chartreuse; Captain Fennel kept a bottle of it and of one or two other choice liqueurs in the little cupboard at the end of the passage, and treated them to a glass sometimes.

"How delightful!" cried Nancy, who liked chartreuse and anything else that was good.

They sat and sipped it, talking pleasantly together. The captain soon finished his, and said he should take a stroll on the pier. It was a bright day with a brisk wind, which seemed to be getting higher.

"The London boat ought to be in about four o'clock," he remarked. "It's catching it sweetly, I know; passengers will look like ghosts. Au revoir; don't get quarrelling." And thus, nodding to the two ladies, he went out gaily.

Not much danger of their quarrelling. They turned their chairs to the fire, and plunged into conversation, which chanced to turn upon Buttermead. In calling up one reminiscence of the old place after another, now Lavinia, now Nancy, the time passed on. Lavinia wore her silver-grey silk dress that day, with some yellowish-looking lace falling at the throat and wrists.

Flore came in to bring the tea-tray; she always put it on the table in readiness on a Sunday afternoon. The water, she said, would be on the boil in the kitchen by the time they wanted it. And then she went away as usual for the rest of the day.

Not long afterwards, Lavinia, who was speaking, suddenly stopped in the middle of a sentence. She started up in her chair, fell back again, and clasped her hands below her chest with a great cry.

"Oh, Nancy!—Nancy!"

Nancy dashed across the hearthrug. "What is it?" she exclaimed. "What is it, Lavinia?"

Lavinia apparently could not say what it was. She seemed to be in the greatest agony; her face had turned livid. Nancy was next door to an imbecile in any emergency, and fairly wrung her hands in her distress.

"Oh, what can be the matter with me?" gasped Lavinia. "Nancy, I think I am dying."

The next moment she had glided from the chair to the floor, and lay there shrieking and writhing. Bursting away, Nancy ran round to the next house, all closed to-day, rang wildly at the private door, and when it was opened by Mariette, rushed upstairs to madame's salon.

Madame Veuve Sauvage, comprehending that something was amiss, without understanding Nancy's frantic words, put a shawl on her shoulders to hasten to the other house, ordering Mariette to follow her. Her sons were out.

There lay Lavinia, in the greatest agony. Madame Sauvage sent Mariette off for Monsieur Dupuis, and told her to fly. "Better bring Monsieur Henri Dupuis, Mariette," she called after her: "he will get quicker over the ground than his old father."

But Monsieur Henri Dupuis, as it turned out, was absent. He had left that morning for Calais with his wife, to spend two days with her friends who lived there, purposing to be back early on Tuesday morning. Old Monsieur Dupuis came very quickly. He thought Mademoiselle Preen must have inward inflammation, he said to Madame Sauvage, and inquired what she had eaten for dinner. Nancy told him as well as she could between her sobs and her broken speech.

A fricandeau of veal, potatoes, a cauliflower au gratin, and a frangipane tart from the pastrycook's. No fruit or any other dessert. They took a little Bordeaux wine with dinner, and a liqueur glass of chartreuse afterwards.

All very wholesome, pronounced Monsieur Dupuis, with satisfaction; not at all likely to disagree with mademoiselle. Possibly she had caught a chill.

Mariette had run for Flore, who came in great consternation. Between them all they got Lavinia upstairs, undressed her and laid her in bed, applying hot flannels to the pain—and Monsieur Dupuis administered in a wine-glass of water every quarter-of-an-hour some drops from a glass phial which he had brought in his pocket.

It was close upon half-past five when Captain Fennel came in. He expressed much surprise and concern, saying, like the doctor, that she must have eaten something which had disagreed with her. The doctor avowed that he could not otherwise account for the seizure; he did not altogether think it was produced by a chill; and he spoke again of the dinner. Captain Fennel observed that as to the dinner they had all three partaken of it, one the same as another; he did not see why it should affect his sister-in-law and not himself or his wife. This reasoning was evident, admitted Monsieur Dupuis; but Miss Preen had touched nothing since her breakfast, except at dinner. In point of fact, he felt very much at a loss, he did not scruple to add; but the more acute symptoms were showing a slight improvement, he was thankful to perceive, and he trusted to bring her round.

As he did. In a few hours the pain had so far abated, or yielded to remedies, that poor Lavinia, worn out, dropped into a comfortable sleep. Monsieur Dupuis was round again early in the morning, and found her recovered, though still feeling tired and very weak. He advised her to lie in bed until the afternoon; not to get up then unless she felt inclined; and he charged her to take chiefly milk food all the day—no solids whatever.

Lavinia slept again all the morning, and awoke very much refreshed. In the afternoon she felt quite equal to getting up, and did so, dressing herself in the grey silk she had worn the previous day, because it was nearest at hand. She then penned a line to Madame Degravier, saying she was unable to travel to Boulogne on the morrow, as had been fixed, but hoped to be there on Wednesday, or, at the latest, Thursday.

Captain Fennel, who generally took possession of the easiest chair in the salon, and the warmest place, resigned it to Lavinia the instant she appeared downstairs. He shook her by the hand, said how glad he was that she had recovered from her indisposition, and installed her in the chair with a cushion at her back and a rug over her knees. All she had to dread now, he thought, was cold; she must guard against that. Lavinia replied that she could not in the least imagine what had been the matter with her; she had never had a similar attack before, and had never been in such dreadful pain.

Presently Mary Carimon came in, having heard of the affair from Mariette, whom she had met in the fish-market during the morning. All danger was over, Mariette said, and mademoiselle was then sleeping quietly: so Madame Carimon, not to disturb her, put off calling until the afternoon. Captain Fennel sat talking with her a few minutes, and then went out. For some cause or other he never seemed to be quite at ease in the presence of Madame Carimon.

"I know what it must have been," cried Mary Carimon, coming to one of her rapid conclusions after listening to the description of the illness. "Misled by the sunny spring days last week, you went and left off some of your warm underclothing, Lavinia, and so caught cold."

"Good gracious!" exclaimed Nancy, who had curled herself up on the sofa like a ball, not having yet recovered from her fatigue and fright. "Leave off one's warm things the beginning of April! I never heard of such imprudence! How came you to do it, Lavinia?"

"I did not do it," said Lavinia quietly. "I have not left off anything. Should I be so silly as to do that with a journey before me?"

"Then what caused the attack?" debated Madame Carimon. "Something you had eaten?"

Lavinia shook her head helplessly. "It could hardly have been that, Mary. I took nothing whatever that Nancy and Captain Fennel did not take. I wish I did know—that I might guard, if possible, against a similar attack in future. The pain seized me all in a moment. I thought I was dying."

"It sounds odd," said Madame Carimon. "Monsieur Dupuis does not know either, it seems. That's why I thought you might have been leaving off your things, and did not like to tell him."

"I conclude that it must have been one of those mysterious attacks of sudden illness to which we are all liable, but for which no one can account," sighed Lavinia. "I hope I shall never have it again. This experience has been enough for a lifetime."

Mary Carimon warmly echoed the hope as she rose to take her departure. She advised Lavinia to go to bed early, and promised to come again in the morning.

While Captain Fennel and Nancy dined, Flore made her mistress some tea, and brought in with it some thin bread-and-butter. Lavinia felt all the better for the refreshment, laughingly remarking that by the morning she was sure she should be as hungry as a hunter. She sat chatting, and sometimes dozing between whiles, until about a quarter to nine o'clock, when she said she would go to bed.

Nancy went to the kitchen to make her a cup of arrowroot. Lavinia then wished Captain Fennel good-night, and went upstairs. Flore had left as usual, after washing up the dinner-things.

"Lavinia, shall I— Oh, she has gone on," broke off Nancy, who had come in with the breakfast-cup of arrowroot in her hand. "Edwin, do you think I may venture to put a little brandy into this?"

Captain Fennel sat reading with his face to the fire and the lamp at his elbow. He turned round.

"Brandy?" said he. "I'm sure I don't know. If that pain meant inflammation, brandy might do harm. Ask Lavinia; she had better decide for herself. No, no; leave the arrowroot on the table here," he hastily cried, as Nancy was going out of the room with the cup. "Tell Lavinia to come down, and we'll discuss the matter with her. Of course a little brandy would do her an immense deal of good, if she might take it with safety."

Nancy did as she was told. Leaving the cup and saucer on the table, she went up to her sister. In a minute or two she was back again.

"Lavinia won't come down again, Edwin; she is already half-undressed. She thinks she had better be on the safe side, and not have the brandy."

"All right," replied the captain, who was sitting as before, intent on his book. Nancy took the cup upstairs.

She helped her sister into bed, and then gave her the arrowroot, inquiring whether she had made it well.

"Quite well, only it was rather sweet," answered Lavinia.

"Sweet!" echoed Nancy, in reply. "Why, I hardly put any sugar at all into it; I remembered that you don't like it."

Lavinia finished the cupful. Nancy tucked her up, and gave her a good-night kiss. "Pleasant dreams, Lavinia dear," she called back, as she was shutting the door.

"Thank you, Nancy; but I hope I shall sleep to-night without dreaming," answered Lavinia.

As Nancy went downstairs she turned into the kitchen for her own arrowroot, which she had left all that time in the saucepan. Being fond of it, she had made enough for herself as well as for Lavinia.

XII

It was between half-past ten and eleven, and Captain and Mrs. Fennel were in their bedroom preparing to retire to rest. She stood before the glass doing her hair, having thrown a thin print cotton cape upon her shoulders as usual, to protect her dress; he had taken off his coat.

"What was that?" cried she, in startled tones.

Some sound had penetrated to their room. The captain put his coat on a chair and bent his ear. "I did not hear anything, Nancy," he answered.

"There it is again!" exclaimed Nancy. "Oh, it is Lavinia! I do believe it is Lavinia!"

Flinging the comb from her hand, Nancy dashed out at the room-door, which was near the head of the stairs; Lavinia's door being nearly at the end of the passage. Unmistakable sounds, now a shriek, now a wail, came from Lavinia's chamber. Nancy flew into it, her fair hair falling on her shoulders.

"What is it, Lavinia? Oh, Edwin, Edwin, come here!" called Mrs. Fennel, beside herself with terror. Lavinia was rolling about the bed, as she had the previous day rolled on the salon floor; her face was distorted with pain, her moans and cries were agonizing.

Captain Fennel stayed to put on his coat, came to Lavinia's door, and put his head inside it. "Is it the pain again?" he asked.

"Yes, it is the pain again," gasped Lavinia, in answer. "I am dying, I am surely dying!"

That put the finishing-touch to timorous Nancy. "Edwin, run, run for Monsieur Dupuis!" she implored. "Oh, what shall we do? What shall we do?"

Captain Fennel descended the stairs. When Nancy thought he must have been gone out at least a minute or two, he appeared again with a wine-glass of hot brandy-and-water, which he had stayed to mix.

"Try and get her to take this," he said. "It can't do harm; it may do good. And if you could put hot flannels to her, Nancy, it might be well; they eased the pain yesterday. I'll bring Dupuis here as soon as I can."

Lavinia could not take the brandy-and-water, and it was left upon the grey marble top of the chest of drawers. Her paroxysms increased; Nancy had never seen or imagined such pain, for this attack was worse than the other, and she almost lost her wits with terror. Could she see Lavinia die before her eyes?—no helping hand near to strive to save her? Just as Nancy had done before, she did again now.

Flying down the stairs and out of the house, across the yard and through the dark entry, she seized the bell-handle of Madame Veuve Sauvage's door and pulled it frantically. The household had all retired for the night.

Presently a window above opened, and Monsieur Gustave—Nancy knew his voice—looked out.

"Who's there?" he asked in French. "What's the matter?"

"Oh, Monsieur Gustave, come in for the love of Heaven!" responded poor Nancy, looking up. "She has another attack, worse than the first; she's dying, and there's no one in the house but me."

"Directly, madame; I am with you on the instant," he kindly answered. "I but wait to put on my effects."

He was at the Petite Maison Rouge almost as soon as she; his brother Emile followed him in, and Mariette, whom they had called, came shortly. Miss Preen lay in dreadful paroxysms; it did appear to them that she must die. Nancy and Mariette busied themselves in the kitchen, heating flannels.

The doctor did not seem to come very quickly. Captain Fennel at length made his appearance and said Monsieur Dupuis would be there in a minute or two.

"I am content to hear that," remarked Monsieur Gustave in reply. "I was just about to despatch my brother for the first doctor he could find."

"Never had such trouble in ringing up a doctor before," returned Captain Fennel. "I suppose the old man sleeps too soundly to be easily aroused; many elderly people do."

"I fear she is dying," whispered Monsieur Gustave.

"No, no, surely not!" cried Captain Fennel, recoiling a step at the words. "What can it possibly be? What causes the attacks?"

Whilst Monsieur Gustave was shaking his head at this difficult question, Monsieur Dupuis arrived. Monsieur Emile, anxious to make himself useful, was requested by Mariette to go to Flore's domicile and ring her up. Flore seemed to have been sleeping with her clothes on, for they came back together.

Monsieur Dupuis could do nothing for his patient. He strove to administer drops of medicinal remedies; he caused her to be nearly smothered in scalding-hot flannels—all in vain. He despatched Monsieur Emile Sauvage to bring in another doctor, Monsieur Podevin, who lived near. All in vain. Lavinia died. Just at one o'clock in the morning, before the cocks had begun to crow, Lavinia Preen died.

The shock to those in the house was great. It seemed to stun them, one and all. The brothers Sauvage, leaving a few words of heartfelt sympathy with Captain Fennel, withdrew silently to their own home. Mariette stayed. The two doctors, shut up in the salon, talked with one another, endeavouring to account for the death.

"Inflammation, no doubt," observed Monsieur Dupuis; "but even so, the death has been too speedy."

"More like poison," rejoined the younger man, Monsieur Podevin. He was brother to the proprietor of the Hôtel des Princes, and was much respected by his fellow-citizens as a safe and skilful practitioner.

"The thought of poison naturally occurred to me on Sunday, when I was first called to her," returned Monsieur Dupuis, "but it could not be borne out. You see, she had partaken of nothing, either in food or drink, but what the other inmates had taken; absolutely nothing. This was assured me by them all, herself included."

"She seems to have taken nothing to-day, either, that could in any way harm her," said Monsieur Podevin.

"Nothing. She took a cup of tea at five o'clock, which the servant, Flore, prepared and also partook of herself—a cup out of the same teapot. Later, when the poor lady went to bed, her sister made her a basin of arrowroot, and made herself one at the same time."

"Well, it appears strange."

"It could not have been a chill. The symptoms—"

"A chill?—bah!" interrupted Monsieur Podevin. "We shall know more after the post-mortem," he added, taking up his hat. "Of course there must be one."

Wishing his brother practitioner good-night, he left. Monsieur Dupuis went looking about for Captain Fennel, and found him in the kitchen, standing by the hot stove, and drinking a glass of hot brandy-and-water. The rest were upstairs.

"This event has shaken my nerves, doctor," apologized the captain, in reference to the glass. "I never was so upset. Shall I mix you one?"

Monsieur Dupuis shook his head. He never took anything so strong. The most calming thing, in his opinion, was a glass of eau sucrée, with a teaspoonful of orange-flower water in it.

"Sir," he went on, "I have been conversing with my esteemed confrère. We cannot, either of us, decide what mademoiselle has died of, being unable to see any adequate cause for it; and we wish to hold a post-mortem examination. I presume you will not object to it?"

"Certainly not; I think there should be one," briskly spoke Captain Fennel after a moment's pause. "For our satisfaction, if for nothing else, doctor."

"Very well. Will nine o'clock in the morning suit you, as to time? It should be made early."

"I—expect it will," answered the captain, reflecting. "Do you hold it here?"

"Undoubtedly. In her own room."

"Then wait just one minute, will you, doctor, whilst I speak to my wife. Nine o'clock seems a little early, but I dare say it will suit."

Monsieur Dupuis went back into the salon. He had waited there a short interval, when Mrs. Fennel burst in, wild with excitement. Her hair still hung down her back, her eyes were swollen with weeping, her face was one of piteous distress. She advanced to Monsieur Dupuis, and held up her trembling hands.

The old doctor understood English fairly well when it was quietly spoken; but he did not in the least understand it in a storm. Sobbing, trembling, Mrs. Fennel was beseeching him not to hold a post-mortem on her poor dead sister, for the love of mercy.

Surprised and distressed, he placed her on the sofa, soothed her into calmness, and then bade her tell him quietly what her petition was. She repeated it—begging, praying, imploring him not to disturb her sister now she was at rest; but to let her be put into her grave in peace. Well, well, said the compassionate old man; if it would pain the relatives so greatly to have it done, he and Monsieur Podevin would, of course, abandon the idea. It would be a satisfaction to them both to be able to decide upon the cause of death, but they did not wish to proceed in it against the feelings of the family.

Sainteville woke up in the morning to a shock. Half the townspeople still believed that Miss Preen was leaving that day, Tuesday, for Boulogne; and to hear that she would not go on that journey, that she would never go on any earthly journey again, that she was dead, shook them to the centre.

What had been the matter with her?—what had killed her so quickly in the midst of life and health? Groups asked this; one group meeting another. "Inflammation," was the answer—for that report had somehow started itself. She caught a chill on the Sunday, probably when leaving the church after morning service; it induced speedy and instant inflammation, and she had died of it.

With softened steps and mournful faces, hosts of people made their way to the Place Ronde. Only to take a glimpse at the outside of the Maison Rouge brought satisfaction to excited feelings. Monsieur Gustave Sauvage had caused his white shop window-blinds to be drawn half-way down, out of respect to the dead; all the windows above had the green persiennes closed before them. The calamity had so greatly affected old Madame Sauvage that she lay in bed.

When her sons returned indoors after the death had taken place, their mother called them to her room. Nancy's violent ringing had disturbed her, and she had lain since then in anxiety, waiting for news.

"Better not tell the mother to-night," whispered Emile to his brother outside her door.

But the mother's ears were quick; she was sitting up in bed, and the door was ajar. "Yes, you will tell me, my sons," she said. "I am fearing the worst."

"Well, mother, it is all over," avowed Gustave. "The attack was more violent than the one last night, and the poor lady is gone."

"May the good God have taken her to His rest!" fervently aspirated madame. But she lay down in the bed in her distress and covered her face with the white-frilled pillow and sobbed a little. Gustave and Emile related a few particulars.

"And what was really the malady? What is it that she has died of?" questioned the mother, wiping her eyes.

"That is not settled; nobody seems to know," replied Gustave.

Madame Veuve Sauvage lay still, thinking. "I—hope—that—man—has—not—done—her—any—injury!" she slowly said.

"I hope not either; there is no appearance of it," said Monsieur Gustave. "Any way, mother, she had two skilful doctors with her, honest men and upright. Better not admit such thoughts."

"True, true," murmured madame, appeased. "I fear the poor dear lady must have taken a chill, which struck inwardly. That handsome demoiselle, the cousin of Monsieur le Procureur, died of the same thing, you may remember. Good-night, my sons; you leave me very unhappy."

About eight o'clock in the morning, Monsieur Jules Carimon heard of it. In going through the large iron entrance-gates of the college to his day's work, he found himself accosted by one of two or three young gamins of pupils, who were also entering. It was Dion Pamart. The well-informed reader is of course aware that the French educational colleges are attended by all classes, high and low, indiscriminately.

"Monsieur, have you heard?" said the lad, with timid deprecation. "Mademoiselle is dead."

Monsieur Jules Carimon turned his eyes on the speaker. At first he did not recognize him: his own work lay with the advanced desks.

"Ah, c'est Pamart, n'est-ce-pas?" said he. "What did you say, my boy? Some one is dead?"

Dion Pamart repeated his information. The master, inwardly shocked, took refuge in disbelief.

"I think you must be mistaken, Pamart," said he.

"Oh no, I'm not, sir. Mademoiselle was taken frightfully ill again last night, and they fetched my mother. They had two doctors to her and all; but they couldn't do anything for her, and she died. Grandmother gave me my breakfast just now; she said my mother was crying too much to come home. The other lady, the captain's wife, has been in hysterics all night."

"Go on to your desks," commanded Monsieur Carimon to the small fry now gathered round him.

He turned back home himself. When he entered the salle-à-manger, Pauline was carrying away the last of the breakfast-things. Her mistress stood putting a little water on a musk plant in the window.

"Is it you, Jules?" she exclaimed. "Have you forgotten something?"

Monsieur Jules shut the door. "I have not forgotten anything," he answered. "But I have heard of a sad calamity, and I have come back to prepare you, Marie, before you hear it from others."

He spoke solemnly; he was looking solemn. His wife put down the jug of water on the table. "A calamity?" she repeated.

"Yes. You will grieve to hear it. Your friend, Miss Preen, was—was taken ill last night with the same sort of attack, but more violent; and she—"

"Oh, Jules, don't tell me, don't tell me!" cried Mary Carimon, lifting her hands to ward off the words with a too sure prevision of what they were going to be.

"But, my dear, you must be told sooner or later," remonstrated he; "you cannot go through even this morning without hearing it from one person or another. Flore's boy was my informant. In spite of all that could be done by those about her, poor lady—in spite of the two doctors who were called to her aid—she died."

Madame Carimon was a great deal too much stunned for tears. She sank back in a chair with a face of stone, feeling that the room was turning upside down about her.

An hour later, when she had somewhat gathered her scattered senses together, she set off for the Petite Maison Rouge. Her way lay past the house of Monsieur Podevin; old Monsieur Dupuis was turning out of it as she went by. Madame Carimon stopped.

"Yes," the doctor said, when a few words had passed, "it is a most desolating affair. But, as madame knows, when Death has laid his grasp upon a patient, medical craft loses its power to resist him."

"Too true," murmured Mary Carimon. "And what is it that she has died of?"

Monsieur Dupuis shook his head to indicate that he did not know.

"I could have wished for an examination, to ascertain the true cause of the seizure," continued the doctor, "and I come now from expressing my regrets to my confrère, Monsieur Podevin. He agrees with me in deciding that we cannot press it in opposition to the family. Captain Fennel was quite willing it should take place, but his wife, poor distressed woman, altogether objects to it."

Mary Carimon went on to the house of death. She saw Lavinia, looking so peaceful in her stillness. A happy smile sat on her countenance. On her white attire lay some sweet fresh primroses, which Flore had placed there. Lavinia loved primroses. She used to say that when she looked at them they brought to her mind the woods and dales of Buttermead, always carpeted with the pale, fair blossoms in the spring of the year. Mrs. Fennel lay in a heavy sleep, exhausted by her night of distress, Flore informed Madame Carimon; and the captain, anxious about her, was sitting in her room, to guard against her being disturbed.

On the next day, Wednesday, in obedience to the laws of France relating to the dead, Lavinia Preen was buried. All the English gentlemen in the town, and some Frenchmen, including Monsieur Carimon and the sons of Madame Veuve Sauvage, assembled in the Place Ronde, and fell in behind the coffin when it was brought forth. They walked after it to the portion of the cemetery consecrated to Protestants, and there witnessed the interment. The tears trickled down Charley Palliser's face as he took his last look into the grave, and he was honest enough not to mind who saw them.

XIII

In their new mourning, at the English Church, the Sunday after the interment of Lavinia Preen, appeared Captain and Mrs. Fennel. The congregation looked at them more than at the parson. Poor Nancy's eyes were so blinded with tears that she could not see the letters in her Prayer-book. Only one little week ago when she had sat there, Lavinia was on the bench at her side, alive and well; and now— It was with difficulty Nancy kept herself from breaking down.

Two or three acquaintances caught her hand on leaving the church, whispering a few words of sympathy in her ear. Not one but felt truly sorry for her. The captain's hat, which had a wide band round it, was perpetually raised in acknowledgment of silent greetings, as he piloted his wife back to their house, the Petite Maison Rouge.

A very different dinner-table, this which the two sat down to, from last Sunday's, in the matter of cheerfulness. Nancy was about half-way through the wing of the fowl her husband had helped her to, when a choking sob caught her throat. She dropped her knife and fork.

"Oh, Edwin, I cannot! I cannot eat for my unhappy thoughts! This time last Sunday Lavinia was seated at the table with us. Now—" Nancy's speech collapsed altogether.

"Come, come," said Captain Fennel. "I hope you are not going to be hysterical again, Nancy. It is frightfully sad; I know that; but this prolonged grief will do no good. Go on with your dinner; it is a very nice chicken."

Nancy gave a great sob, and spoke impulsively, "I don't believe you regret her one bit, Edwin!"

Edwin Fennel in turn laid down his knife and fork and stared at his wife. A curious expression sat on his face.

"Not regret her," he repeated with emphasis. "Why, Nancy, I regret her every hour of the day. But I do not make a parade of my regrets. Why should I?—to what end? Come, come, my dear; you will be all the better for eating your dinner."

He went on with his own as he spoke. Nancy took up her knife and fork with a hopeless sigh.

Dinner over, Captain Fennel went to his cupboard and brought in some of the chartreuse. Two glasses, this time, instead of three. He might regret Lavinia, as he said, every hour of the day; possibly he did so; but it did not seem to affect his appetite, or his relish for good things.

Most events have their dark and their light sides. It could hardly escape the mind of Edwin Fennel that by the death of Lavinia the whole income became Nancy's. To him that must have been a satisfactory consolation.

In the afternoon he went with Nancy for a walk on the pier. She did not want to go; said she had no spirits for it; it was miserable at home; miserable out; miserable everywhere. Captain Fennel took her off, as he might have taken a child, telling her she should come and see the fishing-boats. After tea they went to church—an unusual thing for Captain Fennel. Lavinia and Nancy formerly went to evening service; he, never.

That night something curious occurred. Nancy went up to bed leaving the captain to follow, after finishing his glass of grog. He generally took one the last thing. Nancy had taken off her gown, and was standing before the glass about to undo her hair, when she heard him leave the parlour. Her bedroom-door, almost close to the head of the stairs, was not closed, and her ears were on the alert. Since Lavinia died, Nancy had felt timid in the house when alone, and she was listening for her husband to come up. She heard him lock up the spirit bottle in the little cupboard below, and begin to ascend the stairs, and she opened her door wider, that the light might guide him, for the staircase was in darkness.

Captain Fennel had nearly gained the top, when something—he never knew what—induced him to look round sharply, as though he fancied some one was close behind him. In fact, he did fancy it. In a moment, he gave a shout, dashed onwards into the bedroom, shut the door with a bang, and bolted it. Nancy, in great astonishment, turned to look at him. He seemed to have shrunk within himself in a fit of trembling, his face was ghastly, and the perspiration stood upon his brow.

"Edwin!" she exclaimed in a scared whisper, "what is the matter?"

Captain Fennel did not answer at first. He was getting up his breath.

"Has Flore not gone?" he then said.

"Flore!" exclaimed Nancy in surprise. "Why, Edwin, you know Flore goes away on Sundays in the middle of the afternoon! She left before we went on the pier. Why do you ask?"

"I—I thought—some person—followed me upstairs," he replied, in uneasy pauses.

"Oh, my goodness!" cried timid Nancy. "Perhaps a thief has got into the house!"

She went to the door, and was about to draw it an inch open, intending to peep out gingerly and listen, when her husband pulled her back with a motion of terror, and put his back against it. This meant, she thought, that he knew a thief was there. Perhaps two of them!

"Is there more than one?" she whispered. "Lavinia's silver—my silver, now—is in the basket on the console in the salon."

He did not answer. He appeared to be listening. Nancy listened also. The house seemed still as death.

"Perhaps I was mistaken," said Captain Fennel, beginning to recover himself after a bit. "I dare say I was."

"Well, I think you must have been, Edwin; I can't hear anything. We had better open the door."

She undid the bolt as she spoke, and he moved away from it. Nancy cautiously took a step outside, and kept still. Not a sound met her ear. Then she brought forth the candle and looked down the staircase. Not a sign of anything or any one met her eye.

"Edwin, there's nothing, there's nobody; come and see. You must have fancied it."

"No doubt," answered Captain Fennel. But he did not go to see, for all that.

Nancy went back to the room. "Won't you just look downstairs?" she said. "I—I don't much mind going with you."

"Not any necessity," replied he, and began to undress—and slipped the bolt again.

"Why do you bolt the door to-night?" asked Nancy.

"To keep the thief out," said he, in grim tones, which Nancy took for jesting. But she could not at all understand him.

His restlessness kept her awake. "It must have been all fancy," she more than once heard him mutter to himself.

When he rose in the morning, his restlessness seemed still to hang upon him. Remarking to Nancy, who was only half-awake, that his nerves were out of order, and he should be all the better for a sea-bath, he dressed and left the room. Nancy got down at the usual hour, half-past eight; and was told by Flore that monsieur had left word madame was not to wait breakfast for him: he was gone to have a dip in the sea, and should probably take a long country walk after it.

Flore was making the coffee at the kitchen stove; her mistress stood by, as if wanting to watch the process. These last few days, since Lavinia had been carried from the house, Nancy had felt easier in Flore's company than when alone with her own.

"That's to steady his nerves; they are out of order," replied Nancy, who had as much idea of reticence as a child. "Monsieur had a great fright last night, Flore."

"Truly!" said Flore, much occupied just then with her coffee-pot.

"He was coming up to bed between ten and eleven; I had gone on. When nearly at the top of the stairs he thought he heard some one behind him. It startled him frightfully. Not being prepared for it, supposing that the house was empty, you see, Flore, of course it would startle him."

"Naturally, madame."

"He cried out, and dashed into the bedroom and bolted the door. I never saw any one in such a state of terror, Flore; he was trembling all over; his face was whiter than your apron."

"Vraiment!" returned Flore, turning to look at her mistress in a little surprise. "But, madame, what had terrified him? What was it that he had seen?"

"Why, he could have seen nothing," corrected Mrs. Fennel. "There was nothing to see."

"Madame has reason; there could have been nothing, the house being empty. But then, what could have frightened him?" repeated Flore.

"Why, he must have fancied it, I suppose. Any way, he fancied some one was there. The first question he asked me was, whether you were in the house."

"Moi! Monsieur might have known I should not be in the house at that hour, madame. And why should he show terror if he thought it was me?"

Mrs. Fennel shrugged her shoulders. "It was a moment's scare; just that, I conclude; and it upset his nerves. A sea-bath will put him all right again."

Flore carried the coffee into the salon, and her mistress sat down to breakfast.

Now it chanced that this same week a guest came to stay with Madame Carimon. Stella Featherston, from Buttermead, was about to make a sojourn in Paris, and she took Sainteville on her route that she might stay a few days with her cousin, Mary Carimon, whom she had not seen for several years.

Lavinia and Ann Preen had once been very intimate with Miss Featherston, who reached Madame Carimon's on the Thursday. On the Friday morning Mrs. Fennel called to see her—and, in Nancy's impromptu way, she invited her and Mary Carimon to take tea at seven o'clock that same evening at the Petite Maison Rouge.

Nancy went home delighted. It was a little divertissement to her present saddened life. Captain Fennel knitted his brow when he heard of the arrangement, but made no objection in words. His wife shrank at the frown.

"Don't you like my having invited Miss Featherston to tea, Edwin?"

"Oh! I've no objection to it," he carelessly replied. "I am not in love with either Carimon or his wife, and don't care how little I see of them."

"He cannot come, having a private class on to-night. And I could not invite Miss Featherston without Mary Carimon," pleaded Nancy.

"Just so. I am not objecting."

With this somewhat ungracious assent, Nancy had to content herself. She ordered a gâteau Suisse, the nicest sort of gâteau to be had at Sainteville; and told Flore that she must for once remain for the evening.

The guests appeared punctually at seven o'clock. Such a thing as being invited for one hour, and strolling in an hour or two after it, was a mark of English breeding never yet heard of in the simple-mannered French town. Miss Featherston, a smart, lively young woman, wore a cherry-coloured silk; Mary Carimon was in black; she had gone into slight mourning for Lavinia. Good little Monsieur Jules had put a small band on his hat.

Captain Fennel was not at home to tea, and the ladies had it all their own way in the matter of talking. What with items of news from the old home, Buttermead, and Stella's telling about her own plans, the conversation never flagged a moment.

"Yes, that's what I am going to Paris for," said Stella, explaining her plans. "I don't seem likely to marry, for nobody comes to ask me, and I mean to go out in the world and make a little money. It is a sin and a shame that a healthy girl, the eldest of three sisters, should be living upon her poor mother in idleness. Not much of a girl, you may say, for I was three-and-thirty last week! but we all like to pay ourselves compliments when age is in question."

Nancy laughed. Almost the first time she had laughed since Lavinia's death.

"So you are going to Paris to learn French, Stella!"

"I am going to Paris to learn French, Nancy," assented Miss Featherston. "I know it pretty well, but when I come to speak it I am all at sea; and you can't get out as a governess now unless you speak it fluently. At each of the two situations I applied for in Worcestershire, it was the one fatal objection: 'We should have liked you, Miss Featherston, but we can only engage a lady who will speak French with the children.' So I made my mind up to speak French; and I wrote to good Monsieur Jules Carimon, and he has found me a place to go to in Paris, where not a soul in the household speaks English. He says, and I say, that in six months I shall chatter away like a native," she concluded, laughing.

XIV

About nine o'clock Captain Fennel came home. He was gracious to the visitors. Stella Featherston thought his manners were pleasing. Shortly afterwards Charley Palliser called. He apologized for the lateness of the hour, but his errand was a good-natured one. His aunt, Mrs. Hardy, had received a box of delicious candied fruits from Marseilles; she had sent him with a few to Mrs. Fennel, if that lady would kindly accept them. The truth was, every one in Sainteville felt sorry just now for poor Nancy Fennel.

Nancy looked as delighted as a child. She called to Flore to bring plates, turned out the fruits and handed them round. Flore also brought in the gâteau Suisse and glasses, and a bottle of Picardin wine, that the company might regale themselves. Charley Palliser suddenly spoke; he had just thought of something.

"Would it be too much trouble to give me back that book which I lent you a week or two ago—about the plans of the fortifications?" he asked, turning to Captain Fennel. "I want it sometimes for reference in my studies."

"Not at all; I ought to have returned it to you before this—but the trouble here has driven other things out of my head," replied Captain Fennel. "Let me see—where did I put it? Nancy, do you remember where that book is?—the heavy one, you know, with red edges and a mottled cover."

"That book? Why, it is on the drawers in our bedroom," replied Nancy.

"To be sure; I'll get it," said Captain Fennel.

His wife called after him to bring down the dominoes also; some one might like a game. The captain did not intend to take the trouble of going himself; he meant to send Flore. But Flore was not in the kitchen, and he took it for granted she was upstairs. In fact, Flore was in the yard at the pump; but he never thought of the yard or the pump. Lighting a candle, he strode upstairs.

He was coming down again, the open box of dominoes and Charley Palliser's book in one hand, the candlestick in the other, when the same sort of thing seemed to occur which had occurred on Sunday night. Hearing, as he thought, some one close behind him, almost treading, as it were, upon his heels, and thinking it was Flore, he turned his head round, intending to tell her to keep her distance.

Then, with a frightful yell, down dashed Captain Fennel the few remaining stairs, the book, the candlestick, and the box of dominoes all falling in the passage from his nerveless hands. The dominoes were hard and strong, and made a great crash. But it was the yell which had frightened the company in the salon.

They flocked out in doubt and wonder. The candle had gone out; and Charley Palliser was bringing forth the lamp to light up the darkness, when he was nearly knocked down by Captain Fennel. Flore, returning from the pump with her own candle, much damaged by the air of the yard, held it up to survey the scene.

Captain Fennel swept past Charley into the salon, and threw himself into a chair behind the door, after trying to dash it to; but they were trooping in behind him. His breath was short, his terrified face looked livid as one meet for the grave.

"Why, what has happened to you, sir?" asked Charles, intensely surprised.

"Oh! he must have seen the thief again!" shrieked Nancy.

"Shut the door; bolt it!" called out the stricken man.

They did as they were bid. This order, as it struck them all, could only have reference to keeping out some nefarious intruder, such as a thief. Flore had followed them in, after picking up the débris. She put the book and the dominoes on the table, and stood staring over her mistress's shoulder.

"Has the thief got in again, Edwin?" repeated Mrs. Fennel, who was beginning to tremble. "Did you see him?—or hear him?"

"My foot slipped; it sent me headforemost down the stairs," spoke the captain at last, conscious, perhaps, that something must be said to satisfy the inquisitive faces around him. "I heard Flore behind me, and—"

"Not me, sir," put in Flore in her best English. "I was not upstairs at all; I was out at the pump. There is nobody upstairs, sir; there can't be." But Captain Fennel only glared at her in answer.

"What did you cry out at?" asked Charles Palliser, speaking soothingly, for he saw that the man was pitiably unstrung. "Have you had a thief in the house? Did you think you saw one?"

"I saw no thief; there has been no thief in the house that I know of; I tell you I slipped—and it startled me," retorted the captain, his tones becoming savage.

"Then—why did you have the door bolted, captain?" struck in Miss Stella Featherston, who was extremely practical and matter-of-fact, and who could not understand the scene at all.

This time the captain glared at her. Only for a moment; a sickly smile then stole over his countenance.

"Somebody here talked about a thief: I said bolt him out," answered he.

With this general explanation they had to be contented; but to none of them did it sound natural or straightforward.

Order was restored. The ladies took a glass of wine each and some of the gâteau, which Flore handed round. Charles Palliser said good-night and departed with his book. Captain Fennel went out at the same time. He turned into the café on the Place Ronde, and drank three small glasses of cognac in succession.

"Nancy, what did you mean by talking about a thief?" began Madame Carimon, the whole thing much exercising her mind.

Upon which, Mrs. Fennel treated them all, including Flore, to an elaborate account of her husband's fright on the Sunday night.

"It was on the stairs; just as it was again now," she said. "He thought he heard some one following behind him as he came up to bed. He fancied it was Flore; but Flore had left hours before. I never saw any one show such terror in all my life. He said it was Flore behind him to-night, and you saw how terrified he was."

"But if he took it to be Flore, why should he be frightened?" returned Mary Carimon.

"Pardon, mesdames, but it is the same argument I made bold to use to madame," interposed Flore from the background, where she stood. "There is not anything in me to give people fright."

"I—think—it must have been," said Mrs. Fennel, speaking slowly, "that he grew alarmed when he found it was not Flore he saw. Both times."

"Then who was it that he did see—to startle him like that?" asked Mary Carimon.

"Why, he must have thought it was a thief," replied Nancy. "There's nothing else for it."

At this juncture the argument was brought to a close by the entrance of Monsieur Jules Carimon, who had come to escort his wife and Stella Featherston home.

These curious attacks of terror were repeated; not often, but at a few days' interval; so that at length Captain Fennel took care not to go about the house alone in the dark. He went up to bed when his wife did; he would not go to the door, if a ring came after Flore's departure, without a light in his hand. By-and-by he improvised a lamp, which he kept on the slab.

What was it that he was scared at? An impression arose in the minds of the two or three people who were privy to this, that he saw, or fancied he saw, in the house the spectre of one who had just been carried out of it, Lavinia Preen. Nancy had no such suspicion as yet; she only thought her husband could not be well. She was much occupied about that time, having at length nerved herself to the task of looking over her poor sister's effects.

One afternoon, when sitting in Lavinia's room (Flore—who stayed with her for company—had run down to the kitchen to see that the dinner did not burn), Nancy came upon a small, thin green case. Between its leaves she found three one-hundred-franc notes—twelve pounds in English value. She rightly judged that it was all that remained of her sister's nest-egg, and that she had intended to take it with her to Boulogne.

"Poor Lavinia!" she aspirated, the tears dropping from her eyes. "Every farthing remaining of the quarter's money she left with me for housekeeping."

But now a thought came to Nancy. Placing the case on the floor near her, intending to show it to her husband—she was sitting on a stool before one of Lavinia's boxes—it suddenly occurred to her that it might be as well to say nothing to him about it. He would be sure to appropriate the money to his own private uses: and Nancy knew that she should need some for hers. There would be her mourning to pay for; and—

The room-door was wide open, and at this point in her reflections Nancy heard the captain enter the house with his latch-key, and march straight upstairs. In hasty confusion, she thrust the little case into the nearest hiding-place, which happened to be the front of her black dress bodice.

"Nancy, I have to go to England," cried the captain. "How hot you look! Can't you manage to do that without stooping?"

"To go to England!" repeated Nancy, lifting her flushed face.

"Here's a letter from my brother; the postman gave it me as I was crossing the Place Ronde. It's only a line or two," he added, tossing it to her. "I must take this evening's boat."

Nancy read the letter. Only a line or two, as he said, just telling the captain to go over with all speed upon a pressing matter of business, and that he could return before the week was ended.

"Oh, but, Edwin, you can't go," began Nancy, in alarm. "I cannot stay here by myself."

"Not go! Why, I must go," he said very decisively. "How do I know what it is that I am wanted for? Perhaps that property which we are always expecting to fall in."

"But I should be so lonely. I could not stay here alone."

"Nonsense!" he sharply answered. "I shall not be away above one clear day; two days at the furthest. This is Thursday, and I shall return by Sunday's boat. You will only be alone to-morrow and Saturday."

He turned away, thus putting an end to the discussion, and entered their own room. As Nancy looked after him in despair, it suddenly struck her how very thin and ill he had become; his face worn and grey.

"He wants a change," she said to herself; "our trouble here has upset him as much as it did me. I'll say no more; I must not be selfish. Poor Lavinia used to warn me against selfishness."

So Captain Fennel went off without further opposition, his wife enjoining him to be sure to return on Sunday. The steamer was starting that night at eight o'clock; it was a fine evening, and Nancy walked down to the port with her husband and saw him on board. Nancy met an acquaintance down there; no other than Charley Palliser. They strolled a little in the wake of the departing steamer; Charley then saw her as far as the Place Ronde, and there wished her good-night.

And now an extraordinary thing happened. As Mrs. Fennel opened the door with her latch-key, Flore having left, and was about to enter the dark passage, the same curious and unaccountable terror seized her which had been wont to attack Lavinia. Leaving the door wide open, she dashed up the passage, felt for the match-box, and struck a light. Then, candle in hand, she returned to shut the door; but her whole frame trembled with fear.

"Why, it's just what poor Lavinia felt!" she gasped. "What on earth can it be? Why should it come to me? I will take care not to go out to-morrow night or Saturday."

And she held to her decision. Mrs. Hardy sent Charley Palliser to invite her for either day, or both days; Mary Carimon sent Pauline with a note to the same effect; but Nancy returned a refusal in both cases, with her best thanks.

The boat came in on Sunday night, but it did not bring Captain Fennel. On the Sunday morning the post had brought Nancy a few lines from him, saying he found the business on which he had been called to London was of great importance, and he was obliged to remain another day or two.

Nancy was frightfully put out: not only vexed, but angry. Edwin had no business to leave her alone like that so soon after Lavinia's death. She bemoaned her hard fate to several friends on coming out of church, and Mrs. Smith carried her off to dinner. The major was not out that morning—a twinge of gout in the right foot had kept him indoors.

This involved Nancy's going home alone in the evening, for the major could not walk with her. She did not like it. The same horror came over her before opening the door. She entered somehow, and dashed into the kitchen, hoping the stove was alight: a very silly hope, for Flore had been gone since the afternoon.

Nancy lighted the candle in the kitchen, and then fancied she saw some one looking at her from the open kitchen-door. It looked like Lavinia. It certainly was Lavinia. Nancy stood spell-bound; then she gave a cry of desperate horror and dropped the candlestick.

How she picked it up she never knew; the light had not gone out. Nothing was to be seen then. The apparition, if it had been one, had vanished. She got up to bed somehow, and lay shivering under the bedclothes until morning.

Quite early, when Nancy was at breakfast, Madame Carimon came in. She had already been to the fish-market, and came on to invite Nancy to her house for the day, having heard that Mr. Fennel was still absent. With a scared face and trembling lips, Nancy told her about the previous night—the strange horror of entering which had begun to attack her, the figure of Lavinia at the kitchen-door.

Madame Carimon, listening gravely, took, or appeared to take, a sensible view of it. "You have caught up this fear of entering the house, Nancy, through remembering that it attacked poor Lavinia," she said. "Impressionable minds—and yours is one of them—take fright just as children catch measles. As to thinking you saw Lavinia—"

"She had on the gown she wore the Sunday she was taken ill: her silver-grey silk, you know," interrupted Nancy. "She looked at me with a mournful, appealing gaze, just as if she wanted something."

"Ay, you were just in the mood to fancy something of the kind," lightly spoke Madame Carimon. "The fright of coming in had done that for you. I dare say you had been talking of Lavinia at Major Smith's."

"Well, so we had," confessed Nancy.

"Just so; she was already on your mind, and therefore that and the fright you were in caused you to fancy you saw her. Nancy, my dear, you cannot imagine the foolish illusions our fancies play us."

Easily persuaded, Mrs. Fennel agreed that it might have been so. She strove to forget the matter, and went out there and then with Mary Carimon.

But this state of things was to continue. Captain Fennel did not return, and Nancy grew frightened to death at being alone in the house after dark. Flore was unable to stay longer than the time originally agreed for, her old mother being dangerously ill. As dusk approached, Nancy began to hate her destiny. Apart from nervousness, she was sociably inclined, and yearned for company. Now and again the inclination to accept an invitation was too strong to be resisted, or she went out after dinner, uninvited, to this friend or that. But the pleasure was counterbalanced by having to go in again at night; the horror clung to her.

If a servant attended her home, or any gentleman from the house where she had been, she made them go indoors with her whilst she lighted her candle; once she got Monsieur Gustave's errand-boy to do so. But it was almost as bad with the lighted candle—the first feeling of being in the lonely house after they had gone. She wrote letter after letter, imploring her husband to return. Captain Fennel's replies were rich in promises: he would be back the very instant business permitted; probably "to-morrow, or the next day." But he did not come.

One Sunday, when he had been gone about three weeks, and Nancy had been spending the day in the Rue Pomme Cuite, Mary Carimon walked home with her in the evening. Monsieur Jules had gone to see his cousin off by the nine-o'clock train—Mademoiselle Priscille Carimon, who had come in to spend the day with them. She lived at Drecques.

"You will come in with me, Mary?" said Ann Fennel, as they gained the door.

"To be sure I will," replied Madame Carimon, laughing lightly, for none knew about the fears better than she.

Nancy took her hand as they went up the passage. She lighted the candle at the slab, and they went into the salon. Madame Carimon sat down for a few minutes, by way of reassuring her. Nancy took off her bonnet and mantle. On the table was a small tray with the tea-things upon it. Flore had left it there in readiness, not quite certain whether her mistress would come in to tea or not.

"I had such a curious dream last night," began Nancy; "those tea-things put me in mind of it. Lavinia—"

"For goodness' sake don't begin upon dreams to-night!" interposed Madame Carimon. "You know they always frighten you."

"Oh, but this was a pleasant dream, Mary. I thought that I and Lavinia were seated at a little table, with two teacups between us full of tea. The cups were very pretty; pale amber with gilt scrolls, and the china so thin as to be transparent. I can see them now. And Lavinia said something which made me smile; but I don't remember what it was. Ah, Mary! if she were only back again with us!"

"She is better off, you know," said Mary Carimon in tender tones.

"All the same, it was a cruel fate that took her; I shall never think otherwise. I wish I knew what it was she died of! Flore told me one day that Monsieur Podevin quite laughed at the idea of its being a chill."

"Well, Nancy, it was you who stopped it, you know."

"Stopped what?" asked Nancy.

"The investigation the doctors would have made after death. Both of them were much put out at your forbidding it: for their own satisfaction they wished to ascertain particulars. I may tell you now that I thought you were wrong to interfere."

"It was Captain Fennel," said Nancy calmly.

"Captain Fennel!" echoed Mary Carimon. "Monsieur Dupuis told me that Captain Fennel wished for it as much as he and Monsieur Podevin."

Captain Fennel's wife shook her head. "They asked him about it before they left, after she died. He came to me, and I said, Oh, let them do what they would; it could not hurt her now she was dead. I was in such terrible distress, Mary, that I hardly knew or cared what I said. Then Edwin drew so dreadful a picture of what post-mortems are, and how barbarously her poor neck and arms would be cut and slashed, that I grew sick and frightened."

"And so you stopped it—by reason of the picture he drew?"

"Yes. I came running down here to Monsieur Dupuis—Monsieur Podevin had gone—for Edwin said it must be my decision, not his, and his name had better not be mentioned; and I begged and prayed Monsieur Dupuis not to hold it. I think I startled him, good old man. I was almost out of my mind; quite wild with agitation; and he promised me it should be as I wished. That's how it all was, Mary."

Mary Carimon's face wore a curious look. Then she rallied, speaking even lightly.

"Well, well; it could not have brought her back to life; and I repeat that we must remember she is better off. And now, Nancy, I want you to show me the pretty purse that Miss Perry has knitted for you, if you have it at hand."

Nancy rose, opened her workbox, which stood on the side-table, and brought forth the purse. Of course Madame Carimon's motive had been to change her thoughts. After admiring the purse, and talking of other pleasant matters, Mary took her departure.

And the moment the outer door had closed upon her that feeling of terror seized upon Nancy. Catching up her mantle with one hand and the candle with the other, she made for the staircase, leaving her bonnet and gloves in the salon. The staircase struck cold to her, and she could hear the wind whistling, for it was a windy night. As to the candle, it seemed to burn with a pale flame and not to give half its usual light.

In her nervous agitation, just as she gained the uppermost stair, she dropped her mantle. Raising her head from stooping to pick it up, she suddenly saw some figure before her at the end of the passage. It stood beyond the door of her own room, close to that which had been her sister's.

It was Lavinia. She appeared to be habited in the silver-grey silk already spoken of. Her gaze was fixed upon Nancy, with the same imploring aspect of appeal, as if she wanted something; her pale face was inexpressibly mournful. With a terrible cry, Nancy tore into her own room, the mantle trailing after her. She shut the door and bolted it, and buried her face in the counterpane in wild agony.

And in that moment a revelation came to Ann Fennel. It was this apparition which had been wont to haunt her husband in the house and terrify him beyond control. Not a thief; not Flore—but Lavinia!

XV

On the Monday morning Flore found her mistress in so sick and suffering and strange a state, that she sent for Madame Carimon. In vain Mary Carimon, after hearing Nancy's tale, strove to convince her that what she saw was fancy, the effect of diseased nerves. Nancy was more obstinate than a mule.

"What I saw was Lavinia," she shivered. "Lavinia's apparition. No good to tell me it was not; I have seen it now twice. It was as clear and evident to me, both times, as ever she herself was in life. That's what Edwin used to see; I know it now; and he became unable to bear the house. I seem to read it all as in a book, Mary. He got his brother to send for him, and he is staying away because he dreads to come back again. But you know I cannot stay here alone now."

Madame Carimon wrote off at once to Captain Fennel, Nancy supplying the address. She told him that his wife was ill; in a nervous state; fancying she saw Lavinia in the house. Such a report, she added, should if possible be kept from spreading to the town, and therefore she must advise him to return without delay.

The letter brought back Captain Fennel, Flore having meanwhile remained entirely at the Petite Maison Rouge. Perhaps the captain did not in secret like that little remark of its being well to keep it from the public; he may have considered it suggestive, coming from Mary Carimon. He believed she read him pretty correctly, and he hated her accordingly. Any way, he deemed it well to be on the spot. Left to herself, there was no telling what ridiculous things Nancy might be saying or fancying.

Edwin Fennel did not return alone. His brother's wife was with him. Mrs. James, they called her, James being the brother's Christian name. Mrs. James was not a lady in herself or in manner; but she was lively and very good-natured, and these qualities were what the Petite Maison Rouge wanted in it just now; and perhaps that was Captain Fennel's motive in bringing her. Nancy was delighted. She almost forgot her fears and fancies. Flore was agreeable also, for she was now at liberty to return to ordinary arrangements. Thus there was a lull in the storm. They walked out with Mrs. James on the pier, and took her to see the different points of interest in the town; they even gave a little soirée for her, and in return were invited to other houses.

One day, when the two ladies were gossiping together, Nancy, in the openness of her heart, related to Mrs. James the particulars of Lavinia's unexpected and rather mysterious death, and of her appearing in the house again after it. Captain Fennel disturbed them in the midst of the story. His wife was taking his name in vain at the moment of his entrance, saying how scared he had been at the apparition.

"Hold your peace, you foolish woman!" he thundered, looking as if he meant to strike her. "Don't trouble Mrs. James's head with such miserable rubbish as that."

Mrs. James did not appear to mind it. She burst into a hearty laugh. She never had seen a ghost, she said, and was sure she never should; there were no such things. But she should like to hear all about poor Miss Preen's death.

"There was nothing else to hear," the captain growled. "She caught a chill on the Sunday, coming out of the hot church after morning service. It struck inwardly, bringing on inflammation, which the medical men could not subdue."

"But you know, Edwin, the church never is hot, and you know the doctors decided it was not a chill. Monsieur Podevin especially denied it," dissented Nancy, who possessed about as much insight as a goose, and a little less tact.

"Then what did she die of?" questioned Mrs. James. "Was she poisoned?"

"Oh, how can you suggest so dreadful a thing!" shrieked Nancy. "Poisoned! Who would be so wicked as to poison Lavinia? Every one loved her."

Which again amused the listening lady. "You have a quick imagination, Mrs. Edwin," she laughed. "I was thinking of mushrooms."

"And I of tinned meats and copper saucepans," supplemented Captain Fennel. "However, there could be no suspicion even of that sort in Lavinia's case, since she had touched nothing but what we all partook of. She died of inflammation, Mrs. James."

"Little doubt of it," acquiesced Mrs. James. "A friend of mine went, not twelve months ago, to a funeral at Brompton Cemetery; the ground was damp, and she caught a chill. In four days she was dead."

"Women have no business at funerals," growled Edwin Fennel. "Why should they parade their grief abroad? You see nothing of the kind in France."

"In truth I think you are not far wrong," said Mrs. James. "It is a fashion which has sprung up of late. A few years ago it was as much unknown with us as it is with the French."

"They will be catching it up next, I suppose," retorted the captain, as if the thing were a personal grievance to him.

"Little doubt of it," laughed Mrs. James.

After staying at Sainteville for a month, Mrs. James Fennel took her departure for London. Captain Fennel proposed to escort her over; but his wife went into so wild a state at the mere mention of it, that he had to give it up.

"I dare not stay in the house by myself, Edwin," she shuddered. "I should go to the Vice-Consul and to other influential people here, and tell them of my misery—that I am afraid of seeing Lavinia."

And Captain Fennel believed she would be capable of doing it. So he remained with her.

That the spectre of the dead-and-gone Lavinia did at times appear to them, or else their fancies conjured up the vision, was all too certain. Three times during the visit of Mrs. James the captain had been betrayed into one of his fits of terror: no need to ask what had caused it. After her departure the same thing took place. Nancy had not again seen anything, but she knew he had.

"We shall not be able to stay in the house, Edwin," his wife said to him one evening when they were sitting in the salon at dusk after Flore's departure; nothing having led up to the remark.

"I fancy we should be as well out of it," replied he.

"Oh, Edwin, let us go! If we can! There will be all the rent to pay up first."

"All the what?" said he.

"The rent," repeated Nancy; "up to the end of the term we took it for. About three years longer, I think, Edwin. That would be sixty pounds."

"And where do you suppose the sixty pounds would come from?"

"I don't know. There's the impediment, you see," remarked Nancy blankly. "We cannot leave without paying up."

"Unless we made a moonlight flitting of it, my dear."

"That I never will," she rejoined, with a firmness he could not mistake. "You are only jesting, Edwin."

"It would be no jesting matter to pay up that claim, and others; for there are others. Our better plan, Nancy, will be to go off by the London boat some night, and not let any one know where we are until I can come back to pay. You may see it is the only thing to be done, and you must bring your mind to it."

"Never by me," said Nancy, strong in her innate rectitude. "As to hiding ourselves anywhere, that can never be; I should not conceal my address from Mary Carimon—I could not conceal it from Colonel Selby."

Captain Fennel ground his teeth. "Suppose I say that this shall be, that we will go, and order you to obey me? What then?"

"No, Edwin, I could not. I should go in to Monsieur Gustave Sauvage, and say to him, 'We were thinking of running away, but I cannot do it; please put me in prison until I can pay the debt.' And then—"

"Are you an idiot?" asked Captain Fennel, staring at her.

"And then, when I was in prison," went on Nancy, "I should write to tell William Selby; and perhaps he would come over and release me. Please don't talk in this kind of way again, Edwin. I should keep my word."

Mr. Edwin Fennel could not have felt more astounded had his wife then and there turned into a dromedary before his eyes. She had hitherto been tractable as a child. But he had never tried her in a thing that touched her honour, and he saw that the card which he had intended to play was lost.

Captain Fennel played another. He went away himself.

Making the best he could of the house and its haunted state (though day by day saw him looking more and more like a walking skeleton) throughout the greater part of June, for the summer had come in, he despatched his wife to Pontipette one market day—Saturday—to remain there until the following Wednesday. Old Mrs. Hardy had gone to the homely but comfortable hotel at Pontipette for a change, and she wrote to invite Nancy to stay a short time with her. Charles Palliser was in England. Captain Fennel proceeded to London by that same Saturday night's boat, armed with a letter from his wife to Colonel Selby, requesting the colonel to pay over to her husband her quarterly instalment instead of sending it to herself. Captain Fennel had bidden her do this; and Nancy, of strict probity in regard to other people's money, could not resist signing over her own.

"But you will be sure to bring it all back, won't you, Edwin? and to be here by Wednesday, the day I return?" she said to him.

"Why, of course I shall, my dear."

"It will be a double portion now—thirty-five pounds."

"And a good thing, too; we shall want it," he returned.

"Indeed, yes; there's such a heap of things owing for," concluded Nancy.

Thus the captain went over to England in great glee, carrying with him the order for the money. But he was reckoning without his host.

Upon presenting himself at the bank in the City on Monday morning, he found Colonel Selby absent; not expected to return before the end of that week, or the beginning of the next. This was a check for Captain Fennel. He quite glared at the gentleman who thus informed him—Mr. West, who sat in the colonel's room, and was his locum tenens for the time being.

"Business is transacted all the same, I conclude?" said he snappishly.

"Why, certainly," replied Mr. West, marvelling at the absurdity of the question. "What can I do for you?"

Captain Fennel produced his wife's letter, requesting that her quarter's money should be paid over to him, and handed in her receipt for the same. Mr. West read them both, the letter twice, and then looked direct through his silver-rimmed spectacles at the applicant.

"I cannot do this," said he; "it is a private matter of Colonel Selby's."

"It is not more private than any other payment you may have to make," retorted Captain Fennel.

"Pardon me, it is. This really does not concern the bank at all. I cannot pay it without Colonel Selby's authority: he has neither given it nor mentioned it to me. Another thing: the payment, as I gather from the wording of Mrs. Ann Fennel's letter, is not yet due. Upon that score, apart from any other, I should decline to pay it."

"It will be due in two or three days. Colonel Selby would not object to forestall the time by that short period."

"That would, of course, be for the colonel's own consideration."

"I particularly wish to receive the money this morning."

Mr. West shook his head in answer. "If you will leave Mrs. Fennel's letter and receipt in my charge, sir, I will place them before the colonel as soon as he returns. That is all I can do. Or perhaps you would prefer to retain the latter," he added, handing back the receipt over the desk.

"Business men are the very devil to stick at straws," muttered Captain Fennel under his breath. He saw it was no use trying to move the one before him, and went out, saying he would call in a day or two.

Now it happened that Colonel Selby, who was only staying at Brighton for a rest (for he had been very unwell of late), took a run up to town that same Monday morning to see his medical attendant. His visit paid, he went on to the bank, surprising Mr. West there about one o'clock. After some conference upon business matters, Mr. West spoke of Captain Fennel's visit, and handed over the letter he had left.

Colonel Selby drew in his lips as he read it. He did not like Mr. Edwin Fennel; and he would most assuredly not pay Ann Fennel's money to him. He returned the letter to Mr. West.

"Should the man come here again, West, tell him, as you did this morning, that he can see me on my return—which will probably be on this day week," said the colonel. "No need to say I have been up here to-day."

And on the following day, Tuesday, Colonel Selby, being then at Brighton, drew out a cheque for the quarter almost due and sent it by post to Nancy at Sainteville.

Thus checkmated in regard to the money, Captain Fennel did not return home at the time he promised, even if he had had any intention of doing so. When Nancy returned to Sainteville on the Wednesday from Pontipette, he was not there. The first thing she saw waiting for her on the table was Colonel Selby's letter containing the cheque for five-and-thirty pounds.

"How glad I am it has come to me so soon!" cried Nancy; "I can pay the bills now. I suppose William Selby thinks it would not be legal to pay it to Edwin."

The week went on. Each time a boat came in, Nancy was promenading the port, expecting to see her husband land from it. On the Sunday morning Nancy received a letter from him, in which he told her he was waiting to see Colonel Selby, to get the money paid to him. Nancy wrote back hastily, saying it had been received by herself, and that she had paid it nearly all away in settling the bills. She begged him to come back by the next boat. Flore was staying in the house altogether, but at an inconvenience.

On the Monday evening Mrs. Fennel had another desperate fright. She went to take tea with an elderly lady and her daughter, Mrs. and Miss Lambert, bidding Flore to come for her at half-past nine o'clock. Half-past nine came, but no Flore; ten o'clock came, and then Mrs. Fennel set off alone, supposing Flore had misunderstood her and would be found waiting for her at home. The moonlit streets were crowded with promenaders returning from their summer evening walk upon the pier.

Nancy rang the bell; but it was not answered. She had her latch-key in her pocket, but preferred to be admitted, and she rang again. No one came. "Flore must have dropped asleep in the kitchen," she petulantly thought, and drew out her key.

"Flore!" she called out, pushing the door back. "Flore, where are you?"

Flore apparently was nowhere, very much to the dismay of Mrs. Fennel. She would have to go in alone, all down the dark passage, and wake her up. Leaving the door wide open, she advanced in the dark with cautious steps, the old terror full upon her.

The kitchen was dark also, so far as fire or candlelight went, but a glimmer of moonlight shone in at the window. "Are you not here, Flore?" shivered Nancy. But there was no response.

Groping for the match-box on the mantel-shelf over the stove, and not at once finding it, Nancy suddenly took up an impression that some one was standing in the misty rays of the moon. Gazing attentively, it seemed to assume the shadowy form of Lavinia. And with a shuddering cry Nancy Fennel fell down upon the brick floor of the kitchen.

XVI

It was a lovely summer's day, and Madame Carimon's neat little slip of a kitchen was bright and hot with the morning sun. Madame, herself, stood before the paste-board, making a green-apricot tart. Of pies and tarts à la mode Anglaise, Monsieur Jules was more fond than a schoolboy; and of all tarts known to the civilized world, none can equal that of a green apricot.

Madame had put down the rolling-pin, and stood for the moment idle, looking at Flore Pamart, and listening to something that Flore was saying. Flore, whisking out of the Petite Maison Rouge a few minutes before, ostensibly to do her morning's marketings, had whisked straight off to the Rue Pomme Cuite, and was now seated at the corner of the pastry-table, telling a story to Madame Carimon.

"It was madame's own fault," she broke off in her tale to remark. "Madame will give me her orders in French, and half the time I can't understand them. She had an engagement to take tea at Madame

Smith's in the Rue Lambeau, was what I thought she said to me, and that I must present myself there at half-past nine to walk home with her. Well, madame, I went accordingly, and found nobody at home there but the bonne, Thomasine. Her master was dining out at the Sous-préfet's, and her mistress had gone out with some more ladies to walk on the pier, as it was so fine an evening. Naturally I thought my mistress was one of the ladies, and sat there waiting for her and chatting with Thomasine. Madame Smith came in at ten o'clock, and then she said that my lady had not been there and that she had not expected her."

"She must have gone to tea elsewhere," observed Madame Carimon.

"Clearly, madame; as I afterwards found. It was to Madame Lambert's, in the Rue Lothaire, that I ought to have gone. I could only go home, as madame sees; and when I arrived there I found the house-door wide open. Just as I entered, a frightful cry came from the kitchen, and there I found her dropped down on the floor, half senseless with terror. Madame, she avowed to me that she had seen Mademoiselle Lavinia standing near her in the moonlight."

Madame Carimon took up her rolling-pin slowly before she spoke. "I know she has a fancy that she appears in the house."

"Madame Carimon, I think she is in the house," said Flore solemnly. And for a minute or two Madame Carimon rolled her paste in silence.

"Monsieur Fennel used to see her—I am sure he did—and now his wife sees her," went on the woman. "I think that is the secret of his running away so much: he can't bear the house and what is haunting it."

"It is altogether a dreadful thing; I lie awake thinking of it," bewailed Mary Carimon.

"But it cannot be let go on like this," said Flore; "and that's what has brought me running here this morning—to ask you, madame, whether anything can be done. If she is left alone to see these sights, she'll die of it. When she got up this morning she was shivering like a leaf in the wind. Has madame noticed that she is wasting away? For the matter of that, so was Monsieur Fennel."

Madame Carimon, beginning to line her shallow dish with paste, nodded in assent. "He ought to be here with her," she remarked.

"Catch him," returned Flore, in a heat. "Pardon, madame, but I must avow I trust not that gentleman. He is no good. He will never come back to stay at the house so long as there is in it—what is there. He dare not; and I would like to ask him why not. A man with the conscience at ease could not be that sort of coward. Honest men do not fly away, all scared, when they fancy they see a revenant."

Deeming it might be unwise to pursue the topic from this point, Madame Carimon said she would go and see Mrs. Fennel in the course of the day, and Flore clattered off, her wooden shoes echoing on the narrow pavement of the Rue Pomme Cuite.

But, as Madame Carimon was crossing the Place Ronde in the afternoon to pay her visit, she met Mrs. Fennel. Of course, Flore's communication was not to be mentioned.

"Ah," said Madame Carimon readily, "is it you? I was coming to ask if you would like to take a walk on the pier with me. It is a lovely afternoon, and not too hot."

"Oh, I'll go," said Nancy. "I came out because it is so miserable at home. When Flore went off to the fish-market after breakfast, I felt more lonely than you would believe. Mary," dropping her voice, "I saw Lavinia last night."

"Now I won't listen to that," retorted Mary Carimon, as if she were reprimanding a child. "Once give in to our nerves and fancies, there's no end to the tricks they play us. I wish, Ann, your house were in a more lively situation, where you might sit at the window and watch the passers-by."

"But it isn't," said Nancy sensibly. "It looks upon nothing but the walls."

Walking on, they sat down upon a bench that stood back from the port, facing the harbour. Nearly opposite lay the English boat, busily loading for London. The sight made Nancy sigh.

"I wish it would bring Edwin the next time it comes in," she said in low tones.

"When do you expect him?"

"I don't know when," said poor Nancy with emphasis. "Mary, I am beginning to think he stays away because he is afraid of seeing Lavinia."

"Men are not afraid of those foolish things, Ann."

"He is. Recollect those fits of terror he had. He used to hear her following him up and downstairs; used to see her on the landings."

Madame Carimon found no ready answer. She had witnessed one of those fits of terror herself.

"Last night," went on Mrs. Fennel, after a pause, "when Flore had left me and I could only shiver in my bed, and not expect to sleep, I became calm enough to ask myself why Lavinia should come back again, and what it is she wants. Can you think why, Mary?"

"Not I," said Madame Carimon lightly. "I shall only believe she does come when she shows herself to me."

"And I happened on the thought that, possibly, she may be wanting us to inquire into the true cause of her death. It might have been ascertained at the time, but for my stopping the action of the doctors, you know."

"Ann, my dear, you should exercise a little common sense. I would ask you what end ascertaining it now would answer, to her, dead, or to you, living?"

"It might be seen that she could have been cured, had we only known what the malady was."

"But you did not know; the doctors did not know. It could only have been discovered, even at your showing, after her death, not in time to save her."

"I wish Monsieur Dupuis had come more quickly on the Monday night!" sighed Nancy. "I am always wishing it. You can picture what it was, Mary—Lavinia lying in that dreadful agony and no doctor coming near her. Edwin was gone so long—so long! He could not wake up Monsieur Dupuis. I think now that the bell was out of order."

"Why do you think that now? Captain Fennel must have known whether the bell answered to his summons, or not."

"Well," returned Nancy, "this morning when Flore returned with the fish, she said I looked very ill. She had just seen Monsieur Dupuis in the Place Ronde, and she ran out again and brought him in—"

"Did you mention to him this fancy of seeing Lavinia?" hastily interrupted Madame Carimon.

"No, no; I don't talk of that to people. Only to you and Flore; and—yes—I did tell Mrs. Smith. I let Monsieur Dupuis think I was ill with grieving after Lavinia, and we talked a little about her. I said how I wished he could have been here sooner on the Monday night, and that my husband had rung several times before he could arouse him. Monsieur Dupuis said that was a mistake; he had got up and come as soon as he was called; he was not asleep at the time, and the bell had rung only once."

"What an extraordinary thing!" exclaimed Mary Carimon. "I know your husband said he rang many times."

"That's why I now think the bell must have been out of order; but I did not say so to Monsieur Dupuis," returned Nancy. "He is a kind old man, and it would grieve him: for of course we know doctors ought to keep their door-bells in order."

Madame Carimon rose in silence, but full of thought, and they continued their walk. It was low water in the harbour, but the sun was sparkling and playing on the waves out at sea. On the pier they found Rose and Anna Bosanquet; and in chatting with them Nancy's mood became more cheerful.

That same evening, on that same pier, Mary Carimon spoke a few confidential words to her husband. They sat at the end of it, and the beauty of the night, so warm and still, induced them to linger. The bright moon sailed grandly in the heavens and glittered upon the water that now filled the harbour, for the tide was in. Most of the promenaders had turned down the pier again, after watching out the steamer. What a fine passage she would make, and was making, cutting there so smoothly through the crystal sea!

Mary Carimon began in a low voice, though no one was near to listen and the waves could not hear her. She spoke pretty fully of a haunting doubt that lay upon her mind, as to whether Lavinia had died a natural death.

"If we make the best of it," she concluded, "her dying in that strangely sudden way was unusual; you know that, Jules; quite unaccountable. It never has been accounted for."

Monsieur Jules, gazing on the gentle waves as they rose and fell in the moonlight at the mouth of the harbour, answered nothing.

"He had so much to wish her away for, that man: all the money would become Nancy's. And I'm sure there was secret enmity between them—on both sides. Don't you see, Jules, how suspicious it all looks?"

The moonbeams, illumining Monsieur Jules Carimon's face, showed it to be very impassive, betraying no indication that he as much as heard what his wife was talking about.

"I have not forgotten, I can never forget, Jules, the very singular Fate-reading, or whatever you may please to call it, spoken by the Astrologer Talcke last winter at Miss Bosanquet's soirée. You were not in the room, you know, but I related it to you when we arrived home. He certainly foretold Lavinia's death, as I, recalling the words, look upon it now. He said there was some element of evil in their house, threatening and terrible; he repeated it more than once. In their house, Jules, and that it would end in darkness; which, as every one understood, meant death: not for Mrs. Fennel; he took care to tell her that; but for another. He said the cards were more fateful than he had ever seen them. That evil in the house was Fennel."

Still Monsieur Jules offered no comment.

"And what could be the meaning of those dreams Lavinia had about him, in which he always seemed to be preparing to inflict upon her some fearful ill, and she knew she never could and never would escape from it?" ran on Mary Carimon, her eager, suppressed tones bearing a gruesome sound in the stillness of the night. "And what is the explanation of the fits of terror which have shaken Fennel since the death, fancying he sees Lavinia? Flore said to me this morning that she is sure Lavinia is in the house."

Glancing at her husband to see that he was at least listening, but receiving no confirmation of it by word or motion, Mary Carimon continued:

"Those dreams came to warn her, Jules. To warn her to get out of the house while she could. And she made arrangements to go, and in another day or two would have been away in safety. But he was too quick for her."

Monsieur Jules Carimon turned now to face his wife. "Mon amie, tais toi," said he with authority. "Such a topic is not convenable," he added, still in French, though she had spoken in English. "It is dangerous."

"But, Jules, I believe it to have been so."

"All the same, and whether or no, it is not your affair, Marie. Neither must you make it so. Believe me, my wife, the only way to live peaceably ourselves in the world is to let our neighbours' sins alone."

XVII

Captain Edwin Fennel was certainly in no hurry to return to Sainteville, for he did not come. Nancy, ailing, weak, wretchedly uncomfortable, wrote letter after letter to him, generally sending them over by some friend or other who might be crossing, to be put in a London letter-box, and so evade the foreign postage. Once or twice she had written to Mrs. James, telling of her lonely life and that she wanted Edwin either to take her out of the dark and desolate house, or else to come back to it himself. Captain Fennel would answer now and again, promising to come—she would be quite sure to see him on one of the first boats if she looked out for their arrival. Nancy did look, but she had not yet seen him. She was growing visibly thinner and weaker. Sainteville said how ill Mrs. Fennel was looking.

One evening at the end of July, when the London steamer was due about ten o'clock, Nancy went to watch it in, as usual, Flore attending her. The port was gay, crowded with promenaders. There had been a concert at the Rooms, and the company was coming home from it. Mrs. Fennel had not made one: latterly she had felt no spirit for amusement. Several friends met her; she did not tell them she had come down to meet her husband, if haply he should be on the expected boat; she had grown tired and half ashamed of saying that; she let them think she was only out for a walk that fine evening. There was a yellow glow still in the sky where the sun had set; the north-west was clear and bright with its opal light.

The time went on; the port became deserted, excepting a few passing stragglers. Ten o'clock had struck, eleven would soon strike. Flore and her mistress, tired of pacing about, sat down on one of the benches facing the harbour. One of two young men, passing swiftly homewards from the pier, found himself called to.

"Charley! Charley Palliser!"

Charles turned, and recognized Mrs. Fennel. Stepping across to her, he shook hands.

"What do you think can have become of the boat?" she asked. "It ought to have been in nearly an hour ago."

"Oh, it will be here shortly," he replied. "The boat often makes a slow passage when there's no wind. What little wind we have had to-day has been dead against it."

"As I've just said to madame," put in Flore, always ready to take up the conversation. "Mr. Charles knows there's no fear it has gone down, though it may be a bit late."

"Why, certainly not," laughed Charley. "Are you waiting here for it, Mrs. Fennel?"

"Ye—s," she answered, but with hesitation.

"And as it's not even in sight yet, madame had much better go home and not wait, for the air is getting chilly," again spoke Flore.

"We can't see whether it's in sight or not," said her mistress. "It is dark out at sea."

"Shall I wait here with you, Mrs. Fennel?" asked Charley in his good nature.

"Oh no, no; no, thank you," she answered quickly. "If it does not come in soon, we shall go home."

He wished them good-night, and went onwards.

"She is hoping the boat may bring that mysterious brute, Fennel," remarked Charles to his companion.

"Brute, you call him?"

"He is no better than one, to leave his sick wife alone so long," responded Charles in hearty tones. "She has picked up an idea, I hear, that the house is haunted, and shakes in her shoes in it from morning till night."

The two watchers sat on, Flore grumbling. Not for herself, but for her mistress. A sea-fog was rising, and Flore thought madame might take cold. Mrs. Fennel wrapped her light fleecy shawl closer about her chest, and protested she was quite hot. The shawl was well enough for a warm summer's night, but not for a cold sea-fog. About half-past eleven there suddenly loomed into view through the mist the lights of the steamer, about to enter the harbour.

"There she is!" exultingly cried Nancy, who had been shivering inwardly for some time past, and doing her best not to shiver outwardly for fear of Flore. "And now, Flore, you go home as quickly as you can and make a fire in the salon to warm us. I'm sure he will need one—at sea in this cold fog."

"If he is come," mentally returned Flore in her derisive heart. She had no faith in the return of Monsieur Fennel by any boat, a day or a night one. But she needed no second prompting to hasten away; was too glad to do it.

Poor Nancy waited on. The steamer came very slowly up the port, or she fancied so; one must be cautious in a fog; and it seemed to her a long time swinging round and settling itself into its place. Then the passengers came on shore one by one, Nancy standing close to look at them. There were only about twenty in all, and Captain Fennel was not one of them. With misty eyes and a rising in her throat and spiritless footsteps, Nancy arrived at her home, the Petite Maison Rouge. Flore had the fire burning in the salon; but Nancy was too thoroughly chilled for any salon fire to warm her.

The cold she caught that night stuck to her chest. For some days afterwards she was very ill indeed. Monsieur Dupuis attended her, and brought his son once or twice, Monsieur Henri. Nancy got up again, and was, so to say, herself once more; but she did not get up her strength.

She would lie on the sofa in the salon those August days, which were very hot ones, too languid to get off it. Friends would call in to see her; Major and Mrs. Smith, the Miss Bosanquets, the Lamberts, and so on. Madame Carimon was often there. They would ask her why she did not "make an effort" and sit up and occupy herself with a book or a bit of work, or go out a little; and Nancy's answer was nearly always the same—she would do all that when the weather was somewhat cooler. Charley Palliser was quite a constant visitor. An English damsel, who was casting a covetous eye to Charles, though she might have spared herself the pains, took a fit of jealousy and said one might think sick Nancy Fennel was his sweetheart, going there so often. Charley rarely went empty-handed either. Now it would be half-a-dozen nectarines in their red-ripe loveliness, now some choice peaches, then a bunch of hot-house grapes, "purple and gushing," and again an amusing novel just out in England.

"Mary, she is surely dying!"

The sad exclamation came from Stella Featherston. She and Madame Carimon, going in to take tea at the Petite Maison Rouge, had been sent by its mistress to her chamber above to take off their bonnets. The words had broken from Stella the moment they were alone.

"Sometimes I fear it myself," replied Madame Carimon. "She certainly grows weaker instead of stronger."

"Does any doctor attend her?"

"Monsieur Dupuis; a man of long experience, kind and clever. I was talking to him the other day, and he as good as said his skill and care seemed to avail nothing: were wasted on her."

"Is it consumption?"

"I think not. She caught a dreadful cold about a month ago through being out in a night fog, thinly clad; and there's no doubt it left mischief behind; but it seems to me that she is wasting away with inward fever."

"I should get George to run over to see her, if I were you, Mary," remarked Stella. "French doctors are very clever, I believe, especially as surgeons; but for an uncertain case like this they don't come up to the English. And George knows her constitution."

They went down to the salon, Mary Carimon laughing a little at the remark. Stella Featherston had not been long enough in France to part with her native prejudices. The family with whom she lived in Paris had journeyed to Sainteville for a month for what they called "les eaux," and Stella accompanied them. They were in lodgings on the port.

Mrs. Fennel seemed more like her old self that evening than she had been for some time past. The unexpected presence of her companion of early days changed the tone of her mind and raised her spirits. Stella exerted all her mirth, talked of their doings in the past, told of Buttermead's doings in the present. Nancy was quite gay.

"Do you ever sing now, Stella?" she suddenly asked.

"Why, no," laughed Stella, "unless I am quite alone. Who would care to hear old ditties sung without music?"

"I should. Oh, Stella, sing me a few!" urged the invalid, her tone quite imploring. "It would bring the dear old days back to me."

Stella Featherston had a most melodious voice, but she did not play. It was not unusual in those days for girls to sing without any accompaniment, as Stella had for the most part done.

"Have you forgotten your Scotch songs, Stella?" asked Mary Carimon.

"Not I; I like them best of all," replied Miss Featherston. And without more ado she broke into "Ye banks and braes."

It was followed by "The Banks of Allan Water," and others. Flore stole to the parlour-door, and thought she had never heard so sweet a singer. Last of all, Stella began a quaint song that was more of a chant than anything else, low and subdued:

"Woe's me, for my heart is breakin',
I think on my brither sma',
And on my sister greetin',
When I cam' from home awa'.
And O, how my mither sobbit,
As she took from me her hand,
When I left the door of our old house
To come to this stranger land.

"There's nae place like our ain home,
O, I would that I were there!
There's nae home like our ain home
To be met wi' onywhere.
And O, that I were back again
To our farm and fields sae green,
And heard the tongues of our ain folk,
And was what I hae been!"

A feeling of despair ran through the whole words; and the tears were running down Ann Fennel's hectic cheeks as the melody died away in a plaintive silence.

"It is what I shall never see again, Stella," she murmured—"the green fields of our home; or hear the tongues of all the dear ones there. In my dreams, sometimes, I am at Selby Court, light-hearted and happy, as I was before I left it for this 'stranger land.' Woe's me, also, Stella!"

And now I come into the story—I, Johnny Ludlow. For what I have told of it hitherto has not been from any personal knowledge of mine, but from diaries, and from what Mary Carimon related to me, and from Featherston. It may be regarded as singular that I should have been, so to say, present at its ending, but that I was there is as true as anything I ever wrote. The story itself is true in all its chief facts; I have already said that; and it is true that I saw the close of it.

XVIII

To say that George Featherston, Doctor-in-ordinary at Buttermead, felt as if he were standing on his head instead of his heels, would not in the least express his mental condition as he stood in his surgery that September afternoon and read a letter, just delivered, from his sister, Madame Carimon.

"Wants me to go to Sainteville to see Ann Preen; thinks she will die if I refuse, for the French doctors can do nothing for her!" commented Featherston, staring at the letter in intense perplexity, and then looking off it to stare at me.

I wonder whether anything in this world happens by chance? In the days and years that have gone by since, I sometimes ask myself whether that did: that I should be at that particular moment in Featherston's surgery. Squire Todhetley was staying with Sir John Whitney for partridge shooting. He had taken me with him, Tod being in Gloucestershire; and on this Friday afternoon I had run in to say "How-d'ye-do" to Featherston.

"Sainteville!" repeated he, quite unable to collect his senses. "Why, I must cross the water to get there!"

I laughed. "Did you think Sainteville would cross to you, sir?"

"Bless me! just listen to this," he went on, reading parts of the letter aloud for my benefit. "'It is a dreadful story, George; I dare not enter into details here. But I may tell you this much: that she is dying of fright as much as of fever—or whatever it may be that ails her physically. I am sure it is not consumption, though some of the people here think it is. It is fright and superstition. She lives in the belief that the house is haunted: that Lavinia's ghost walks in it.'"

"Now what on earth can Mary mean by that?" demanded the doctor, looking off to ask me. "Ann Preen's wits must have left her. And Mary's too, to repeat so nonsensical a thing."

Turning to the next page of the letter, Featherston read on.

"'To see her dying by inches before my eyes, and not make any attempt to, save her is what I cannot reconcile myself to, George. I should have it on my conscience afterwards. I think there is this one chance for her: that you, who have attended her before and must know her constitution, would see her now. You might be able to suggest some remedy or mode of treatment which would restore her. It might even be that the sight of a home face, of her old home doctor, would do for her what the strange doctors here cannot do. No one knows better than you how marvellously in illness the mind influences the body.'

"True enough," broke off Featherston. "But it seems to me there must be something mysterious about the sickness." He read on again.

"'Stella, who is here, was the first to suggest your seeing her, but it was already exercising my thoughts. Do come, George! the sooner the better. I and Jules will be delighted to have you with us.'"

Featherston slowly folded up the letter. "What do you think of all this, Johnny Ludlow? Curious, is it not?"

"Very. Especially that hint about the house being haunted by the dead-and-gone Miss Preen."

"I have never heard clearly what it was Lavinia Preen died of," observed Featherston, leaving, doctor-like, the supernatural for the practical. "Except that she was seized with some sort of illness one day and died the next."

"But that's no reason why her ghost should walk. Is it?"

"Nancy's imagination," spoke Featherston slightingly. "She was always foolish and fanciful."

"Shall you go to Sainteville, Mr. Featherston?"

He gave his head a slow, dubious shake, but did not speak.

"Don't I wish such a chance were offered to me!"

Featherston sat down on a high stool, which stood before the physic shelves, to revolve the momentous question. And by the time he took over it, he seemed to find it a difficult task.

"One hardly likes to refuse the request, put as Mary writes it," remarked he presently. "Yet I don't see how I can go all the way over there; or how I could leave my patients here. What a temper some of them would be in!"

"They wouldn't die of it. It would be a rare holiday for you. Set you up in health for a year to come."

"I've not had a holiday since that time at Pumpwater," he rejoined dreamily; "when I went over for a day or two to see poor John Whitney. You remember it, Johnny; you were there."

"Ay, I remember it."

"Not that this is a question of a holiday for me or no holiday, and I wonder you should put it so, Johnny Ludlow; it turns upon Ann Preen. Ann Fennel, that's to say. If I thought I could do her any good, and those French doctors can't, why, I suppose I ought to make an effort to go."

"To be sure. Make one also to take me with you!"

"I dare say!" laughed Featherston. "What would the Squire say to that?"

"Bluster a bit, and then see it was the very thing for me, and ask what the cost would be. Mr. Featherston, I shall be ready to start when you are. Please let me go!"

Of course I said this half in jest. But it turned out to be earnest. Whether Featherston feared he might get lost if he crossed the sea alone, I can't say; but he said I might put the question to the Squire if I liked, and he would see him later and second it.

Featherston did another thing. He carried Mary Carimon's letter that evening to Selby Court. Colonel Selby was staying with his brother for a week's shooting. Mr. Selby, a nervous valetudinarian, would not have gone out with a gun if bribed to it, but he invited his friends to do so. They had just finished dinner when Featherston arrived; the two brothers, and a short, dark, younger man with a rather keen but good-natured face and kindly dark eyes. He was introduced as Mr. David Preen, and turned out to be a cousin, more or less removed, of all the Preens and all the Selbys you have ever heard of, dead or living.

Featherston imparted his news to them, and showed his sister's letter. It was pronounced to be a very curious letter, and was read over more than once. Colonel Selby next told them what he knew and what he thought of Edwin Fennel: how he had persistently schemed to get the quarterly money of the two ladies into his own covetous hands, and what a shady sort of individual he was believed to be. Mr. Selby, nervous at the best of times, let alone the worst, became painfully impressed: he seemed to fear poor Nancy was altogether in a hornet's nest, and gave an impulsive opinion that some one of the family ought to go over with Featherston to look into things.

"Lavinia can't have been murdered, can she?" cried he, his thoughts altogether confused; "murdered by that man for her share of the money? Why else should her ghost come back?"

"Don't make us laugh, Paul," said the colonel to his brother. "Ghosts are all moonshine. There are no such things."

"I can tell you that there are, William," returned the elder. "Though mercifully the power to see them is accorded to very few mortals on earth. Can you go with Mr. Featherston to look into this strange business, William?"

"No," replied the colonel, "I could not possibly spare the time. Neither should I care to do it. Any inquiry of that kind would be quite out of my line."

"I will go," quietly spoke David Preen.

"Do so, David," said Mr. Selby eagerly. "It shall cost you nothing, you know." By which little speech, Featherston gathered that Mr. David Preen was not more overdone with riches than were many of the other Preens.

"Look into it well, David. See the doctor who attended Lavinia; see all and every one able to throw any light upon her death," urged Mr. Selby. "As to Ann, she was lamentably, foolishly blamable to marry as she did, but she must not be left at the villain's mercy now things have come to this pass."

To which Mr. David Preen nodded an emphatic assent.

The Squire gave in at last. Not to my pleading—he accused me of having lost my head only to think of it—but to Featherston. And when the following week was wearing away, the exigencies of Featherston's patients not releasing him sooner, we started for Sainteville; he, I, and David Preen. Getting in at ten at night after a boisterous passage, Featherston took up his quarters at Monsieur Carimon's, we ours at the Hôtel des Princes.

She looked very ill. Ill and changed. I had seen Ann Preen at Buttermead when she lived there, but the Ann Preen (or Fennel) I saw now was not much like her. The once bright face was drawn and fallen in, and very nearly as long and grey as Featherston's. Apart from that, a timid, shrinking look sat upon it, as though she feared some terror lay very near to her.

The sick have to be studied, especially when suffering from whims and fancies. So they invented a little fable to Mrs. Fennel—that Featherston and David Preen were taking an excursion together for their recreation, and the doctor had extended it as far as Sainteville to see his sister Mary; never allowing her to think that it was to see her. I was with them, but I went for nobody—and in truth that's all I was in the matter.

It was the forenoon of the day after we arrived. David Preen had gone in first, her kinsman and distant cousin, to the Petite Maison Rouge, paving the way, as it were, for Featherston. We went in presently. Mrs. Fennel sat in a large armchair by the salon fire, wrapped in a grey shawl; she was always cold now, she told us; David Preen sat on the sofa opposite, talking pleasantly of home news. Featherston joined him on the sofa, and I sat down near the table.

Oh, she was glad to see us! Glad to see us all. Ours were home faces, you see. She held my hands in hers, and the tears ran down her face, betraying her state of weakness.

"You have not been very well of late, Mary tells me," Featherston said to her in a break of the conversation. "What has been the matter?"

"I—it came on from a bad cold I caught," she answered with some hesitation. "And there was all the trouble about Lavinia's death. I could not get over the grief."

"Well, I must say you don't look very robust," returned Featherston, in a half-joking tone. "I think I had better take you in hand whilst I am here, and set you up."

"I do not think you can set me up; I do not suppose any one can," she replied, shaking back her curls, which fell on each side of her face in ringlets, as of old.

Featherston smiled cheerily. "I'll try," said he. "Some of my patients say the same when I am first called in to them; but they change their tone after I have brought back their roses. So will you; never fear. I'll come in this afternoon and have a professional chat with you."

That settled, they went on with Buttermead again; David Preen giving scraps and revelations of the Preen and Selby families; Featherston telling choice items of the rural public in general. Mrs. Fennel's spirits went up to animation.

"Shall you be able to do anything for her, sir?" I asked the doctor as we came away and went through the entry to the Place Ronde.

"I cannot tell," he answered gravely. "She has a look on her face that I do not like to see there."

Betrayed into confidence, I suppose, by the presence of the old friend of her girlhood, Ann Fennel related everything to Mr. Featherston that afternoon, as they sat on the sofa side by side, her hand occasionally held soothingly in his own. He assured her plainly that what she was chiefly suffering from was a disorder of the nerves, and that she must state to him explicitly the circumstances which brought it on before he could decide how to treat her for it.

Nancy obeyed him. She yearned to get well, though a latent impression lay within her that she should not do so. She told him the particulars of Lavinia's unexpected death just when on the point of leaving Sainteville; and she went on to declare, glancing over her shoulders with frightened eyes, that she (Lavinia) had several times since then appeared in the house.

"What did Lavinia die of?" inquired the doctor at this juncture.

"We could not tell," answered Mrs. Fennel. "It puzzled us. At first Monsieur Dupuis thought it must be inflammation brought on by a chill; but Monsieur Podevin quite put that opinion aside, saying it was nothing of the sort. He is a younger and more energetic practitioner than Monsieur Dupuis."

"Was it never suggested that she might, in one way or another, have taken something which poisoned her?"

"Why, yes, it was; I believe Monsieur Dupuis did think so—I am sure Monsieur Podevin did. But it was impossible it could have been the case, you see, because Lavinia touched nothing either of the days that we did not also partake of."

"There ought to have been an examination after death. You objected to that, I fancy," continued Featherston, who had talked a little with Madame Carimon.

"True—I did; and I have been sorry for it since," sighed Ann Fennel. "It was through what my husband said to me that I objected. Edwin thought it would be distasteful to me. He did not like the idea of it either. Being dead, he held that she should be left in reverence."

Featherston coughed. She was evidently innocent as any lamb of suspicion against him.

"And now," went on Mr. Featherston, "just tell me what you mean by saying you see your sister about the house."

"We do see her," said Nancy.

"Nonsense! You don't. It is all fancy. When the nerves are unstrung, as yours are, they play us all sorts of tricks. Why, I knew a man once who took up a notion that he walked upon his head, and he came to me to be cured!"

"But it is seeing Lavinia's apparition, and the constant fear of seeing it which lies upon me, that has brought on this nervousness," pleaded Nancy. "It is to my husband, when he is here, that she chiefly appears; nothing but that is keeping him away. I have seen her only three or four times."

She spoke quietly and simply, evidently grounded in the belief. Mr. Featherston wondered how he was to deal with this: and perhaps he was not himself so much of a sceptic in the supernatural as he thought fit to pretend. Nancy continued:

"It was to my husband she appeared first. Exactly a week after her death. No; a week after the evening she was first taken ill. He was coming upstairs to bed—I had gone on—when he suddenly fancied that some one was following him, though only he and I were in the house. Turning quickly round, he saw Lavinia. That was the first time; and I assure you I thought he would have died of it. Never before had I witnessed such mortal terror in man."

"Did he tell you he had seen her?"

"No; never. I could not imagine what brought on these curious attacks of fright, for he had others. He put it upon his health. It was only when I saw Lavinia myself after he went to England that I knew. I knew then what it must have been."

Mr. Featherston was silent.

"She always appears in the same dress," continued Nancy; "a silver-grey silk that she wore at church that Sunday. It was the last gown she ever put on: we took it off her when she was first seized with the pain. And in her face there is always a sad, beseeching aspect, as if she wanted something and were imploring us to get it for her. Indeed we see her, Mr. Featherston."

"Ah, well," he said, perceiving it was not from this quarter that light could be thrown on the suspicious darkness of the past, "let us talk of yourself. You are to obey my orders in all respects, Mistress Nancy. We will soon have you flourishing again."

Brave words. Perhaps the doctor half believed in them himself. But he and they received a check all too soon.

That same evening, after David Preen had left—for he went in to spend an hour at the little red house to gossip about the folks at home—Nancy was taken with a fit of shivering. Flore hastily mixed her a glass of hot wine-and-water, and then went upstairs to light a fire in the bedroom, thinking her mistress would be the better for it. Nancy, who could hear Flore moving about overhead, suddenly remembered something that she wanted brought down. Rising from her chair, she went to the door of the salon, intending to call out. A sort of side light, dim and indistinct, fell upon her as she stood in the recess at the foot of the stairs from the lamp in the salon and from the stove in the kitchen, for both doors were open.

"Flore," she was beginning, "will you bring down my—"

And there Ann Fennel's words ended. With a wild cry, which reached the ears of Flore and nearly startled her into fits, Mrs. Fennel collapsed. The servant came dashing downstairs, expecting to hear that the ghost had appeared again.

It was not that. Her mistress was looking wild and puzzled; and when she recovered herself sufficiently to speak, declared that she had been startled by some animal. Either a cat or a rabbit, she could not tell which, the glimpse she caught of it was so brief and slight; it had run against her legs as she was calling out.

Flore did not know what to make of this. She looked about, but neither cat nor rabbit was to be seen; and she told her mistress it could have been nothing but fancy. Mrs. Fennel thought she knew better.

"Why, I felt it and saw it," she said. "It came right against me and ran over my feet. It seemed to be making for the passage, as if it wanted to get out by the front-door."

We were gathered together in the salon of the Petite Maison Rouge the following morning, partly by accident. Ann Fennel, exceedingly weak and nervous, lay in bed. Featherston and Monsieur Dupuis were both upstairs. She put down her illness to the fright, which she talked of to them freely. They did not assure her it was only "nerves"—to what purpose? I waited in the salon with David Preen, and just as the doctors came down Madame Carimon came in.

David Preen seized upon the opportunity. Fearing that one so favourable might not again occur, unless formally planned, he opened the ball. Drawing his chair to the table, next to that of Madame Carimon, the two doctors sitting opposite, David Preen avowed, with straightforward candour, that he, with some other relatives, held a sort of doubt as to whether it might not have been something Miss Lavinia Preen took which caused her death; and he begged Monsieur Dupuis to say if any such doubt had crossed his own mind at the time.

The fair-faced little médecin shook his head at this appeal, as much as to say he thought that the subject was a puzzling one. Naturally the doubt had crossed him, and very strongly, he answered; but the difficulty in assuming that view of the matter lay in her having partaken solely of the food which the rest of the household had partaken of; that and nothing else. His confrère, Monsieur Podevin, held a very conclusive opinion—that she had died of poison.

David Preen drew towards him a writing-case which lay on the table, took a sheet of paper from it, and a pencil from his pocket. "Let us go over the facts quietly," said he; "it may be we shall arrive at some decision."

So they went over the facts, the chief speakers being Madame Carimon and Flore, who was called in. David Preen dotted down from time to time something which I suppose particularly impressed him.

Miss Preen was in perfectly good health up to that Sunday—the first after Easter. On the following Tuesday she was about to quit Sainteville for Boulogne, her home at the Petite Maison Rouge having become intolerable to her through the residence in it of Captain Fennel.

"Pardon me if I state here something which is not positively in the line of facts; rather, perhaps, in that of imagination," said Madame Carimon, looking up. "Lavinia had gradually acquired a most painful dread of Captain Fennel. She had dreams which she could only believe came to warn her against him, in which he appeared to be threatening her with some evil that she could not escape from. Once or twice—and this I cannot in any way account for—she saw him in the house when he was not in it, not even at Sainteville—"

"What! saw his apparition?" cried Featherston. "When the man was living! Come, come, Mary, that is going too far!"

"Quelle drôle d'idée!" exclaimed the little doctor.

"He appeared to her twice, she told me," continued Mary Carimon. "She had been spending the evening out each time; had come into the house, this house, closing the street-door behind her. When she lighted a candle at the slab, she saw him standing just inside the door, gazing at her with the same dreadful aspect that she saw afterwards in her dreams. You may laugh, George; Monsieur Dupuis, I think you are already laughing; but I fully believe that she saw what she said she did, and dreamt what she did dream."

"But it could not have been the man's apparition when he was not dead; and it could not have been the man himself when he was not at Sainteville," contended Featherston.

"And I believe that it all meant one of those mysterious warnings which are vouchsafed us from our spiritual guardians in the unseen world," added Madame Carimon, independently pursuing her argument. "And that it came to Lavinia to warn her to escape from this evil house."

"And she did not do it," remarked David Preen. "She was not quick enough. Well, let us go on."

"As Lavinia came out of church, Charles Palliser ran after her to ask her to go home to dine with him and his aunt," resumed Madame Carimon. "If she had only accepted it! The dinner here was a very simple one, and they all partook of it, including Flore—"

"And it was Flore who cooked and served it?" interrupted David Preen, looking at her.

"Mais oui, monsieur. The tart excepted; that was frangipane, and did come from the pastrycook," added Flore, plunging into English. "Then I had my own dinner, and I had of every dish; and I drank of the wine. Miss Lavinia would give me a glass of wine on the Sunday, and she poured it out for me herself that day from the bottle of Bordeaux on their own table. Nothing was the matter with any of all that. The one thing I did not have of was the liqueur."

"What liqueur was that?"

"It was chartreuse, I believe," said Flore. "While I was busy removing the dinner articles from the salon, monsieur was busy at his cupboard outside there, where he kept his bottles. He came into the kitchen just as I had sat down to eat, and asked me for three liqueur glasses, which I gave to him on a plate. I heard him pour the liqueur into them, and he carried them to the ladies."

Mr. David Preen wrote something down here.

"After that the captain went out to walk, saying he would see the English boat enter; and when I had finished washing up I carried the tea-tray to the salon-table and went home. Miss Lavinia was quite well then; she sat in her belle robe of grey silk talking with her sister. Then, when I was giving my boy Dion his collation, a tartine and a cooked apple, I was fetched back here, and found the poor lady fighting with pain for her life."

"Did you wash those liqueur glasses?" asked Mr. Featherston.

"But yes, sir. I had taken them away when I carried in the tea-things, and washed them at once, and put them on the shelf in their places."

"You see," observed Monsieur Dupuis, "the ill-fated lady appears to have taken nothing that the others did not take also. I applied my remedies when I was called to her, and the following day she had, as I believed, recovered from the attack; nothing but the exhaustion left by the agony was remaining. But that night she was again seized, and I was again fetched to her. The attack was even more violent than the first one. I made a request for another doctor, and Monsieur Podevin was brought. He at once set aside my suggestion of inflammation from a chill, and said it looked to him more like a case of poison."

"She had had nothing but slops all day, messieurs, which I made and carried to her," put in Flore; "and when I left, at night, she was, as Monsieur le Médecin put it, 'all well to look at.'"

"Flore did not make the arrowroot which she took later," said Mary Carimon, taking up the narrative. "When Lavinia went up to bed, towards nine o'clock, Mrs. Fennel made her a cup of arrowroot in the kitchen—"

"And a cup for herself at the same time, as I was informed, madame," spoke the little doctor.

"Oh yes, I know that, Monsieur Dupuis. Mrs. Fennel brought her sister's arrowroot, when it was ready, into this room, asking her husband whether she might venture to put a little brandy into it. He sent her to ask the question of Lavinia, bidding her leave the arrowroot on the table here. She came down for it, saying Lavinia declined the brandy, carried it up to her and saw her take it. Mrs. Fennel wished her good-night and came down for her own portion, which she had left in the kitchen. Before eleven o'clock, when they were going to bed, cries were heard in Lavinia's room; she was seized with the second attack, and—and died in it."

"This second attack was so violent, so unmanageable," said Monsieur Dupuis, as Mary Carimon's voice faltered into silence, "that I feel convinced I could not have saved her had I been present when it came on. I hear that Captain Fennel says he rang several times at my door before he could arouse me. Such was not the case. I am a very light sleeper, waking, from habit, at the slightest sound. But in this case I had not had time to fall asleep when I fancied I heard the bell sound very faintly. I thought I must be mistaken, as the bell is a loud bell, and rings easily; and people who ring me up at night generally ring pretty sharply. I lay listening, and some time afterwards, not immediately, it did ring. I opened my window, saw Captain Fennel outside, and was dressed and with him in two minutes."

"That sounds as if he did not want you to go to her too quickly, monsieur," observed Mr. Featherston, which went, as the French have it, without saying. "And I have heard of another suspicious fact: that he put his wife up to stop the medical examination after death."

"It amounts to this," spoke David Preen, "according to our judgment, if anything wrong was administered to her, it was given in the glass of liqueur on the Sunday afternoon, and in the cup of arrowroot on the Monday evening. They were the only things affording an opportunity of being tampered with; and in each case the pain came on about two hours afterwards."

Grave suspicion, as I am sure they all felt it to be. But not enough, as Featherston remarked, to accuse a man of murder. There was no proof to be brought forward, especially now that months had elapsed.

"What became of the cup which had contained the arrowroot?" inquired David Preen, looking at Flore. "Was it left in the bedroom?"

"That cup, sir, I found in a bowl of water in the kitchen, and also the other one which had been used. The two were together in the wooden bowl. I supposed Madame Fennel had put them there; but she said she had not."

"Ah!" exclaimed David Preen, drawing a deep breath.

He had come over to look into this suspicious matter; but, as it seemed, nothing could be done. To stir in it, and fail, would be worse than letting it alone.

"Look you," said David Preen, as he put up his note-book. "If it be true that Lavinia cannot rest now she's dead, but shows herself here in the house, I regard it as a pretty sure proof that she was sent out of the world unjustly. But—"

"Then you hold the belief that spirits revisit the earth, monsieur," interrupted Monsieur Dupuis, "and that revenants are to be seen?"

"I do, sir," replied David. "We Preens see them. But I cannot stir in this matter, I was about to say, and the man must be left to his conscience."

And so the conference broke up.

The thing which lay chiefly on hand now was to try to bring health back to Ann Fennel. It was thought well to take her out of the house for a short time, as she had such fancies about it; so Featherston gave up his room at Madame Carimon's, and Ann was invited to move into it, whilst he joined us at the hotel. I thought her very ill, as we all did. But after her removal there, she recovered her spirits wonderfully, and went out for short walks and laughed and chatted: and when Featherston and David Preen took the boat back to return home, she went to the port to see them steam off.

"Will it be all right with her?" was the last question Mary Carimon whispered to her brother.

"I'm afraid not," he answered. "A little time will show one way or the other. Depends somewhat, perhaps, upon how that husband of hers allows things to go on. I have done what I can, Mary; I could not do more."

Does the reader notice that I did not include myself in those who steamed off? For I did not go. Good, genial little Jules Carimon, who was pleased to say he had always liked me much at school, invited me to make a stay at his house, if I did not mind putting up with a small bedroom in the mansarde. I did not mind it at all; it was large enough for me. Nancy was delighted. We had quite a gay time of it; and I made the acquaintance of Major and Mrs. Smith, the Misses Bosanquet and Charley Palliser, who was shortly to quit Sainteville. Charley's impression of Mrs. Fennel was that she would quit it before he did, but in a different manner.

One fine afternoon, when we were coming off the pier, Nancy was walking between me and Mary Carimon, for she needed the support of two arms if she went far—yes, she was as weak as that—some one called out that the London boat was coming in. Turning round, we saw her gliding smoothly up the harbour. No one in these Anglo-French towns willingly misses that sight, and we drew up on the quay to watch the passengers land. There were only eight or ten of them.

Suddenly Nancy gave a great cry, which bore a sound both of fear and of gladness—"Oh, there's Edwin!"—and the next moment began to shake her pocket-handkerchief frantically.

A thin, grey, weasel of a man, whose face I did not like, came stalking up the ladder. Yes, it was the ex-captain, Edwin Fennel.

"He has not come for her sake; he has come to grab the quarter's money," spoke Mary, quite savagely, in my ear. No doubt. It would be due the end of September, which was at hand.

The captain was elaborately polite; quite effusive in his greeting to us. Nancy left us and took his arm. At the turning where we had to branch off to the Rue Pomme Cuite, she halted to say good-bye.

"But you are coming back to us, are you not?" cried Madame Carimon to her.

"Oh, I could not let Edwin go home alone," said she. "Nobody's there but Flore, you know."

So she went back there and then to the Petite Maison Rouge, and never came out of it again. I think he was kind to her, that man. He had sometimes a scared look upon his face, and I guessed he had been seeing sights. The man would have given his head to be off again; to remain in that haunted house must have been to him a most intolerable penance; but he had some regard (policy dictating it) for public opinion, and could not well run away from his wife in her failing health.

It was curious how quickly Nancy declined. From the very afternoon she entered the house it seemed to begin. He had grabbed the money, as Mary Carimon called it, and brought her nice and nourishing things; but nothing availed. And a fine way he must have been in, to see that; for with his wife's death the money would go away from him for evermore.

Monsieur Dupuis, sometimes Monsieur Henry Dupuis, saw her daily; and Captain Fennel hastily called in another doctor who had the reputation of being the best in the town, next to Monsieur Podevin; one Monsieur Lamirand. Mary Carimon spent half her time there; I went in most days. It could not be said that she had any special complaint, but she was too weak to live.

In less than three weeks it was all over. The end, when it came, was quite sudden. For a day or two she had seemed so much better that we told her she had taken a turn at last. On the Thursday evening, quite late—it was between eight and nine o'clock—Madame Carimon asked me to run there with some jelly which she had made, and which was only then ready. When I arrived, Flore said she was sure her mistress would like me to go up to her room; she was alone, monsieur having stepped out.

Nancy, wrapped in a warm dressing-gown, sat by the fire in an easy-chair and a great shawl. Her fair curls were all put back under a small lace cap, which was tied at the chin with grey ribbon; her pretty blue eyes were bright. I told her what I had come for, and took the chair in front of her.

"You look so well this evening, Nancy," I said heartily—for I had learnt to call her so at Madame Carimon's, as they did. "We shall have you getting well now all one way."

"It is the spurt of the candle before going out," she quietly answered. "I have not the least pain left anywhere—but it is only that."

"You should not say or think so."

"But I know it; I cannot mistake my own feelings. Fancy any one, reduced as I am, getting well again!"

I am a bad one to keep up "make-believes." Truth to say, I felt as sure of it as she did.

"And it will not be very long first. Johnny," she went on, in a half-whisper, "I saw Lavinia to-day."

I looked at her, but made no reply.

"I have never seen her since I came back here. Edwin has, though; I am sure of it. This afternoon at dusk I woke up out of a doze, for getting up to sit here quite exhausts me, and I was moving forward to touch the hand-bell on the table there, to let Flore know I was ready for my tea, when I saw Lavinia. She was standing over there, just in the firelight. I thought she seemed to be holding out her hand to me, as if inviting me to go to her, and on her face there was the sweetest smile of welcome; sweeter than could be seen on any face in life. All the sad, mournful, beseeching look had left it. She stood there for about a minute, and then vanished."

"Were you very much frightened?"

"I had not a thought of fear, Johnny. It was the contrary. She looked radiantly happy; and it somehow imparted happiness to me. I think—I think," added Nancy impressively, though with some hesitation, "that she came to let me know I am going to her. I believe I have seen her for the last time. The house has, also, I fancy; she and I will shortly go out of it together."

What could I answer to that?

"And so it is over at last," she murmured, more to herself than to me. "Very nearly over. The distress and the doubt, the terror and the pain. I brought it all on; you know that, Johnny Ludlow. I feel sure now that she has pardoned me. I humbly hope that God has."

She caught up her breath with a long-drawn sigh.

"And you will give my dear love to all the old friends in England, Johnny, beginning with Mr. Featherston; he has been very kind to me; you will see them again, but I shall not. Not in this life. But we shall be together in the Life which has no ending."

At twelve o'clock that night Nancy Fennel died. At least, it was as near twelve as could be told. Just after that hour Flore went into the room, preparatory to sitting up with her, and found her dead—just expired, apparently—with a sweet smile on her face, and one hand stretched out as if in greeting. Perhaps Lavinia had come to greet her.

We followed her to the grave on Saturday. Captain Fennel walked next the coffin—and I wondered how he liked it. I was close behind him with Monsieur Carimon. Charley Palliser came next with little Monsieur le Docteur Dupuis and Monsieur Gustave Sauvage. And we left Nancy in the cemetery, side by side with her sister.

Captain Edwin Fennel disappeared. On the Sunday, when we English were looking for him in church, he did not come—his grief not allowing him, said some of the ladies. But an English clerk in the broker's office, hearing this, told another tale. Fennel had gone off by the boat which left the port for London the previous night at midnight.

And he did not come back again. He had left sundry debts behind him, including that owing to Madame Veuve Sauvage. Monsieur Carimon, later, undertook the payment of these at the request of Colonel Selby. It was understood that Captain Edwin Fennel had emigrated to South America. If he had any conscience at all, it was to be hoped he carried it with him. He did not carry the money. The poor little income which he had schemed for, and perhaps worse, went back to the Selbys.

And that is the story. It is a curious history, and painful in more ways than one. But I repeat that it is true.

WATCHING ON ST MARK'S EVE

Easter-Day that year was nearly as late as it could be—the twenty-third of April. That brought St. Mark's Day (the twenty-fifth) on the Tuesday; and Easter Monday was St. Mark's Eve.

There is a superstitious belief in our county, and in some others—more thought of in our old grannies' days than in these—that if you go to the churchyard on St. Mark's Eve and watch the gate, the shadows, or phantoms, of those fated to die that year, and destined there to be buried, will be seen to enter it.

Easter Monday is a great holiday with us; the greatest in all the year. Christmas-Day and Good Friday are looked upon more in a religious light; but on Easter Monday servants and labourers think themselves at liberty to take their swing. The first day of the wake is nothing to it.

Now Squire Todhetley gave in to these holidays: they did not come often, he said. Our servants in the country are not a bit like yours in town; yours want a day's holiday once a month, oftener sometimes, and strike if they don't get it; ours have one or two in a year. On Easter Monday the work was got over by mid-day; there was no cooking, and the household could roam abroad at will. No ill had ever come of it; none would have come of it this time, but for St. Mark's Eve falling on the day.

Tod and I got home from school on the Thursday. It was a despicable old school, taking no heed of Passion Week. Other fellows from other schools could have a fortnight at Easter; we but a week. Tod entered on a remonstrance with the pater this time; he had been planning it as we drove home, and thought he'd put it in a strongish point of view.

"It is sinful, you know, sir; awfully so. Passion Week is Passion Week. We have no right to pass it at school at our desks."

"Well, Joe, I don't quite see that," returned the pater, twisting his lip. "Discipline and lessons are more in accordance with the season of Passion Week than kicking up your heels at large in all sorts of mischief; and that's what you'd be at, you know, if you were at home. What's the matter with Johnny."

"He has been ill for three days, with a cold or something," said Tod. "Tell it for yourself, Johnny."

I had no more to tell than that. For three or four days I had felt ill, feverish; yesterday (Wednesday) had done no lessons. Mrs. Todhetley thought it was an attack of influenza. She sent me to bed, and called in the doctor, Mr. Duffham.

I was better the next day—Good Friday. Old Duff—as Tod and I called him for short—came in while they were at church, and said I might get up. It was slow work, I told him, lying in bed for one's holidays. He was a wiry little man, with black hair; good in the main, but pompous, and always carried a gold-headed cane.

"Not to go out, you know," he said. "You must promise that, Johnny."

I promised readily. I only wanted to be downstairs with the rest. They returned home from church, saying they had promised to go over and take tea with the Sterlings; Mrs. Todhetley looked grave at seeing me, and thought the doctor was wrong. At which I put on a gay air, like a fellow suddenly cured.

But I could not eat any dinner. They had salt fish and cold boiled beef at two o'clock—our usual way of fasting on Good Friday. Not a morsel could I swallow, and Hannah brought me some mutton-broth.

"Do you mind our leaving you, Johnny?" Mrs. Todhetley said to me in her kind way—which Tod never believed in. "If you do—if you think you shall feel lonely, I'll stay at home."

I answered that I should feel very jolly, not lonely at all; and so they started, going over in the large carriage, drawn by Bob and Blister. Mr. and Mrs. Todhetley, with Lena, in front, Tod and Hugh behind. Standing at the window to watch the start, I saw Roger Monk looking on from the side of the house.

He was a small, white-faced chap of twenty or so, with a queer look in his eyes, and black sprouting whiskers. Looking full at the eyes, when you could get the chance, which was not very often, for they rarely looked at you, there was nothing wrong to be seen with them, and yet they gave a sinister cast to the face. Perhaps it was that they were too near together. Roger Monk was not one of our regular men; for the matter of that, he was above the condition; but was temporarily filling the head-gardener's place, who was ill with rheumatism. Seeing me, he walked up to the window, and I opened it to speak to him. "Are you here still, Monk?"

"And likely to be, Mr. Ludlow, if it depends upon Jenkins's coming on again," was the answer. "Fine cattle, those that the governor has just driven off."

He meant Bob and Blister, and they were fine; but I did not like the tone, or the word "governor," as applied to Mr. Todhetley. "I can't keep the window up," I said; "I'm not well."

"All right, sir; shut it. As for me, I must be about my work. There's enough to do with the gardens, one way or another; and the responsibility lies on my shoulders."

"You must not work to-day, Monk. Squire Todhetley never allows it on Good Friday."

He laughed pleasantly; as much as to say, what Squire Todhetley allowed, or did not allow, was no concern of his; and went briskly away across the lawn. And not once, during the short interview, had his eyes met mine.

Wasn't it dull that afternoon! I took old Duffham's physic, and drank the tea Hannah brought me, and was hot, and restless, and sick. Never a soul to talk to; never a book to read—my eyes and head ached too much for that; never a voice to be heard. Most of the servants were out; all of them, for what I knew, except Hannah; and I was fit to die of weariness. At dusk I went up to the nursery. Hannah was not there. The fire was raked—if you understand what that means, though it is generally applied only to kitchen fires in our county—which proved that she was off somewhere on a prolonged expedition. Even old Hannah's absence was a disappointment. I threw myself down on the faded sofa at the far end of the room, and, I suppose, went to sleep.

For when I became alive again to outward things, Hannah was seated in one chair at the fire, cracking up the coal; Molly, the cook with the sharp tongue and red-brown eyes, in another. It was dark and late; my head ached awfully, and I wished them and their clatter somewhere. They were talking of St. Mark's Eve, and its popular superstition. Molly was telling a tale of the past, the beginning of which I had not heard.

"I can't believe it," exclaimed Hannah; "I can't believe that the shadows come."

"Did ye ever watch for 'em, woman?" asked Molly, who had been born in the North.

"No," acknowledged Hannah.

"Then how can ye speak of what ye don't know? It is as true as that you and me be a-sitting here. Two foolish, sickly girls they was, both of 'em sweet upon the same young man. Leastways, he was sweet upon both of them, the deceiver, which comes to the same thing. My sister Becky was five-and-twenty that same year; she had a constant pain and a cough, which some said was windpipe and some said was liver. The other was Mary Clarkson, who was subject to swimmings in the head and frightful dartings. Any way, they'd got no health to brag on, either of 'em, and they were just eat up with jealousy, the one of the other. Tom Town, he knew this; and he played 'em off again' each other nicely, little thinking what his own punishment was to be."

Hannah gently put the poker inside the bars to raise the coal, and some more light came out. Molly went on.

"Now, Hannah, you mustn't think bad of them two young women. They did not wish one another dead—far from it; but each thought the other couldn't live. In natural course, if the one went off, poor thing, Tom Town, he would be left undivided for the other."

"Was Tom Town handsome?" interrupted Hannah.

"Well, middling for that. He was under-sized, not up to their shoulders, with big bushy red whiskers; but he had a taking way with him. He was in a shop for himself, and doing well, so that more young women nor the two I am telling of would have said Yes to his asking. Becky, she thought Mary Clarkson couldn't live the year out; Mary, she told a friend that she was sure Becky wouldn't. And what should they do but go to watch the graveyard on St. Mark's Eve, to see the other's shadow pass!"

"Together?"

"No; but they met there. Awk'ard, wasn't it? Calling up their wits, each of 'em, they pretended to have come out promiskous, just on the spree, not expecting to see nobody's shadow in particular. As they had come, they stopped; standing back again' the hedge near the graveyard, holding on to each other's arms for company, and making belief not to be scared. Hannah, woman, I don't care to tell this. I've never told it many times."

Molly's face had a hard, solemn look, in the fire's blaze, and Hannah suddenly drew her chair close to her. I could have laughed out loud.

"Just as the clock struck—ten, I think it was," went on Molly, in a half-whisper, "there was a faint rustle heard, like a flutter in the air, and somebody came along the road. At first the women's eyes were dazed, and they didn't see distinct, but as the gate opened to let him in, he turned his face, and they saw it was Tom Town. Both the girls thought it was himself, Hannah; and they held their breath and kept quite still, hoping he'd not notice them, for they'd have felt ashamed to be caught watching there."

"And it was not himself?" asked Hannah, catching up her breath.

Molly gave her head a shake. "No more than it was you or me: it was his shadow. He walked on up the path, looking neither to the right nor left, and they lost sight of him. I was with mother when they came home. Mary Clarkson, she came in with Beck, and they said they had seen Tom Town, and supposed he had gone out watching, too. Mother advised them to hold their tongues: it didn't look well, she said, for them two, only sickly young girls, to have run out to the graveyard alone. A short while after, Tom Town, in talking of that night, mother having artfully led to it, said he had gone up to bed at nine with a splitting headache, and forgot all about its being St. Mark's Eve. When mother heard that, she turned the colour o' chalk, and looked round at me."

"And Tom Town died?"

"He died that blessed year; the very day that folks was eating their Michaelmas gooses. A rapid decline took him off."

"It's very strange," said Hannah, musingly. "People believe here that the shadows appear, and folks used to go watching, as it's said. I don't think many go now. Did the two young women die?"

"Not they. Becky's married, and got half-a-dozen children; and Mary Clarkson, she went off to America. Shouldn't you like to watch?"

"Well, I should," acknowledged Hannah; "I would, too, if I thought I should see anything. I've said more than once in my life that I should just like to go out on St. Mark's Eve, and see whether there is anything in it or not. My mother went, I know."

"If you'll go, I'll go."

Hannah made no answer to this at first. She sat looking at the fire with a cross face. It had always a cross look when she was deep in thought. "The mistress would think me such a fool, Molly, if she came to know of it."

"If! How could she come to know of it? Next Monday will be the Easter holidays, and we mayn't never have the opportunity again. I shouldn't wonder but the lane's full o' watchers. St. Mark's Eve don't often come on a Easter Monday."

There's no time to go on with what they said. A good half-hour the two sat there, laying their plans: when once Hannah had decided to go in for the expedition, she made no more bones over it. The nursery-windows faced the front, and when the carriage was heard driving in, they both decamped downstairs—Hannah to the children, Molly to her kitchen. I found Tod, and told him the news: Hannah and Molly were going to watch in the churchyard for the shadows on St. Mark's Eve.

"We'll have some fun over this, Johnny," said he, when he had done laughing. "You and I will be on to them."

Monday came; and, upon my word, it seemed as if things turned out on purpose. Mr. Todhetley went off to Worcester with Dwarf Giles, on some business connected with the Quarter Sessions, and was not expected home until midnight, as he stayed to dine at Worcester. Mrs. Todhetley had one of her excruciating face-aches, and she went to bed when the children did—seven o'clock. Hannah had said in the morning that she and Molly were going to spend an hour or two with Goody Picker after the children were in bed; upon which Mrs. Todhetley told her to get them to bed early. It was something rare for Hannah to take any holiday; she generally said she did not want it. Goody Picker's husband used to be a gamekeeper—not ours. Since his death she lived how she could, on her vegetables, or by letting her odd room; Roger Monk had it now. Sometimes she had her grandchild with her; and the parents, well-to-do shopkeepers at Alcester, paid her well. Goody Picker was thought well of at our house, and came up occasionally to have tea in the nursery with Hannah.

I was well by Monday; nothing but a bit of a cough left; and Tod and I looked forward to the night's fun. Not a word had we heard since; but we had seen the two women-servants whispering together whenever they got the chance; and so we knew they were going. What Tod meant to do, he wouldn't tell me; I think he hardly knew himself. The big turnips were all gone, or he might have scooped one out for a death's head, and stuck it on the gate-post, with a candle in it.

The night came. A clear night, with a miserable moon. Miserable for our sport, because it was so bright.

"A pitch-dark night would have had some sense in it, you know, Johnny," Tod remarked to me, as we stood at the door, looking out. "The moon should hide her face on St. Mark's Eve."

Just as he spoke, the clock struck nine. Time to be going. There was nobody to let or hinder us. Mrs. Todhetley was in bed groaning with toothache; old Thomas and Phoebe, neither of whom had cared to take holiday, were at supper in the kitchen. She was a young girl lately had in to help the housemaid.

"You go on, Johnny; I'll follow presently. Take your time; they won't go on the watch for this half-hour yet."

"But, Tod, what is it that you are going to do?"

"Never you mind. If you hear a great noise, and see a light blaze up, don't you be scared."

"I scared, Tod! That's good."

"All right, Johnny. Take care not to be seen. It might spoil sport."

The church was about half-a-mile from our house, whether you crossed the fields to it or took the highway. It stood back from the road, in its big churchyard. A narrow lane, between two dwarf hedges, led up from the road to the gate; it was hardly wide enough for carriages; they wound round the open road further on. A cross-path, shut in by two stiles, led right across the lane near to the churchyard gate. Stories went that a poor fellow who had hung himself about twenty years ago was buried by torchlight under that very crossing, with never a parson to say a prayer over him.

We guessed where the women would stand—at one of these crossing stiles, with the gate and the churchyard in full view. As Tod said, it stood to reason that shadows and the watchers for them would not choose the broader road, where all was open, and not so much as a tree grew for shelter.

I stole along cautiously, taking the roadway and keeping under shade of the hedge, and got there all right. Not a creature was about. The old grey church, built of stone, the many-shaped graves in the churchyard, stood white and cold in the moonlight. I went behind the cross-stile at the side furthest from our house, and leaned over it, looking up and down the lane. That the women would be on the opposite side was certain, because the churchyard gate could not be seen so well from this.

The old clock did not tell the quarters, only struck the hour; time went on, and I began to wonder how long I was to wait. It must be turned half-past nine; getting nearer to a quarter to ten; and still nobody came. Where were the watchers? And where was Tod? The shadows of the trees, of the hedges, of the graves, fell in distinct lines on the grass; and I don't mind confessing that it felt uncommonly lonely.

"Hou-ou-ou-ou-ou-ou-ou!" burst forth over my head with a sudden and unearthly sound. I started back in a fright for one moment, and called myself an idiot the next, for it was only an owl. It had come flying forth from the old belfry, and went rushing on with its great wings, crying still, but changing its note. "Tu-whit; tu-whoo."

And while I watched the owl, other sounds, as of whispering, made themselves manifest, heralding the approach of the women from the opposite field, making for the stile in front of me, through the little copse. Drawing behind the low hedge, to sit down on the stump of a tree, I pushed my head forward, and took a look at them through the lower bars of the stile. They were standing at the other, in their light shawls and new Easter straw-bonnets; Molly's trimmed with green, Hannah's with primrose. The moonlight fell full on their faces—mine was in the shade. But they might see me, and I drew back again.

Presently they began to gabble; in low tones at first, which increased, perhaps unconsciously to themselves, to higher ones. They said how lonely it was, especially with "them grave-marks" in view close by; and they speculated upon whether any shadows would appear to them. My sense of loneliness had vanished. To have two practical women, each of them a good five-and-thirty, for neighbours, took it off. But I wondered what had become of Tod.

Another owl! or perhaps the last one coming back again. It was not so startling a noise as before, and created no alarm. I thought it a good opportunity to steal another look, and propelled my head forward an inch at a time. Their two faces were turned upwards, watching the owl's flight towards the belfry.

But to my intense astonishment there was a third face. A face behind them peeping out from the close folds of a mantle, and almost resting on their shoulders. At the first moment I thought of Tod; but soon the features became familiar to me in the bright light, and I knew them for Phoebe's. Phoebe, whom I had left in the kitchen, supping quietly! That she had stolen up unseen and unheard while they talked, was apparent.

A wild screech! Two wild screeches. Phoebe had put her hands on the startled women, and given vent to a dismal groan. She laughed: but the others went into a desperate passion. First at having been frightened, next at having been followed. When matters came to be investigated later, it turned out that Phoebe had overheard a conversation between Molly and Hannah, which betrayed what they were about to do, and had come on purpose to startle them.

A row ensued. Bitter words on both sides; mutual abusings. The elder servants ordered Phoebe home; she refused to go, and gave them some sauce. She intended to stay and see what there was to be seen, she said; for all she could tell, their shadows might pass, and a good thing if they did; let alone that she'd not dare to go back by herself at that hour and meet the ghosts. Hannah and Molly cut the matter short by leaving the stile to her; they went round, and took up their places by the churchyard gate.

It seems very stupid to be writing of this, I dare say; it must read like an old ghost-story out of a fable-book; but every word is true, as the people that lived round us then could tell you.

There we waited; Hannah and Molly gathered close against the hedge by the churchyard gate; Phoebe, wrapped in her shawl, leaning on the top of the stile; I on the old tree stump, feeling inclined to go to sleep. It seemed a long time, and the night grew cold. Evidently there were no watchers for St. Mark's shadows abroad that night, except ourselves. Without warning, the old clock boomed out the strokes of the hour. Ten.

Did you ever have the opportunity of noticing how long it takes for a sound like this to die quite away on the calm night-air? I seemed to hear it still, floating off in the distance, when I became aware that some figure was advancing up the lane towards us with a rather swift step. It's Tod this time, I thought, and naturally looked out; and I don't mind telling that I caught hold of the bars of the stile for companionship, in my shock of terror.

I had never seen the dead walking; but I do believe I thought I saw it then. It looked like a corpse in its winding-sheet; whether man or woman, none could tell. An ashey-white, still, ghastly face, enveloped around with bands of white linen, was turned full to the moonlight, that played upon the rigid features. The whole person, from the crown of the head to the soles of the feet, was enshrouded in a white garment. All thoughts of Tod went out of me; and I'm not sure but my hair rose up on end as the thing came on. You may laugh at me, all of you, but just you go and try it.

My fear went for nothing, however; it didn't damage me. Of all the awful cries ever heard, shrill at first, changing to something like the barking of a dog afterwards, those were the worst that arose opposite. They came from Phoebe. The girl had stood petrified, with straining eyes and laboured breath, like one who has not the power to fly, while the thing advanced. Only when it stopped close and looked at her did the pent-up cries come forth. Then she turned to fly, and the white figure leaped the stile, and went after her into the copse. What immediately followed I cannot remember—never could remember it; but it seemed that not more than a minute had elapsed when I and Molly and Hannah were standing over Phoebe, lying in convulsions on the ground, and the creature nowhere to be seen. The cries had been heard in the road, and some people passing came running up. They lifted the girl in their arms, and bore her homewards.

My senses were coming to me, showing plainly enough that it was no "shadow," but some ill-starred individual dressed up to personate one. Poor Phoebe! I could hear her cries still, though the group was already out of the copse and crossing the open field beyond. Somebody touched me on the shoulder.

"Tod! Did you do it?"

"Do what?" asked Tod, who was out of breath with running. "What was all that row?"

I told him. Somebody had made himself into a ghost, with a tied-up whitened face, just as the dead have, and came up the Green Lane in a sheet; and Phoebe was being carried home in convulsions.

"You are a fool, Johnny," was his wrathful answer. "I am not one to risk a thing of that sort, not even for those two old women we came out to frighten. Look here."

He went to the edge of the copse near the road, and showed me some things—the old pistol from the stable, and gunpowder lights that went off with a crash yards high. It's not of much use going into it now. Tod had meant, standing at a safe distance, to set a light to the explosive articles, and fire off his pistol at the same time.

"It would have been so good to see the women scutter off in their fright, Johnny; and it couldn't have hurt them. They might have looked upon it as the blue-light from below."

"What made you so late?"

"Late!" returned Tod, savagely; "I am late, and the fun's spoilt. That confounded old Duff and his cane came in to see you, Johnny, just as I was starting; there was nobody else, and I couldn't leave him. I said you were in bed and asleep, but it didn't send him away. Down he sat, telling a tale of how hard-worked he'd been all day, and asking for brandy-and-water. The dickens take him!"

"And, Tod, it was really not you?"

"If you repeat that again, Johnny, I'll strike you. I swear it was not me. There! I never told you a lie yet."

He never had; and from that moment of strong denial I know that Tod had no more to do with the matter than I had.

"I wonder who it could have been?"

"I'll find that out, as sure as my name's Todhetley," he said, catching up his pistols and lights.

We ran all the way home, looking out in vain for the ghost on our way, and got in almost as soon as the rest. What a hullabaloo it was! They put a mattress on the kitchen floor, and laid Phoebe on it. Mr. Duffham was upon the scene in no time; the Squire had returned earlier than was thought for, and Mrs. Todhetley came down with her face smothered in a woollen handkerchief.

As to any concealment now, it was useless to think of it. None was attempted, and Molly and Hannah had to confess that they went out to watch for the shadows. The Squire blustered at them a little, but Mrs. Todhetley said the keenest thing, in her mild way:

"At your age, Hannah!"

"I have known a person rendered an idiot for life with a less fright than this," said old Duff, turning round to speak. "It was the following her that did the mischief."

Nothing could be done that night as to investigation; but with the morning the Squire entered upon it in hot anger. "Couldn't the fool have been contented with what he'd already done, without going over the stile after her? If I spend a fifty-pound note, I'll unearth him. It looks to me uncommonly like a trick you two boys would play," he added, turning sharply upon me and Tod.

And the suspicion made us all the more eager to find out the real fox. But not a clue could we discover. Nobody had known of the proposed expedition except Goody Picker; and she, as everybody testified, was true to the backbone. As the day went on, and nothing came of it, Tod had one of his stamping fits.

"If one could find out whether it was man or woman! If one could divine how they got at the knowledge!" stamped Tod. "The pater does not look sure about us yet."

"I wonder if it could have been Roger Monk?" I said, speaking out a thought that had been dimly creeping up in my mind by starts all day.

"Roger Monk!" repeated Tod, "why pitch upon him?"

"Only that it's just possible he might have got it out of Goody Picker."

Away went Tod, in his straightforward fashion, to look for Roger Monk. He was in the hot-house, doing something to his plants.

"Monk, did you play that trick last night?"

"What trick, sir?" asked Monk, twitching a good-for-nothing leaf off a budding geranium.

"What trick! As if there were more tricks than one played! I mean dressing yourself up like a dead man, and frightening Phoebe."

"I have too much to do with my work, Mr. Todhetley, to find time to play tricks. I took no holiday at all yesterday, day or night, but was about my business till I went to bed. They were saying out here this morning that the Squire thought you had done it."

"Don't you be insolent, Monk. That won't answer with me."

"Well, sir, it is not pleasant to be accused point-blank of a crime, as you've just accused me. I know nothing at all about the matter. 'Twasn't me. I had no grudge against Phoebe, that I should harm her."

Tod was satisfied; I was not. He never once looked in either of our faces as he was speaking. We leaped the wire-fence and went across to Goody Picker's, bursting into her kitchen without ceremony.

"I say, Mrs. Picker, we can't find out anything about that business last night," began Tod.

"And you never will, gentlemen, as is my opinion," returned Mrs. Picker, getting up in a bustle and dusting two wooden chairs. "Whoever did that, have took himself off for a bit; never doubt it. 'Twas some one o' them village lads."

"We have been wondering whether it was Roger Monk."

"Lawk-a-mercy!" cried she, dropping a basin on the brick floor. And if ever I saw a woman change colour, she did.

"What's the matter now?"

"Why, you sent me into a tremble, gentlemen, saying that," she answered, stooping to pick up the broken crockery. "A young man lodging in my place, do such a villain's trick! I'd not like to think it; I shouldn't rest in my bed. The two servants having started right out from here for the churchyard have cowed-down my heart bad enough, without more ill news."

"What time did Monk come in last night?" questioned Tod. "Do you remember?"

"He come in after Mrs. Hannah and the other had gone," she replied, taking a moment's pause. "Close upon it; I'd hardly shut my door on them when I had to open it to him."

"Did he go out again?"

"Not he, sir. He eat his supper, telling me in a grumbling tone about the extra work he'd had to do in the greenhouses and places, because the other man had took holiday best part o' the day. And then he went up to bed. Right tired he seemed."

We left her fitting the pieces of the basin together, and went home. "It wasn't Monk," said Tod. "But now—where to look for the right man, Johnny?"

Look as we might, we did not find him. Phoebe was better in a day or two, but the convulsive fits stuck to her, coming on at all sorts of unexpected times. Old Duff thought it might end in insanity.

And that's what came of Watching for the Shadows on St. Mark's Eve!

SANKER'S VISIT

His name was Sanker, and he was related to Mrs. Todhetley. Not expecting to go home for the holidays—for his people lived in some far-off district of Wales, and did not afford him the journey—Tod invited him to spend them with us at Dyke Manor: which was uncommonly generous, for he disliked Sanker beyond everything. Having plenty of money himself, Tod could not bear that a connection of his should be known as nearly the poorest and meanest in the school, and resented it awfully. But he could not be ill-natured, for all his prejudices, and he asked Sanker to go home with us.

"It's slow there," he said; "not much going on in summer besides haymaking; but it may be an improvement on this. So, if you'd like to come, I'll write and tell them."

"Thank you," said Sanker; "I should like it very much."

Things had been queer at school as the term drew to its close. Petty pilferings were taking place; articles and money alike disappeared. Tod lost half-a-sovereign; one of the masters some silver; Bill Whitney put sevenpence halfpenny and a set of enamelled studs into his desk one day, never to see either again; and Snepp, who had been home to his sister's marriage, lost a piece of wedding-cake out of his box the night he came back. There was a thief in the school, and no clue to him. One might mentally accuse this fellow, another that; but not a shadow of proof was there against any. Altogether we were not sorry to get away.

But the curious thing was, that soon after we got home pilferings began there. Ned Banker was well received; and Tod, regarding himself in the capacity of host, grew more cordial with him than he had been at school. It was a sort of noblesse oblige feeling. Sanker was sixteen; stout and round; not tall; with pale eyes and a dull face. He was to be a clergyman; funds at his home permitting. His father lived at some mines in Wales. Tod wondered in what capacity.

"Mr. Sanker was a gentleman born and bred," explained Mrs. Todhetley. "He never had much money; but what little it was he lost, speculating in this very mine. After that, when he had nothing in the world left to live upon, and a wife and several young children to keep, he was thankful to take a situation as over-looker at a small yearly salary."

We had been home about a week when the first thing was missed. At one side of the house, in a sort of nook, was a square room, its glass-doors opening on the gravel-path that skirted the hedge of the vegetable garden. Squire Todhetley kept his farming accounts there and wrote his letters. A barometer and two county maps, Worcestershire and Warwickshire, on its walls, a square of matting on its floor, an upright bureau, a table, some chairs; and there you have the picture of the room.

One afternoon—mind! we did not know this for a week after, but it is as well to tell of it as it occurred— he was sitting at the table in this room, his account-books, kept in the bureau, open before him; his inkstand and cash-box at hand. Lying near the cash-box was a five-pound note, open; the Squire had put it out for Dwarf Giles to get changed at Alcester. He was writing an order for some things that Giles would have to bring back, when Rimmell, who acted as working bailiff on the estate, came to the glass-doors, open to the warm June air, saying he had received an offer for the wheat that had spurted. The Squire stepped outside on the gravel-path while he talked with Rimmell, and then strolled round with him to the fold-yard. He was away—that is, out of sight of the room—about three minutes, and when he got back the note was gone.

He could not believe his own eyes. It was a calm day; no wind stirring. He lifted the things on the table; he lifted the matting on the floor; he shook his loose coat; all in vain. Standing at the door, he shouted aloud; he walked along the path to the front of the house, and shouted there; but was not answered. So far as could be seen, no person whatever was about who could have come round to the room during his short absence.

Striding back to the room, he went through it, and up the passage to the hall, his boots creaking. Molly was in the kitchen, singing over her work; Phoebe and Hannah were heard talking upstairs; and Mrs. Todhetley stood in the store-room, doing something to the last year's pots of jam. She said, on being questioned, that no one had passed to the passage leading to the Squire's room.

It happened at that moment, that I, coming home from the Dyke, ran into the hall, full butt against the Squire.

"Johnny," said he, "where are you all? What are you up to?"

I had been at the Dyke all the afternoon with Tod and Hugh; they were there still. Not Sanker: he was outside, on the lawn, reading. This I told the pater, and he said no more. Later, when we came to know what had happened, he mentioned to us that, at this time, no idea of robbery had entered his head; he thought one of us might have hidden the money in sport.

So much an impossibility did it appear of the note's having been lifted by human hands, that the Squire went back to his room in a maze. He could only think that it must have attached itself to his clothes, and dropped off them in the fold-yard. What had become of it, goodness knew; whether it had fluttered into the pond, or the hens had scratched it to pieces, or the turkeys gobbled it up; he searched fruitlessly.

That was on a Thursday. On the following Thursday, when Tod was lying on the lawn bench on his back, playing with his tame magpie, and teasing Hugh and Lena, the pater's voice was heard calling to him in a sharp, quick tone, as if something was the matter. Tod got up and went round by the gravel-path to whence the sound came, and I followed. The Squire was standing at the window of the room, half in, half out.

"I don't want you, Johnny. Stay, though," he added, after a moment, "you may as well be told—why not?"

He sat down in his place at the table. Tod stood just inside the door, paying more attention to the magpie, which he had brought on his arm, than to his father: I leaned against the bureau. There was a minute's silence, waiting for the Squire to speak.

"Put that wretched bird down," he said; and we knew something had put him out, for he rarely spoke with sharpness to Tod.

Tod sent the magpie off, and came in. The first day we got home from school, Tod had rescued the magpie from Goody Picker's grandson; he caught him pulling the feathers out of its tail; gave him sixpence for it, and brought it home. A poor, miserable, half-starved thing, that somebody had taught to say continually, "Now then, Peter." Tod meant to feed it into condition; but the pater had not taken kindly to the bird; he said it would be better dead than alive.

"What was that I heard you boys talking of the other day, about some petty pilferings in your school?" he asked, abruptly. And we gave him the history.

"Well, as it seems to me, the same thing is going on here," he continued, looking at us both. "Johnny, sit down; I can't talk while you sway about like that."

"The same thing going on here, sir?"

"I say that it seems so," said the pater, thrusting both his hands deep into his trousers' pockets, and rattling the silver in them. "Last Thursday, this day week, a bank-note lay on my table here. I just went round to the yard with Rimmell, and when I got back the note was gone."

"Where did it go to?" asked Tod, practically.

"That is just the question—where? I concluded that it must have stuck to my coat in some unaccountable way, and got lost out-of-doors. I don't conclude so now."

Tod seemed to take the news in his usual careless fashion, and kept privately telegraphing signs to the magpie, sitting now on the old tree-stump opposite.

"Yes, sir. Well?"

"I think now, Joe, that somebody came in at these open doors, and took the note," said the pater, impressively. "And I want to find out who it was."

"Now then, Peter!" cried the bird, hopping down on the gravel; at which Tod laughed. The Squire got up in a rage, and shut the doors with a bang.

"If you can't be serious for a few moments, you had better say so. I can tell you this is likely to turn out no laughing business."

Tod turned his back to the glass-doors, and left the magpie to its devices.

"Whoever it was, contrived to slip round here from the front, during my temporary absence; possibly without ill intention: the sight of the note lying open might have proved too strong a temptation for him."

"Him!" put in Tod, critically. "It might have been a woman."

"You might be a jackass: and often are one," said the pater. And it struck us both, from the affable retort, that his suspicions were pointing to some particular person of the male gender.

"This morning, after breakfast, I was here, writing a letter," he went on. "While sealing it, Thomas called me away in a hurry, and I was absent the best part of an hour. When I got back, my ring had disappeared."

"Your ring, sir!" cried Tod.

"Yes, my ring, sir," mocked the pater; for he thought we were taking up the matter lightly, and it nettled him. "I left it on the seal, expecting to find it there when I returned. Not so. The ring had gone, and the letter lay on the ground. We have got a thief about the house, boys—a thief—within or without. Just the same sort of thief, as it seems to me, that you had at school."

Tod suddenly leaned forward, his elbow on his knee, his whole interest aroused. Some unpleasant doubt had struck him, as was evident by the flush upon his face.

"Of course, anybody that might be about, back or front, could find their way down here if they pleased," he slowly said. "Tramps get in sometimes."

"Rarely, without being noticed. Who did you boys see about the place that afternoon—tramp or gentleman? Come! You were at the house, Johnny: you bolted into it, head foremost, saying you had come from the Dyke."

"I never saw a soul but Sanker: he was on the bench on the lawn, reading. I said so at the time, sir."

"Ah! yes; Sanker was there reading," quietly assented the Squire. "What were you hastening home for, Johnny?"

As if that mattered, or could have had anything to do with it! He had a knack of asking unpleasant questions; and I looked at Tod.

"Hugh got his blouse torn, and Johnny came in to get another," acknowledged Tod, readily. The fact was, Hugh's clothes that afternoon had come to uncommon grief. Hannah had made one of her usual rows over it, and afterwards shown the things to Mrs. Todhetley.

"Well, and now for to-day," resumed the pater. "Where have you all been?"

Where had we not? In the three-cornered paddock; with Monk in the pine-house; away in the rick-yard; once to the hay-field; at the rabbit-hutches; round at the stables; oh, everywhere.

"You two, and Sanker?"

"Not Sanker," I said. Sanker stayed on the lawn with his book. We had all been on the lawn for the last half-hour: he, us, Hugh, Lena, and the magpie. But not a suspicious character of any sort had we seen about the place.

"Sanker's fond of reading on the lawn," remarked Mr. Todhetley, in a careless tone. But he got no answer: we had been struck into silence.

He took one hand out of his pocket, and drummed on the table, not looking at either of us. Tod had laid hold of a piece of blotting-paper and was pulling it to pieces. I wondered what they were thinking of: I know what I was.

"At any rate, the first thing is to find the ring; that only went this morning," said the Squire, as he left us. Tod sat on where he was, dropping the bits of paper.

"I say, Tod, do you think it could be—?"

"Hold your tongue, Johnny!" he shouted. "No, I don't think it. The bank-note—light, flimsy thing—must have been lost in the yard, and the ring will turn up. It's somewhere on the floor here."

In five minutes the news had spread. Mr. Todhetley had told his wife, and summoned the servants to the search. Both losses were made known; consternation fell on the household; the women-servants searched the room; old Thomas bent his back double over the frame outside the glass-doors. But there was no ring.

"This is just like the mysterious losses we had at school," exclaimed Sanker, as a lot of us were standing in the hall.

"Yes, it is," said the Squire.

"Perhaps, sir, your ring is in a corner of some odd pocket?" went on Sanker.

"Perhaps it may be," answered the Squire, rather emphatically; "but not in mine."

Happening to look at Mrs. Todhetley, I saw her face had turned to a white fright. Whether the remark of Sanker or the peculiarity of the Squire's manner brought to her mind the strange coincidence of the losses, here and at school, certain it was the doubt had dawned upon her. Later, when I and Tod were hunting in the room on our own account, she came to us with her terror-stricken face.

"Joseph, I see what you are thinking," she said; "but it can't be; it can't be. If the Sankers are poor, they are honest. I wish you knew his father and mother."

"I have not accused any one, Mrs. Todhetley."

"No; neither has your father; but you suspect."

"Perhaps we had better not talk of it," said Tod.

"Joseph, I think we must talk of it, and see what can be done. If—if he should have done such a thing, of course he cannot stay here."

"But we don't know that he has, therefore he ought not to be accused of it."

"Oh! Joseph, don't you see the pain? None of you can feel this as I do. He is my relative."

I felt so sorry for her. With the trouble in her pale, mild eyes, and the quivering of her thin, meek lips. It was quite evident that she feared the worst: and Tod threw away concealment with his step-mother.

"We must not accuse him; we must not let it be known that we suspect him," he said; "the matter here can be hushed up—got over—but were suspicion once directed to him on the score of the school losses, the disgrace would never be lived down, now or later. It would cling to him through life."

Mrs. Todhetley clasped her slender and rather bony fingers, from which the wedding-ring looked always ready to drop off. "Joseph," she said, "you assume confidently that he has done it; I see that. Perhaps you know he has? Perhaps you have some proof that you are concealing?"

"No, on my honour. But for my father's laying stress on the curious coincidence of the disappearances at school I should not have thought of Sanker. 'Losses there; losses here,' he said—"

"Now then, Peter!" mocked the bird, from his perch on the old tree.

"Be quiet!" shouted Tod. "And then the Squire went on adroitly to the fact, without putting it into words, that nobody else seems to have been within hail of this room either time."

"He has had so few advantages; he is kept so short of money," murmured poor Mrs. Todhetley, seeking to find an excuse for him. "I would almost rather have found my boy Hugh—when he shall be old enough—guilty of such a thing, than Edward Sanker."

"I'd a great deal rather it had been me," I exclaimed. "I shouldn't have felt half so uncomfortable. And we are not sure. Can't we keep him here, after all? It will be an awful thing to turn him out—a thief."

"He is not going to be turned out, a thief. Don't put in your oar, Johnny. The pater intends to hush it up. Why! had he suspected any other living mortal about the place, except Sanker, he'd have accused them outright, and sent for old Jones in hot haste."

Mrs. Todhetley, holding her hand to her troubled face, looked at Tod as he spoke. "I am not sure, Joseph—I don't quite know whether to hush it up entirely will be for the best. If he— Oh!"

The exclamation came out with a shriek. We turned at it, having been standing together at the table, our backs to the window. There stood Sanker. How long he had been there was uncertain; quite long enough to hear and comprehend. His face was livid with passion, his voice hoarse with it.

"Is it possible that I am accused of taking the bank-note and the ring?—of having been the thief at school? I thank you, Joseph Todhetley."

Mrs. Todhetley, always for peace, ran before him, and took his hands. Her gentle words were drowned—Tod's were overpowered. When quiet fellows like Sanker do get into a rage, it's something bad to witness.

"Look here, old fellow," said Tod, in a breath of silence; "we don't accuse you, and don't wish to accuse you. The things going here, as they did at school, is an unfortunate coincidence; you can't shut your eyes to it; but as to—"

"Why are you not accused?—why's Ludlow not accused?—you were both at school, as well as I; and you are both here," raved Sanker, panting like a wild animal. "You have money, both of you; you don't want helping on in life; I have only my good name. And that you would take from me!"

"Edward, Edward! we did not wish to accuse you; we said we would not accuse you," cried poor Mrs. Todhetley in her simplicity. But his voice broke in.

"No; you only suspected me. You assumed my guilt, and would not be honest enough to accuse me, lest I refuted it. Not another hour will I stay in this house. Come with me."

"Don't be foolish, Sanker! If we are wrong—"

"Be silent!" he cried, turning savagely on Tod. "I'm not strong; no match for you, or I would pound you to atoms! Let me go my own way now. You go yours."

Half dragging, half leading Mrs. Todhetley with him, the angry light in his eyes frightening her, he went to his bedroom. Taking off his jacket; turning his pockets inside out; emptying the contents of his trunk on the floor, he scattered the articles, one by one, with the view of showing that he had nothing concealed belonging to other people. Mrs. Todhetley, great in quiet emergencies, had her senses hopelessly scared away in this; she could only cry, and implore of him to be reasonable. He flung back his things, and in five minutes was gone. Dragging his box down the stairs by its stout cord, he managed to hoist it on his shoulders, and they saw him go fiercely off across the lawn.

I met him in the plantation, beyond the Dyke. Mrs. Todhetley, awfully distressed, sent me flying away to find the pater; she mistakenly thought he might be at Rimmell's, who lived in a cottage beyond it. Running home through the trees, I came upon Sanker. He was sitting on his box, crying; great big sobs bursting from him. Of course he could not carry that far. Down I sat by him, and put my hand on his.

"Don't, Sanker! don't, old fellow! Come back and have it cleared up. I dare say they are all wrong together."

His angry mood had changed. Those fierce whirlwinds of passion are generally followed by depression. He did not seem to care an atom for his sobs, or for my seeing them.

"It's the cruelest wrong I ever had dealt to me, Johnny. Why should they pitch upon me? What have they seen in me that they should set me down as a thief?—and such a thief! Why, the very thought of it, if they send her word, will kill my mother."

"You didn't do it, Sanker. I—"

He got up, and raised his hand solemnly to the blue sky, just as a man might have done.

"I swear I did not. I swear I never laid finger on a thing in your house, or at school, that was not mine. God hears me say it."

"And now you'll come back with me, Ned. The box will take no harm here till we send for it."

"Go back with you! that I never will. Fare you well, Johnny: I'll wish it to you."

"But where are you going?"

"That's my business. Look here; I was more generous than some of you have been. All along, I felt as sure who it was, cribbing those things at school, as though I had seen it done; but I never told. I just whispered to the fellow, when we were parting: 'Don't you go in for the same game next half, or I shall have you dropped upon;' and I don't think he will."

"Who—which was it?" I cried, eagerly.

"No: give him a chance. It was neither you nor me, and that's enough to know."

Hoisting the box up on to the projecting edge of a tree, he got it on his shoulders again. Certain of his innocence then, I was in an agony to get him back.

"It's of no use, Johnny. Good-bye."

"Sanker! Ned! The Squire will be fit to smother us all, when he finds you are off; Mrs. Todhetley is in dreadful grief. Such an unpleasant thing has never before happened with us."

"Good-bye," was all he repeated, marching resolutely off, with the black box held safe by the cord.

Fit to smother us? I thought the pater would have done it, when he came home late in the afternoon; laying the blame of Sanker's going, first on Mrs. Todhetley, then on Tod, then on me.

"What is to be done?" he asked, looking at us all helplessly. "I wouldn't have had it come out for the world. Think of his parents—of his own prospects."

"He never did it, sir," I said, speaking up; "he swore it to me."

The pater gave a sniff. "Swearing does not go for much in such cases, I'm afraid, Johnny."

It was so hopeless, the making them understand Sanker's solemn truth as he did swear it, that I held my tongue. I told Tod; also, what he had said about the fellow he suspected at school; but Tod only curled his lip, and quietly reminded me that I should never be anything but a muff.

Three or four days passed on. We could not learn where Sanker went to, or what had become of him; nothing about him except the fact that he had left his box at Goody Picker's cottage, asking her to take charge of it until it was sent for. Mrs. Todhetley would not write to Wales, or to the school, for fear of making mischief. I know this: it was altogether a disagreeable remembrance, whichever way we looked at it, but I was the only one who believed in his innocence.

On the Monday another loss occurred; not one of value in itself, but uncommonly significant. Since the explosion, Mrs. Todhetley had moved about the house restlessly, more like a fish out of water than a reasonable woman, following the Squire to his room, and staying there to talk with him, as she never had before. It was always in her head to do something to mend matters; but, what, she could not tell; hence her talkings with the pater. As each day passed, bringing no news of Sanker, she grew more anxious and fidgety. While he was in his room on the Monday morning, she came in with her work. It was the unpicking some blue ribbons from a white body of Lena's. There had been a child's party at the Stirlings' (they were always giving them), and Lena had a new frock for it. The dressmaker had put a glistening glass thing, as big as a pea, in the bows that tied up the sleeves. They looked like diamonds. The pater made a fuss after we got home, saying it was inconsistent at the best; she was too young for real diamonds, and he would not have her wear mock rubbish. Well, Mrs. Todhetley had the frock in her hand, taking these bows off, when she came to the Squire on the Monday morning, chattering and lamenting. I saw and heard her. On going away she accidentally left one of them on the table. The Squire went about as usual, dodging in and out of the room at intervals like a dog in a fair. I sat on the low seat, on the other side of the hedge, in the vegetable garden, making a fishing-line and flinging stones at the magpie whenever he came up to his perch on the old tree's stump. All was still; nothing to be heard but his occasional croak, "Now then, Peter!" Presently I caught a soft low whistle behind me. Looking through the hedge, I saw Roger Monk coming out of the room with stealthy steps, and going off towards his greenhouses. I thought nothing of it; it was his ordinary way of walking; but he must have come up to the room very quietly.

"Johnny," came the Squire's voice by-and-by, and I ran round: he had seen me sitting there.

"Johnny, have you a mind for a walk to—"

He had got thus far when Mrs. Todhetley came in by the inner door, and began looking on the table. Nothing in the world was on it except the inkstand, the Worcester Herald, and the papers before the Squire.

"I must have left one of the blue knots here," she said.

"You did; I saw it," said the Squire; and he took up his papers one by one, and shook the newspaper.

Well, the blue shoulder-knot was gone. Just as we had searched for the ring, we searched for that: under the matting, and above the matting, and everywhere; I and those two. A grim look came over the Squire's face.

"The thief is amongst us still. He has taken that glittering paste thing for a diamond. This clears Sanker."

Mrs. Todhetley burst into glad sobs. I had never seen her so excited; you might have thought her an hysterical girl. She would do all sorts of things at once; the least of which was, starting in a post-chaise-and-four for Wales.

"Do nothing," said the Squire, with authority. "I had news of Sanker this morning, and he's back at school. He wrote me a letter."

"Oh, why did you not show it me?" asked Mrs. Todhetley, through her tears.

"Because it's a trifle abusive; actionable, a lawyer might say," he answered, stopping a laugh. "Ah! ha! a big diamond! I'm as glad of this as if anybody had left me a thousand pounds," continued the good old pater. "I've not had that boy out of my head since, night or day. We'll have him back to finish his holidays—eh, Johnny?"

Whether I went along on my head or my tail, doing the Squire's errand, I didn't exactly know. To my mind the thief stood disclosed—Roger Monk. But I did not much like to betray him to the Squire. As a compromise between duty and disinclination, I told Tod. He went straight off to the Squire, and Roger Monk was ordered to the room.

He did not take the accusation as Sanker took it—noisily. About as cool and hardy as any fellow could be, stood he; white, angry retaliation shining from his sullen face. And, for once, he looked full at the Squire as he spoke.

"This is the second time I have been accused wrongfully by you or yours, sir. You must prove your words. A bank-note, a ring, a false diamond (taken to be a true one), in a blue ribbon; and I have stolen them. If you don't either prove your charge to be true, or withdraw the imputation, the law shall make you, Mr. Todhetley. I am down in the world, obliged to take a common situation for a while; but that's no reason why I should be browbeat and put upon."

Somehow, the words, or the manner, told upon the Squire. He was not feeling sure of his grounds. Until then he had never cast a thought of ill on Roger Monk.

"What were you doing here, Monk? What made you come up stealthily, and creep stealthily away again?" demanded Tod, who had assumed the guilt out and out.

"As to what I was doing here, I came to ask a question about my work," coolly returned Monk. "I walked slowly, not stealthily; the day's hot."

"You had better turn out your pockets, Monk," said the Squire.

He did so at once, just as Sanker had done unbidden, biting his lips to get some colour into them. Lots of odds and ends of things were there; string, nails, a tobacco-pipe, halfpence, and such like; but no blue bow. I don't think the Squire knew whether to let him off as innocent, or to give him into custody as guilty. At any rate, he seemed to be in hesitation, when who should appear on the scene but Goody Picker. The turned-out pockets, Monk's aspect, and the few words she caught, told the tale.

"If you please, Squire—if you please, young masters," she began, dropping a curtsy to us in succession; "the mistress told me to come round here. Stepping up this morning about a job o' work I'm doing—for Mrs. Hannah, I heard of the losses that have took place, apperiently thefts. So I up and spoke; and Hannah took me to the mistress; and the mistress, who had got her gownd off a-changing of it, listened to what I had to say, and told me to come round at once to Mr. Todhetley. (Don't you be frighted, Monk.) Sir, young gentlemen, I think it might have been the magpie."

"Think who might have been the magpie?" asked the Squire, puzzled.

"What stole the things. Sir, that there pie, bought only t'other day from my gran'son by young Mr. Todhetley, was turned out o' my son Peter's home at Alcester for thieving. He took this, and he took that; he have been at it for weeks, ever since they'd had him. They thought it was the servant, and sent her away. (A dirty young drab she was, so 'twere no loss.) Not her, though; it were that beast of a magpie. A whole nest of goods he had got hid away in the brewhouse: but for having a brewing on, he might never ha' been found out. The woman was drawing off her second mash when she see him hop in with a new shirt wristban' and drop it into the old iron pot."

Tod, who believed the story to be utterly unreasonable—got up, perhaps, by Mother Picker to screen the real thief—resented the imputation on his magpie. The bird came hopping up to us, "Now, then, Peter."

"That's rather too good, Mrs. Picker, that is. I have heard of lodging-house cats effecting wonders in the way of domestic disappearances, but not of magpies. Look at him, poor old fellow! He can't speak to defend himself."

"Yes, look at him, sir," repeated Mother Picker; "and a fine objec' of a half-fed animal he is, to look at! My opinion is, he have got something wrong o' the inside of him, or else it's his sins that troubles his skin, for the more he's give to eat the thinner he gets. No feathers, no flesh; nothing but a big beak, and them bright eyes, and the deuce's own tongue for impedence. Which is begging pard'n for speaking up free," concluded Mother Picker, as Mrs. Todhetley came in, fastening her waistband.

A little searching, not a tithe of what had been before again and again, and the creature's nest was discovered. In a cavity of the old tree-stump, so conveniently opposite, lay the articles: the bank-note, the ring, the blue bow, and some other things, most of which had not been missed. One was a bank receipt, that the house had been hunted for high and low.

"Now, then, Peter!" cried the magpie, hopping about on the gravel as he watched the raid on his treasures.

"He must be killed to-day, Joe," said Mr. Todhetley; "he has made mischief enough. I never took kindly to him. Monk, I am sorry for the mistake I was led into; but we suspected others before you—ay, and accused them."

"Don't mention it, sir," replied Monk, his eye catching mine. And if ever I saw revenge written in a face, it was in his as he turned away.

ROGER MONK

I'd never seen such a scene before; I have not seen one since. Perhaps, in fact, the same thing had never happened.

What had done it nobody could imagine. It was as if the place had been smoked out with some deleterious stuff; some destructive or poisoning gases, fatal to vegetable life.

On the previous day but one, Tuesday, there had been a party at the Manor. Squire and Mrs. Todhetley did not go in for much of that kind of thing, but some girls from London were staying with the Jacobsons, and we all went over to a dance there on the Friday. After supper some of them got talking to Mrs. Todhetley, asking in a laughing sort of way why she did not give them one? she shook her head, and answered that we were quiet people. Upon that Tod spoke up, and said he had no doubt the Squire would give one if asked; would like to do it. Had Mrs. Todhetley gone heartily into the proposal at once, Tod would have thrown cold water on it. That was his obstinacy. The girls attacked the Squire, and the thing was settled; the dance being fixed for the following Tuesday.

I know Mrs. Todhetley thought it an awful trouble; the Squire openly said it was when we got home; and he grumbled all day on Saturday. You see, our servants were not used to fashionable parties; neither in truth were their masters. However, if it had to be done at all, it was to be done well. The laundry was cleared out for dancing; the old square ironing-stove taken away, and a few pictures were done round with wreaths of green and hung on the yellow-washed walls. The supper-table was laid in the dining-room; leaving the drawing-room free for reception.

It was the Squire thought of having the plants brought into the hall. He never could say afterwards it was anybody but him. His grumbling was got over by the Tuesday morning, and he was as eager as any of us. He went about in his open nankeen coat and straw hat, puffing and blowing, and saying he hoped we should relish it—he wouldn't dance in the dog-days.

"I should like to see you dance in any days now, sir," cried Tod.

"You impudent rascals! You must laugh, too, must you, Johnny! I can tell you young fellows what—you'll neither of you dance a country dance as we'd used to do it. You should have seen us at the wake. Once when we militia chaps were at the Ram, at Gloucester, for a week's training, we gave a ball there, and footed it till daylight. 'We bucks at the Ram;' that's what we called ourselves: but most of us are dead and gone now. Look here, boys," continued the pater after a pause, "I'll have the choice plants brought into the hall. If we knock up a few sconces for candles on the walls, their colours will show out well."

He went out to talk to Roger Monk about it. Mrs. Todhetley was in the kitchen over the creams and jellies and things, fit to faint with heat. Jenkins, the head-gardener was back then, but he was stiff yet, not likely to be of permanent good; so Roger Monk was kept on as chief. Under the pater's direction the sets of green steps were brought in and put on either side of the hall, as many sets as there was space for; and the plants were arranged upon them.

I'd tell you the different sorts but that you might think it tedious. They were choice and beautiful. Mr. Todhetley took pride in his flowers, and spared no expense. Geraniums of all colours, tulips, brilliant roses, the white lily and the purple iris; and the rarer flowers, with hard names that nobody can spell. It was like a lovely garden, rising tier upon tier; a grove of perfume that the guests would pass through. They managed the wax-lights well; and the colours, pink, white, violet, green, orange, purple, scarlet, blue, shone out as the old east window in Worcester Cathedral used to do when it sparkled in the morning sun.

It went off first-rate. Some of the supper sweet dishes fell out of shape with the heat; but they were just as good to eat. In London, the thing you call "society" is made up of form and coldness, and artificialism; with us county people it is honest openness. There, any failure on the table is looked away from, not supposed to be seen; at the supper at Squire Todhetley's the tumble-down dishes were introduced as a topic of regret. "And to think it should be so, after all the pains I bestowed on them!" added Mrs. Todhetley, not hesitating to say that she had been the confectioner and pastry-cook.

But it is not of the party I have to tell you. It was jolly; and everyone said what a prime ball-room the laundry made. I dare say if we had been London fashionables we should have called it the "library," and made believe we'd had the books taken out.

Getting ready for company is delightful; but putting things to rights the next day is rather another thing. The plants were carried back to their places again in the greenhouse—a large, long, commodious greenhouse—and appeared none the worse for their show. The old folks, whose dancing-days were over, had spent half the night in the cool hall, admiring these beautiful plants; and the pater told this to Roger Monk as he stood with him in the greenhouse after they were put back. I was there, too.

"I'm glad they were admired, sir," said Monk in answer. "I've taken pains with them, and I think they do the Manor credit."

"Well, truth to say, Monk, it's a better and brighter collection than Jenkins ever got. But you must not tell him I say so. I do take a pride in my greenhouse; my father did before me. I remember your mother spending a day here once, Johnny, before you were born, and she said of all the collections in the two counties of Warwick and Worcester, ours was the finest. It came up to Lord Coventry's; not as large, of course, but the plants in the same prime condition."

"Yes, sir: I've seen the conservatories at Croome," returned Monk, who generally went in for large names.

"The late Lord Coventry—Yes! Here! Who's calling?"

Tod's voice outside, shouting for the Squire, caused the break. He had got Mr. Duffham with him; who wanted to ask about some parish business; and they came to the greenhouse.

So that made another admirer. Old Duff turned himself and his cane about, saying the colours looked brighter by daylight than waxlight; and he had not thought it possible the night before that they could do it. He stole a piece of geranium to put in his button-hole.

"By the way, Monk, when are you going over to Evesham about those seeds and things?" asked the Squire, as he was departing with old Duff.

"I can go when you like, sir."

"Go to-morrow, then. Start with the cool of the morning. Jenkins can do what has to be done, for once. You had better take the light cart."

"Very well, sir," answered Monk. But he had never once looked in the Squire's face as he answered.

The next morning was Thursday. Tod and I were up betimes to go fishing. There was a capital stream—but I've not time for that now. It was striking six as we went out of the house, and the first thing I saw was Jenkins coming along, his face as white as a sheet. He was a big man once, of middle height, but thin and stooping since his last bout of rheumatism; grey whiskers, blue eyes, and close upon fifty.

"I say, Tod, look at old Jenkins! He must be ill again."

Not ill but frightened. His lips were of a bluey grey, like one whom some great terror has scared. Tod stared as he came nearer, for they were trembling as well as blue.

"What's up, Jenkins?"

"I don't know what, Mr. Joe. The devil has been at work."

"Whereabouts?" asked Tod.

"Come and see, sir."

He turned back towards the greenhouse, but not another word would he say, only pointed to it. Leaving the fishing-rods on the path, we set off to run.

Never had I seen such a scene before; as I told you at the beginning. The windows were shut, every crevice where a breath of air might enter seemed to be hermetically closed; a smell as of some sulphurous acid pervaded the air; and the whole show of plants had turned to ruin.

A wreck complete. Colour was gone; leaves and stems were gone; the sweet perfume was gone; nothing remained, so to say, but the pots. It was as if some burning blast had passed through the greenhouse, withering to death every plant that stood in it, and the ripening grapes above.

"What on earth can have done this?" cried Tod to Jenkins, when he was able to speak.

"Well, Mr. Joseph, I say nothing could have done it but the—"

"Don't talk rubbish about the devil, Jenkins. He does not work in quite so practical a way. Open the windows."

"I was on by half-past five, sir, not coming here at first, but—"

"Where's Monk this morning?" again interrupted Tod, who had turned imperative.

"The Squire sent him over to Evesham for the seeds. I heard him go by in the light cart."

"Sent him when?"

"Yesterday, I suppose; that is, told him to go. Monk came to me last evening and said I must be on early. He started betimes; it was long afore five when I heard the cart go by. I should know the rattle of that there light cart anywhere, Mr. Joe."

"Never mind the cart. What has done this?"

That was the question. What had done it? Some blasting poison must have been set to burn in the greenhouse. Such substances might be common enough, but we knew nothing of them. We examined the place pretty carefully, but not a trace of any proof was discovered.

"What's this?" cried out Jenkins, presently.

Some earthenware pot-stands were stacked on the ground at the far end of the greenhouse—Mrs. Todhetley always called them saucers—Jenkins had been taking two or three of the top ones off, and came upon one that contained a small portion of some soft, white, damp substance, smelling just like the smell that pervaded the greenhouse—a suffocating smell that choked you. Some sulphuric acid was in the tool-house; Tod fetched the bottle, poured a little on the stuff, and set it alight.

Instantly a white smoke arose, and a smell that sent us off. Jenkins, looking at it as if it were alive and going to bite him, carried it at arm's length out to the nearest bed, and heaped mould upon it.

"That has done it, Mr. Joseph. But I should like to know what the white stuff is. It's some subtle poison."

We took the stack of pot-stands off one by one. Six or eight of them were perfectly clean, as if just wiped out. Jenkins gave his opinion again.

"Them clean saucers have all had the stuff burning in 'em this night, and they've done their work well. Somebody, which it must be the villain himself, has been in and cleaned 'em out, overlooking one of 'em. I can be upon my word the stands were all dusty enough last Tuesday, when the greenhouse was emptied for the ball, for I stacked 'em myself one upon another."

Tod took up his perch on the edge of the shut-in brick stove, and surveyed the wreck. There was not a bit of green life remaining, not a semblance of it. When he had done looking he stared at me, then at Jenkins; it was his way when puzzled or perplexed.

"Have you seen anybody about here this morning, Jenkins?"

"Not a soul," responded Jenkins, ruefully. "I was about the beds and places at first, and when I came up here and opened the door, the smoke and smell knocked me back'ards. When I see the plants—leastways what was the plants—with their leaves and blossoms and stems all black and blasted, I says to myself, 'The devil must have been in here;' and I was on my way to tell the master so when you two young gents met me."

"But it's time some of them were about," cried Tod. "Where's Drew? Is he not come?"

"Drew be hanged for a lazy vagabond!" retorted old Jenkins. "He never comes on much afore seven, he doesn't. Monk threatened last week to get his wages stopped for him. I did stop 'em once, afore I was ill."

Drew was the under-gardener, an active young fellow of nineteen. There was a boy as well, but it happened that he was away just now. Almost as Jenkins spoke, Drew came in view, leaping along furiously towards the vegetable garden, as though he knew he was late.

"Halloa, Drew!"

He recognized Tod's voice, turned, and came into the greenhouse. His look of amazement would have made a picture.

"Sakes alive! Jenkins, what have done this?"

"Do you know anything about it, Drew?" asked Tod.

"Me, sir?" answered Drew, turning his wide-open eyes on Tod, in surprise at the question. "I don't as much as know what it is."

"Mr. Joe, I think the master ought to be told of this," said Jenkins. "As well get it over."

He meant the explosion of wrath that was sure to come when the Squire saw the ravages. Tod never stirred. Who was to tell him? It was like the mice proposing to bell the cat: nobody offered to do it.

"You go, Johnny," said Tod, by-and-by. "Perhaps he's getting up now."

I went. I always did what he ordered me, and heard Mrs. Todhetley in her dressing-room. She had her white petticoats on, doing her hair. When I told her, she just backed into a chair and turned as white as Jenkins.

"What's that, Johnny?" roared out the Squire from his bed. I hadn't noticed that the door between the rooms was open.

"Something is wrong in the greenhouse, sir."

"Something wrong in the greenhouse! What d'ye mean, lad?"

"He says the plants are spoiled, and the grapes," interrupted Mrs. Todhetley, to help me.

"Plants and grapes spoiled! You must be out of your senses, Johnny, to say such a thing. What has spoiled them?"

"It looks like some—blight," I answered, pitching upon the word. "Everything's dead and blackened."

Downstairs I rushed for fear he should ask more. And down came the pater after me, hardly anything on, so to say; not shaved, and his nankeen coat flying behind him.

I let him go on to get the burst over. When I reached them, they were talking about the key. It was customary for the head-gardener to lock the greenhouse at night. For the past month or so there had been, as may be said, two head-gardeners, and the key had been left on the ledge at the back of the greenhouse, that whichever of them came on first in the morning might get in.

The Squire stormed at this—with that scene before his eyes he was ready to storm at everything. Pretty gardeners, they were! leaving the key where any tramp, hiding about the premises for a night's lodging, might get into the greenhouse and steal what he chose! As good leave the key in the door, as hang it up outside it! The world had nothing but fools in it, as he believed.

Jenkins answered with deprecation. The key was not likely to be found by anybody but those that knew where to look for it. It always had a flower-pot turned down upon it; and so he had found it that morning.

"If all the tramps within ten miles got into the greenhouse, sir, they'd not do this," affirmed Tod.

"Hold your tongue," said the Squire; "what do you know about tramps? I've known them to do the wickedest things conceivable. My beautiful plants! And look at the grapes! I've never had a finer crop of grapes than this was, Jenkins," concluded the pater, in a culminating access of rage. "If I find this has arisen through any neglect of yours and Monk's, I'll—I'll hang you both."

The morning went on; breakfast was over, and the news of the strange calamity spread. Old Jones, the constable, had been sent for by the Squire. He stared, and exclaimed, and made his comments; but he was not any the nearer hitting upon the guilty man.

About ten, Roger Monk got home from Evesham. We heard the spring-cart go round to the stables, and presently he appeared in the gardens, looking at objects on either side of the path, as was his usual wont. Then he caught sight of us, standing in and about the greenhouse, and came on faster. Jenkins was telling the story of his discovery to Mr. Duffham. He had told it a good fifty times since early morning to as many different listeners.

They made way for Monk to come in, nobody saying a word. The pater stood inside, and Monk, touching his hat, was about to report to him of his journey, when the strange aspect of affairs seemed to strike him dumb. He looked round with a sort of startled gaze at the walls, at the glass and grapes above, at the destroyed plants, and then turned savagely on Jenkins, speaking hoarsely.

"What have you been up to here?"

"Me been up to! That's good, that is! What had you, been up to afore you went off? You had the first chance. Come, Mr. Monk."

The semi-accusation was spoken by Jenkins on the spur of the moment, in his anger at the other's words. Monk was in a degree Jenkins's protégé, and it had not previously occurred to him that he could be in any way to blame.

"What do you know of this wicked business, Monk?" asked the Squire.

"What should I know of it, sir? I have only just come in from Evesham. The things were all right last night."

"How did you leave the greenhouse last night?"

"Exactly as I always leave it, sir. There was nothing the matter with it then. Drew—I saw him outside, didn't I? Step here, Drew. You were with me when I locked up the greenhouse last night. Did you see anything wrong with it?"

"It were right enough then," answered Drew.

Monk turned himself about, lifting his hands in dismay, as one blackened object after another came under view. "I never saw such a thing!" he cried piteously. "There has been something wrong at work here; or else—"

Monk came to a sudden pause. "Or else what?" asked the Squire.

"Or else, moving the plants into the hall on Tuesday has killed them."

"Moving the plants wouldn't kill them. What are you thinking of, Monk?"

"Moving them would not kill them, sir, or hurt them either," returned Monk, with a stress on the first word; "but it might have been the remote cause of it."

"I don't understand you!"

"I saw some result of the sort once, sir. It was at a gentleman's place at Chiswick. All the choice plants were taken indoors to improvise a kind of conservatory for a night fête. They were carried back the next day, seemingly none the worse, and on the morrow were found withered."

"Like these?"

"No, sir, not so bad as these. They didn't die; they revived after a time. A great fuss was made over it; the gentleman thought it must be wilful damage, and offered twenty pounds reward for the discovery of the offenders. At last it was found they had been poisoned by the candles."

"Poisoned by the candles!"

"A new sort of candle, very beautiful to look at, but with a great quantity of arsenic in it," continued Monk. "A scientific man gave it as his opinion that the poison thrown out from the candles had been fatal to the plants. Perhaps something of the same kind has done the mischief here, sir. Plants are such delicate things!"

"And what has been fatal to the grapes? They were not taken into the house."

The question came from the surgeon, Mr. Duffham. He had stood all the while against the end of the far steps, looking fixedly at Monk over the top of his cane. Monk put his eyes on the grapes above, and kept them there while he answered.

"True, sir; the grapes, as you say, didn't go in. Perhaps the poison brought back by the plants may have acted on them."

"Now, I tell you what, Monk, I think that's all nonsense," cried the Squire, testily.

"Well, sir, I don't see any other way of accounting for this state of things."

"The greenhouse was filled with some suffocating, smelling, blasting stuff that knocked me back'ards," put in Jenkins. "Every crack and crevice was stopped where a breath of air could have got in. I wish it had been you to find it; you'd not have liked to be smothered alive, I know."

"I wish it had been," said Monk. "If there was any such thing here, and not your fancy, I'll be bound I'd have traced it out."

"Oh, would you! Did you do anything to them there pot-stands?" continued Jenkins, pointing to them.

"No."

"Oh! Didn't clean 'em out?"

"I wiped a few out on Wednesday morning before we brought back the plants. Somebody—Drew, I suppose—had stacked them in the wrong place. In putting them right, I began to wipe them. I didn't do them all; I was called away."

"'Twas me stacked 'em," said Jenkins. "Well—them stands are what had held the poison; I found a'most one-half of 'em filled with it."

Monk cast a rapid glance around. "What was the poison?" he asked.

Jenkins grunted, but gave no other reply. The fact was, he had been so abused by the Squire for having put away the trace of the "stuff," that it was a sore subject.

"Did you come on here, Monk, before you started for Evesham this morning?" questioned the Squire.

"I didn't come near the gardens, sir. I had told Jenkins last night to be on early," replied Monk, bending over a blackened row of plants while he spoke. "I went the back way to the stables through the lane, had harnessed the horse to the cart, and was away before five."

We quitted the greenhouse. The pater went out with Mr. Duffham, Tod and I followed. I, looking quietly on, had been struck with the contrast of manner between old Duff and Monk—he peering at Monk with his searching gaze, never once taking it off him; and Monk meeting nobody's eyes, but shifting his own anywhere rather than meet them.

"About this queer arsenic tale Monk tells?" began the Squire. "Is there anything in it? Will it hold water?"

"Moonshine!" said old Duff, with emphasis.

The tone was curious, and we all looked at him. He had got his lips drawn in, and the top of his cane pressing them.

"Where did you take Monk from, Squire? Get a good character with him?"

"Jenkins brought him here. As to character, he had never been in any situation before. Why? Do you suspect him?"

"Um-m-m!" said the doctor, prolonging the sound as though in doubt. "If I do suspect him, he has caused me to. I never saw such a shifty manner in all my life. Why, he never once looked at any of us! His eyes are false, and his tones are false!"

"His tones? Do you mean his words?"

"I mean the tone his words are spoken in. To an apt ear, the sound of a man's voice, or woman's either, can be read off like a book; a man's voice is honest or dishonest according to his nature; and you can't make a mistake about it. Monk's has a false ring in it, if ever I heard one. Now, master Johnny, what are you looking so eager about?"

"I think Monk's voice false, too, Mr. Duffham; I have thought himself false all along. Tod knows I have."

"I know that you are just a muff, Johnny, going in for prejudices against people unreasonably," said Tod, putting me down as usual.

Old Duff pushed my straw hat up, and passed his fingers over the top of my forehead. "Johnny, my boy," he said, "you have a strong and good indication here for reading the world. Trust to it."

"I couldn't trust Monk. I never have trusted him. That was one reason why I suspected him of stealing the things the magpie took."

"Well, you were wrong there," said Tod.

"Yes. But I'm nearly sure I was right in the thing before."

"What thing?" demanded old Duff, sharply.

"Well, I thought it was Monk that frightened Phoebe."

"Oh," said Mr. Duffham. "Dressed himself up in a sheet, and whitened his face, and went up the lane when the women were watching for the shadows on St. Mark's Eve! What else do you suspect, Johnny?"

"Nothing else, sir; except that I fancied Mother Picker knew of it. When Tod and I went to ask her whether Monk was out that night, she looked frightened to death, and broke a basin."

"Did she say he was out?"

"She said he was not out; but I thought she said it more eagerly than truthfully."

"Squire, when you are in doubt as to people's morals, let this boy read them for you," said old Duff, in his quaint way. The Squire, thinking of his plants, looked as perplexed as could be.

"It is such a thing, you know, Duffham, to have one's whole hothouse destroyed in a night. It's no better than arson."

"And the incendiary who did it would have no scruple in attacking the barns next; therefore, he must be bowled out."

The pater looked rueful. He could bluster and threaten, but he could not do much; he never knew how to set about it. In all emergencies he would send for Jones—the greatest old woman going.

"You don't seriously think it could have been Monk, Duffham?"

"I think there's strong suspicion that it was. Look here:" and the doctor began to tell off points with his cane and fingers. "Somebody goes into the greenhouse to set the stuff alight in the pot-stands—for that's how it was done. Monk and Jenkins alone knew where the key was; Jenkins, a trusty man, years in the employ, comes on at six and finds the state of things. Where's Monk? Gone off by previous order to Evesham at five. Why should it happen the very morning he was away? What was to prevent his stealing into the greenhouse after dark last night putting his deleterious stuff to work, leaving it to burn, and stealing in again at four this morning to put all traces away? He thought he cleaned out all the tale-telling earthen saucers, but he overlooks one, as is usually the case. When he comes back, finding the wreck and the commotion consequent upon it, he relates a glib tale of other plants destroyed by arsenic from candles, and he never looks honestly into a single face as he tells it!"

The Squire drew a deep breath. "And you say Monk did all this?"

"Nonsense, Squire. I say he might have done it. I say, moreover, that it looks very like it. Putting Monk aside, your scent would be wholly at fault."

"What is to be done?"

"I'll go and see Mother Picker; she can tell what time he went in last night, and what time he came out this morning," cried Tod, who was just as hasty as the pater. But old Duff caught him as he was vaulting off.

"I had better see Mother Picker. Will you let me act in this matter, Squire, and see what can be made of it?"

"Do, Duffham. Take Jones to help you?"

"Jones be shot," returned Duff in a passion. "If I wanted any one—which I don't—I'd take Johnny. He is worth fifty Joneses. Say nothing—nothing at all. Do you understand?"

He went off down a side path, and crossed Jenkins, who was at work now. Monk stayed in the greenhouse.

"This is a sad calamity, Jenkins."

"It's the worst I ever met with, sir," cried Jenkins, touching his hat. "And what have done it is the odd thing. Monk, he talks of the candles poisoning of 'em; but I don't know."

"Well, there's not a much surer poison than arsenic, Jenkins," said the doctor, candidly. "I hope it will be cleared up. Monk, too, has taken so much pains with the plants. He is a clever young man in his vocation. Where did you hear of him?"

Jenkins's answer was a long one. Curtailed, it stated that he had heard of Monk "promiskeous." He had thought him a gentleman till he asked if he, Jenkins, could help him to a place as ornamental gardener. He had rather took to the young man, and recommended the Squire to employ him "temporay," for he, Jenkins, was just then falling sick with rheumatism.

Mr. Duffham nodded approvingly. "Didn't think it necessary to ask for references?"

"Monk said he could give me a cart-load a'most of them, sir, if I'd wanted to see 'em."

"Just so! Good-day, Jenkins, I can't stay gossiping my morning away."

He went straight to Mrs. Picker's, and caught her taking her luncheon off the kitchen-table—bread-and-cheese, and perry.

"It's a little cask o' last year's my son have made me a present of, sir; if you'd be pleased to drink a cup, Dr. Duff'm," said she, hospitably.

She drew a half-pint cup full; bright, sparkling, full-bodied perry, never better made in Gloucestershire. Mr. Duffham smacked his lips, and wished some of the champagne at gentlemen's tables was half as good. He talked, and she talked; and, it may be, he took her a little off her guard. Evidently, she was not cognizant of the mishap to the greenhouse.

A nice young man that lodger of hers? Well, yes, he was; steady and well-conducted. Talked quite like a gentleman, but wasn't uppish 'cause o' that, and seemed satisfied with all she did for him. He was gone off to Evesham after seeds and other things. Squire Todhetley put great confidence in him.

"Ay," said Mr. Duffham, "to be sure. One does put confidence in steady young men, you know, Goody. He was off by four o'clock, wasn't he?"

Earlier nor that, Goody Picker thought. Monk were one o' them who liked to take time by the forelock, and get his extra work forrard when he were put on to any.

"Nothing like putting the shoulder to the wheel. This is perry! The next time I call to see your son Peter, at Alcester, I shall ask him if he can't get some for me. As to Monk—you might have had young fellows here who'd have idled their days away, and paid no rent, Goody. Monk was at his work late last night, too, I fancy?"

Goody fancied he had been; leastways he went out after supper, and were gone an hour or so. What with the fires, and what with the opening and shutting o' the winders to keep the hot-houses at proper temperture, an head-gardener didn't sit on a bed o' idle roses, as Dr. Duff'm knew.

Mr. Duffham was beginning to make pretty sure of winning his game. His manner suddenly changed. Pushing the empty cup from him, he leaned forward, and laid hold of Mrs. Picker by the two wrists. Between the perry and the doctor's sociability and Monk's merits, her eyes had begun to sparkle.

"Don't be alarmed, Mrs. Picker. I have come here to ask you a question, and you must answer me. But you have nothing to fear on your own score, provided you tell me the truth honestly. Young men will do foolish things, however industrious they may be. Why did Monk play that prank on Easter Monday?"

The sparkle in the eyes faded with fright. She would have got away, but could not, and so put on an air of wonder.

"On Easter Monday! What were it he did on Easter Monday?"

"When he put himself and his face into white, and went to the churchyard by moonlight to represent the dead, you know, Mrs. Picker."

She gave a shrill scream, got one of her hands loose and flung it up to her face.

"Come, Goody, you had better answer me quietly than be taken to confess before Squire Todhetley. I dare say you were not to blame."

Afore Squire Todhetley! O-o-o-o-o-h! Did they know it at the Manor?

"Well," said Mr. Duffham, "you see I know it, and I have come straight from there. Now then, my good woman, I have not much time."

Goody Picker's will was good to hold out longer, but she surrendered à coup de main, as so many of us have to do when superior power is brought to bear. Monk overheered it, was the substance of her answer. On coming in from work that there same blessed evening—and look at him now! at his work on a Easter Monday till past dark!—he overheered the two servants, Molly and Hannah, talking of what they was going out to watch for—the shadows in the churchyard. He let 'em go, never showing hisself till they'd left the house. Then he got the sheets from his bed, and put the flour on his face, and went on there to frighten 'em; all in fun. He never thought of hurting the women; he never knowed as the young girl, Phoebe, was to be there. Nobody could be more sorry for it nor he was; but he'd never meant to do harm more nor a babby unborn.

Mr. Duffham released the hands. Looking back in reflection, he had little doubt it was as she said—that Monk had done it out of pure sport, not intending ill.

"He might have confessed: it would have been more honest. And you! why did you deny that it was Monk?"

Mrs. Picker at first could only stare in reply. Confess to it? Him? What, and run the risk o' being put into ancuffs by that there Jones with his fat legs? And she! a poor old widder? If Monk went and said he didn't do it, she couldn't go and say he did. Doctor Duff'm might see as there were no choice left for her. Never should she forget the fright when the two young gents come in with their querries the next day; her fingers was took with the palsy and dropped the pudd'n basin, as she'd had fifteen year. Monk, poor fellow, couldn't sleep for a peck o' nights after, thinking o' Phoebe.

"There; that's enough," said Mr. Duffham. "Who is Monk? Where does he come from?"

From the moon, for all Mrs. Picker knew. A civiler young man she'd not wish to have lodging with her; paid reg'lar as the Saturdays come round; but he never told her nothing about hisself.

"Which is his room? The one at the back, I suppose."

Without saying with your leave, or by your leave, as Mrs. Picker phrased it in telling the story a long while afterwards, Mr. Duffham penetrated at once into the lodger's room. There he took the liberty of making a slight examination, good Mrs. Picker standing by with round eyes and open mouth. And what he discovered caused him to stride off at once to the pater.

Roger Monk was not Monk at all, but somebody else. He had been implicated in some crime (whether guilty or not remained yet a question), and to avoid exposure had come away into this quiet locality under a false name. In short, during the time he had been working as gardener at Dyke Manor and living at Mother Picker's, he was in hiding. As the son of a well-known and most respectable landscape and ornamental nursery-man, he had become thoroughly conversant with the requisite duties.

"They are fools, at the best, these fellows," remarked Duffham, as he finished his narrative. "A letter written to him by some friend betrayed to me all this. Now why should not Monk have destroyed that letter, instead of keeping it in his room, Squire?"

The Squire did not answer. All he could do just now was to wipe his hot face and try to get over his amazement. Monk not a gardener or servant at all, but an educated man! Only living there to hide from the police; and calling himself by any name that came uppermost—which happened to be Monk!

"I must say there's a certain credit due to him for his patient industry, and the perfection to which he has brought your grounds," said Mr. Duffham.

"And for blighting all my hot-house plants at a blow—is there credit due to him for that?" roared out the Squire. "I'll have him tried for it, as sure as my name's Todhetley."

It was easier said than done. For when Mr. Jones, receiving his private orders from the pater, went, staff in hand, to arrest Monk, that gentleman had already departed.

"He come into the house just as Dr. Duff'm left it," explained Mrs. Picker. "Saying he had got to take a short journey, he put his things into his port-manty, and went off carrying of it, leaving me a week's rent on the table."

"Go and catch him, Jones," sternly commanded the Squire, when the constable came back with the above news.

"Yes, your worship," replied Jones. But how he was to do it, taking the gouty legs into consideration, was quite a different thing.

The men were sent off various ways. And came back again, not having come up with Monk. Squire Todhetley went into a rage, abused old Jones, and told him he was no longer worth his salt. But the strangest thing occurred in the evening.

The pater walked over to the Court after tea, carrying the grievance of his destroyed plants to the Sterlings. In coming up Dyke Lane as he returned at night, where it was always darker than in other places because the trees hid the moonlight, somebody seemed to walk right out of the hedge upon him.

It was Roger Monk. He raised his hat to the Squire as a gentleman does—did not touch it as a gardener—and began pleading for clemency.

"Clemency, after destroying a whole hot-houseful of rare plants!" cried the Squire.

"I never did it, sir," returned Monk, passionately. "On my word as a man—I will not to you say as a gentleman—if the plants were not injured by the candles, as I fully believe, I know not how they could have been injured."

The pater was staggered. At heart he was the best man living. Suppose Monk was innocent?

"Look here, Monk. You know your name is—"

"Hush, sir!" interposed Monk, hastily, as if to prevent the hedges hearing the true name. "It is of that I have waited to speak to you; to beseech your clemency. I have no need to crave it in the matter of plants which I never harmed. I want to ask you to be silent, sir; not to proclaim to the world that I am other than what I appeared to be. A short while longer and I should have been able to prove my innocence; things are working round. But if you set the hue-and-cry upon me—"

"Were you innocent?" interposed the Squire.

"I was; I swear it to you. Oh, Mr. Todhetley, think for a moment! I am not so very much older than your son; he is not more innocent than I was; but it might happen that he—I crave your pardon, sir, but it might—that he should become the companion of dissipated young men, and get mixed up unwittingly in a disgraceful affair, whose circumstances were so complicated that he could only fly for a time and hide himself. What would you say if the people with whom he took refuge, whether as servant or else, were to deliver him up to justice, and he stood before the world an accused felon? Sir, it is my case. Keep my secret; keep my secret, Mr. Todhetley."

"And couldn't you prove your innocence?" cried the Squire, as he followed out the train of ideas suggested.

"Not at present—that I see. And when once a man has stood at a criminal bar, it is a ban on him for life, although it may be afterwards shown he stood there wrongly."

"True," said the Squire, softening.

Well—for there's no space to go on at length—the upshot was that Monk went away with a promise; and the Squire came home to the Manor and told Duffham, who was waiting there, that they must both be silent. Only those two knew of the discovery; they had kept the particulars and Monk's real name to themselves. Duff gave his head a toss, and told the pater he was softer than old Jones.

"How came you to suspect him, Johnny?" he continued, turning on me in his sharp way.

"I think just for the same things that you did, Mr. Duffham—because neither his face nor his voice is true."

And—remembering his look of revenge when accused in mistake for the magpie—I suspected him still.

THE EBONY BOX

I

In one or two of the papers already written for you, I have spoken of "Lawyer Cockermuth," as he was usually styled by his fellow-townspeople at Worcester. I am now going to tell of something that happened in his family; that actually did happen, and is no invention of mine.

Lawyer Cockermuth's house stood in the Foregate Street. He had practised in it for a good many years; he had never married, and his sister lived with him. She had been christened Betty; it was a more common name in those days than it is in these. There was a younger brother named Charles. They were tall, wiry men with long arms and legs. John, the lawyer, had a smiling, homely face; Charles was handsome, but given to be choleric.

Charles had served in the militia once, and had been ever since called Captain Cockermuth. When only twenty-one he married a young lady with a good bit of money; he had also a small income of his own; so he abandoned the law, to which he had been bred, and lived as a gentleman in a pretty little house on the outskirts of Worcester. His wife died in the course of a few years, leaving him with one child, a son, named Philip. The interest of Mrs. Charles Cockermuth's money would be enjoyed by her husband until his death, and then would go to Philip.

When Philip left school he was articled to his uncle, Lawyer Cockermuth, and took up his abode with him. Captain Cockermuth (who was of a restless disposition, and fond of roving), gave up his house then and went travelling about. Philip Cockermuth was a very nice steady young fellow, and his father was liberal to him in the way of pocket-money, allowing him a guinea a-week. Every Monday morning Lawyer Cockermuth handed (for his brother) to Philip a guinea in gold; the coin being in use then. Philip spent most of this in books, but he saved some of it; and by the time he was of age he had sixty golden guineas put aside in a small round black box of carved ebony. "What are you going to do with it, Philip?" asked Miss Cockermuth, as he brought it down from his room to show her. "I don't know what yet, Aunt Betty," said Philip, laughing. "I call it my nest-egg."

He carried the little black box (the sixty guineas quite filled it), back to his chamber and put it back into one of the pigeon-holes of the old-fashioned bureau which stood in the room, where he always kept it, and left it there, the bureau locked as usual. After that time, Philip put his spare money, now increased by a salary, into the Old Bank; and it chanced that he did not again look at the ebony box of gold, never supposing but that it was safe in its hiding-place. On the occasion of his marriage some years later, he laughingly remarked to Aunt Betty that he must now take his box of guineas into use; and he went up to fetch it. The box was not there.

Consternation ensued. The family flocked upstairs; the lawyer, Miss Betty, and the captain—who had come to Worcester for the wedding, and was staying in the house—one and all put their hands into the deep, dark pigeon-holes, but failed to find the box. The captain, a hot-tempered man, flew into a passion and swore over it; Miss Betty shed tears; Lawyer Cockermuth, always cool and genial, shrugged his shoulders and absolutely joked. None of them could form the slightest notion as to how the box had gone or who was likely to have taken it, and it had to be given up as a bad job.

Philip was married the next day, and left his uncle's house for good, having taken one out Barbourne way. Captain Cockermuth felt very sore about the loss of the box, he strode about Worcester talking of it, and swearing that he would send the thief to Botany Bay if he could find him.

A few years more yet, and poor Philip became ill. Ill of the disorder which had carried off his mother—decline. When Captain Cockermuth heard that his son was lying sick, he being (as usual) on his travels, he hastened to Worcester and took up his abode at his brother's—always his home on these visits. The disease was making very quick progress indeed; it was what is called "rapid decline." The captain called in all the famed doctors of the town—if they had not been called before: but there was no hope.

The day before Philip died, his father spoke to him about the box of guineas. It had always seemed to the captain that Philip must have, or ought to have, some notion of how it went. And he put the question to him again, solemnly, for the last time.

"Father," said the dying man—who retained all his faculties and his speech to the very end—"I declare to you that I have none. I have never been able to set up any idea at all upon the loss, or attach suspicion to a soul, living or dead. The two maids were honest; they would not have touched it; the clerks had no opportunity of going upstairs. I had always kept the key safely, and you know that we found the lock of the bureau had not been tampered with."

Poor Philip died. His widow and four children went to live at a pretty cottage on Malvern Link—upon a hundred pounds a-year, supplied to her by her father-in-law. Mr. Cockermuth added the best part of another hundred. These matters settled, Captain Cockermuth set off on his rovings again, considering himself hardly used by Fate at having his limited income docked of nearly half its value. And yet some more years passed on.

This much has been by way of introduction to what has to come. It was best to give it.

Mr. and Mrs. Jacobson, our neighbours at Dyke Manor, had a whole colony of nephews, what with brothers' sons and sisters' sons; of nieces also; batches of them would come over in relays to stay at Elm Farm, which had no children of its own. Samson Dene was the favourite nephew of all; his mother was sister to Mr. Jacobson, his father was dead. Samson Reginald Dene he was christened, but most people called him "Sam." He had been articled to the gentleman who took to his father's practice; a lawyer in a village in Oxfordshire. Later, he had gone to a firm in London for a year, had passed, and then came down to his uncle at Elm Farm, asking what he was to do next. For, upon his brother-in-law's death, Mr. Jacobson had taken upon himself the expenses of Sam, the eldest son.

"Want to know what you are to do now, eh?" cried old Jacobson, who was smoking his evening pipe by the wide fire of the dark-wainscoted, handsome dining-parlour, one evening in February. He was a tall, portly man with a fresh-coloured, healthy face; and not, I dare say, far off sixty years old. "What would you like to do?—what is your own opinion upon it, Sam?"

"I should like to set up in practice for myself, uncle."

"Oh, indeed! In what quarter of the globe, pray?"

"In Worcester. I have always wished to practise at Worcester. It is the assize town: I don't care for pettifogging places: one can't get on in them."

"You'd like to emerge all at once into a full-blown lawyer there? That's your notion, is it, Sam?"

Sam made no answer. He knew by the tone his notion was being laughed at.

"No, my lad. When you have been in some good office for another year or two maybe, then you might think about setting-up. The office can be in Worcester if you like."

"I am hard upon twenty-three, Uncle Jacobson. I have as much knowledge of law as I need."

"And as much steadiness also, perhaps?" said old Jacobson.

Sam turned as red as the table-cover. He was a frank-looking, slender young fellow of middle height, with fine wavy hair almost a gold colour and worn of a decent length. The present fashion—to be cropped as if you were a prison-bird and to pretend to like it so—was not favoured by gentlemen in those days.

"You may have been acquiring a knowledge of law in London, Sam; I hope you have; but you've been kicking up your heels over it. What about those sums of money you've more than once got out of your mother?"

Sam's face was a deeper red than the cloth now. "Did she tell you of it, uncle?" he gasped.

"No, she didn't; she cares too much for her graceless son to betray him. I chanced to hear of it, though."

"One has to spend so much in London," murmured Sam, in lame apology.

"I dare say! In my past days, sir, a young man had to cut his coat according to his cloth. We didn't rush into all kinds of random games and then go to our fathers or mothers to help us out of them. Which is what you've been doing, my gentleman."

"Does aunt know?" burst out Sam in a fright, as a step was heard on the stairs.

"I've not told her," said Mr. Jacobson, listening—"she is gone on into the kitchen. How much is it that you've left owing in London, Sam?"

Sam nearly choked. He did not perceive this was just a random shot: he was wondering whether magic had been at work.

"Left owing in London?" stammered he.

"That's what I asked. How much? And I mean to know. 'Twon't be of any use your fencing about the bush. Come! tell it in a lump."

"Fifty pounds would cover it all, sir," said Sam, driven by desperation into the avowal.

"I want the truth, Sam."

"That is the truth, uncle, I put it all down in a list before leaving London; it comes to just under fifty pounds."

"How could you be so wicked as to contract it?"

"There has not been much wickedness about it," said Sam, miserably, "indeed there hasn't. One gets drawn into expenses unconsciously in the most extraordinary manner up in London. Uncle Jacobson, you may believe me or not, when I say that until I added it up, I did not think it amounted to twenty pounds in all."

"And then you found it to be fifty! How do you propose to pay this?"

"I intend to send it up by instalments, as I can."

"Instead of doing which, you'll get into deeper debt at Worcester. If it's Worcester you go to."

"I hope not, uncle. I shall do my best to keep out of debt. I mean to be steady."

Mr. Jacobson filled a fresh pipe, and lighted it with a spill from the mantelpiece. He did not doubt the young fellow's intentions; he only doubted his resolution.

"You shall go into some lawyer's office in Worcester for two years, Sam, when we shall see how things turn out," said he presently. "And, look here, I'll pay these debts of yours myself, provided you promise me not to get into trouble again. There, no more"—interrupting Sam's grateful looks—"your aunt's coming in."

Sam opened the door for Mrs. Jacobson. A little pleasant-faced woman in a white net cap, with small flat silver curls under it. She carried a small basket lined with blue silk, in which lay her knitting.

"I've been looking to your room, my dear, to see that all's comfortable for you," she said to Sam, as she sat down by the table and the candles. "That new housemaid of ours is not altogether to be trusted. I suppose you've been telling your uncle all about the wonders of London?"

"And something else, too," put in old Jacobson gruffly. "He wanted to set up in practice for himself at Worcester: off-hand, red-hot!"

"Oh dear!" said Mrs. Jacobson.

"That's what the boy wanted, nothing less. No. Another year or two's work in some good house, to acquire stability and experience, and then he may talk about setting up. It will be all for the best, Sam; trust me."

"Well, uncle, perhaps it will." It was of no use for him to say perhaps it won't: he could not help himself. But it was a disappointment.

Mr. Jacobson walked over to Dyke Manor the next day, to consult the Squire as to the best lawyer to place Sam with, himself suggesting their old friend Cockermuth. He described all Sam's wild ways (it was how he put it) in that dreadful place, London, and the money he had got out of amidst its snares. The Squire took up the matter with his usual hearty sympathy, and quite agreed that no practitioner in the law could be so good for Sam as John Cockermuth.

John Cockermuth proved to be agreeable. He was getting to be an elderly man then, but was active as ever, saving when a fit of the gout took him. He received young Dene in his usual cheery manner, upon the day appointed for his entrance, and assigned him his place in the office next to Mr. Parslet. Parslet had been there more than twenty years; he was, so to say, at the top and tail of all the work that went on in it, but he was not a qualified solicitor. Samson Dene was qualified, and could therefore represent Mr. Cockermuth before the magistrates and what not: of which the old lawyer expected to find the benefit.

"Where are you going to live?" he questioned of Sam that first morning.

"I don't know yet, sir. Mr. and Mrs. Jacobson are about the town now, I believe, looking for lodgings for me. Of course they couldn't let me look; they'd think I should be taken in," added Sam.

"Taken in and done for," laughed the lawyer. "I should not wonder but Mr. Parslet could accommodate you. Can you, Parslet?"

Mr. Parslet looked up from his desk, his thin cheeks flushing. He was small and slight, with weak brown hair, and had a patient, sad sort of look in his face and in his meek, dark eyes.

James Parslet was one of those men who are said to spoil their own lives. Left alone early, he was looked after by a bachelor uncle, a minor canon of the cathedral, who perhaps tried to do his duty by him in a mild sort of manner. But young Parslet liked to go his own ways, and they were not very good ways. He did not stay at any calling he was put to, trying first one and then another; either the people got tired of him, or he of them. Money (when he got any) burnt a hole in his pocket, and his coats grew shabby and his boots dirty. "Poor Jamie Parslet! how he has spoilt his life" cried the town, shaking its pitying head at him: and thus things went on till he grew to be nearly thirty years of age. Then, to the public astonishment, Jamie pulled up. He got taken on by Lawyer Cockermuth as copying clerk at twenty shillings a-week, married, and became as steady as Old Time. He had been nothing but steady from that day to this, had forty shillings a-week now, instead of twenty, and was ever a meek, subdued man, as if he carried about with him a perpetual repentance for the past, regret for the life that might have been.

He lived in Edgar Street, which is close to the cathedral, as every one knows, Edgar Tower being at the top of it. An old gentleman attached to the cathedral had now lodged in his house for ten years, occupying the drawing-room floor; he had recently died, and hence Lawyer Cockermuth's suggestion.

Mr. Parslet looked up. "I should be happy to, sir," he said; "if our rooms suited Mr. Dene. Perhaps he would like to look at them?"

"I will," said Sam. "If my uncle and aunt do not fix on any for me."

Is there any subtle mesmeric power, I wonder, that influences things unconsciously? Curious to say, at this very moment Mr. and Mrs. Jacobson were looking at these identical rooms. They had driven into Worcester with Sam very early indeed, so as to have a long day before them, and when breakfast was over at the inn, took the opportunity, which they very rarely got, of slipping into the cathedral to hear the beautiful ten-o'clock service. Coming out the cloister way when it was over, and so down Edgar Street, Mrs. Jacobson espied a card in a window with "Lodgings" on it. "I wonder if they would suit Sam?" she cried to her husband. "Edgar Street is a nice, wide, open street, and quiet. Suppose we look at them?"

A young servant-maid, called by her mistress "Sally," answered the knock. Mrs. Parslet, a capable, bustling woman of ready speech and good manners, came out of the parlour, and took the visitors to the floor above. They liked the rooms and they liked Mrs. Parslet; they also liked the moderate rent asked, for respectable country people in those days did not live by shaving one another; and when it came out that the house's master had been clerk to Lawyer Cockermuth for twenty years, they settled the matter off-hand, without the ceremony of consulting Sam. Mrs. Jacobson looked upon Sam as a boy still. Mr. Jacobson might have done the same but for the debts made in London.

And all this, you will say, has been yet more explanation; but I could not help it. The real thing begins now, with Sam Dene's sojourn in Mr. Cockermuth's office, and his residence in Edgar Street.

The first Sunday of his stay there, Sam went out to attend the morning service in the cathedral, congratulating himself that that grand edifice stood so conveniently near, and looking, it must be confessed, a bit of a dandy, for he had put a little bunch of spring violets into his coat, and "button-holes" were quite out of the common way then. The service began with the Litany, the earlier service of prayers being held at eight o'clock. Sam Dene has not yet forgotten that day, for it is no imaginary person I am telling you of, and never will forget it. The Reverend Allen Wheeler chanted, and the prebendary in residence (Somers Cocks) preached. While wondering when the sermon (a very good one) would be over, and thinking it rather prosy, after the custom of young men, Sam's roving gaze was drawn to a young lady sitting in the long seat opposite to him on the other side of the choir, whose whole attention appeared to be given to the preacher, to whom her head was turned. It is a nice face, thought Sam; such a sweet expression in it. It really was a nice face, rather pretty, gentle and thoughtful, a patient look in the dark brown eyes. She had on a well-worn dark silk, and a straw bonnet; all very quiet and plain; but she looked very much of a lady. Wonder if she sits there always? thought Sam.

Service over, he went home, and was about to turn the handle of the door to enter (looking another way) when he found it turned for him by some one who was behind and had stretched out a hand to do it. Turning quickly, he saw the same young lady.

"Oh, I beg your pardon," said Sam, all at sea; "did you wish to come in here?"

"If you please," she answered—and her voice was sweet and her manner modest.

"Oh," repeated Sam, rather taken aback at the answer. "You did not want me, did you?"

"Thank you, it is my home," she said.

"Your home?" stammered Sam, for he had not seen the ghost of any one in the house yet, saving his landlord and landlady and Sally. "Here?"

"Yes. I am Maria Parslet."

He stood back to let her enter; a slender, gentle girl of middle height; she looked about eighteen, Sam thought (she was that and two years on to it), and he wondered where she had been hidden. He had to go out again, for he was invited to dine at Lawyer Cockermuth's, so he saw no more of the young lady that day; but she kept dancing about in his memory. And somehow she so fixed herself in it, and as the time went on so grew in it, and at last so filled it, that Sam may well hold that day as a marked day—the one that introduced him to Maria Parslet. But that is anticipating.

On the Monday morning all his ears and eyes were alert, listening and looking for Maria. He did not see her; he did not hear a sound of her. By degrees he got to learn that the young lady was resident teacher in a lady's school hard by; and that she was often allowed to spend the whole day at home on Sundays. One Sunday evening he ingeniously got himself invited to take tea in Mrs. Parslet's parlour, and thus became acquainted with Maria; but his opportunities for meeting her were rare.

There's not much to tell of the first twelvemonth. It passed in due course. Sam Dene was fairly steady. He made a few debts, as some young men, left to themselves, can't help making—at least, they'd tell you they can't. Sundry friends of Sam's in Worcester knew of this, and somehow it reached Mr. Cockermuth's ears, who gave Sam a word of advice privately.

This was just as the first year expired. According to agreement, Sam had another year to stay. He entered upon it with inward gloom. On adding up his scores, which he deemed it as well to do after his master's lecture, he again found that they amounted to far more than he had thought for, and how he should contrive to pay them out of his own resources he knew no more than the man in the moon. In short, he could not do it; he was in a fix; and lived in perpetual dread of its coming to the ears of his uncle Jacobson.

The spring assize, taking place early in March, was just over; the judges had left the town for Stafford, and Worcester was settling down again to quietness. Miss Cockermuth gave herself and her two handmaidens a week's rest—assize time being always a busy and bustling period at the lawyer's, no end of chance company looking in—and then the house began its spring cleaning, a grand institution with our good grandmothers, often lasting a couple of weeks. This time, at the lawyer's house, it was to be a double bustle; for visitors were being prepared for.

It had pleased Captain Cockermuth to write word that he should be at home for Easter; upon which, the lawyer and his sister decided to invite Philip's widow and her children also to spend it with them; they knew Charles would be pleased. Easter-Day was very early indeed that year, falling at the end of March.

To make clearer what's coming, the house had better have a word or two of description. You entered from the street into a wide passage; no steps. On the left was the parlour and general sitting-room, in which all meals were usually taken. It was a long, low room, its two rather narrow windows looking upon the street, the back of the room being a little dark. Opposite the door was the fireplace. On the other side the passage, facing the parlour-door, was the door that opened to the two rooms (one front, one back) used as the lawyer's offices. The kitchens and staircase were at the back of the passage, a garden lying beyond; and there was a handsome drawing-room on the first floor, not much used.

The house, I say, was in a commotion with the spring cleaning, and the other preparations. To accommodate so many visitors required contrivance: a bedroom for the captain, a bedroom for his daughter-in-law, two bedrooms for the children. Mistress and maids held momentous consultations together.

"We have decided to put the three little girls in Philip's old room, John," said Miss Betty to her brother, as they sat in the parlour after dinner on the Monday evening of the week preceding Passion Week; "and little Philip can have the small room off mine. We shall have to get in a child's bed, though; I can't put the three little girls in one bed; they might get fighting. John, I do wish you'd sell that old bureau for what it will fetch."

"Sell the old bureau!" exclaimed Mr. Cockermuth.

"I'm sure I should. What good does it do? Unless that bureau goes out of the room, we can't put the extra bed in. I've been in there half the day with Susan and Ann, planning and contriving, and we find it can't be done any way. Do let Ward take it away, John; there's no place for it in the other chambers. He'd give you a fair price for it, I dare say."

Miss Betty had never cared for this piece of furniture, thinking it more awkward than useful: she looked eagerly at her brother, awaiting his decision. She was the elder of the two; tall, like him; but whilst he maintained his thin, wiry form, just the shape of an upright gas-post with arms, she had grown stout with no shape at all. Miss Betty had dark, thick eyebrows and an amiable red face. She wore a "front" of brown curls with a high and dressy cap perched above it. This evening her gown was of soft twilled shot-green silk, a white net kerchief was crossed under its body, and she had on a white muslin apron.

"I don't mind," assented the lawyer, as easy in disposition as Miss Betty was; "it's of no use keeping it that I know of. Send for Ward and ask him, if you like, Betty."

Ward, a carpenter and cabinet-maker, who had a shop in the town and sometimes bought second-hand things, was sent for by Miss Betty on the following morning; and he agreed, after some chaffering, to buy the old bureau. It was the bureau from which Philip's box of gold had disappeared—but I dare say you have understood that. In the midst of all this stir and clatter, just as Ward betook himself away after concluding the negotiation, and the maids were hard at work above stairs with mops and pails and scrubbing-brushes, the first advance-guard of the visitors unexpectedly walked in: Captain Cockermuth.

Miss Betty sat down in an access of consternation. She could do nothing but stare. He had not been expected for a week yet; there was nothing ready and nowhere to put him.

"I wish you'd take to behaving like a rational being, Charles!" she exclaimed. "We are all in a mess; the rooms upside down, and the bedside carpets hanging out at the windows."

Captain Cockermuth said he did not care for bedside carpets, he could sleep anywhere—on the brewhouse-bench, if she liked. He quite approved of selling the old bureau, when told it was going to be done.

Ward had appointed five o'clock that evening to fetch it away. They were about to sit down to dinner when he came, five o'clock being the hour for late dinners then in ordinary life. Ward had brought a man with him and they went upstairs.

Miss Betty, as carver, sat at the top of the dining-table, her back to the windows, the lawyer in his place at the foot, Charles between them, facing the fire. Miss Betty was cutting off the first joint of a loin of veal when the bureau was heard coming down the staircase, with much bumping and noise.

Mr. Cockermuth stepped out of the dining-room to look on. The captain followed: being a sociable man with his fellow-townspeople, he went to ask Ward how he did.

The bureau came down safely, and was lodged at the foot of the stairs; the man wiped his hot face, while Ward spoke with Captain Cockermuth. It seemed quite a commotion in the usual quiet dwelling. Susan, a jug of ale in her hand, which she had been to the cellar to draw, stood looking on from the passage; Mr. Dene and a younger clerk, coming out of the office just then to leave for the evening, turned to look on also.

"I suppose there's nothing in here, sir?" cried Ward, returning to business and the bureau.

"Nothing, I believe," replied Mr. Cockermuth.

"Nothing at all," called out Miss Betty through the open parlour-door. "I emptied the drawers this morning."

Ward, a cautious man and honest, drew back the lid and put his hand in succession into the pigeon-holes; which had not been used since Philip's time. There were twelve of them; three above, and three below on each side, and a little drawer that locked in the middle. "Halloa!" cried Ward, when his hand was in the depth of one of them: "here's something."

And he drew forth the lost box. The little ebony box with all the gold in it.

Well now, that was a strange thing. Worcester thinks so, those people who are still living to remember it, to this day. How it was that the box had appeared to be lost and was searched for in vain over and over again, by poor Philip and others; and how it was that it was now recovered in this easy and natural manner, was never explained or accounted for. Ward's opinion was that the box must have been put in, side upwards, that it had in some way stuck to the back of the deep, narrow pigeon-hole, which just about held the box in width, that those who had searched took the box for the back of the hole when their fingers touched it and that the bumping of the bureau now in coming downstairs had dislodged the box and brought it forward. As a maker of bureaus, Ward's opinion was listened to with deference. Any way, it was a sort of theory, serving passably well in the absence of any other. But who knew? All that was certain about it was the fact; the loss and the recovery after many years. It happened just as here described, as I have already said.

Sam Dene had never heard of the loss. Captain Cockermuth, perfectly beside himself with glee, explained it to him. Sam laughed as he touched with his forefinger the closely packed golden guineas, lying there so snug and safe, offered his congratulations, and walked home to tea.

It chanced that on that especial Tuesday evening, matters were at sixes and sevens in the Parslets' house. Sally had misbehaved herself and was discharged in consequence; and the servant engaged in her place, who was to have entered that afternoon, had not made her appearance. When Sam entered, Maria came out of the parlour, a pretty blush upon her face. And to Sam the unexpected sight of her, it was not often he got a chance of it, and the blush and the sweet eyes came like a gleam of Eden, for he had grown to love her dearly. Not that he had owned it to himself yet.

Maria explained. Her school had broken up for the Easter holidays earlier than it ought, one of the girls showing symptoms of measles; and her mother had gone out to see what had become of the new servant, leaving a request that Mr. Dene would take his tea with them in the parlour that evening, as there was no one to wait on him.

Nothing loth, you may be sure, Mr. Dene accepted the invitation, running up to wash his hands, and give a look at his hair, and running down in a trice. The tea-tray stood in readiness on the parlour table, Maria sitting behind it. Perhaps she had given a look at her hair, for it was quite more lovely, Sam thought, more soft and silken than any hair he had ever seen. The little copper kettle sang away on the hob by the fire.

"Will papa be long, do you know?" began Maria demurely, feeling shy and conscious at being thus thrown alone into Sam's company. "I had better not make the tea until he comes in."

"I don't know at all," answered Sam. "He went out on some business for Mr. Cockermuth at half-past four, and was not back when I left. Such a curious thing has just happened up there, Miss Parslet!"

"Indeed! What is it?"

Sam entered on the narrative. Maria, who knew all about the strange loss of the box, grew quite excited as she listened. "Found!" she exclaimed. "Found in the same bureau! And all the golden guineas in it!"

"Every one," said Sam: "as I take it. They were packed right up to the top!"

"Oh, what a happy thing!" repeated Maria, in a fervent tone that rather struck Sam, and she clasped her fingers into one another, as one sometimes does in pleasure or in pain.

"Why do you say that, Miss Parslet?"

"Because papa—but I do not think I ought to tell you," added Maria, breaking off abruptly.

"Oh yes, you may. I am quite safe, even if it's a secret. Please do."

"Well," cried the easily persuaded girl, "papa has always had an uncomfortable feeling upon him ever since the loss. He feared that some people, knowing he was not well off, might think perhaps it was he who had stolen upstairs and taken it."

Sam laughed at that.

"He has never said so, but somehow we have seen it, my mother and I. It was altogether so mysterious a loss, you see, affording no clue as to when it occurred, that people were ready to suspect anything, however improbable. Oh, I am thankful it is found!"

The kettle went on singing, the minutes went on flitting, and still nobody came. Six o'clock struck out from the cathedral as Mr. Parslet entered. Had the two been asked the time, they might have said it was about a quarter-past five. Golden hours fly quickly; fly on angels' wings.

Now it chanced that whilst they were at tea, a creditor of Sam's came to the door, one Jonas Badger. Sam went to him: and the colloquy that ensued might be heard in the parlour. Mr. Badger said (in quite a fatherly way) that he really could not be put off any longer with promises; if his money was not repaid to him before Easter he should be obliged to take steps about it, should write to Mr. Jacobson, of Elm Farm, to begin with. Sam returned to the tea-table with a wry face.

Soon after that, Mrs. Parslet came in, the delinquent servant in her rear. Next, a friend of Sam's called, Austin Chance, whose father was a solicitor in good practice in the town. The two young men, who were very intimate and often together, went up to Sam's room above.

"I say, my good young friend," began Chance, in a tone that might be taken for jest or earnest, "don't you go and get into any entanglement in that quarter."

"What d'you mean now?" demanded Sam, turning the colour of the rising sun.

"I mean Maria Parslet," said Austin Chance, laughing. "She's a deuced nice girl; I know that; just the one a fellow might fall in love with unawares. But it wouldn't do, Dene."

"Why wouldn't it do?"

"Oh, come now, Sam, you know it wouldn't. Parslet is only a working clerk at Cockermuth's."

"I should like to know what has put the thought in your head?" contended Sam. "You had better put it out again. I've never told you I was falling in love with her; or told herself, either. Mrs. Parslet would be about me, I expect, if I did. She looks after her as one looks after gold."

"Well, I found you in their room, having tea with them, and—"

"It was quite an accident; an exceptional thing," interrupted Sam.

"Well," repeated Austin, "you need not put your back up, old fellow; a friendly warning does no harm. Talking of gold, Dene, I've done my best to get up the twenty pounds you wanted to borrow of me, and I can't do it. I'd let you have it with all my heart if I could; but I find I am harder up than I thought for."

Which was all true. Chance was as good-natured a young man as ever lived, but at this early stage of his life he made more debts than he could pay.

"Badger has just been here, whining and covertly threatening," said Sam. "I am to pay up in a week, or he'll make me pay—and tell my uncle, he says, to begin with."

"Hypocritical old skinflint!" ejaculated Chance, himself sometimes in the hands of Mr. Badger—a worthy gentleman who did a little benevolent usury in a small and quiet way, and took his delight in accommodating safe young men. A story was whispered that young M., desperately hard-up, borrowed two pounds from him one Saturday night, undertaking to repay it, with two pounds added on for interest, that day month; and when the day came and M. had not got the money, or was at all likely to get it, he carried off a lot of his mother's plate under his coat to the pawnbroker's.

"And there's more besides Badger's that is pressing," went on Dene. "I must get money from somewhere, or it will play the very deuce with me. I wonder whether Charley Hill could lend me any?"

"Don't much think so. You might ask him. Money seems scarce with Hill always. Has a good many ways for it, I fancy."

"Talking of money, Chance, a lot has been found at Cockermuth's to-day. A boxful of guineas that has been lost for years."

Austin Chance stared. "You don't mean that box of guineas that mysteriously disappeared in Philip's time?"

"Well, they say so. It is a small, round box of carved ebony, and it is stuffed to the brim with old guineas. Sixty of them, I hear."

"I can't believe it's true; that that's found."

"Not believe it's true, Chance! Why, I saw it. Saw the box found, and touched the guineas with my fingers. It has been hidden in an old bureau all the time," added Sam, and he related the particulars of the discovery.

"What an extraordinary thing!" exclaimed young Chance: "the queerest start I ever heard of." And he fell to musing.

But the "queer start," as Mr. Austin Chance was pleased to designate the resuscitation of the box, did not prove to be a lucky one.

II

The sun shone brightly on Foregate Street, but did not yet touch the front-windows on Lawyer Cockermuth's side of it. Miss Betty Cockermuth sat near one of them in the parlour, spectacles on nose, and hard at work unpicking the braid off some very old woollen curtains, green once, but now faded to a sort of dingy brown. It was Wednesday morning, the day following the wonderful event of finding the box, lost so long, full of its golden guineas. In truth nobody thought of it as anything less than marvellous.

The house-cleaning, in preparation for Easter and Easter's visitors, was in full flow to-day, and would be for more than a week to come; the two maids were hard at it above. Ward, who did not disdain to labour with his own hands, was at the house, busy at some mysterious business in the brewhouse, coat off, shirt-sleeves stripped up to elbow, plunging at that moment something or other into the boiling water of the furnace.

"How I could have let them remain up so long in this state, I can't think," said Miss Betty to herself, arresting her employment, scissors in hand, to regard the dreary curtains. She had drawn the table towards her from the middle of the room, and the heavy work was upon it. Susan came in to impart some domestic news.

"Ward says there's a rare talk in the town about the finding of that box, missis," cried she, when she had concluded it. "My! how bad them curtains look, now they're down!"

Servants were on more familiar terms with their mistresses in those days without meaning, or showing, any disrespect; identifying themselves, as it were, with the family and its interests. Susan, a plump, red-cheeked young woman turned thirty, had been housemaid in her present place for seven years. She had promised a baker's head man to marry him, but never could be got to fix the day. In winter she'd say to him, "Wait till summer;" and when summer came, she'd say, "Wait till winter." Miss Betty commended her prudence.

"Yes," said she now, in answer to the girl, "I've been wondering how we could have kept them up so long; they are not fit for much, I'm afraid, save the ragbag. Chintz will make the room look much nicer."

As Susan left the parlour, Captain Cockermuth entered it, a farmer with him who had come in from Hallow to the Wednesday's market. The captain's delighted excitement at the finding of the box had not at all subsided; he had dreamt of it, he talked of it, he pinned every acquaintance he could pick up this morning and brought him in to see the box of gold. Independently of its being a very great satisfaction to have had the old mysterious loss cleared up, the sixty guineas would be a huge boon to the captain's pocket.

"But how was it that none of you ever found it, if it remained all this while in the pigeon-hole?" cried the wondering farmer, bending over the little round box of guineas, which the captain placed upon the table open, the lid by its side.

"Well, we didn't find it, that's all I know; or poor Philip, either," said Captain Cockermuth.

The farmer took his departure. As the captain was showing him to the front-door, another gentleman came hustling in. It was Thomas Chance the lawyer, father of the young man who had been the previous night with Samson Dene. He and Lawyer Cockermuth were engaged together just then in some complicated, private, and very disagreeable business, each acting for a separate client, who were the defendants against a great wrong—or what they thought was one.

"Come in, Chance, and take a look at my box of guineas, resuscitated from the grave," cried the captain, joyously. "You can go into the office to John afterwards."

"Well, I've hardly time this morning," answered Mr. Chance, turning, though, into the parlour and shaking hands with Miss Betty. "Austin told me it was found."

Now it happened that Lawyer Cockermuth came then into the parlour himself, to get something from his private desk-table which stood there. When the box had been discussed, Mr. Chance took a letter from his pocket and placed it in his brother practitioner's hands.

"What do you think of that?" he asked. "I got it by post this morning."

"Think! why, that it is of vital importance," said Mr. Cockermuth when he had read it.

"Yes; no doubt of that. But what is to be our next move in answer to it?" asked the other.

Seeing they were plunging into business, the captain strolled away to the front-door, which stood open all day, for the convenience of those coming to the office, and remained there whistling, his hands in his pockets, on the look out for somebody else to bring in. He had put the lid on the box of guineas, and left the box on the table.

"I should like to take a copy of this letter," said Mr. Cockermuth to the other lawyer.

"Well, you can take it," answered Chance. "Mind who does it, though—Parslet, or somebody else that's confidential. Don't let it go into the office."

"You are wanted, sir," said Mr. Dene, from the door.

"Who is it?" asked his master.

"Mr. Chamberlain. He says he is in a hurry."

"I'm coming. Here, Dene!" he called out as the latter was turning away: and young Dene came back again.

"Sit down here, now, and take a copy of this letter," cried the lawyer, rapidly drawing out and opening the little writing-desk table that stood against the wall at the back of the room. "Here's pen, ink and paper, all ready: the letter is confidential, you perceive."

He went out of the room as he spoke, Mr. Chance with him; and Sam Dene sat down to commence his task, after exchanging a few words with Miss Betty, with whom he was on good terms.

"Charles makes as much fuss over this little box as if it were filled with diamonds from Golconda, instead of guineas," remarked she, pointing with her scissors to the box, which stood near her on the table, to direct the young man's attention to it. "I don't know how many folks he has not brought in already to have a look at it."

"Well, it was a capital find, Miss Betty; one to be proud of," answered Sam, settling to his work.

For some little time nothing was heard but the scratching of Mr. Dene's pen and the clicking of Miss Betty's scissors. Her task was nearing completion. A few minutes more, and the last click was given, the last bit of the braid was off. "And I'm glad of it," cried she aloud, flinging the end of the curtain on the top of the rest.

"This braid will do again for something or other," considered Miss Betty, as she began to wind it upon an old book. "It was put on fresh only three or four years ago. Well brushed, it will look almost like new."

Again Susan opened the door. "Miss Betty, here's the man come with the chintz: five or six rolls of it for you to choose from," cried she. "Shall he come in here?"

Miss Betty was about to say Yes, but stopped and said No, instead. The commotion of holding up the chintzes to the light, to judge of their different merits, might disturb Mr. Dene; and she knew better than to interrupt business.

"Let him take them to the room where they are to hang, Susan; we can judge best there."

Tossing the braid to Susan, who stood waiting at the door, Miss Betty hastily took up her curtains, and Susan held the door open for her mistress to pass through.

Choosing chintz for window-curtains takes some time; as everybody knows whose fancy is erratic. And how long Miss Betty and Susan and the young man from the chintz-mart had been doubting and deciding and doubting again, did not quite appear, when Captain Cockermuth's voice was heard ascending from below.

"Betty! Are you upstairs, Betty?"

"Yes, I'm here," she called back, crossing to the door to speak. "Do you want me, Charles?"

"Where have you put the box?"

"What box?"

"The box of guineas."

"It is on the table."

"It is not on the table. I can't see it anywhere."

"It was on the table when I left the parlour. I did not touch it. Ask Mr. Dene where it is: I left him there."

"Mr. Dene's not here. I wish you'd come down."

"Very well; I'll come in a minute or two," concluded Miss Betty, going back to the chintzes.

"Why, I saw that box on the table as I shut the door after you had come out, ma'am," observed Susan, who had listened to the colloquy.

"So did I," said Miss Betty; "it was the very last thing my eyes fell on. If young Mr. Dene finished what he was about and left the parlour, I dare say he put the box up somewhere for safety. I think, Susan, we must fix upon this light pea-green with the rosebuds running up it. It matches the paper: and the light coming through it takes quite a nice shade."

A little more indecision yet; and yet a little more, as to whether the curtains should be lined, or not, and then Miss Cockermuth went downstairs. The captain was pacing the passage to and fro impatiently.

"Now then, Betty, where's my box?"

"But how am I to know where the box is, Charles, if it's not on the table?" she remonstrated, turning into the parlour, where two friends of the captain's waited to be regaled with the sight of the recovered treasure. "I had to go upstairs with the young man who brought the chintzes; and I left the box here"— indicating the exact spot on the table. "It was where you left it yourself. I did not touch it at all."

She shook hands with the visitors. Captain Cockermuth looked gloomy—as if he were at sea and had lost his reckoning.

"If you had to leave the room, why didn't you put the box up?" asked he. "A boxful of guineas shouldn't be left alone in an empty room."

"But Mr. Dene was in the room; he sat at the desk there, copying a letter for John. As to why didn't I put the box up, it was not my place to do so that I know of. You were about yourself, Charles—only at the front-door, I suppose."

Captain Cockermuth was aware that he had not been entirely at the front-door. Two or three times he had crossed over to hold a chat with acquaintances on the other side the way; had strolled with one of them nearly up to Salt Lane and back. Upon catching hold of these two gentlemen, now brought in, he had found the parlour empty of occupants and the box not to be seen.

"Well, this is a nice thing—that a man can't put his hand upon his own property when he wants to, or hear where it is!" grumbled he. "And what business on earth had Dene to meddle with the box?"

"To put it in safety—if he did meddle with it, and a sensible thing to do," retorted Miss Betty, who did not like to be scolded unjustly. "Just like you, Charles, making a fuss over nothing! Why don't you go and ask young Dene where it is?"

"Young Dene is not in. And John's not in. Nobody is in but Parslet; and he does not know anything about it. I must say, Betty, you manage the house nicely!" concluded the captain ironically, giving way to his temper.

This was, perhaps the reader may think, commotion enough "over nothing," as Miss Betty put it. But it was not much as compared with the commotion which set in later. When Mr. Cockermuth came in, he denied all knowledge of it, and Sam Dene was impatiently waited for.

It was past two o'clock when he returned, for he had been home to dinner. The good-looking young fellow turned in at the front-door with a fleet step, and encountered Captain Cockermuth, who attacked him hotly, demanding what he had done with the box.

"Ah," said Sam, lightly and coolly, "Parslet said you were looking for it." Mr. Parslet had in fact mentioned it at home over his dinner.

"Well, where is it?" said the captain. "Where did you put it?"

"I?" cried young Dene. "Not anywhere. Should I be likely to touch the box, sir? I saw the box on that table while I was copying a letter for Mr. Cockermuth; that's all I know of it."

The captain turned red, and pale, and red again. "Do you mean to tell me to my face, Mr. Dene, that the box is gone?"

"I'm sure I don't know," said Sam in the easiest of all easy tones. "It seems to be gone."

The box was gone. Gone once more with all its golden guineas. It could not be found anywhere; in the house or out of the house, upstairs or down. The captain searched frantically, the others helped him, but no trace of it could be found.

At first it was impossible to believe it. That this self-same box should mysteriously have vanished a second time, seemed to be too marvellous for fact. But it was true.

Nobody would admit a share in the responsibility. The captain left the box safe amidst (as he put it) a roomful of people: Miss Betty considered that she left it equally safe, with Mr. Dene seated at the writing-table, and the captain dodging (as she put it) in and out. Mr. Cockermuth had not entered the parlour since he left it, when called to Mr. Chamberlain, with whom he had gone out. Sam Dene reiterated that he had not meddled with the box; no, nor thought about it.

Sam's account, briefly given, was this. After finishing copying the letter, he closed the little table-desk and pushed it back to its place against the wall, and had carried the letter and the copy into the office. Finding Mr. Cockermuth was not there, he locked them up in his own desk, having to go to the Guildhall upon some business. The business there took up some time, in fact until past one o'clock, and he then went home to dinner.

"And did you consider it right, Sam Dene, to leave a valuable box like that on the table, unguarded?" demanded Captain Cockermuth, as they all stood together in the parlour, after questioning Sam; and the captain had been looking so fierce and speaking so sharply that it might be thought he was taking Sam for the thief, off-hand.

"To tell the truth, captain, I never thought of the box," answered Sam. "I might not have noticed that the box was in the room at all but for Miss Betty's drawing my attention to it. After that, I grew so much interested in the letter I was copying (for I know all about the cause, as Mr. Cockermuth is aware, and it was curious news) that I forgot everything else."

Lawyer Cockermuth nodded to confirm this. The captain went on.

"Betty drew your attention to it, did she? Why did she draw it? In what way?"

"Well, she remarked that you made as much fuss over that box as if it were filled with diamonds," replied the young man, glad to pay out the captain for his angry and dictatorial tone. But the captain was in truth beginning to entertain a very ominous suspicion.

"Do you wish to deny, Samson Dene, that my sister Betty left that box on the table when she quitted the room?"

"Why, who does?" cried Sam. "When Miss Betty says she left the box on the table, of course she did leave it. She must know. Susan, it seems, also saw that it was left there."

"And you could see that box of guineas standing stark staring on the table, and come out of the room and leave it to its fate!" foamed the captain. "Instead of giving me a call to say nobody was on guard here!"

"I didn't see it," returned Sam. "There's no doubt it was there, but I did not see it. I never looked towards the table as I came out, that I know of. The table, as I dare say you remember, was not in its usual place; it was up there by the window. The box had gone clean out of my thoughts."

"Well, Mr. Dene, my impression is that you have got the box," cried the angry captain.

"Oh, is it!" returned Sam, with supreme good humour, and just the least suspicion of a laugh. "A box like that would be uncommonly useful to me."

"I expect, young man, the guineas would!"

"Right you are, captain."

But Captain Cockermuth regarded this mocking pleasantry as particularly ill-timed. He believed the young man was putting it on to divert suspicion from himself.

"Who did take the box?" questioned he. "Tell me that."

"I wish I could, sir."

"How could the box vanish off the table unless it was taken, I ask you?"

"That's a puzzling question," coolly rejoined Sam. "It was too heavy for the rats, I expect."

"Oh dear, but we have no rats in the house," cried Miss Betty. "I wish we had, I'm sure—and could find the box in their holes." She was feeling tolerably uncomfortable. Placid and easy in a general way, serious worry always upset her considerably.

Captain Cockermuth's suspicions were becoming certainties. The previous night, when his brother had been telling him various items of news of the old town, as they sat confidentially over the fire after Miss Betty had gone up to bed, Mr. Cockermuth chanced to mention the fact that young Dene had been making a few debts. Not speaking in any ill-natured spirit, quite the contrary, for he liked the young man amazingly. Only a few, he continued; thoughtless young men would do so; and he had given him a lecture. And then he laughingly added the information that Mr. Jacobson had imparted to him twelve months ago, in their mutual friendship—of the debts Sam had made in London.

No sensible person can be surprised that Charles Cockermuth recalled this now. It rankled in his mind. Had Sam Dene taken the box of guineas to satisfy these debts contracted during the past year at Worcester? It looked like it. And the longer the captain dwelt on it, the more and more likely it grew to look.

All the afternoon the search was kept up by the captain. Not an individual article in the parlour but was turned inside out; he wanted to have the carpet up. His brother and Sam Dene had returned to their work in the office as usual. The captain was getting to feel like a raging bear; three times Miss Betty had to stop him in a dreadful fit of swearing; and when dinner-time came he could not eat. It was a beautiful slice of Severn salmon, which had its price, I can tell you, in Worcester then, and minced veal, and a jam tart, all of which dishes Charles Cockermuth especially favoured. But the loss of the sixty guineas did away with his appetite. Mr. Cockermuth, who took the loss very coolly, laughed at him.

The laughing did not mend the captain's temper: neither did the hearing that Sam Dene had departed for home as usual at five o'clock. Had Sam been innocent, he would at least have come to the parlour and inquired whether the box was found, instead of sneaking off home to tea.

Fretting and fuming, raging and stamping, disturbing the parlour's peace and his own, strode Charles Cockermuth. His good-humoured brother John bore it for an hour or two, and then told him he might as well go outside and stamp on the pavement for a bit.

"I will," said Charles. Catching up his hat, saying nothing to anybody, he strode off to see the sergeant of police—Dutton—and laid the case concisely before him: The box of guineas was on the table where his sister sat at work; her work being at one end, the box at the other. Sam Dene was also in the room, copying a letter at the writing-table. Miss Betty was called upstairs; she went, leaving the box on the table. It was the last thing she saw as she left the room; the servant, who had come to call her, also saw it standing there. Presently young Dene also left the room and the house; and from that moment the box was never seen.

"What do you make of that, Mr. Dutton?" summed up Captain Cockermuth.

"Am I to understand that no other person entered the room after Mr. Dene quitted it?" inquired the sergeant.

"Not a soul. I can testify to that myself."

"Then it looks as though Mr. Dene must have taken the box."

"Just so," assented the complainant, triumphantly. "And I shall give him into custody for stealing it."

Mr. Dutton considered. His judgment was cool; the captain's hot. He thought there might be ins and outs in this affair that had not yet come to the surface. Besides that, he knew young Dene, and did not much fancy him the sort of individual likely to do a thing of this kind.

"Captain Cockermuth," said he, "I think it might be best for me to come up to the house and see a bit into the matter personally, before proceeding to extreme measures. We experienced officers have a way of turning up scraps of evidence that other people would never look at. Perhaps, after all, the box is only mislaid."

"But I tell you it's lost," said the captain. "Clean gone. Can't be found high or low."

"Well, if that same black box is lost again, I can only say it is the oddest case I ever heard of. One would think the box had a demon inside it."

"No, sergeant, you are wrong there. The demon's inside him that took it. Listen while I whisper something in your ear—that young Dene is over head and ears in debt: he has debts here, debts there, debts everywhere. For some little time now, as I chance to know, he has been at his very wits' end to think where or how he could pick up some money to satisfy the most pressing; fit to die of fear, lest they should travel to the knowledge of his uncle at Elm Farm."

"Is it so?" exclaimed Mr. Dutton, severely. And his face changed, and his opinion also. "Are you sure of this, sir?"

"Well, my informant was my brother; so you may judge whether it is likely to be correct or not," said the captain. "But, if you think it best to make some inquiries at the house, come with me now and do so."

They walked to Foregate together. The sergeant looked a little at the features of the parlour, where the loss had taken place, and heard what Miss Betty had to say, and questioned Susan. This did not help the suspicion thrown on Sam Dene, saving in one point—their joint testimony that he and the box were left alone in the room together.

Mr. Cockermuth had gone out, so the sergeant did not see him: but, as he was not within doors when the loss occurred, he could not have aided the investigation in any way.

"Well, Dutton, what do you think now?" asked Captain Cockermuth, strolling down the street with the sergeant when he departed.

"I confess my visit has not helped me much," said Dutton, a slow-speaking man, given to be cautious. "If nobody entered the room between the time when Miss Cockermuth left it and you entered it, why then, sir, there's only young Dene to fall back upon."

"I tell you nobody did enter it," cried the choleric captain; "or could, without my seeing them. I stood at the front-door. Ward was busy at the house that morning, dodging perpetually across the top of the passage, between the kitchen and brewhouse: he, too, is sure no stranger could have come in without being seen by him."

"Did you see young Dene leave the room, sir?"

"I did. Hearing somebody come out of the parlour, I looked round and saw it was young Dene with some papers in his hand. He went into the office for a minute or two, and then passed me, remarking, with all the impudence in life, that he was going to the town hall. He must have had my box in his pocket then."

"A pity but you had gone into the parlour at once, captain," remarked the sergeant. "If only to put the box in safety—provided it was there."

"But I thought it was safe. I thought my sister was there. I did go in almost directly."

"And you never stirred from the door—from first to last?"

"I don't say that. When I first stood there I strolled about a little, talking with one person and another. But I did not stir from the door after I saw Sam Dene leave the parlour. And I do not think five minutes elapsed before I went in. Not more than five, I am quite certain. What are you thinking about, Dutton?— you don't seem to take me."

"I take you well enough, sir, and all you say. But what is puzzling me in the matter is this; strikes me as strange, in fact: that Mr. Dene should do the thing (allowing that he has done it) in so open and barefaced a manner, laying himself open to immediate suspicion. Left alone in the room with the box by Miss Betty, he must know that if, when he left it, the box vanished with him, only one inference would be drawn. Most thieves exercise some caution."

"Not when they are as hard up as Dene is. Impudence with them is the order of the day, and often carries luck with it. Nothing risk, nothing win, they cry, and they do risk—and win. Dene has got my box, sergeant."

"Well, sir, it looks dark against him; almost too dark; and if you decide to give him into custody, of course we have only to— Good-evening, Badger!"

They had strolled as far as the Cross, and were standing on the wide pavement in front of St. Nicholas' Church, about to part, when that respectable gentleman, Jonas Badger, passed by. A thought struck the captain. He knew the man was a money-lender in a private way.

"Here, Badger, stop a minute," he hastily cried. "I want to ask you a question about young Dene—my brother's clerk, you know. Does he owe you money?—Much?"

Mr. Badger, wary by nature and by habit, glanced first at the questioner and then at the police-sergeant, and did not answer. Whereupon Captain Cockermuth, as an excuse for his curiosity, plunged into the history of what had occurred: the finding of the box of guineas yesterday and the losing it again to-day, and the doubt of Sam.

Mr. Badger listened with interest; for the news of that marvellous find had not yet reached his ears. He had been shut up in his office all the morning, very busy over his account-books; and in the afternoon had walked over to Kempsey, where he had a client or two, getting back only in time for tea.

"That long-lost box of guineas come to light at last!" he exclaimed. "What an extraordinary thing! And Mr. Dene is suspected of— Why, good gracious!" he broke off in fresh astonishment, "I have just seen him with a guinea in his pocket!"

"Seen a guinea in Sam Dene's pocket!" cried Captain Cockermuth, turning yellow as the gas-flame under which they were standing.

"Why yes, I have. It was—"

But there Mr. Badger came to a full stop. It had suddenly struck him that he might be doing harm to Sam Dene; and the rule of his life was not to harm any one, or to make an enemy, if his own interest allowed him to avoid it.

"I won't say any more, Captain Cockermuth. It is no business of mine."

But here Mr. Sergeant Dutton came to the fore. "You must, Badger. You must say all you know that bears upon the affair; the law demands it of you. What about the guinea?"

"Well, if you force me to do so—putting it in that way," returned the man, driven into a corner.

Mr. Badger had just been down to Edgar Street to pay another visit to Sam. Not to torment him; he did not do that more than he could help; but simply to say he would accept smaller instalments for the liquidation of his debt—which of course meant giving to Sam a longer time to pay the whole in. This evening he was admitted to Sam's sitting-room. During their short conversation, Sam, searching impatiently for a pencil in his waistcoat-pocket, drew out with it a few coins in silver money, and one coin in gold. Mr. Badger's hungry eyes saw that it was an old guinea. These particulars he now imparted.

"What did he say about the guinea?" cried Captain Cockermuth, his own eyes glaring.

"Not a word," said Badger; "neither did I. He slipped it back into his pocket."

"I hope you think there's some proof to go upon now," were Charles Cockermuth's last words to the police-officer as he wished him good-night.

On the following morning, Sam Dene was apprehended, and taken before the magistrates. Beyond being formally charged, very little was done; Miss Betty was in bed with a sick headache, brought on by the worry, and could not appear to give evidence; so he was remanded on bail until Saturday.

III

I'm sure you might have thought all his rick-yards were on fire by the way old Jacobson came bursting in. It was Saturday morning, and we were at breakfast at Dyke Manor. He had run every step of the way from Elm Farm, two miles nearly, not having patience to wait for his gig, and came in all excitement, the Worcester Herald in his hand. The Squire started from his chair; Mrs. Todhetley, then in the act of pouring out a cup of coffee, let it flow over on to the tablecloth.

"What on earth's amiss, Jacobson?" cried the Squire.

"Ay, what's amiss," stuttered Jacobson in answer; "this is amiss," holding out the newspaper. "I'll prosecute the editor as sure as I'm a living man. It is a conspiracy got up to sell it; a concocted lie. It can't be anything else, you know, Todhetley. And I want you to go off with me to Worcester. The gig's following me."

When we had somewhat collected our senses, and could look at the newspaper, there was the account as large as life. Samson Reginald Dene had been had up before the magistrates on Thursday morning on a charge of stealing a small box of carved ebony, containing sixty guineas in gold, from the dwelling house of Lawyer Cockermuth; and he was to be brought up again that day, Saturday, for examination.

"A pretty thing this is to see, when a man opens his weekly newspaper at his breakfast-table!" gasped Jacobson, flicking the report with his angry finger. "I'll have the law of them—accusing my nephew of such a thing as that! You'll go with me, Squire!"

"Go! of course I'll go!" returned the Squire, in his hot partisanship. "We were going to Worcester, any way; I've things to do there. Poor Sam! Hanging would be too good for the printers of that newspaper, Jacobson."

Mr. Jacobson's gig was heard driving up to the gate at railroad speed; and soon our own carriage was ready. Old Jacobson sat with the Squire, I behind with Giles; the other groom, Blossom, drove Tod in the gig; and away we went in the blustering March wind. Many people, farmers and others, were on the road, riding or driving to Worcester market.

Well, we found it was true. And not the mistake of the newspapers: they had but reported what passed before the magistrates at the town hall.

The first person we saw was Miss Cockermuth. She was in a fine way, not knowing what to think or believe, and sat in the parlour in that soft green gown of twilled silk (that might have been a relic of the silk made in the time of the Queen of Sheba), her cap and front all awry. Rumour said old Jacobson had been a sweetheart of hers in their young days; but I'm sure I don't know. Any way they were very friendly with one another, and she sometimes called him "Frederick." He sat down by her on the horse-hair sofa, and we took chairs.

She recounted the circumstances (ramblingly) from beginning to end. Not that the end had come yet by a long way. And—there it was, she wound up, when the narrative was over: the box had disappeared, just for all the world as mysteriously as it disappeared in the days gone by.

Mr. Jacobson had listened patiently. He was a fine, upright man, with a healthy colour and bright dark eyes. He wore a blue frock-coat to-day with metal buttons, and top-boots. As yet he did not see how they had got up grounds for accusing Sam, and he said so.

"To be sure," cried the Squire. "How's that, Miss Betty?"

"Why, it's this way," said Miss Betty—"that nobody was here in the parlour but Sam when the box vanished. It is my brother Charles who has done it all; he is so passionate, you know. John has properly quarrelled with him for it."

"It is not possible, you know, Miss Betty, that Sam Dene could have done it," struck in Tod, who was boiling over with rage at the whole thing. "Some thief must have stolen in at the street-door when Sam had left the room."

"Well, no, that could hardly have been, seeing that Charles never left the street-door after that," returned Miss Betty, mildly. "It appears to be a certain fact that not a soul entered the room after the young man left it. And there lies the puzzle of it."

Putting it to be as Miss Betty put it—and I may as well say here that nothing turned up, then or later, to change the opinion—it looked rather suspicious for Sam Dene. I think the Squire saw it.

"I suppose you are sure the box was on the table when you left the room, Miss Betty?" said he.

"Why, of course I am sure, Squire," she answered. "It was the last thing my eyes fell on; for, as I went through the door, I glanced back to see that I had left the table tidy. Susan can bear witness to that. Dutton, the police-sergeant, thinks some demon of mischief must be in that box—meaning the deuce, you know. Upon my word it looks like it."

Susan came in with some glasses and ale as Miss Betty spoke, and confirmed the testimony—which did not need confirmation. As she closed the parlour-door, she said, after her mistress had passed out, she noticed the box standing on the table.

"Is Sam here to-day—in the office?" asked Mr. Jacobson.

"Oh, my goodness, no," cried Miss Betty in a fluster. "Why, Frederick, he has not been here since Thursday, when they had him up at the Guildhall. He couldn't well come while the charge is hanging over him."

"Then I think we had better go out to find Sam, and hear what he has to say," observed Mr. Jacobson, drinking up his glass of ale.

"Yes, do," said Miss Betty. "Tell poor Sam I'm as sorry as I can be—pestered almost out of my mind over it. And as to their having found one of the guineas in his pocket, please just mention to him that I say it might have slipped in accidentally."

"One of the guineas found in Sam's pocket!" exclaimed Mr. Jacobson, taken aback.

"Well, I hear so," responded Miss Betty. "The police searched him, you see."

As the Squire and Mr. Jacobson went out, Mr. Cockermuth was coming in. They all turned into the office together, while we made a rush to Sam Dene's lodgings in Edgar Street: as much of a rush, at least, as the Saturday's streets would let us make. Sam was out, the young servant said when we got there, and while parleying with her Mrs. Parslet opened her sitting-room door.

"I do not suppose Mr. Dene will be long," she said. "He has to appear at the town hall this morning, and I think it likely he will come home first. Will you walk in and wait?"

She handed us into her parlour, where she had been busy, marking sheets and pillow-cases and towels with "prepared" ink; the table was covered with them. Tod began telling her that Mr. Jacobson was at Worcester, and went on to say what a shame it was that Sam Dene should be accused of this thing.

"We consider it so," said Mrs. Parslet; who was a capable, pleasant-speaking woman, tall and slender. "My husband says it has upset Mr. Cockermuth more than anything that has occurred for years past. He tells his brother that he should have had it investigated privately, not have given Mr. Dene into custody."

"Then why did he let him do it, Mrs. Parslet?"

She looked at Tod, as if surprised at the question. "Mr. Cockermuth knew nothing of it; you may be sure of that. Captain Cockermuth had the young man at the Guildhall and was preferring the charge, before Mr. Cockermuth heard a word of what was agate. Certainly that is a most mysterious box! It seems fated to give trouble."

At this moment the door opened, and a young lady came into the parlour. It was Maria. What a nice face she had!—what sweet thoughtful eyes!—what gentle manners! Sam's friends in the town were accusing him of being in love with her—and small blame to him.

But Sam did not appear to be coming home, and time was getting on. Tod decided not to wait longer, and said good-morning.

Flying back along High Street, we caught sight of the tray of Dublin buns, just put fresh on the counter in Rousse's shop, and made as good a feast as time allowed. Some people called them Doubling buns (from their shape, I take it), and I don't know to this day which was right.

Away with fleet foot again, past the bustle round the town hall, and market house, till we came to the next confectioner's and saw the apple-tarts. Perhaps somebody remembers yet how delicious those apple-tarts were. Bounding in, we began upon them.

While the feast was in progress, Sam Dene went by, walking very fast. We dashed out to catch him. Good Mrs. Mountford chanced to be in the shop and knew us, or they might have thought we were decamping without payment.

Sam Dene, in answer to Tod's hasty questions, went into a passion; swearing at the world in general, and Captain Cockermuth in particular, as freely as though the justices, then taking their places in the Guildhall, were not as good as within earshot.

"It is a fearful shame, Todhetley!—to bring such a charge against me, and to lug me up to the criminal bar like a felon. Worse than all, to let it go forth to the town and county in to-day's glaring newspapers that I, Sam Dene, am a common thief!"

"Of course it is a fearful shame, Sam—it's infamous, and all your friends know it is," cried Tod, with eager sympathy. "My father wishes he could hang the printers. I say, what do you think has become of the box?"

"Become of it!—why, that blundering Charles Cockermuth has got it. He was off his head with excitement at its being found. He must have come into the room and put it somewhere and forgotten it: or else he put it into his pocket and got robbed of it in the street. That's what I think. Quite off his head, I give you my word."

"And what fable is it the wretches have got up about finding one of the guineas in your pocket, Sam?"

"Oh, bother that! It was my own guinea. I swear it—there! I can't stay now," went on Sam, striding off down High Street. "I am due at the town hall this minute; only out on bail. You'll come with me."

"You go in and pay for the tarts, Johnny," called back Tod, as he put his arm within Sam Dene's. I looked in, pitched a shilling on the counter, said I didn't know how many we had eaten; perhaps ten; and that I couldn't wait for change.

Crushing my way amidst the market women and their baskets in the Guildhall yard, I came upon Austin Chance. His father held some post connected with the law, as administered there, and Austin said he would get me in.

"Can it be true that the police found one of the guineas about him?" I asked.

Chance pulled a long face. "It's true they found one when they searched him—"

"What right had they to search him?"

"Well, I don't know," said Austin, laughing a little; "they did it. To see perhaps whether all the guineas were about him. And I am afraid, Johnny Ludlow, that the finding of that guinea will make it rather hard for Sam. It is said that Maria Parslet can prove the guinea was Sam's own, and that my father has had a summons served on her to appear here to-day. He has taken Sam's case in hand; but he is closer than wax, and tells me nothing."

"You don't think he can have stolen the box, Chance?"

"I don't. I shouldn't think him capable of anything so mean; let alone the danger of it. Not but that there are circumstances in the case that tell uncommonly strong against him. And where the deuce the box can have got to, otherwise, is more than mortal man can guess at. Come along."

IV

Not for a long while had Worcester been stirred as it was over this affair of Samson Dene's. What with the curious discovery of the box of guineas after its mysterious disappearance of years, and then its second no less mysterious loss, with the suspicion that Sam Dene stole it, the Faithful City was so excited as hardly to know whether it stood on its head or its heels.

When the police searched the prisoner on Thursday morning, after taking him into custody, and found the guinea upon him (having been told that he had one about him), his guilt was thought to be as good as proved. Sam said the guinea was his own, an heirloom, and stood to this so indignantly resolute that the police let him have it back. But now, what did Sam go and do? When released upon bail by the magistrates—to come up again on the Saturday—he went straight off to a silversmith's, had a hole stamped in the guinea and hung it to his watch-chain across his waistcoat, that the public might feast their eyes upon it. It was in this spirit of defiance—or, as the town called it, bravado—that he met the charge. His lodgings had been searched for the rest of the guineas, but they were not found.

The hour for the Saturday's examination—twelve o'clock—was striking, as I struggled my way with Austin Chance through the crush round the Guildhall. But that Austin's father was a man of consequence with the door-keepers, we should not have got in at all.

The accused, arraigned by his full name, Samson Reginald Dene, stood in the place allotted to prisoners, cold defiance on his handsome face. As near to him as might be permitted, stood Tod, just as defiant as he. Captain Charles Cockermuth, a third in defiance, stood opposite to prosecute; while Lawyer Cockermuth, who came in with Sam's uncle, Mr. Jacobson, openly wished his brother at Hanover. Squire Todhetley, being a county magistrate, sat on the bench with the City magnates, but not to interfere.

The proceedings began. Captain Cockermuth related how the little box, his property, containing sixty golden guineas, was left on the table in a sitting-room in his brother's house, the accused being the only person in the room at the time, and that the box disappeared. He, himself (standing at the front-door), saw the accused quit the room; he went into it almost immediately, but the box was gone. He swore that no person entered the room after the prisoner left it.

Miss Betty Cockermuth, flustered and red, appeared next. She testified that she was in the room nearly all the morning, the little box being upon the table; when she left the room, Mr. Dene remained in it alone, copying a letter for her brother; the box was still on the table. Susan Edwards, housemaid at Lawyer Cockermuth's, spoke to the same fact. It was she who had fetched her mistress out, and she saw the box standing upon the table.

The accused was asked by one of the magistrates what he had to say to this. He answered, speaking freely, that he had nothing to say in contradiction, except that he did not know what became of the box.

"Did you see the box on the table?" asked the lawyer on the opposite side, Mr. Standup.

"I saw it there when I first went into the room. Miss Betty made a remark about the box, which drew my attention to it. I was sitting at the far end of the room, at Mr. Cockermuth's little desk-table. I did not notice the box afterwards."

"Did you not see it there after Miss Cockermuth left the room?"

"No, I did not; not that I remember," answered Sam. "Truth to say, I never thought about it. My attention was confined to the letter I was copying, to the exclusion of everything else."

"Did any one come into the room after Miss Cockermuth left it?"

"No one came into it. Somebody opened the door and looked in."

This was fresh news. The town hall pricked up its ears.

"I do not know who it was," added Sam. "My head was bent over my writing, when the door opened quickly, and as quickly shut again. I supposed somebody had looked in to see if Mr. or Miss Cockermuth was there, and had retreated on finding they were not."

"Could that person, whomsoever it might be, have advanced to the table and taken the box?" asked the chief of the magistrates.

"No, sir. For certain, no!"—and Sam's tone here, he best knew why, was aggravatingly defiant. "The person might have put his head in—and no doubt did—but he did not set a foot inside the room."

Captain Cockermuth was asked about this: whether he observed any one go to the parlour and look in. He protested till he was nearly blue with rage (for he regarded it as Sam's invention), that such a thing never took place, that no one whatever went near the parlour-door.

Next came up the question of the guinea, which was hanging from his watch-guard, shining and bold as if it had been brass. Sam had been questioned about this by the justices on Thursday, and his statement in answer to them was just as bold as the coin.

The guinea had been given him by his late father's uncle, old Thomas Dene, who had jokingly enjoined him never to change it, always to keep it by him, and then he would never be without money. Sam had kept it; kept it from that time to this. He kept it in the pocket of an old-fashioned leather case, which contained some letters from his father, and two or three other things he valued. No, he was not in the habit of getting the guinea out to look at, he had retorted to a little badgering; had not looked at it (or at the case either, which lay in the bottom of his trunk) for months and months—yes, it might be years, for all he recollected. But on the Tuesday evening, when talking with Miss Parslet about guineas, he fetched it to show to her; and slipped it into his pocket afterwards, where, the police found it on the Thursday. This was the substance of his first answer, and he repeated it now.

"Do you know who is said to be the father of lies, young man?" asked Justice Whitewicker in a solemn tone, suspecting that the prisoner was telling an out-and-out fable.

"I have heard," answered Sam. "Have never seen him myself. Perhaps you have, sir." At which a titter went round the court, and it put his worship's back up. Sam went on to say that he had often thought of taking his guinea into wear, and had now done it. And he gave the guinea a flick in the face of us all.

Evidently little good could come of a hardened criminal like this; and Justice Whitewicker, who thought nothing on earth so grand as the sound of his own voice from the bench, gave Sam a piece of his mind. In the midst of this a stir arose at the appearance of Maria Parslet. Mr. Chance led her in; her father, sad and shrinking as usual, walked behind them. Lawyer Cockermuth—and I liked him for it—made a place for his clerk next to himself. Maria looked modest, gentle and pretty. She wore black silk, being in slight mourning, and a dainty white bonnet.

Mr. Dene was asked to take tea with them in the parlour on the Tuesday evening, as a matter of convenience, Maria's evidence ran, in answer to questions, and she briefly alluded to the reason why. Whilst waiting together, he and she, for her father to come in, Mr. Dene told her of the finding of the ebony box of guineas at Mr. Cockermuth's. She laughingly remarked that a guinea was an out-of-date coin now, and she was not sure that she had ever seen one. In reply to that, Mr. Dene said he had one by him, given him by an old uncle some years before; and he went upstairs and brought it down to show to her. There could be no mistake, Maria added to Mr. Whitewicker, who wanted to insinuate a word of doubt, and her sweet brown eyes were honest and true as she said it; she had touched the guinea and held it in her hand for some moments.

"Held it and touched it, did you, Miss Parslet?" retorted Lawyer Standup. "Pray what appearance had it?"

"It was a thin, worn coin, sir," replied Maria; "thinner, I think, than a sovereign, but somewhat larger; it seemed to be worn thin at the edge."

"Whose image was on it?—what king's?"

"George the Third's. I noticed that."

"Now don't you think, young lady, that the accused took this marvellous coin from his pocket, instead of from some receptacle above stairs?" went on Mr. Standup.

"I am quite sure he did not take it from his pocket when before me," answered Maria. "He ran upstairs quickly, saying he would fetch the guinea: he had nothing in his hands then."

Upon this Lawyer Chance inquired of his learned brother why he need waste time in useless questions; begging to remind him that it was not until Wednesday morning the box disappeared, so the prisoner could not well have had any of its contents about him on Tuesday.

"Just let my questions alone, will you," retorted Mr. Standup, with a nod. "I know what I am about. Now, Miss Parslet, please attend to me. Was the guinea you profess to have seen a perfect coin, or was there a hole in it?"

"It was a perfect coin, sir."

"And what became of it?"

"I think Mr. Dene put it in his waistcoat-pocket: I did not particularly notice. Quite close upon that, my father came home, and we sat down to tea. No, sir, nothing was said to my father about the guinea; if it was, I did not hear it. But he and Mr. Dene talked of the box of guineas that had been found."

"Who was it that called while you were at tea?"

"Young Mr. Chance called. We had finished tea then, and Mr. Dene took him upstairs to his own sitting-room."

"I am not asking you about young Mr. Chance; we shall come to him presently," was the rough-toned, but not ill-natured retort. "Somebody else called: who was it?"

Maria, blushing and paling ever since she stood up to the ordeal, grew white now. Mr. Badger had called at the door, she answered, and Mr. Dene went out to speak to him. Worried by Lawyer Standup as to whether he did not come to ask for money, she said she believed so, but she did not hear all they said.

Quiet Mr. Parslet was the next witness. He had to acknowledge that he did hear it. Mr. Badger appeared to be pressing for some money owing to him; could not tell the amount, knew nothing about that. When questioned whether the accused owed him money, Parslet said not a shilling; Mr. Dene had never sought to borrow of him, and had paid his monthly accounts regularly.

Upon that, Mr. Badger was produced; a thin man with a neck as stiff as a poker; who gave his reluctant testimony in a sweet tone of benevolence. Mr. Dene had been borrowing money from him for some time; somewhere about twenty pounds, he thought, was owing now, including interest. He had repeatedly asked for its repayment, but only got put off with (as he believed) lame excuses. Had certainly gone to ask for it on the Tuesday evening; was neither loud nor angry, oh dear, no; but did tell the accused he thought he could give him some if he would, and did say that he must have a portion of it within a week, or he should apply to Mr. Jacobson, of Elm Farm. Did not really mean to apply to Mr. Jacobson, had no wish to do any one an injury, but felt vexed at the young man's off-handedness, which looked like indifference. Knew besides that Mr. Dene had other debts.

Now I'll leave you to judge how this evidence struck on the ears of old Jacobson. He leaped to the conclusion that Sam had been going all sorts of ways, as he supposed he went when in London, and might be owing, the mischief only knew how much money; and he shook his fist at Sam across the justice-room.

Mr. Standup next called young Chance, quite to young Chance's surprise; perhaps also to his father's. He was questioned upon no end of things—whether he did not know that the accused was owing a great deal of money, and whether the accused had shown any guinea to him when he was in Edgar Street on the Tuesday night. Austin answered that he believed Mr. Dene owed a little money, not a great deal, so far as he knew; and that he had not seen the guinea or heard of it. And in saying all this, Austin's tone was just as resentfully insolent to Mr. Standup as he dared to make it.

Well, it is of no use to go on categorically with the day's proceedings. When they came to an end, the magistrates conferred pretty hotly in a low tone amongst themselves, some apparently taking up one opinion, as to Sam's guilt, or innocence, and some the other. At length they announced their decision, and it was as follows.

"Although the case undoubtedly presents grave grounds of suspicion against the accused, Samson Reginald Dene—'Very grave indeed,' interjected Mr. Whitewicker, solemnly—we do not consider them to be sufficient to commit him for trial upon; therefore, we give him the benefit of the doubt, and discharge him. Should any further evidence transpire, he can be brought up again."

"It was Maria Parslet's testimony about the guinea that cleared him," whispered the crowd, as they filed out.

And I think it must have been. It was just impossible to doubt her truth, or the earnestness with which she gave it.

Mr. Jacobson "interviewed" Sam, as the Americans say, and the interview was not a loving one. Being in the mood, he said anything that came uppermost. He forbade Sam to appear at Elm Farm ever again, as "long as oak and ash grew;" and he added that as Sam was bent on going to the deuce head foremost, he might do it upon his own means, but that he'd never get any more help from him.

The way the Squire lashed up Bob and Blister when driving home—for, liking Sam hitherto, he was just as much put out as old Jacobson—and the duet they kept together in abuse of his misdeeds, was edifying to hear. Tod laughed; I did not. The gig was given over this return journey to the two grooms.

"I do not believe Sam took the box, sir," I said to old Jacobson, interrupting a fiery oration.

He turned round to stare at me. "What do you say, Johnny Ludlow? You do not believe he took the box?"

"Well, to me it seems quite plain that he did not take it. I've hardly ever felt more sure of anything."

"Plain!" struck in the Squire. "How is it plain, Johnny? What grounds do you go upon?"

"I judge by his looks and his tones, sir, when denying it. They are to be trusted."

They did not know whether to laugh or scoff at me. It was Johnny's way, said the Squire; always fancying he could read the riddles in a man's face and voice. But they'd have thrown up their two best market-going hats with glee to be able to think it true.

V

Samson Reginald Dene was relieved of the charge, as it was declared "not proven;" all the same, Samson Reginald Dene was ruined. Worcester said so. During the following week, which was Passion Week, its citizens talked more of him than of their prayers.

Granted that Maria Parslet's testimony had been honestly genuine, a theory cropped up to counteract it. Lawyer Standup had been bold enough to start it at the Saturday's examination: a hundred tongues were repeating it now. Sam Dene, as may be remembered, was present at the finding of the box on Tuesday; he had come up the passage and touched the golden guineas in it with the tips of his fingers; those fingers might have deftly extracted one of the coins. No wonder he could show it to Maria when he went home to tea! Captain Cockermuth admitted that in counting the guineas subsequently he had thought he counted sixty; but, as he knew there were (or ought to be) that number in the box, probably the assumption misled him, causing him to reckon them as sixty when in fact there were only fifty-nine. Which was a bit of logic.

Still, popular opinion was divided. If part of the town judged Sam to be guilty, part believed him to be innocent. A good deal might be said on both sides. To a young man who does not know how to pay his debts from lack of means, and debts that he is afraid of, too, sixty golden guineas may be a great temptation; and people did not shut their eyes to that. It transpired also that Mr. Jacobson, his own uncle, his best friend, had altogether cast Sam off and told him he might now go to the dogs his own way.

Sam resented it all bitterly, and defied the world. Far from giving in or showing any sense of shame, he walked about with an air, his head up, and that brazen guinea dangling in front of him. He actually had the face to appear at college on Good Friday (the congregation looking askance at him), and sat out the cold service of the day: no singing, no organ, and the little chorister-boys in black surplices instead of white ones.

But the crowning act of boldness was to come. Before Easter week had lapsed into the past, Sam Dene had taken two rooms in a conspicuous part of the town and set-up in practice. A big brass plate on the outer door displayed his name: "Mr. Dene, Attorney-at-law." Sam's friends extolled his courage; Sam's enemies were amazed at his impudence. Captain Cockermuth prophesied that the ceiling of that office would come tumbling down on its crafty occupant's head: it was his gold that was paying for it.

The Cockermuths, like the town, were divided in opinion. Mr. Cockermuth could not believe Sam guilty, although the mystery as to where the box could be puzzled him as few things had ever puzzled him in this life. He would fain have taken Sam back again, had it been a right thing to do. What the captain thought need not be enlarged upon. While Miss Betty felt uncertain; veering now to this belief, now to that, and much distressed either way.

There is one friend in this world that hardly ever deserts us—and that is a mother. Mrs. Dene, a pretty little woman yet, had come flying to Worcester, ready to fight everybody in it on her son's behalf. Sam of course made his own tale good to her; whether it was a true one or not he alone knew, but not an angel from heaven could have stirred her faith in it. She declared that, to her positive knowledge, the old uncle had given Sam the guinea.

It was understood to be Mrs. Dene who advanced the money to Sam to set up with; it was certainly Mrs. Dene who bought a shutting-up bed (at old Ward's), and a gridiron, and a tea-pot, and a three-legged table, and a chair or two, all for the back-room of the little office, that Sam might go into housekeeping on his own account, and live upon sixpence a-day, so to say, until business came in. To look at Sam's hopeful face, he meant to do it, and to live down the scandal.

Looking at the thing impartially, one might perhaps see that Sam was not swayed by impudence in setting-up, so much as by obligation. For what else lay open to him?—no firm would engage him as clerk with that doubt sticking to his coat-tails. He paid some of his debts, and undertook to pay the rest before the year was out. A whisper arose that it was Mrs. Dene who managed this. Sam's adversaries knew better; the funds came out of the ebony box: that, as Charles Cockermuth demonstrated, was as sure as heaven.

But now there occurred one thing that I, Johnny Ludlow, could not understand, and never shall: why Worcester should have turned its back, like an angry drake, upon Maria Parslet. The school, where she was resident teacher, wrote her a cool, polite note, to say she need not trouble herself to return after the Easter recess. That example was followed. Pious individuals looked upon her as a possible story-teller, in danger of going to the bad in Sam's defence, nearly as much as Sam had gone.

It was just a craze. Even Charles Cockermuth said there was no sense in blaming Maria: of course Sam had deceived her (when pretending to show the guinea as his own), just as he deceived other people. Next the town called her "bold" for standing up in the face and eyes of the Guildhall to give her evidence. But how could Maria help that? It was not her own choice: she'd rather have locked herself up in the cellar. Lawyer Chance had burst in upon her that Saturday morning (not ten minutes after we left the house), giving nobody warning, and carried her off imperatively, never saying "Will you, or Won't you." It was not his way.

Placid Miss Betty was indignant when the injustice came to her ears. What did people mean by it? she wanted to know. She sent for Maria to spend the next Sunday in Foregate Street, and marched with her arm-in-arm to church (St. Nicholas'), morning and evening.

As the days and the weeks passed, commotion gave place to a calm; Sam and his delinquencies were let alone. One cannot be on the grumble for ever. Sam's lines were pretty hard; practice held itself aloof from him; and if he did not live upon the sixpence a-day, he looked at every halfpenny that he had to spend beyond it. His face grew thin, his blue eyes wistful, but he smiled hopefully.

"You keep up young Dene's acquaintance, I perceive," remarked Lawyer Chance to his son one evening as they were finishing dinner, for he had met the two young men together that day.

"Yes: why shouldn't I?" returned Austin.

"Think that charge was a mistaken one, I suppose?"

"Well I do, father. He has affirmed it to me in terms so unmistakable that I can but believe him. Besides, I don't think Dene, as I have always said, is the sort of fellow to turn rogue: I don't, indeed."

"Does he get any practice?"

"Very little, I'm afraid."

Mr. Chance was a man with a conscience. On the whole, he felt inclined to think Sam had not helped himself to the guineas, but he was by no means sure of it: like Miss Betty Cockermuth, his opinion veered, now on this side, now on that, like a haunted weathercock. If Sam was not guilty, why, then, Fate had dealt hardly with the young fellow—and what would the end be? These thoughts were running through the lawyer's mind as he talked to his son and sat playing with his bunch of seals, which hung down by a short, thick gold chain, in the old-fashioned manner.

"I should like to say a word to him if he'd come to me," he suddenly cried. "You might go and bring him, Austin."

"What—this evening?" exclaimed Austin.

"Ay; why not? One time's as good as another."

Austin Chance started off promptly for the new office, and found his friend presiding over his own tea-tray in the little back-room; the loaf and butter on the table, and a red herring on the gridiron.

"Hadn't time to get any dinner to-day; too busy," was Sam's apology, given briefly with a flush of the face. "Mr. Chance wants me? Well, I'll come. What is it for?"

"Don't know," replied Austin. And away they went.

The lawyer was standing at the window, his hands in the pockets of his pepper-and-salt trousers, tinkling the shillings and sixpences there. Austin supposed he was not wanted, and shut them in.

"I have been thinking of your case a good bit lately, Sam Dene," began Mr. Chance, giving Sam a seat and sitting down himself; "and I should like to feel, if I can, more at a certainty about it, one way or the other."

"Yes, sir," replied Sam. And you must please to note that manners in those days had not degenerated to what they are in these. Young men, whether gentle or simple, addressed their elders with respect;

young women also. "Yes, sir," replied Sam. "But what do you mean about wishing to feel more at a certainty?"

"When I defended you before the magistrates, I did my best to convince them that you were not guilty: you had assured me you were not: and they discharged you. I believe my arguments and my pleadings went some way with them."

"I have no doubt of it, sir, and I thanked you at the time with all my heart," said Sam warmly. "Some of my enemies were bitter enough against me."

"But you should not speak in that way—calling people your enemies!" reproved the lawyer. "People were only at enmity with you on the score of the offence. Look here, Sam Dene—did you commit it, or did you not?"

Sam stared. Mr. Chance had dropped his voice to a solemn key, his head was pushed forward, gravity sat on his face.

"No, sir. No."

The short answer did not satisfy the lawyer. "Did you filch that box of guineas out of Cockermuth's room; or were you, and are you, as you assert, wholly innocent?" he resumed. "Tell me the truth as before Heaven. Whatever it be, I will shield you still."

Sam rose. "On my sacred word, sir, and before Heaven, I have told nothing but the truth. I did not take or touch the box of guineas. I do not know what became of it."

Mr. Chance regarded Sam in silence. He had known young men, when under a cloud, prevaricate in a most extraordinary and unblushing manner: to look at them and listen to them, one might have said they were fit to be canonized. But he thought truth lay with Sam now.

"Sit down, sit down, Dene," he said. "I am glad to believe you. Where the deuce could the box have got to? It could not take flight through the ceiling up to the clouds, or down to the earth through the floor. Whose hands took it?"

"The box went in one of two ways," returned Sam. "If the captain did not fetch it out unconsciously, and lose it in the street, why, somebody must have entered the parlour after I left it and carried off the box. Perhaps the individual who looked into the room when I was sitting there."

"A pity but you had noticed who that was."

"Yes, it is. Look here, Mr. Chance; a thought has more than once struck me—if that person did not come back and take the box, why has he not come forward openly and honestly to avow it was himself who looked in?"

The lawyer gave his head a dissenting shake. "It is a ticklish thing to be mixed up in, he may think, one that he had best keep out of—though he may be innocent as the day. How are you getting on?" he asked, passing abruptly from the subject.

"Oh, middling," replied Sam. "As well, perhaps, as I could expect to get on at first, with all the prejudice abroad against me."

"Earning bread-and-cheese?"

"Not quite—yet."

"Well, see here, Dene—and this is what I chiefly sent for you to say, if you could assure me on your conscience you deserved it—I may be able to put some little business in your hands. Petty matters are brought to us that we hardly care to waste time upon: I'll send them to you in future. I dare say you'll be able to rub on by dint of patience. Rome was not built in a day, you know."

"Thank you, sir; I thank you very truly," breathed Sam. "Mr. Cockermuth sent me a small matter the other day. If I can make a bare living of it at present, that's all I ask. Fame and fortune are not rained down upon black sheep."

Which was so true a remark as to need no contradiction.

May was nearing its close then, and the summer evenings were long and lovely. As Sam went forth from the interview, he thought he would take a walk by the river, instead of turning in to his solitary rooms. Since entering upon them he had been as steady as old Time: the accusation and its attendant shame seemed to have converted him from a heedless, youthful man into a wise old sage of age and care. Passing down Broad Street towards the bridge, he turned to the left and sauntered along beside the Severn. The water glittered in the light of the setting sun; barges, some of them bearing men and women and children, passed smoothly up and down on it; the opposite fields, towards St. John's, were green as an emerald: all things seemed to wear an aspect of brightness.

All on a sudden things grew brighter—and Sam's pulses gave a leap. He had passed the grand old red-stoned wall that enclosed the Bishop's palace, and was close upon the gates leading up to the Green, when a young lady turned out of them and came towards him with a light, quick step. It was Maria Parslet, in a pretty summer muslin, a straw hat shading her blushing face. For it did blush furiously at sight of Sam.

"Mr. Dene!"

"Maria!"

She began to say, hurriedly, that her mother had sent her with a message to the dressmaker on the Parade, and she had taken that way, as being the shortest—as if in apology for having met Sam.

He turned with her, and they paced slowly along side by side, the colour on Maria's cheeks coming and going with every word he spoke and every look he gave her—which seemed altogether senseless and unreasonable. Sam told her of his conversation with Austin Chance's father, and his promise to put a few things in his way.

"Once let me be making two hundred a-year, Maria, and then—"

"Then what?" questioned Maria innocently.

"Then I should ask you to come to me, and we'd risk it together."

"Risk what?" stammered Maria, turning her head right round to watch a barge that was being towed by.

"Risk our luck. Two hundred a-year is not so bad to begin upon. I should take the floor above as well as the ground-floor I rent now, and we should get along. Any way, I hope to try it."

"Oh, Mr. Dene!"

"Now don't 'Mr. Dene' me, young lady, if you please. Why, Maria, what else can we do? A mean, malicious set of dogs and cats have turned their backs upon us both; the least we should do is to see if we can't do without them. I know you'd rather come to me than stay in Edgar Street."

Maria held her tongue, as to whether she would or not. "Mamma is negotiating to get me a situation at Cheltenham," she said.

"You will not go to Cheltenham, or anywhere else, if I get any luck," he replied dictatorially. "Life would look very blue to me now without you, Maria. And many a man and wife, rolling in riches at the end, have rubbed on with less than two hundred a-year at the beginning. I wouldn't say, mind, but we might risk it on a hundred and fifty. My rent is low, you see."

"Ye—es," stammered Maria "But—I wish that mystery of the guineas could be cleared up!"

Sam stood still, turned, and faced her. "Why do you say that? You are not suspecting that I took them?"

"Oh dear, NO," returned Maria, losing her breath. "I know you did not take them: could not. I was only thinking of your practice: so much more would come in."

"Cockermuth has sent me a small matter or two. I think I shall get on," repeated Sam.

They were at their journey's end by that time, at the dressmaker's door. "Good-evening," said Maria, timidly holding out her hand.

Sam Dene took it and clasped it. "Good-bye, my darling. I am going home to my bread-and-cheese supper, and I wish you were there to eat it with me!"

Maria sighed. She wondered whether that wonderful state of things would ever come to pass. Perhaps no; perhaps yes. Meanwhile no living soul knew aught of these treasonable aspirations; they were a secret between her and Sam. Mr. and Mrs. Parslet suspected nothing.

Time went on. Lawyer Chance was as good as his word, and put a few small matters of business into the hands of Sam Dene. Mr. Cockermuth did the same. The town came down upon him for it; though it let Chance alone, who was not the sort of man to be dictated to. "Well," said Cockermuth in answer, "I don't believe the lad is guilty; never have believed it. Had he been of a dishonest turn, he could have helped himself before, for a good deal of my cash passed at times through his hands. And, given that he was innocent, he has been hardly dealt by."

Sam Dene was grateful for these stray windfalls, and returned his best thanks to the lawyers for them. But they did not amount to much in the aggregate; and a gloomy vision began to present itself to his apprehension of being forced to give up the struggle, and wandering out in the world to seek a better fortune. The summer assizes drew near. Sam had no grand cause to come on at them, or small one either; but it was impossible not to give a thought now and again to what his fate might have been, had he stood committed to take his trial at them. The popular voice said that was only what he merited.

VI

The assizes were held, and passed. One hot day, when July was nearing its meridian, word was brought to Miss Cockermuth—who was charitable—that a poor sick woman whom she befriended, was worse than usual, so she put on her bonnet and cloak to pay her a visit. The bonnet was a huge Leghorn, which shaded her face well from the sun, its trimming of straw colour; and the cloak was of thin black "taffeta," edged with narrow lace. It was a long walk on a hot afternoon, for the sick woman lived but just on this side Henwick. Miss Betty had got as far as the bridge, and was about to cross it when Sam Dene, coming over it at a strapping pace, ran against her.

"Miss Betty!" he cried. "I beg your pardon."

Miss Betty brought her bonnet from under the shade of her large grass-green parasol. "Dear me, is it you, Sam Dene?" she said. "Were you walking for a wager?"

Sam laughed a little. "I was hastening back to my office, Miss Betty. I have no clerk, you know, and a client might come in."

Miss Betty gave her head a twist, something between a nod and a shake; she noticed the doubtful tone in the "might." "Very hot, isn't it?" said she. "I'm going up to see that poor Hester Knowles; she's uncommon bad, I hear."

"You'll have a warm walk."

"Ay. Are you pretty well, Sam? You look thin."

"Do I? Oh, that's nothing but the heat of the weather. I am quite well, thank you. Good-afternoon, Miss Betty."

She shook his hand heartily. One of Sam's worst enemies, who might have run in a curricle with Charles Cockermuth, as to an out-and-out belief in his guilt, was passing at the moment, and saw it.

Miss Betty crossed the bridge, turned off into Turkey, for it was through those classical regions that her nearest and coolest way lay, and so onwards to the sick woman's room. There she found the blazing July sun streaming in at the wide window, which had no blind, no shelter whatever from it. Miss Betty had had enough of the sun out-of-doors, without having it in. Done up with the walk and the heat, she sat down on the first chair, and felt ready to swoon right off.

"Dear me, Hester, this is bad for you!" she gasped.

"Did you mean the sun, ma'am?" asked the sick woman, who was sitting full in it, wrapped in a blanket or two. "It is a little hot just now, but I don't grumble at it; I'm so cold mostly. As soon as the sun goes off the window, I shall begin to shiver."

"Well-a-day!" responded Miss Betty, wishing she could be cool enough to shiver. "But if you feel it cold now, Hester, what will you do when the autumn winds come on?"

"Ah, ma'am, please do not talk of it! I just can't tell what I shall do. That window don't fit tight, and the way the wind pours in through it upon me as I sit here at evening, or lie in my little bed there, passes belief. I'm coughing always then."

"You should have some good thick curtains put up," said Miss Betty, gazing at the bare window, which had a pot of musk on its sill. "Woollen ones."

The sick woman smiled sadly. She was very poor now, though it had not always been so; she might as well have hoped to buy the sun itself as woollen curtains—or cotton curtains either. Miss Betty knew that.

"I'll think about it, Hester, and see if I've any old ones that I could let you have. I'm not sure; but I'll look," repeated she—and began to empty her capacious dimity pockets of a few items of good things she had brought.

By-and-by, when she was a little cooler, and had talked with Hester, Miss Betty set off home again, her mind running upon the half-promised curtains. "They are properly shabby," thought she, as she went along, "but they'll serve to keep the sun and the wind off her."

She was thinking of those warm green curtains that she had picked the braid from that past disastrous morning—as the reader heard of, and all the town as well. Nothing had been done with them since.

Getting home, Miss Betty turned into the parlour. Susan—who had not yet found leisure to fix any time for her wedding—found her mistress fanning her hot face, her bonnet untied and tilted back.

"I've been to see that poor Hester Knowles, Susan," began Miss Betty.

"Law, ma'am!" interposed Susan. "What a walk for you this scorching afternoon! All up that wide New Road!"

"You may well say that, girl: but I went Turkey away. She's very ill, poor thing; and that's a frightfully staring window of hers, the sun on it like a blazing fire, and not as much as a rag for a blind; and the window don't fit, she says, and in cold weather the biting wind comes in and shivers her up. I think I might give her those shabby old curtains, Susan—that were up in Mr. Philip's room, you know, before we got the new chintz ones in."

"So you might, ma'am," said Susan, who was not a bad-hearted girl, excepting to the baker's man. "They can't go up at any of our windows as they be; and if you had 'em dyed, I don't know as they'd answer much, being so shabby."

"I put them—let me see—into the spare ottoman, didn't I? Yes, that was it. And there I suppose they must be lying still."

"Sure enough, Miss Betty," said Susan. "I've not touched 'em."

"Nor I," said Miss Betty. "With all the trouble that got into our house at that time, I couldn't give my mind to seeing after the old things, and I've not thought about them since. Come upstairs with me now, Susan; we'll see what sort of a state they are in."

They went up; and Miss Betty took off her bonnet and cloak and put her cap on. The spare ottoman, soft, and red, and ancient, used as a receptacle for odds and ends that were not wanted, stood in a spacious linen-closet on the first-floor landing. It was built out over the back-door, and had a skylight above. Susan threw back the lid of the ottoman, and Miss Betty stood by. The faded old brown curtains, green once, lay in a heap at one end, just as Miss Betty had hastily flung them in that past day in March, when on her way to look at the chintzes.

"They're in a fine rabble, seemingly," observed Susan, pausing to regard the curtains.

"Dear me!" cried Miss Betty, conscience-stricken, for she was a careful housewife, "I let them drop in any way, I remember. I did mean to have them well shaken out-of-doors and properly folded, but that bother drove it all out of my head. Take them out, girl."

Susan put her strong arms underneath the heap and lifted it out with a fling. Something heavy flew out of the curtains, and dropped on the boarded floor with a crash. Letting fall the curtains, Susan gave a wild shriek of terror and Miss Betty gave a wilder, for the floor was suddenly covered with shining gold coins. Mr. Cockermuth, passing across the passage below at the moment, heard the cries, wondered whether the house was on fire, and came hastening up.

"Oh," said he coolly, taking in the aspect of affairs. "So the thief was you, Betty, after all!"

He picked up the ebony box, and bent his head to look at the guineas. Miss Betty sank down on a three-legged stool—brought in for Philip's children—and grew as white as death.

Yes, it was the missing box of guineas, come to light in the same extraordinary and unexpected manner that it had come before, without having been (as may be said) truly lost. When Miss Betty gathered her curtains off the dining-room table that March morning, a cumbersome and weighty heap, she had unwittingly gathered up the box with them. No wonder Sam Dene had not seen the box on the table after Miss Betty's departure! It was a grievous misfortune, though, that he failed to take notice it was not there.

She had no idea she was not speaking truth in saying she saw the box on the table as she left the room. Having seen the box there all the morning she thought it was there still, and that she saw it, being quite unconscious that it was in her arms. Susan, too, had noticed the box on the table when she opened the door to call her mistress, and believed she was correct in saying she saw it there to the last: the real fact being that she had not observed it was gone. So there the box with its golden freight had lain undisturbed, hidden in the folds of the curtains. But for Hester Knowles's defective window, it might have stayed there still, who can say how long?

Susan, no less scared than her mistress, stood back against the closet wall for safety, out of reach of those diabolical coins; Miss Betty, groaning and half-fainting on the three-legged stool, sat pushing back her cap and her front. The lawyer picked up the guineas and counted them as he laid them flat in the box. Sixty of them: not one missing. So Sam's guinea was his own! He had not, as Worcester whispered, trumped up the story with Maria Parslet.

"John," gasped poor Miss Betty, beside herself with remorse and terror, "John, what will become of me now? Will anything be done?"

"How 'done'?" asked he.

"Will they bring me to trial—or anything of that—in poor Sam's place?"

"Well, I don't know," answered her brother grimly; "perhaps not this time. But I'd have you take more care in future, Betty, than to hide away gold in old curtains."

Locking the box securely within his iron safe, Mr. Cockermuth put on his hat and went down to the town hall, where the magistrates, after dispensing their wisdom, were about to disperse for the day. He told them of the wonderful recovery of the box of guineas, of how it had been lost, and that Sam Dene was wholly innocent. Their worships were of course charmed to hear it, Mr. Whitewicker observing that they had only judged Sam by appearances, and that appearances had been sufficient (in theory) to hang him.

From the town hall, Mr. Cockermuth turned off to Sam's office. Sam was making a great show of business, surrounded by a tableful of imposing parchments, but with never a client to the fore. His old master grasped his hand.

"Well, Sam, my boy," he said, "the tables have turned for you. That box of guineas is found."

Sam never spoke an answering word. His lips parted with expectation: his breath seemed to be a little short.

"Betty had got it all the time. She managed somehow to pick it up off the table with those wretched old curtains she had there, all unconsciously, of course, and it has lain hidden with the curtains upstairs in a lumber-box ever since. Betty will never forgive herself. She'll have a fit of the jaundice over this."

Sam drew a long breath. "You will let the public know, sir?"

"Ay, Sam, without loss of an hour. I've begun with the magistrates—and a fine sensation the news made amidst 'em, I can tell you; and now I'm going round to the newspapers; and I shall go over to Elm Farm the first thing to-morrow. The town took up the cause against you, Sam: take care it does not eat you now in its repentance. Look here, you'll have to come round to Betty, or she'll moan her heart out: you won't bear malice, Sam?"

"No, that I won't," said Sam warmly. "Miss Betty did not bear it to me. She has been as kind as can be all along."

The town did want to eat Sam. It is the custom of the true Briton to go to extremes. Being unable to shake Sam's hands quite off, the city would fain have chaired him round the streets with honours, as it used to chair its newly returned members.

Captain Cockermuth, sent for post haste, came to Worcester all contrition, beseeching Sam to forgive him fifty times a-day, and wanting to press the box of guineas upon him as a peace-offering. Sam would not take it: he laughingly told the captain that the box did not seem to carry luck with it.

And then Sam's troubles were over. And no objection was made by his people (as it otherwise might have been) to his marrying Maria Parslet, by way of recompense. "God never fails to bring good out of evil, my dear," said old Mrs. Jacobson to Maria, the first time they had her on a visit at Elm Farm. As to Sam, he had short time for Elm Farm, or anything else in the shape of recreation. Practice was flowing in quickly: litigants arguing, one with another, that a young man, lying for months under an imputation of theft, and then coming out of it with flying colours, must needs be a clever lawyer.

"But, Johnny," Sam said to me, when talking of the past, "there's one thing I would alter if I made the laws. No person, so long as he is only suspected of crime, should have his name proclaimed publicly. I am not speaking of murder, you understand, or charges of that grave nature; but of such a case as mine. My name appeared in full, in all the local newspapers, Samson Reginald Dene, coupled with theft, and of course it got a mark upon it. It is an awful blight upon a man when he is innocent, one that he may never quite live down. Suspicions must arise, I know that, of the innocent as well as the guilty, and they must undergo preliminary examinations in public and submit to legal inquiries: but time enough to proclaim who the man is when evidence strengthens against him, and he is committed for trial; until then let his name be suppressed. At least that is my opinion."

And it is mine as well as Sam's.

OUR FIRST TERM AT OXFORD

I

It was Friday night at the Oxford terminus, and all the world scrambling for cabs. Sir John and the Squire, nearly lifted off their legs, and too much taken aback to fight for themselves, stood against the wall, thinking the community had gone suddenly mad. Bill Whitney and Tod, tall, strong young fellows, able to hold their own anywhere, secured a cab at length, and we and our luggage got in and on it.

"To the Mitre."

"If this is a specimen of Oxford manners, the sooner the lads are at home the better," growled the Squire. Sir John Whitney was settling his spectacles on his nose—nearly lost off it in the scuffle.

"Snepp told me it was a regular shindy at the terminus the first day of term, with all the students coming back," said Bill Whitney.

There had been no end of discussion as to our college career. Sir John Whitney said William must go to Oxford, as he had been at Oxford himself; whereas Brandon stood out against Oxford for me; would not hear of it. He preferred Cambridge he said: and to Cambridge Johnny Ludlow should go: and he, as my guardian, had full power over me. The Squire cared not which university was chosen; but Tod went in for Oxford with all his strong will: he said the boating was best there. The result was that Mr. Brandon gave way, and we were entered at Christchurch.

Mr. Brandon had me at his house for two days beforehand, giving me counsel. He had one of his bad colds just then and kept his room, and his voice was never more squeaky. The last evening, I sat up there with him while he sipped his broth. The fire was large enough to roast us, and he had three flannel night-caps on. It was that night that he talked to me most. He believed with all his heart, he said, that the temptations to young men were greater at Oxford than at Cambridge; that, of the two, the more reckless set of men were there: and that was one of the reasons why he had objected to Oxford for me. And then he proceeded to put the temptations pretty strongly before me, and did not mince things, warning me that it would require all the mental and moral strength I possessed to resist them, and steer clear of a course of sin and shame. He then suddenly opened the Bible, which was on the table at his elbow, and read out a line or two from the thirtieth chapter of Deuteronomy.

"'See, I have set before you this day life and good, and death and evil: therefore choose life, that both thou and thy seed may live.'"

"That's what I have been striving to set before you, Johnny Ludlow. Read that chapter, the whole of it, often; treasure its precepts in your heart; and may God give you grace to keep them!"

He shook hands with me in silence. I took up my candle and waited a moment, for I thought he was going to speak again.

"Will you try to keep them, lad?"

"I will try, sir."

We were fortunate in getting good rooms at Christchurch. Tod's and mine were close together; Bill Whitney's on the floor above. Our sitting-room was pleasant; it had an old cracked piano in it, which turned out to be passably fair when it had been tinkered and tuned. The windows looked out on the trees of the Broad Walk and to the meadows beyond; but trees are bare in winter, and the month was January. I had never stayed at Oxford before: and I saw that I should like it, with its fine, grand old colleges. The day after we got there, Saturday, we wrote our names in the dean's book, and saw our tutor. The rest of the day was spent in seeing about battels and getting into the new ways. Very new to us. A civil young fellow, who waited on us as scout, was useful; they called him "Charley" in the college. Tod pulled a long face at some of the rules, and did not like the prospect of unlimited work.

"I'll go in for the boating and fishing and driving, Johnny; and you can go in for the books."

"All right, Tod." I knew what he meant. It was not that he did not intend to take a fair amount of work: but to exist without a good share of out-of-door life also, would have been hard lines for Tod.

The Sunday services were beautiful. The first Sunday of term was a high day, and the cathedral was filled. Orders of admission to the public were not necessary that day, and a general congregation mixed with the students. Sir John and the Squire were staying at the Mitre until Monday. After service we went to promenade in the Broad Walk—and it seemed that everybody else went.

"Look there!" cried the Squire, "at this tall clergyman coming along. I am sure he is one of the canons of Worcester."

It was Mr. Fortescue—Honourable and Reverend. He halted for a minute to exchange greetings with Sir John Whitney, whom he knew, and then passed on his way.

"There's some pretty girls about, too," resumed the Squire, gazing around. "Not that I'd advise you boys to look much at them. Wonder if they often walk here?"

Before a week had gone by, we were quite at home; had shaken down into our new life as passengers shake down in their places in an omnibus; and made lots of friends. Some I liked; some I did not like. There was one fellow always coming in—a tall dark man with crisp hair; his name Richardson. He had plenty of money and kept dogs and horses, and seemed to go in for every kind of fast life the place afforded. Of work he did none; and report ran that he was being watched by the proctor, with whom he was generally in hot water. Altogether he was not in good odour: and he had a way of mocking at religion as though he were an atheist.

"I heard a bit about Richardson just now," cried Whitney, one morning that he had brought his commons in to breakfast with us—and the fields outside were white with snow. "Mayhew says he's a scamp."

"Don't think he's much else, myself," said Tod. "I say, just taste this butter! It's shockingly strong. Wonder what it is made of?"

"Mayhew says he's a liar as well as a villain. There's no speaking after him. Last term a miserable affair occurred in the town; the authorities could not trace it home to Richardson though they suspected he was the black sheep. Lots of fellows knew he was: but he denied it out-and-out. I think we had better not have much to do with him."

"He entertains jolly well," said Tod. "Johnny, you've boiled these eggs too hard. And his funds seem to spring from some perpetual gold mine—"

The door opened, and two bull-dogs burst in, leaping and howling. Richardson—they were his—followed, with little Ford; the latter a quiet, inoffensive man, who stuck to his work.

"Be quiet, you two devils!" cried Richardson, kicking his dogs. "Lie down, will you? I say, I've a wine-coach on to-night in my rooms, after Hall. Shall be glad to see you all at it."

Considering the conversation he had broken in upon, none of us had a very ready answer at hand.

"I have heaps of letters to answer to-night, and must do it," said Whitney. "Thank you all the same."

Richardson might have read coolness in the tone; I don't know; but he turned the back of his chair on Bill to face Tod.

"You have not letters to write, I suppose, Todhetley?"

"Not I. I leave letters to Ludlow."

"You'll come, then?"

"Can't," said Tod candidly. "Don't mean to go in for wine-parties."

"Oh," said Richardson. "You'll tell another tale when you've been here a bit longer. Will you be still, you brutes?"

"Hope I shan't," said Tod. "Wine plays the very mischief with work. Should never get any done if I went in for it."

"Do you intend to go up for honours?" went on Richardson.

"'Twould be a signal failure if I did. I leave all that to Ludlow—as I said by the letters. See to the dogs, Richardson."

The animals had struck up a fight. Richardson secured the one and sent the other out with a kick. Our scout was coming in, and the dog flew at him. No damage; but a great row.

"Charley," cried Tod, "this butter's not fit to eat."

"Is it not, sir? What's the matter with it?"

"The matter with it?—everything's the matter with it."

"Is that your scout?" asked Richardson, when the man had gone again, holding his dog between his knees as he sat.

"Yes," said Tod. "And your dogs all but made mincemeat of him. You should teach them better manners."

"Serve him right if they had. His name's Tasson."

"Tasson, is it? We call him Charley here."

"I know. He's a queer one."

"How is he queer?"

"He's pious."

"He's what?"

"Pious," repeated Richardson, twisting his mouth. "A saint; a cant; a sneak."

"Good gracious!" cried Bill Whitney.

"You think I'm jesting! Ask Ford here. Tell it, Ford."

"Oh, it's true," said Ford: "true that he goes in for piety. Last term there was a freshman here named Carstairs. He was young; rather soft; no experience, you know, and he began to go the pace. One night this Charley, his scout, fell on his knees, and besought him with tears not to go to the bad; to pull up in time and remember what the end must be; and—and so on."

"What did Carstairs do?"

"Do! why turned him out," put in Richardson. "Carstairs, by the way, has taken his name off the books, or had to take it off."

"Charley is civil and obliging to us," said Whitney. "Never presumes."

How much of the tale was gospel we knew not; but for my own part, I liked Charley. There was something about him quite different from scouts and servants in general—and by the way, I don't think Charley was a scout, only a scout's help—but in appearance and diction and manner he was really superior. A slim, slight young fellow of twenty, with straight fine light hair and blue eyes, and a round spot of scarlet on his thin cheeks.

"I say, Charley, they say you are pious," began Bill Whitney that same day after lecture, when the man was bringing in the bread-and-cheese from the buttery.

He coloured to the roots of his light hair, and did not answer. Bill never minded what he said to any one.

"You were scout to Mr. Carstairs. Did you take his morals under your special protection?"

"Be quiet, Whitney," said Tod in an undertone.

"And constitute yourself his guardian-angel-in-ordinary? Didn't you go down on your knees to him with tears and sobs, and beseech him not to go to the bad?" went on Bill.

"There's not a word of truth in it, sir. One evening when Mr. Carstairs was lying on his sofa, tired and ill—for he was beginning to lead a life that had no rest in it, hardly, day or night, a folded slip of paper was brought in from Mr. Richardson, and Mr. Carstairs bade me read it to him. It was to remind him of some appointment for the night. Mr. Carstairs was silent for a minute, and then burst out with a kind of sharp cry, painful to hear. 'By Heaven, if this goes on, they'll ruin me, body and soul! I've a great mind not to go.' I did speak then, sir; I told him he was ill, and had better stay at home; and I said that it was easy enough for him to pull up then, but that when one got too far on the down-hill path it was more difficult."

"Was that all?" cried Whitney.

"Every word, sir. I should not have spoken at all but that I had known Mr. Carstairs before we came here. Mr. Richardson made a great deal of it, and gave it quite a different colouring."

"Did Mr. Carstairs turn you away for that?" I asked of Charley; when he came back for the things, and the other two had gone out.

"Three or four days after it happened, sir, Mr. Carstairs stopped my waiting on him again. I think it was through Mr. Richardson. Mr. Carstairs had refused to go out with him the evening it occurred."

"You knew Mr. Carstairs before he came to Oxford. Where was it?"

"It was—" he hesitated, and then went on. "It was at the school he was at in London, sir. I was a junior master there."

Letting a plate fall—for I was helping to pack them, wanting the table—I stared at the fellow. "A master there and—" and a servant here, I all but said, but I stopped the words.

"Only one of the outer masters, attending daily," he went on quietly. "I taught writing and arithmetic, and English to the juniors."

"But how comes it that you are here in this post, Charley?"

"I had reasons for wishing to come to live at Oxford, sir."

"But why not have sought out something better than this?"

"I did seek, sir. But nothing of the kind was to be had, and this place offered. There's many a one, sir, falls into the wrong post in life, and can never afterwards get into the right one."

"But—do you—like this?"

"Like it, sir; no! But I make a living at it. One thing I shall be always grateful to Mr. Carstairs for: that he did not mention where he had known me. I should not like it to be talked of in the college, especially by Mr. Richardson."

He disappeared with his tray as he spoke. It sounded quite mysterious. But I took the hint, and said nothing.

The matter passed. Charley did not put on any mentorship to us, and the more we saw of him the more we liked him. But an impression gradually dawned upon us that he was not strong enough for his place. Carrying a heavy tray upstairs would set him panting like an old man, and he could not run far or fast.

One day I was hard at work, Tod and Whitney being off somewhere, driving tandem, when a queer, ugly-sounding cough kept annoying me from outside: but whether it came from dog or man I could not tell. Opening the door at last, there sat Charley on the stairs, his head resting against the wall, and his cheeks brighter than a red leaf in autumn.

"What, is it you, Charley? Where did you pick up that cough?"

"I beg your pardon, sir," said he, starting up. "I thought your rooms were empty."

"Come in till the fit's over. You are in a regular draught there. Come along," for he hesitated—"I want to shut the door."

He came in, coughing finely, and I gave him the chair by the fire. It was nothing, he said, and would soon be gone. He had caught it a day or two back in the bleak east wind: the college was draughty, and he had to be on the run out-of-doors in all sorts of weather.

"Well, you know, Charley, putting east winds and draughts aside, you don't seem to be quite up to your work here in point of strength."

"I was up to it, sir, when I took it. It's a failing in some of our family, sir, to have weak lungs. I shall be all right again, soon."

The coughing was over, and he got up to go away, evidently not liking to intrude. There was a degree of sensitiveness about him that, of itself, might have shown he was superior to his position.

"Take a good jorum of treacle-posset, Charley, at bed-time."

Spring weather came in with February. The biting cold and snow of January disappeared, and genial sunshine warmed the earth again. The first Sunday in this same February month, from my place at morning service, looking out on the townsfolk who had come in with orders, I saw a lady, very little and pretty, staring fixedly at me from afar. The face—where had I seen her face? It seemed familiar, but I could not tell how or where I had known it. A small slight face of almost an ivory white, and wide-open light blue eyes that had plenty of confidence in them.

Sophie Chalk! I should have recognized her at the first moment but for the different mode in which her hair was dressed. Wonderful hair! A vast amount of it, and made the most of. She wore it its natural colour to-day, brown, and the red tinge on it shone like burnished gold. She knew me; that was certain; and I could not help watching her. Her eyes went roving away presently, possibly in search of Tod. I stole a glance at him; but he did not appear to see her. What brought her to Oxford?

We got out of church. I took care to hold my tongue. Tod had cared for Sophie Chalk—there could be little doubt of it—as one never cares for anybody again in life: and it might be just as well—in spite of the exposé of mademoiselle's false ways and misdoings—that they did not meet. Syrens are syrens all the world over.

The day went on to a bright moonlight night. Tod and I, out for a stroll, were standing within the shade of the fine old Magdalen Tower, talking to a fellow of Trinity, when there came up a lady of delicate presence, the flowers in her bonnet exhaling a faint odour of perfume.

"I think I am not mistaken—I am sure—yes, I am sure it is Mr. Ludlow. And—surely that cannot be Mr. Todhetley?"

Tod wheeled round at the soft, false voice. The daintily gloved hand was held out to him; the fair, false face was bent close: and his own face turned red and white with emotion. I saw it even in the shade of the moonlight. Had she been strolling about to look for us? Most likely. A few moments more, and we were all three walking onwards together.

"Only fancy my position!" she gaily said. "Here am I, all forlorn, set down alone in this great town, and must take care of myself as I best can. The formidable gowns and caps frighten me."

"The gowns and caps will do you no harm—Miss Chalk," cried Tod—and he only just saved himself from saying "Sophie."

"Do you think not," she returned, touching the sleeve of her velvet jacket, as if to brush off a fly. "But I beg you will accord me my due style and title, Mr. Todhetley, and honour me accordingly. I am no longer Miss Chalk. I am Mrs. Everty."

So she had married Mr. Everty after all! She minced along between us in her silk gown, her hands in her ermine muff that looked made for a doll. At the private door of a shop in High Street she halted, rang the bell, and threw the door open.

"You will walk up and take a cup of tea with me. Nay, but you must—or I shall think you want to hold yourselves above poor little me, now you are grand Oxford men."

She went along the passage and up the stairs: there seemed no resource but to follow. In the sitting-room, which was very well furnished and looked out upon the street, a fire burned brightly; and a lamp and tea-things stood on the table.

"Where have you been?—keeping me waiting for my tea in this way! You never think of any one but yourself: never."

The querulous complaint, and thin, shrill voice came from a small dark girl who sat at the window, peering out into the lighted street. I had not forgotten the sharp-featured sallow face and the deep-set eyes. It was Mabel Smith, the poor little lame and deformed girl I had seen in Torriana Square. She really did not look much older or bigger, and she spoke as abruptly as ever.

"I remember you, Johnny Ludlow."

Mrs. Everty made the tea. Her dress, white one way, green the other, gleamed like silver in the lamplight. It had a quantity of white lace upon it: light green ribbons were twisted in her hair. "I should think it would be better to have those curtains drawn, Mabel. Your tea's ready: if you will come to it."

"But I choose to have the curtains open and I'll take my tea here," answered Mabel. "You may be going out again for hours, and what company should I have but the street? I don't like to be shut up in a strange room: I might see ghosts. Johnny Ludlow, that's a little coffee-table by the wall: if you'll put it here it will hold my cup and saucer."

I put it near her with her tea and plate of bread-and-butter.

"Won't you sit by me? I am very lonely. Those other two can talk to one another."

So I carried my cup and sat down by Mabel. The "other two," as Mabel put it, were talking and laughing. Tod was taking a lesson in tea-making from her, and she called him awkward.

"Are you living here?" I asked of Mabel under cover of the noise.

"Living here! no," she replied in her old abrupt fashion. "Do you think papa would let me be living over a shop in Oxford? My grandmamma lives near the town, and she invited me down on a visit to her. There was no one to bring me, and she said she would"—indicating Sophie—"and we came yesterday. Well, would you believe it? Grandmamma had meant next Saturday, and she could not take us in, having visitors already. I wanted to go back home; but she said she liked the look of Oxford, and she took these rooms for a week. Two guineas without fires and other extras: I call it dear. How came she to find you out, Johnny?"

"We met just now. She tells us she is Mrs. Everty now."

"Oh yes, they are married. And a nice bargain Mr. Everty has in her! Her dresses must cost twenty pounds apiece. Some of them thirty pounds! Look at the lace on that one. Mrs. Smith, papa's wife, gives her a good talking-to sometimes, telling her Mr. Everty's income won't stand it. I should think it would not!—though I fancy he has a small share in papa's business now."

"Do they live in London?"

"Oh yes, they live in London. Close to us, too! In one of the small houses in Torriana Street. She wanted to take a large house in the square like ours, but Mr. Everty was too wise."

Talking to this girl, my thoughts back in the past, I wondered whether Sophie's people had heard of the abstraction of Miss Deveen's emeralds. But it was not likely. To look at her now: watching her fascinating ease, listening to her innocent reminiscences of the time we had all spent together at Lady Whitney's, I might have supposed she had taken a dose of the waters of Lethe, and that Sophie Chalk had always been guileless as a child; an angel without wings.

"She has lost none of her impudence, Tod," I said as we went home. "In the old days, you know, we used to say she'd fascinate the hair off our heads, give her the chance. She'd wile off both ears as well now. A good thing she's married!"

Tod broke into a whistle, and went striding on.

Before the week was out, Sophie Chalk—we generally called her by the old name—had become intimate with some of the men of different colleges. Mabel Smith went to her grandmother's, and Sophie had nothing to do but exhibit her charms in the Oxford streets and entertain her friends. The time went on. Hardly an evening passed but Tod was there; Bill Whitney went sometimes; I rarely. Sophie did not fascinate me, whatever she might do by others. Sophie treated her guests to wine and spirits, and to unlimited packs of cards. Bill Whitney said one night in a joking way that he was not sure but she might be indicted for keeping a private gaming-house. Richardson was one of her frequent evening visitors, and she would let him take his bull-dogs to make a morning call. There would be betting over the cards in the evenings, and she did not attempt to object. Sophie would not play herself; she dispersed her fascinations amidst the company while they played, and sang songs at the piano—one of the best pianos to be found in Oxford. There set in a kind of furore for pretty Mrs. Everty; the men who had the entrée there went wild over her charms, and vied with each other in making her costly presents. Sophie broke into raptures of delight over each with the seeming simplicity of a child, and swept all into her capacious net.

I think it was receiving those presents that was keeping her in Oxford; or helping to keep her. Some of them were valuable. Very valuable indeed was a set of diamonds, brooch and ear-rings, that soft young calf, Gaiton, brought her; but what few brains the viscount had were clean dazzled away by Sophie's attractions: and Richardson gave her a bejewelled fan that must have cost a small fortune. If Sophie Chalk did spend her husband's money, she was augmenting her stock of precious stones—and she had not lost her passion for them.

One morning my breakfast was brought in by a strange fellow, gloomy and grim. Tod had gone to breakfast with Mayhew.

"Where's Charley?" I asked.

"Sick," was the short answer.

"What's the matter with him?"

"Down with a cold, or something."

And we had this surly servant for ever so long to come: and I'm sorry to say got so accustomed to seeing his face as to forget sick Charley.

II

"Will you go up the river for a row, Johnny?"

"I don't mind if I do."

The questioner was Bill Whitney; who had come in to look for Tod. I had nothing particular on hand that afternoon, and the skies were blue and the sun golden. So we went down to the river together.

"Where has Tod got to?" he asked.

"Goodness knows. I've not seen him since lecture this morning."

We rowed up to Godstowe. Bill disappeared with some friend of his from Merton's, who had watched us put in. I strolled about. Every one knows the dark pool of water there. On the bench under the foliage, so thick in summer, but bare yet in this early season, warm and sunny though it was, sat a man wrapped in a great-coat, whom I took at first to be a skeleton with painted cheeks. But one does not care to stare at skeletons, knowing they'd help their looks if they could; and I was passing him with my face turned the other way.

"Good-afternoon, sir."

I turned at the hollow words—hollow in sound as though they came out of a drum. It was Charley: the red paint on his thin cheeks was nothing but natural hectic, and the blue of his eyes shone painfully bright.

"Why, what's the matter, Charley?"

"A fly-man, who had to drive here and back, brought me with him for a mouthful of fresh air, it being so warm and bright. It is the first time I have been able to get out, sir."

"You are poorly, Charley." I had all but said "dying." But one can only be complimentary to a poor fellow in that condition.

"Very ill I have been, sir; but I'm better. At one time I never thought I should get up again. It's this beautiful warm weather coming in so early that has restored me."

"I don't know about restored? You don't look great things yet."

"You should have seen me a short while ago, sir! I'm getting on."

Lying by his side, on a piece of paper, was a thick slice, doubled, of bread-and-butter, that he must have brought with him. He broke a piece off, and ate it.

"You look hungry, Charley."

"That's the worst of it, sir; I'm always hungry," he answered, and his tone from its eagerness was quite painful to hear, and his eyes grew moist, and the hectic spread on his cheeks. "It is the nature of the complaint, I'm told: and poor mother was the same. I could be eating and drinking every hour, sir, and hardly be satisfied."

"Come along to the inn, and have some tea."

"No, sir; no, thank you," he said, shrinking back. "I answered your remark thoughtlessly, sir, for it's the truth; not with any notion that it would make you ask me to take anything. And I've got some bread-and-butter here."

Going indoors, I told them to serve him a good tea, with a big dish of bacon and eggs, or some relishing thing of that sort. Whitney came in and heard me.

"You be hanged, Johnny! We are not going in for all that, here!"

"It's not for us, Bill; it's for that poor old scout, Charley. He's as surely dying as that you and I are talking. Come and look at him: you never saw such an object. I don't believe he gets enough to eat."

Whitney came, and did nothing but stare. Charley went indoors with a good deal of pressing, and we saw him sit down to the feast. Whitney stayed; I went out-of-doors again.

I remembered a similar case. It was that of a young woman who used to make Lena's frocks. She fell into a decline. Her appetite was wonderful. Anything good and substantial to eat and drink, she was always craving for: and it all seemed to do her no good. Charley Tasson's sickness must be of the same nature. She died: and he—

I was struck dumb! Seated on the bench under the trees, my thoughts back in that past time, there came two figures over the rustic bridge. A lady and gentleman, arm-in-arm: she in a hat and blue feather and dainty lace parasol; and he with bent head and words softened to a whisper. Tod!—and Sophie Chalk!

"Good gracious! There's Johnny Ludlow!"

She loosed his arm as she spoke, and came sailing up to me, her gold bracelets jingling as she gave her hand. I don't believe there are ten women in England who could get themselves up as effectively as did Sophie Chalk. Tod looked black as thunder.

"What the devil brings you here, Johnny?"

"I rowed up with Whitney."

A pause. "Who else is here?"

"Forbes of Merton: Whitney has been about with him. And I suppose a few others. We noticed a skiff or two waiting. Perhaps one was yours."

I spoke indifferently, determined he should not know I was put out. Seeing him there—I was going to say on the sly—with that beguiling syren, who was to foretell what pitfalls she might charm him into? He took Madame Sophie on his arm again to continue their promenade, and I lost sight of them.

I did not like it. It was not satisfactory. He had rowed her up—or perhaps driven her up—and was marching about with her tête-à-tête under the sweet spring sunshine. No great harm in itself this pastime: but he might grow too fond of it. That she had reacquired all her strong influence over Tod's heart was clear as the stars on a frosty night. Whitney called out to me that it was time to think of going back. I got into the boat with him, saying nothing.

Charley told me where he lived—"Up Stagg's Entry"—for I said I would call to see him. Just for a day or two there seemed to be no time; but I got there one evening when Tod had gone to the syren's. It was a dark, dusky place, this Stagg's Entry, and, I think, is done away with now, with several houses crowded into it. Asking for Charles Tasson, of a tidy, motherly woman on the stairs, she went before me, and threw open a door.

"Here's a gentleman to see you, Mr. Charley."

He was lying in a bed at the end of the room near the fire, under the lean-to roof. If I had been shocked at seeing him in the open air, in the glad sunshine, I was doubly so now in the dim light of the tallow candle. He rose in bed.

"It's very kind of you to come here, sir! I'm sure I didn't expect you to remember it."

"Are you worse, Charley?"

"I caught a fresh cold, sir, that day at Godstowe. And I'm as weak as a rat too—hardly able to creep out of bed. Nanny, bring a chair for this gentleman."

One of the handiest little girls I ever saw, with the same shining blue eyes that he had, and plump, pretty cheeks, laid hold of a chair. I took it from her and sat down.

"Is this your sister, Charley?"

"Yes, sir. There's only us two left together. We were eight of us once. Three went abroad, and one is in London, and two dead."

"What doctor sees you?"

"One comes in now and then, sir. My illness is not much in a doctor's way. There's nothing he could do: nothing for me but to wait patiently for summer weather."

"What have you had to eat to-day?"

"He had two eggs for his dinner: I boiled them," said little Nanny. "And Mrs. Cann brought us in six herrings, and I cooked one for tea; and he'll have some ale and bread-and-butter for supper."

She spoke like a little important housekeeper. But I wondered whether Charley was badly off.

Mrs. Cann, the same woman who had spoken to me, came out of her room opposite as I was going away. She followed me downstairs, and began to talk in an undertone. "A sad thing, ain't it, sir, to see him a-lying there so helpless; and to know that it has laid hold of him for good and all. He caught it from his mother."

"How do you mean?"

"She died here in that room, just as the winter come in, with the same complaint—decline they call it; and he waited on her and nursed her, and must have caught it of her. A good son he was. They were well off once, sir, but the father just brought 'em to beggary; and Charley—he had a good education of his own—came down from London when his mother got ill, and looked out for something to do here that he might stay with her. At first he couldn't find anything; and when he was at a sore pinch, he took a place at Christchurch College as scout's helper. He had to pocket his pride: but there was Nanny as well as his mother."

"I see."

"He'd been teacher in a school up in London, sir, by day, and in the evenings he used to help some young clergyman as scripture-reader to the poor in one of them crowded parishes we hear tell of: he was always one for trying to do what good he could. Naturally he'd be disheartened at falling to be a bed-maker in a college, and I'm afraid the work was too hard for him: but, as I say, he was a good son. The mother settled in Oxford after her misfortunes."

"How is he supported now? And the little girl?"

"It's not over much of a support," said Mrs. Cann with disparagement. "Not for him, that's a-craving for meat and drink every hour. The eldest brother is in business in London, sir, and he sends them what they have. Perhaps he's not able to do more."

It was not late. I thought I would, for once, pay Mrs. Everty a visit. A run of three minutes, and I was at her door.

They were there—the usual set. Tod, and Richardson, and Lord Gaiton, and the two men from Magdalen, and—well, it's no use enumerating—seven or eight in all. Richardson and another were quarrelling at écarté, four were at whist; Tod was sitting apart with Sophie Chalk.

She was got up like a fairy at the play, in a cloud of thin white muslin; her hair hanging around and sparkling with gold dust, and little gleams of gold ornaments shining about her. If ever Joseph Todhetley had need to pray against falling into temptation, it was during the weeks of that unlucky term.

"This is quite an honour, Johnny Ludlow," said Madame Sophie, rising to meet me, her eyes sparkling with what might have been taken for the most hearty welcome. "It is not often you honour my poor little room, sir."

"It is not often I can find the time for it, Mrs. Everty. Tod, I came in to see whether you were ready to go in."

He looked at his watch hastily, fearing it might be later than it was; and answered curtly and coolly.

"Ready?—no. I have not had my revenge yet at écarté."

Approaching the écarté table, he sat down. Mrs. Everty drew a chair behind Lord Gaiton, and looked over his hand.

The days passed. I had two cares on my mind, and they bothered me. The one was Tod and his dangerous infatuation; the other, poor dying Charley Tasson. Tod was losing frightfully at those card-tables. Night after night it went on. Tod's steps were drawn thither by a fascination irresistible: and whether the cards or their mistress were the more subtle potion for him, or what was to be the ending of it all, no living being could tell.

As to Stagg's Entry, my visits to it had grown nearly as much into a habit as Tod's had to High Street. When I stayed away for a night, little Nanny would whisper to me the next that Charley had not taken his eyes off the door. Sick people always like to see visitors.

"Don't let him want for anything, Johnny," said Tod. "The pater would blow us up."

The time ran on, and the sands of Charley's life ran with it. One Wednesday evening upon going in late, and not having many minutes to stay, I found him on the bed in a dead faint, and the candle guttering in the socket. Nanny was nowhere. I went across the passage to Mrs. Cann's, and she was nowhere. It was an awkward situation; for I declare that for the moment I thought he was gone.

Knowing most of Nanny's household secrets, I looked in the candle-box for a fresh candle. Charley was stirring then, and I gave him some wine. He had had a similar fainting-fit at mid-day, he said, which had frightened them, and Nanny had fetched the doctor. She was gone now, he supposed, to fetch some medicine.

"Is this the end, sir?"

He asked it quite calmly. I could not tell: but to judge by his wan face I thought it might be. And my time was up and more than up: and neither Nanny nor Mrs. Cann came. The wine revived him and he seemed better; quite well again: well, for him. But I did not like to leave him alone.

"Would you mind reading to me, sir?" he asked.

"What shall I read, Charley?"

"It may be for the last time, sir. I'd like to hear the service for the burial of the dead."

So I read it every word, the long lesson, and all. Nanny came in before it was finished, medicine in hand, and sat down in silence with her bonnet on. She had been kept at the doctor's. Mrs. Cann was the next to make her appearance, having been abroad on some business of her own: and I got away when it was close upon midnight.

"Your name and college, sir."

"Ludlow. Christchurch."

It was the proctor. He had pounced full upon me as I was racing home. And the clocks were striking twelve!

"Ludlow—Christchurch," he repeated, nodding his head.

"I am sorry to be out so late, sir, against rules, but I could not help it. I have been sitting with a sick man."

"Very good," said he blandly; "you can tell that to-morrow to the dean. Home to your quarters now, if you please, Mr. Ludlow."

And I knew he believed me just as much as he would had I told him I'd been up in a balloon.

"You are a nice lot, Master Johnny!"

The salutation was Tod's. He and Bill Whitney were sitting over the fire in our room.

"I couldn't help being late."

"Of course not! As to late—it's only midnight. Next time you'll come in with the milk."

"Don't jest. I've been with that poor Charley, and I think he's dying. The worst of it is, the proctor has just dropped upon me."

"No!" It sobered them both, and they put aside their mockery. Bill, who had the tongs in his hand, let them go down with a crash.

"It's a thousand pities, Johnny. Not one of us has been before the dean yet."

"I can only tell the dean the truth."

"As if he'd believe you! By Jupiter! Once get one of our names up, and those proctors will track every step of the ground we tread on. They watch a marked man as a starving cat watches a mouse."

With the morning came in the requisition for me to attend before the dean. When I got there, who should be stealing out of the room quite sheepishly, his face down and his ears red, but Gaiton.

"Is it your turn, Ludlow!" he cried, closing the room-door as softly as though the dean had been asleep inside.

"What have you been had up for, Gaiton?"

"Oh, nothing. I got knocking about a bit last night, for Mrs. Everty did not receive, and came across that confounded proctor."

"Is the dean in a hard humour?"

"Hard enough, and be hanged to him! It's not the dean: he's ill, or something; perhaps been making a night of it himself: and Applerigg's on duty for him. Dry old scarecrow! For two pins, Ludlow, I'd take my name off the books, and be free of the lot."

Dr. Applerigg had the reputation of being one of the strictest of college dons. He was like a maypole, just as tall and thin, with a long, sallow face, and enough learning to set up the reputations of three archbishops for life. The doctor was marching up and down the room in his college-cap, and turned his spectacles on me.

"Shut the door, sir."

While I did as I was bid, he sat down at an open desk near the fire and looked at a paper that had some writing on it.

"What age may you be, Mr. Ludlow?" he sternly asked, when a question or two had passed. And I told him my age.

"Oh! And don't you think it a very disreputable thing, a great discredit, sir, for a young fellow of your years to be found abroad by your proctor at midnight?"

"But I could not help being late, sir, last night; and I was not abroad for any purpose of pleasure. I had been staying with a poor fellow who is sick; dying, in fact: and—and it was not my fault, sir."

"Take care, young man," said he, glaring through his spectacles. "There's one thing I can never forgive if deliberately told me, and that's a lie."

"I should be sorry to tell a lie, sir," I answered: and by the annoyance so visible in his looks and tones, it was impossible to help fancying he had found out, or thought he had found out, Gaiton in one. "What I have said is truth."

"Go over again what you did say," cried he, very shortly, after looking at his paper again and then hard at me. And I went over it.

"What do you say the man's name is?"

"Charles Tasson, sir. He was our scout until he fell ill."

"Pray do you make a point, Mr. Ludlow, of visiting all the scouts and their friends who may happen to fall sick?"

"No, sir," I said, uneasily, for there was ridicule in his tone, and I knew he did not believe a word. "I don't suppose I should ever have thought of visiting Tasson, but for seeing him look so ill one afternoon up at Godstowe."

"He must be very ill to be at Godstowe!" cried Dr. Applerigg. "Very!"

"He was so ill, sir, that I thought he was dying then. Some flyman he knew had driven him to Godstowe for the sake of the air."

"But what's your motive, may I ask, for going to sit with him?" He had a way of laying emphasis on certain of his words.

"There's no motive, sir: except that he is lonely and dying."

The doctor looked at me for what seemed ten minutes. "What is this sick man's address, pray?"

I told him the address in Stagg's Entry; and he wrote it down, telling me to present myself again before him the following morning.

That day, I met Sophie Chalk; her husband was with her. She nodded and seemed gay as air: he looked dark and sullen as he took off his hat. I carried the news into college.

"Sophie Chalk has her husband down, Tod."

"Queen Anne's dead," retorted he.

"Oh, you knew it!" And I might have guessed that he did by his not having spent the past evening in High Street, but in a fellow's rooms at Oriel. And he was as cross as two sticks.

"What a fool she must have been to go and throw herself away upon that low fellow Everty!" he exclaimed, putting his shoulders against the mantelpiece and stamping on the carpet with one heel.

"Throw herself away! Well, Tod, opinions vary. I think she was lucky to get him. As to his being low, we don't know that he is. Putting aside that one mysterious episode of his being down at our place in hiding, which I suppose we shall never come to the bottom of, we know nothing of what Everty has, or has not been."

"You shut up, Johnny. Common sense is common sense."

"Everty's being here—we can't associate with him, you know, Tod—affords a good opportunity for breaking off the visits to High Street."

"Who wants to break off the visits to High Street?"

"I do, for one. Madame Sophie's is a dangerous atmosphere."

"Dangerous for you, Johnny?"

"Not a bit of it. You know. Be wise in time, old fellow."

"Of all the muffs living, Johnny, you are about the greatest. In the old days you feared I might go in for marrying Sophie Chalk. I don't see what you can fear now. Do you suppose I should run away with another man's wife?"

"Nonsense, Tod!"

"Well, what else is it? Come! Out with it."

"Do you think our people or the Whitneys would like it if they knew we are intimate with her?"

"They'd not die of it, I expect."

"I don't like her, Tod. It is not a nice thing of her to allow the play and the betting, and to have all those fellows there when they choose to go."

Tod took his shoulder from the mantelpiece, and sat down to his imposition: one he had to write for having missed chapel.

"You mean well, Johnny, though you are a muff."

Later in the day I met Dr. Applerigg. He signed to me to stop. "Mr. Ludlow, I find that what you told me this morning was true. And I withdraw every word of condemnation that I spoke. I wish I had never greater cause to find fault than I have with you, in regard to this matter. Not that I can sanction your being out so late, although the plea of excuse be a dying man. You understand?"

"Yes, sir. It shall not occur again."

Down at the house in Stagg's Entry, that evening, Mrs. Cann met me on the stairs. "One of the great college doctors was here to-day, sir. He came up asking all manner of questions about you—whether you'd been here till a'most midnight yesterday, and what you'd stayed so late for, and—and all about it."

Dr. Applerigg! "What did you tell him, Mrs. Cann?"

"Tell him, sir! what should I tell him but the truth? That you had stayed here late because of Charley's being took worse and nobody with him, and had read the burial service to him for his asking; and that you came most evenings, and was just as good to him as gold. He said he'd see Charley for himself then; and he went in and talked to him, oh so gently and nicely about his soul; and gave little Nanny half-a-crown when he went away. Sometimes it happens, sir, that those who look to have the hardest faces have the gentlest hearts. And Charley's dying, sir. He was took worse again this evening at five o'clock, and I hardly thought he'd have lasted till now. The doctor has been, and thinks he'll go off quietly."

Quietly perhaps in one sense, but it was a restless death-bed. He was not still a minute; but he was quite sensible and calm. Waking up out of a doze when I went in, he held out his hand.

"It is nearly over, sir."

I was sure of that, and sat down in silence. There could be no mistaking his looks.

"I have just had a strange dream," he whispered, between his laboured breath; and his eyes were wet with tears, and he looked curiously agitated. "I thought I saw mother. It was in a wide place, all light and sunshine, too beautiful for anything but heaven. Mother was looking at me; I seemed to be outside in dulness and darkness, and not to know how to get in. Others that I've known in my lifetime, and who have gone on before, were there, as well as mother; they all looked happy, and there was a soft strain of music, like nothing I ever heard in this world. All at once, as I was wondering how I could get in, my sins seemed to rise up before me in a great cloud; I turned sick, thinking of them; for I knew no sinful person might enter there. Then I saw One standing on the brink! it could only have been Jesus; and He held out His hand to me and smiled, 'I am here to wash out your sins,' He said, and I thought He touched me with His finger; and oh, the feeling of delight that came over me, of repose, of bliss, for I knew that all earth's troubles were over, and I had passed into rest and peace for ever."

Nanny came up, and gave him one or two spoonfuls of wine.

"I don't believe it was a dream," he said, after a pause. "I think it was sent to show me what it is I am entering on; to uphold me through the darksome valley of the shadow of death."

"Mother said she should be watching for us, you know, Charley," said the child.

A restless fit came over him again, and he stirred uneasily. When it had passed, he was still for awhile and then looked up at me.

"It was the new heaven and the new earth, sir, that we are told of in the Revelation. Would you mind, sir—just those few verses—reading them to me for the last time?"

Nanny brought the Bible, and put the candle on the stand, and I read what he asked for—the first few verses of the twenty-first chapter. The little girl kneeled down by the bed and joined her hands together.

"That's enough, Nanny," I whispered. "Put the candle back."

"But I did not tell all my dream," he resumed; "not quite all. As I passed over into heaven, I thought I looked down here again. I could see the places in the world; I could see this same Oxford city. I saw the men here in it, sir, at their cards and their dice and their drink; at all their thoughtless folly. Spending their days and nights without a care for the end, without as much as thinking whether they need a Saviour or not. And oh, their condition troubled me! I seemed to understand all things plainly then, sir. And I thought if they would but once lift up their hearts to Him, even in the midst of their sin, He would take care of them even then, and save them from it in the end—for He was tempted Himself once, and knows how sore their temptations are. In my distress, I tried to call out and tell them this, and it awoke me."

"Do you think he ought to talk, sir?" whispered Nanny. But nothing more could harm him now.

My time was up, and I ought to be going. Poor Charley spoke so imploringly—almost as though the thought of it startled him.

"Not yet, sir; not yet! Stay a bit longer with me. It is for the last time."

And I stayed: in spite of my word passed to Dr. Applerigg. It seems to me a solemn thing to cross the wishes of the dying.

So the clock went ticking on. Mrs. Cann stole in and out, and a lodger from below came in and looked at him. Before twelve all was over.

I went hastening home, not much caring whether the proctor met me again, or whether he didn't, for in any case I must go to Dr. Applerigg in the morning, and tell him I had broken my promise to him, and why. Close at the gates some one overtook and passed me.

It was Tod. Tod with a white face, and his hair damp with running. He had come from Sophie Chalk's.

"What is it, Tod?"

I laid my hand upon his arm in speaking. He threw it off with a word that was very like an imprecation.

"What is the matter?"

"The devil's the matter. Mind your own business, Johnny."

"Have you been quarrelling with Everty?"

"Everty be hanged! The man has betaken himself off."

"How much have you lost to-night?"

"Cleaned-out, lad. That's all."

We got to our room in silence. Tod turned over some cards that lay on the table, and trimmed the candle from a thief.

"Tasson's dead, Tod."

"A good thing if some of us were dead," was the answer. And he turned into his chamber and bolted the door.

III

Lunch-time at Oxford, and a sunny day. Instead of college and our usual fare, bread-and-cheese from the buttery, we were looking on the High Street from Mrs. Everty's rooms, and about to sit down to a snow-white damasked table with no end of good things upon it. Madam Sophie had invited four or five of us to lunch with her.

The term had gone on, and Easter was not far off. Tod had not worked much: just enough to keep him out of hot-water. His mind ran on Sophie Chalk more than it did on lectures and chapel. He and the other fellows who were caught by her fascinations mostly spent their spare time there. Sophie dispersed her smiles pretty equally, but Tod contrived to get the largest share. The difference was this: they had lost their heads to her and Tod his heart. The evening card-playing did not flag, and the stakes played for were high. Tod and Gaiton were the general losers: a run of ill-luck had set in from the first for both of them. Gaiton might afford this, but Tod could not.

Tod had his moments of reflection. He'd sit sometimes for an hour together, his head bent down, whistling softly to himself some slow dolorous strain, and pulling at his dark whiskers; no doubt pondering the question of what was to be the upshot of it all. For my part, I devoutly wished Sophie Chalk had been caught up into the moon before an ill-wind had wafted her to Oxford. It was an awful shame of her husband to let her stay on there, turning the under-graduates' brains. Perhaps he could not help it.

We sat down to table: Sophie at its head in a fresh-looking pink gown and bracelets and nicknacks. Lord Gaiton and Tod sat on either side of her; Richardson was at the foot, and Fred Temple and I faced each other. What fit of politeness had taken Sophie to invite me, I could not imagine. Possibly she thought I should be sure to refuse; but I did not.

"So kind of you all to honour my poor little table!" said Sophie, as we sat down. "Being in lodgings, I cannot treat you as I should wish. It is all cold: chickens, meat-patties, lobster-salad, and bread-and-cheese. Lord Gaiton, this is sherry by you, I think. Mr. Richardson, you like porter, I know: there is some on the chiffonier."

We plunged into the dishes without ceremony, each one according to his taste, and the lunch progressed. I may as well mention one thing—that there was nothing in Mrs. Everty's manners at any time to take exception to: never a word was heard from her, never a look seen, that could offend even an old dowager. She made the most of her charms and her general fascinations, and flirted quietly; but all in a lady-like way.

"Thank you, yes; I think I will take a little more salad, Mr. Richardson," she said to him with a beaming smile. "It is my dinner, you know. I have not a hall to dine in to-night, as you gentlemen have. I am sorry to trouble you, Mr. Johnny."

I was holding her plate for Richardson. There happened at that moment to be a lull in the talking, and we heard a carriage of some kind stop at the door, and a loud peal at the house-bell.

"It's that brother of mine," said Fred Temple. "He bothered me to drive out to some confounded place with him, but I told him I wouldn't. What's he bumping up the stairs in that fashion for?"

The room-door was flung open, and Fred Temple put on a savage face, for his brother looked after him more than he liked; when, instead of Temple major, there appeared a shining big brown satin bonnet, and an old lady's face under it, who stood there with a walking-stick.

"Yes, you see I was right, grandmamma; I said she was not gone," piped a shrill voice behind; and Mabel Smith, in an old-fashioned black silk frock and tippet, came into view. They had driven up to look after Sophie.

Sophie was equal to the occasion. She rose gracefully and held out both her hands, as though they had been welcome as is the sun in harvest. The old lady leaned on her stick, and stared around: the many faces seemed to confuse her.

"Dear me! I did not know you had a luncheon-party, ma'am."

"Just two or three friends who have dropped in, Mrs. Golding," said Sophie, airily. "Let me take your stick."

The old lady, who looked like a very amiable old lady, sat down in the nearest chair, but kept the stick in her hand. Mabel Smith was regarding everything with her shrewd eyes and compressing her thin lips.

"This is Johnny Ludlow, grandmamma; you have heard me speak of him: I don't know the others."

"How do you do, sir," said the old lady, politely nodding her brown bonnet at me. "I hope you are in good health, sir?"

"Yes, ma'am, thank you." For she put it as a question, and seemed to await an answer. Tod and the rest, who had risen, began to sit down again.

"I'm sure I am sorry to disturb you at luncheon, ma'am," said the old lady to Mrs. Everty. "We came in to see whether you had gone home or not. I said you of course had gone; that you wouldn't stay away from your husband so long as this; and also because we had not heard of you for a month past. But Mabel thought you were here still."

"I am intending to return shortly," said Sophie.

"That's well: for I want to send up Mabel. And I brought in a letter that came to my house this morning, addressed to you," continued the old lady, lugging out of her pocket a small collection of articles before she found the letter. "Mabel says it is your husband's handwriting, ma'am; if so, he must be thinking you are staying with me."

"Thanks," said Sophie, slipping the letter away unopened.

"Had you not better see what it says?" suggested Mrs. Golding to her.

"Not at all: it can wait. May I offer you some luncheon?"

"Much obleeged, ma'am, but I and Mabel took an early dinner before setting out. And on which day, Mrs. Everty, do you purpose going?"

"I'll let you know," said Sophie.

"What can have kept you so long here?" continued the old lady, wonderingly. "Mabel said you did not know any of the inhabitants."

"I have found it of service to my health," replied Sophie with charming simplicity. "Will you take a glass of sherry, Mrs. Golding?"

"I don't mind if I do. Just half a glass. Thank you, sir; not much more than half"—to me, as I went forward with the glass and decanter. "I'm sure, sir, it is good of you to be attentive to an old lady like me. If you had a mind for a brisk walk at any time, of three miles, or so, and would come over to my house, I'd make you welcome. Mabel, write down the address."

"And I wish you had come while I was there, Johnny Ludlow," said the girl, giving me the paper. "I like you. You don't say smiling words to people with your lips and mock at them in your heart, as some do."

I remembered that she had not been asked to take any wine, and I offered it.

"No, thank you," she said with emphasis. "None for me." And it struck me that she refused because the wine belonged to Sophie.

The old lady, after nodding a farewell around and shaking hands with Mrs. Everty, stood leaning on her stick between the doorway and the stairs. "My servant's not here," she said, looking back, "and these stairs are steep: would any one be good enough to help me down?"

Tod went forward to give her his arm; and we heard the fly drive away with her and Mabel. Somehow the interlude had damped the free go of the banquet, and we soon prepared to depart also. Sophie made no attempt to hinder it, but said she should expect us in to take some tea with her in the evening: and the lot of us filed out together, some going one way, some another. I and Fred Temple kept together.

There was a good-natured fellow at Oxford that term, who had come up from Wales to take his degree, and had brought his wife with him, a nice kind of young girl who put me in mind of Anna Whitney. They had become acquainted with Sophie Chalk, and liked her; she fascinated both. She meant to do it too: for the companionship of staid irreproachable people like Mr. and Mrs. Ap-Jenkyns, reflected credit on herself in the eyes of Oxford.

"I thought we should have met the Ap-Jenkynses, at lunch," remarked Temple. "What a droll old party that was with the stick! She puts me in mind of—I say, here's another old party!" he broke off. "Seems to be a friend of yours."

It was Mrs. Cann. She had stopped, evidently wanting to speak to me.

"I have just been to put little Nanny Tasson in the train for London, sir," she said; "I thought you might like to know it. Her eldest brother, the one that's settled there, has taken to her. His wife wrote a nice letter and sent the fare."

"All right, Mrs. Cann. I hope they'll take good care of her. Good-afternoon."

"Who the wonder is Nanny Tasson?" cried Temple as we went on.

"Only a little friendless child. Her brother was our scout when we first came, and he died."

"Oh, by Jove, Ludlow! Look there!"

I turned at Temple's words. A gig was dashing by as large as life; Tod in it, driving Sophie Chalk. Behind it dashed another gig, containing Mr. and Mrs. Ap-Jenkyns. Fred Temple laughed.

"Mrs. Everty's unmistakably charming," said he, "and we don't know any real harm of her, but if I were Ap-Jenkyns I should not let my wife be quite her bosom companion. As to Todhetley, I think he's a gone calf."

Whitney came to our room as I got in. He had been invited to the luncheon by Mrs. Everty, but excused himself, and she asked Fred Temple in his place.

"Well, Johnny, how did it go off?"

"Oh, pretty well. Lobster-salad and other good things. Why did not you go?"

"Where's Tod?" he rejoined, not answering the question.

"Out on a driving-party. Sophie Chalk and the Ap-Jenkynses."

Whitney whistled through the verse of an old song: "Froggy would a-wooing go." "I say, Johnny," he said presently, "you had better give Tod a hint to take care of himself. That thing will go too far if he does not look out."

"As if Tod would mind me! Give him the hint yourself, Bill."

"I said half a word to him this morning after chapel: he turned on me and accused me of being jealous."

We both laughed.

"I had a letter from home yesterday," Bill went on, "ordering me to keep clear of Madam Sophie."

"No! Who from?"

"The mother. And Miss Deveen, who is staying with them, put in a postscript."

"How did they know Sophie Chalk was here?"

"Through me. One wet afternoon I wrote a long epistle to Harry, telling him, amidst other items, that Sophie Chalk was here, turning some of our heads, especially Todhetley's. Harry, like a flat, let Helen get hold of the letter, and she read it aloud, pro bono publico. There was nothing in it that I might not have written to Helen herself; but Mr. Harry won't get another from me in a hurry. Sophie seems to have fallen to a discount with the mother and Miss Deveen."

Bill Whitney did not know what I knew—the true story of the emeralds.

"And that's why I did not go to the lunch to-day, Johnny. Who's this?"

It was the scout. He came in to bring in a small parcel, daintily done up in white paper.

"Something for you, sir," he said to me. "A boy has just left it."

"It can't be for me—that I know of. It looks like wedding-cake."

"Open it," said Bill. "Perhaps one of the grads has gone and got married."

We opened it together, laughing. A tiny paste-board box loomed out with a jeweller's name on it; inside it was a chased gold cross, attached to a slight gold chain.

"It's a mistake, Bill. I'll do it up again."

Tod came back in time for dinner. Seeing the little parcel on the mantelshelf, he asked what it was. So I told him—something that the jeweller's shop must have sent to our room by mistake. Upon that, he tore the paper open; called the shop people hard names for sending it into college, and put the box in his pocket. Which showed that it was for him.

I went to Sophie's in the evening, having promised her, but not as soon as Tod, for I stayed to finish some Greek. Whitney went with me, in spite of his orders from home. The luncheon-party had all assembled there with the addition of Mr. and Mrs. Ap-Jenkyns. Sophie sat behind the tea-tray, dispensing tea; Gaiton handed the plum-cake. She wore a silken robe of opal tints; white lace fell over her wrists and bracelets; in her hair, brushed off her face, fluttered a butterfly with silver wings; and on her neck was the chased gold cross that had come to our rooms a few hours before.

"Tod's just a fool, Johnny," said Whitney in my ear. "Upon my word, I think he is. And she's a syren!—and it was at our house he met her first!"

After Mr. and Mrs. Ap-Jenkyns left, for she was tired, they began cards. Sophie was engrossing Gaiton, and Tod sat down to écarté. He refused at first, but Richardson drew him on.

"I'll show Tod the letter I had from home," said Whitney to me as we went out. "What can possess him to go and buy gold crosses for her? She's married."

"Gaiton and Richardson buy her things also, Bill."

"They don't know how to spend their money fast enough. I wouldn't: I know that."

Tod and Gaiton came in together soon after I got in. Gaiton just looked in to say good-night, and proposed that we should breakfast with him on the morrow, saying he'd ask Whitney also: and then he went up to his own rooms.

Tod fell into one of his thinking fits. He had work to do, but he sat staring at the fire, his legs stretched out. With all his carelessness he had a conscience and some forethought. I told him Bill Whitney had had a lecture from home, touching Sophie Chalk, and I conclude he heard. But he made no sign.

"I wish to goodness you wouldn't keep up that tinkling, Johnny," he said by-and-by, in a tone of irritation.

The "tinkling" was a bit of quiet harmony. However, I shut down the piano, and went and sat by the fire, opposite to him. His brow looked troubled; he was running his hands through his hair.

"I wonder whether I could raise some money, Johnny," he began, after a bit.

"How much money?"

"A hundred, or so."

"You'd have to pay a hundred and fifty for doing it."

"Confound it, yes! And besides—"

"Besides what?"

"Nothing."

"Look here, Tod: we should have gone on as straightly and steadily as need be but for her. As it is, you are wasting your time and getting out of the way of work. What's going to be the end of it?"

"Don't know myself, Johnny."

"Do you ever ask yourself?"

"Where's the use of asking?" he returned, after a pause. "If I ask it of myself at night, I forget it by the morning."

"Pull up at once, Tod. You'd be in time."

"Yes, now: don't know that I shall be much longer," said Tod candidly. He was in a soft mood that night; an unusual thing with him. "Some awful complication may come of it: a few writs or something."

"Sophie Chalk can't do you any good, Tod."

"She has not done me any harm."

"Yes she has. She has unsettled you from the work that you came to Oxford to do; and the play in her rooms has caused you to run into debt that you don't know how to get out of: it's nearly as much harm as she can do you."

"Is it?"

"As much as she can do any honest fellow. Tod, if you were to lapse into crooked paths, you'd break the good old pater's heart. There's nobody in the world he cares for as he cares for you."

Tod sat twitching his whiskers. I could not understand his mood: all the carelessness and the fierceness had quite gone out of him.

"It's the thought of the father that pulls me up, lad. What a cross-grained world it is! Why should a bit of pleasure be hedged in with thorns?"

"If we don't go to bed we shall not be up for chapel."

"You can go to bed."

"Why do you drive her out, Tod?"

"Why does the sun shine?" was the lucid answer.

"I saw you with her in that gig to-day."

"We only went four miles. Four out and four in."

"You may be driving her rather too far some day—fourteen, or so."

"I don't think she'd be driven. With all her simplicity, she knows how to take care of herself."

Simplicity! I looked at him; and saw he spoke the word in good faith. He was simple.

"She has a husband, Tod."

"Well?"

"Do you suppose he would like to see you driving her abroad?—and all you fellows in her rooms to the last minute any of you dare stop out?"

"That's not my affair. It's his."

"Any way, Everty might come down upon the lot of you some of these fine days, and say things you'd not like. She's to blame. Why, you heard what that old lady in the brown bonnet said—that her husband must think Sophie was staying with her."

"The fire's low, and I'm cold," said Tod. "Good-night, Johnny."

He went into his room, and I to mine.

A few years ago, there appeared a short poem called "Amor Mundi."[1] While reading it, I involuntarily recalled this past experience at Oxford, for it described a young fellow's setting-out on the downward path, as Tod did. Two of life's wayfarers start on their long life journey: the woman first; the man sees and joins her; then speaks to her.

[1] *Christina G. Rossetti.*

"Oh, where are you going, with your love-locks flowing,
And the west wind blowing along the narrow track?"
"This downward path is easy, come with me, an it please ye;
We shall escape the up-hill by never turning back."

So they two went together in the sunny August weather;
The honey-blooming heather lay to the left and right:
And dear she was to dote on, her small feet seemed to float on
The air, like soft twin-pigeons too sportive to alight.

And so they go forth, these two, on their journey, revelling in the summer sunshine and giving no heed to their sliding progress; until he sees something in the path that startles him. But the syren accounts for it in some plausible way; it lulls his fear, and onward they go again. In time he sees something worse, halts, and asks her again:

"Oh, what's that in the hollow, so pale I quake to follow?"
"Oh, that's a thin dead body that waits the Eternal term."

The answer effectually arouses him, and he pulls up in terror, asking her to turn. She answers again, and he knows his fate.

"Turn again, oh my sweetest! Turn again, false and fleetest!
This way, whereof thou westest, is surely Hell's own track!"
"Nay, too late for cost counting, nay too steep for hill-mounting,
This downward path is easy, but there's no turning back."

Shakespeare tells us that there is a tide in the affairs of man, which, taken at the flood, leads on to fortune: omitted, all the voyage of the after life is spent in shoals and miseries. That will apply to other things besides fortune. I fully believe that after a young fellow has set out on the downward path, in almost all cases there's a chance given him of pulling up again, if he only is sufficiently wise and firm to seize upon it. The opportunity was to come for Tod. He had started; there was no doubt of that; but he had not got down very far yet and could go backward almost as easily as forward. Left alone, he would probably make a sliding run of it, and descend into the shoals. But the chance for him was at hand.

Our commons and Whitney's went up to Gaiton's room in the morning, and we breakfasted there. Lecture that day was at eleven, but I had work to do beforehand. So had Tod, for the matter of that; plenty of it. I went down to mine, but Tod stayed up with the two others.

Bursting into our room, as a fellow does when he is late for anything, I saw at the open window somebody that I thought must be Mr. Brandon's ghost. It took me aback, and for a moment I stood staring.

"Have you no greeting for me, Johnny Ludlow?"

"I was lost in surprise, sir. I am very glad to see you."

"I dare say you are!" he returned, as if he doubted my word. "It's a good half-hour that I have waited here. You've been at a breakfast-party!"

He must have got that from the scout. "Not at a party, sir. Gaiton asked us to take our commons up, and breakfast with him in his room."

"Who is Gaiton?"

"He is Lord Gaiton. One of the students at Christchurch."

"Never mind his being a lord. Is he any good?"

I could not say Gaiton was particularly good, so passed the question over, and asked Mr. Brandon when he came to Oxford.

"I got here at mid-day yesterday. How are you getting on?"

"Oh, very well, sir."

"Been in any rows?"

"No, sir."

"And Todhetley? How is he getting on?"

I should have said very well to this; it would never have done to say very ill, but Tod and Bill Whitney interrupted the answer. They looked just as much surprised as I had been. After talking a bit, Mr. Brandon left, saying he should expect us all three at the Mitre in the evening when dinner in Hall was over.

"What the deuce brings him at Oxford?" cried Tod.

Whitney laughed. "I'll lay a crown he has come to look after Johnny and his morals."

"After the lot of us," added Tod, pushing his books about. "Look here, you two. I'm not obliged to go bothering to that Mitre in the evening, and I shan't. You'll be enough without me."

"It won't do, Tod," I said. "He expects you."

"What if he does? I have an engagement elsewhere."

"Break it."

"I shall not do anything of the kind. There! Hold your tongue, Johnny, and push the ink this way."

Tod held to that. So when I and Whitney reached the Mitre after dinner, we said he was unable to get off a previous engagement, putting the excuse as politely as we could.

"Oh," said old Brandon, twitching his yellow silk handkerchief off his head, for he had been asleep before the fire. "Engaged elsewhere, is he! With the lady I saw him driving out yesterday, I suppose: a person with blue feathers on her head."

This struck us dumb. Bill said nothing, neither did I.

"It was Miss Sophie Chalk, I presume," went on old Brandon, ringing the bell. "Sit down, boys; we'll have tea up."

The tea and coffee must have been ordered beforehand, for they came in at once. Mr. Brandon drank four cups of tea, and ate a plate of bread-and-butter and some watercress.

"Tea is my best meal in the day," he said. "You young fellows all like coffee best. Don't spare it. What's that by you, William Whitney?—anchovy toast? Cut that pound-cake, Johnny."

Nobody could say, with all his strict notions, that Mr. Brandon was not hospitable. He'd have ordered up the Mitre's whole larder had he thought we could eat it. And never another word did he say about Tod until the things had gone away.

Then he began, quietly at first: he sitting on one side the fire, I and Bill on the other. Touching gently on this, alluding to that, our eyes opened in more senses than one; for we found that he knew all about Sophie Chalk's sojourn in the town, the attention she received from the undergraduates, and Tod's infatuation.

"What's Todhetley's object in going there?" he asked.

"Amusement, I think, sir," hazarded Bill.

"Does he gamble there for amusement too?"

Where on earth had old Brandon got hold of all this?

"How much has Todhetley lost already?" he continued. "He is in debt, I know. Not for the first time from the same cause."

Bill stared. He knew nothing of that old episode in London with the Clement-Pells. I felt my face flush.

"Tod does not care for playing really, sir. But the cards are there, and he sees others play and gets drawn in to join."

"Well, what amount has he lost this time, Johnny?"

"I don't know, sir."

"But you know that he is in debt?"

"I—yes, sir. Perhaps he is a little."

"Look here, boys," said old Brandon. "Believing that matters were not running in a satisfactory groove with some of you, I came down to Oxford yesterday to look about me a bit—for I don't intend that Johnny Ludlow shall lapse into bad ways, if I can keep him out of them. Todhetley may have made up his mind to go to the deuce, but he shall not take Johnny with him. I hear no good report of Todhetley; he neglects his studies for the sake of a witch, and is in debt over his head and shoulders."

"Who could have told you that, sir?"

"Never you mind, Johnny Ludlow; I dare say you know it's pretty true. Now look here—as I said just now. I mean to see what I can do towards saving Todhetley, for the sake of my good old friend, the Squire, and for his dead mother's sake; and I appeal to you both to aid me. You can answer my questions if you will; and you are not children, that you should make an evasive pretence of ignorance. If I find matters are too hard for me to cope with, I shall send for the Squire and Sir John Whitney; their influence may effect what mine cannot. If I can deal with the affair successfully, and save Todhetley from himself, I'll do so, and say nothing about it anywhere. You understand me?"

"Yes, sir."

"Very well. To begin with, what amount of debt has Todhetley got into?"

It seemed to be a choice of evils: but the least of them was to speak. Bill honestly said he would tell in a minute if he knew. I knew little more than he; only that Tod had been saying the night before he wished he could raise a hundred pounds.

"A hundred pounds!" repeated old Brandon, nodding his head like a Chinese mandarin. "Pretty well, that, for a first term at Oxford. Well, we'll leave that for the present, and go to other questions. What snare and delusion is drawing him on to make visits to this person, this Sophie Chalk? What does he purpose? Is it marriage?"

Marriage! Bill and I both looked up at him.

"She is married already, sir. Did you not know it?"

"Married already! Who says so?"

So I told him all about it—as much as I knew—and that her husband, Mr. Everty, had been to Oxford once or twice to see her.

"Well, that's a relief," cried Mr. Brandon, drawing a deep breath, as though a fear of some kind had been lifted from his mind. And then he fell into a reverie, his head nodding incessantly, and his yellow handkerchief in his hand keeping time to it.

"If it's better in one sense, it's worse in another," he squeaked. "Todhetley's in love with her, I suppose!"

"Something like it, sir," said Bill.

"What brainless fools some of you young men can be!"

But it was then on the stroke of nine, when Old Tom would peal out. Mr. Brandon hurried us away: he seemed to understand the notions of University life as well as we did: ordering us to say nothing to Tod, as he intended to speak to him on the morrow.

And we concluded that he did. Tod came stalking in during the afternoon in a white rage with somebody, and I thought it might be with old Brandon.

The time passed. Mr Brandon stayed on at the Mitre as though he meant to make it his home for good, and was evidently watching. Tod seemed to be conscious of it, and to exist in a chronic state of irritation. Sophie Chalk stayed on also, and Tod was there more than ever. The affair had got wind somehow—I mean Tod's infatuation for her—and was talked of in the colleges. Richardson fell ill about that time: at least, he met with an accident which confined him to his bed: and the play at Mrs. Everty's was not much to speak of: I did not go, Mr. Brandon had interdicted it. Thus the time went on, and Passion Week was coming in.

"Are you running for a wager, Johnny Ludlow?"

I was running down to the river and had nearly run over Mr. Brandon, who was strolling along with his hands under his coat-tails. It was Saturday afternoon, and some of us were going out rowing. Mr. Brandon came down to see us embark.

As we all stood there, who should loom into sight but Sophie Chalk. She was leading a little mouse-coloured dog by a piece of red tape, one that Fred Temple had given her; and her shining hair was a sight to be seen in the sunlight; Tod walked by her with his arms folded. They halted to talk with some of us for a minute, and then went on, Madam Sophie giving old Brandon a saucy stare from her wide-open blue eyes. He had stood as still as a post, giving never a word to either of them.

That same night, when Tod and I were in our room alone, Mr. Brandon walked in. It was pretty late, but Tod was about to depart on his visit to High Street. As if the entrance of Mr. Brandon had been the signal for him to bolt, he put on his trencher and turned to the door. Quick as thought, Mr. Brandon interposed himself.

"If you go out of this room, Joseph Todhetley, it shall be over my body," cried he, a whole hatful of authority in his squeaky voice. "I have come in to hold a final conversation with you; and I mean to do it."

I thought an explosion was inevitable, with Tod's temper. He controlled it, however; and after a moment's hesitation put off his cap. Mr. Brandon sat down in the old big chair by the fire; Tod stood on the other side, his arm on the mantelpiece.

In a minute or two, they were going at it kindly. Old Brandon put Tod's doings before him in the plainest language he could command; Tod retorted insolently in his passion.

"I have warned you enough against your ways and against that woman," said Mr. Brandon. "I am here to do it once again, and to bid you for the last time give up her acquaintanceship. Yes, sir, bid you: I stand in the light of your unconscious father."

"I wouldn't do it for my father," cried Tod, in his fury.

"She is leading you into a gulf of—of brimstone," fired old Brandon. "Day by day you creep down a step lower into it, sir, like a calf that is being wiled to the shambles. Once fairly in, you'll be smothered: the whole world won't be able to pull you out again."

Tod answered with a torrent of words. The chief burden of them was—that if he chose to walk into the brimstone, it was not Mr. Brandon who should keep him out of it.

"Is it not?" retorted Mr. Brandon—and though he was very firm and hard, he gave no sign of losing his temper. "We'll see that. I am in this town to strive to save you, Joseph Todhetley; and if I can't do it by easy means, I'll do it by hard ones. I got you out of one scrape, thanks to Johnny here, and now I'm going to get you out of another."

Tod held his peace. That past obligation was often on his conscience.

"You ought to take shame to yourself, sir," continued old Brandon. "You were placed at Oxford to study, to learn to be a man and a gentleman, to prepare yourself to fight well the battle of life, not to waste the talents God has given you, and fritter away your best days in sin."

"In sin?" retorted Tod, jerking his head fiercely.

"Yes, sir, in sin. What else do you call it—this idleness that you are indulging in? The short space of time that young men spend at the University must be used, not abused. Once it has passed, it can never again be laid hold of. What sort of example are you setting my ward here, who is as your younger brother? Stay where you are, Johnny Ludlow. I choose that you shall be present at this."

"Johnny need not fret himself that he'll catch much harm from my iniquities," said Tod with a sneer.

"Now listen to me, young man," spoke Mr. Brandon. "If you persist in this insane conduct and refuse to hear reason, I'll keep you out of danger by putting you in prison."

Tod stared.

"You owe me a hundred pounds."

"I am quite conscious of that, sir: and of my inability hitherto to repay it."

"For that debt I will shut you up in prison. Headstrong young idiots like you must be saved from themselves."

Tod laughed slightly in his insolence. A defiant, mocking laugh.

"I should like to see you try to shut me up in prison! You have no power to do it, Mr. Brandon: you have never proved the debt."

Mr. Brandon rose, and took a step towards him. "You dare to tell me I cannot do a thing that I say I will do, Joseph Todhetley! I shall make an affidavit before a judge in chambers that you are about to leave the country, and obtain the warrant that will lock you up. And I say to you that I believe you are going to leave it, sooner or later; and that Chalk woman with you!"

"What an awful lie," cried Tod, his face all ablaze.

"Lie or no lie, I believe it. I believe it is what she will bring you to, unless you are speedily separated from her. And if there be no other way of saving you, why, I'll save you by force."

Tod ran his hands through his damp hair: what with wrath and emotion he was in a fine heat. Knowing nothing of the law himself, he supposed old Brandon could do as he said, and it sobered him.

"I am your father's friend, Joseph Todhetley, and I'll take care of you for his sake if I can. I have stayed on here, putting myself, as it were, into his place to save him pain. As his substitute, I have a right to be heard; ay, and to act. Do you know that your dead mother was very dear to me? I will tell you what perhaps I never should have told you but for this crisis in your life, that her sister was to me the dearest friend a man can have in this life; she would have been my wife but that death claimed her. Your mother was nearly equally dear, and loved me to the last. She took my hand in dying, and spoke of you; of you, her only child. 'Should it ever be in your power to shield him from harm or evil, do so, John,' she said, 'do it for my sake.' And with Heaven's help, I will do it now."

Tod was moved. The mention of his mother softened him at all times. Mr. Brandon sat down again.

"Don't let us play at this pitched battle, Joe. Hear a bit of truth from me, of common sense: can't you see that I have your interest at heart? There are two roads that lie before a young man on his setting out in life, either of which he can take: you can take either, even yet. The one leads to honour, to prosperity, to a clear conscience, to a useful career, to a hale and happy old age—and, let us hope, to heaven. The other leads to vice, to discomfort, to miserable self-torment, to a waste of talent and energies; in short, to altogether a lost life. Lost, at any rate, for this world: and—we'll not speculate upon what it may be in the other. Are you attending?"

Tod just lifted his eyes in answer. I sat at the table by my books, silently turning some of their leaves, ready to drop through the floor with annoyance. Mr. Brandon resumed.

"You have come to the Oxford University to perfect your education; to acquire self-reliance, experience, and a tone of good manners; to keep upright ways, to eschew bad company, and to train yourself to be a Christian gentleman. Do this, and you will go home with satisfaction and a sound conscience. In time you will marry, and rear your children to good, and be respected of all men. This is the career expected of you; this is the road you ought to take."

He paused slightly, and then went on.

"I will put the other road before you; the one you seem so eager to rush upon. Ah, boy! how many a one, with as hopeful a future before him as you have, has gone sliding, sliding down unconsciously, never meaning, poor fellow, to slide too far, and been lost in the vortex of sin and shame! You are starting on well for it. Wine, and cards, and betting, and debt; and a singing mermaid to lure you on! That woman, with the hard light eyes, and the seductive airs, has cast her spell upon you. You think her an angel, no doubt; I say she's more of an angel's opposite—"

"Mr. Brandon!"

"There are women in the world who will conjure a man's coat off his back, and his pockets after it," persisted Mr. Brandon, drowning the interruption. "She is one of them. They are bad to the core. They are; and they draw a man into all kinds of irretrievable entanglements. She will draw you: and the end may be that you'd find her saddled on you for good. Who will care to take your hand in friendship then? Will you dare to clasp that of honest people, or hold up your face in the light of day? No: not for very shame. That's what gambling and evil courses will bring a man to: and, his self-respect once gone, it's gone for ever. You will feel that you have raised a barrier between you and your kind: remembrance will be a sting, and your days will be spent in one long cry of too late repentance, 'Oh, that I had been wise in time!'"

"You are altogether mistaken in her," burst out Tod. "There's no harm in her. She is as particular as—as any lady need be."

"No harm in her!" retorted Mr. Brandon. "Is there any good in her? Put it at its best: she induces you to waste your time and your substance. How much money has the card-playing and the present-giving taken out of you, pray? What amount of debt has it involved you in? More than you know how to pay."

Tod winced.

"Be wise in time, lad, now, without further delay, and break off this dangerous connection. I know that in your better moments you must see how fatal it may become. It is a crisis in your life; it may be its turning-point; and, as you choose the evil or the good, so may you be lost or saved in this world and in eternity."

Tod muttered something about his not deserving to be judged so harshly.

"I judge you not harshly yet: I say that evil will come unless you flee from it," said Mr. Brandon. "Don't you care for yourself?—for your good name? Is it nothing to you whether you turn out a scamp or a gentleman?"

To look at Tod just then, it was a great deal.

"Have you any reverence for your father?—for the memory of your mother? Then you will do a little violence to your own inclinations, even though it be hard and difficult—more difficult than to get a double first; harder than having the best tooth in your head drawn—and take your leave of that lady for ever. For your own sake, Joe; for your own sake!"

Tod was pulling gently at his whiskers.

"Send all folly to the wind, Joseph Todhetley! Say to yourself, for God and myself will I strive henceforth! It only needs a little steady resolution; and you can call it up if you choose. You shall always find a friend in me. Write down on a bit of paper the sums you owe, and I'll give you a cheque to cover them. Come, shake hands upon it."

"You are very kind, sir," gasped Tod, letting his hand meet old Brandon's.

"I hope you will let me be kind. Why, lad, you should have had more spirit than to renew an acquaintanceship with a false girl; an adventurer, who has gone about the country stealing jewels."

"Stealing jewels!" echoed Tod.

"Stealing jewels, lad. Did you never know it? She took Miss Deveen's emeralds at Whitney Hall."

"Oh, that was a mistake," said Tod, cheerfully. "She explained it to me."

"A mistake, was it! Explained it to you, did she! When?"

"At Oxford: before she had been here above a day or two. She introduced the subject herself, sir, saying she supposed I had heard something about it, and what an absurd piece of business the suspecting her was; altogether a mistake."

"Ah, she's a wily one, Joe," said Mr. Brandon. "Johnny Ludlow could have told you whether it was a mistake or not. Why, boy, she stole the stones out of Miss Deveen's own dressing-room, and went up to London the next day, or the next but one, and pledged them the same night at a pawnbroker's, in a false name, and gave a false account of herself. Moreover, when it was brought home to her, she confessed all upon her knees to Miss Deveen, and sued for mercy."

Tod looked from Mr. Brandon to me. At the time of the discovery, he had had a hint given him of the fact, with a view of more effectually weaning him from Sophie Chalk, but not the particulars.

"It's true, Todhetley," said Mr. Brandon, nodding his head. "You may judge, therefore, whether she is a nice kind of person for you to be seen beauing about Oxford streets in the face and eyes of the dons." And Tod winced again, and bit his lips.

Mr. Brandon rose, taking both Tod's hands in his, and said a few solemn words in the kindest tone I had ever heard him speak; wrung his hands, nodded good-night to me, and was gone. Tod walked about the room a bit, whistling softly to make a show of indifference, and looking miserably cut up.

"Is what he said true?" he asked me presently, stopping by the mantelpiece again: "about the emeralds?"

"Every word of it."

"Then why on earth could you not open your mouth and tell me, Johnny Ludlow?"

"I thought you knew it. I'm sure you were told of it at the time. Had I brought up the matter again later, you'd have been fit to punch me into next week, Tod."

"Let's hear the details—shortly."

I went over them all; shortly, as he said; but omitting none. Tod stood in silence, never once interrupting.

"Did the Whitneys know of this?"

"Anna did."

"Anna!"

"Yes. Anna had suspected Sophie from the first. She saw her steal out of Miss Deveen's room, and saw her sewing something into her stays at bed-time. But Anna kept it to herself until discovery had come."

Tod could frown pretty well on ordinary occasions, but I never saw a frown like the one on his brow as he listened. And I thought—I thought—it was meant for Sophie Chalk.

"Lady Whitney, I expect, knows it all now, Tod. Perhaps Helen also. Old Brandon went over to the Hall to spend the day, and it was in consequence of what he heard from Lady Whitney and Miss Deveen that he came down here to look us up."

"Meaning me," said Tod. "Not us. Use right words, Johnny."

"They did not know, you see, that Sophie Chalk was married. And they must have noticed that you cared for her."

Tod made no comment. He just leaned against the shelf in silence. I was stacking my books.

"Good-night, Johnny," he quietly said, without any appearance of resentment; and went into his room.

The next day was Palm Sunday. Tod lay in bed with a splitting headache, could not lift his head from the pillow, and his skin was as sallow as an old gander's. "Glad to hear it," said Mr. Brandon, when I told him; "it will give him a quiet day for reflection."

A surprise awaited me that morning, and Mr. Brandon also. Miss Deveen was at Oxford, with Helen and Anna Whitney. They had arrived the evening before, and meant to stay and go up with Bill and with us. I did not tell Tod: in fact, he seemed too ill to be spoken to, his head covered with the bedclothes.

You can't see many a finer sight than the Broad Walk presents on the evening of Palm Sunday. Every one promenades there, from the dean downwards. Our party went together: Miss Deveen, Helen, and Anna; Bill, I, and Mr. Brandon.

We were in the middle of the walk; and it was at its fullest, when Tod came up. He was better, but looked worn and ill. A flush of surprise came into his face when he saw who we had with us, and he shook hands with the ladies nearly in silence.

"Oxford has not mended your looks, Mr. Todhetley," said Miss Deveen.

"I have one of my bad headaches to-day," he answered. "I get them now and then."

The group of us were turning to walk on, when in that moment there approached Sophie Chalk. Sophie in a glistening blue silk, and flowers, and jingling ornaments, and kid gloves. She was coming up to us as bold as brass with her fascinating smile, when she saw Miss Deveen, and stopped short. Miss Deveen passed on without notice of any kind; Helen really did not see her; Anna, always gentle and kind, slightly bowed. Even then Madam Sophie's native impudence came to her aid. She saw they meant to shun her, and she nodded and smiled at Tod, and made as though she would stop him for a chat. He took off his cap to her, and went on. Anna's delicate face had flushed, and his own was white enough for its coffin.

Miss Deveen held Tod's hand in parting. "I am so glad to have met you again," she cordially said; "we are all glad. We shall see you often, I hope, until we go up together. And all you young people are coming to me for a few days in the Easter holidays. Friends cannot afford too long absences from one another in this short life. Good-bye; and mind you get rid of your headache for to-morrow. There; shake hands with Helen and Anna."

He did as he was bid. Helen was gay as usual; Anna rather shy. Her pretty blue eyes glanced up at Tod's, and he smiled for the first time that day. Sophie Chalk might have fascinated three parts of his heart away, but there was a corner in it remaining for Anna Whitney.

I did not do it intentionally. Going into our room the next day, a sheet of paper with some writing on it lay on the table, the ink still wet. Supposing it was some message just left for me by Tod, I went up to read it, and caught the full sense of the lines.

"DEAR MRS. EVERTY,

"I have just received your note. I am sorry that I cannot drive you   out to-day—and fear that I shall not be able to do so at all. Our friends, who are staying here, have to receive the best part of my leisure time.

"Faithfully yours,
"J. TODHETLEY."

And I knew by the contents of the note, by its very wording even, that the crisis was past, and Tod saved.

"Thank you, Johnny! Perhaps you'll read your own letters another time. That's mine."

He had come out of his room with the envelopes and sealing-wax.

"I beg your pardon, Tod. I thought it was a message you had left for me, seeing it lie open."

"You've read it, I suppose?"

"Yes, or just as good. My eyes seemed to take it all in at once; and I am as glad as though I had had a purse of gold given to me."

"Well, it's no use trying to fight against a stream," said he, as he folded the note. "And if I had known the truth about the emeralds, why—there'd have been no bother at all."

"Putting the emeralds out of the question, she is not a nice person to know, Tod. And there's no telling what might have come of it."

"I suppose not. When the two paths, down-hill and up-hill, cross each other, as Brandon put it, and the one is pleasant and the other is not, one has to do a bit of battle with one's self in choosing the right."

And something in his face told me that in the intervening day and nights, he had battled with himself as few can battle; fought strenuously with the evil, striven hard for the good, and come out a conqueror.

"It has cost you pain."

"Somewhat, Johnny. There are few good things in the way of duty but what do cost man pain—as it seems to me. The world and a safe conscience will give us back our recompense."

"And heaven too, Tod."

"Ay, lad; and heaven."

MRS HENRY WOOD (aka ELLEN WOOD) – A CONCISE BIBLIOGRAPHY

Danesbury House (1860)
East Lynne (1861)
The Elchester College Boys (1861)
A Life's Secret (1862)
Mrs. Halliburton's Troubles (1862)
The Channings (1862)
The Foggy Night at Offord: A Christmas Gift for the Lancashire Fund (1863)
The Shadow of Ashlydyat (1863)
Verner's Pride (1863)
Lord Oakburn's Daughters (1864)
Oswald Cray (1864)
Trevlyn Hold; or, Squire Trevlyn's Heir (1864)
William Allair; or, Running away to Sea (1864)
Mildred Arkell: A Novel (1865)

The Argosy (1865)
Elster's Folly: A Novel (1866)
St. Martin's Eve: A Novel (1866)
Lady Adelaide's Oath (1867)
Orville College: A Story (1867)
The Ghost of the Hollow Field (1867)
Anne Hereford: A Novel (1868)
Castle Wafer; or, The Plain Gold Ring (1868)
The Red Court Farm: A Novel (1868)
Roland Yorke: A Novel (1869)
Bessy Rane: A Novel (1870)
George Canterbury's Will (1870)
Dene Hollow (1871)
Within the Maze: A Novel (1872)
The Master of Greylands (1872)
Johnny Ludlow (1874)
Bessy Wells (1875)
Told in the Twilight: Containing 'Parkwater' and nine short stories (1875)
Adam Grainger: A Tale (1876)
Edina (1876)
Our Children (1876)
Parkwater: With four other tales (1876)
Pomeroy Abbey (1878)
Lady Adelaide (1879)
Johnny Ludlow, Second Series (1880)
A Tale of Sin and Other Tales (1881)
Court Netherleigh: A Novel (1881)
About Ourselves (1883)
Johnny Ludlow. Third Series (1885)
Lady Grace and Other Stories (1887)
The Story of Charles Strange (1888)
Featherston's Story. A Tale by Johnny Ludlow (1889)
The Unholy Wish and Other Stories (1890)
The House of Halliwell. A Novel (1890)
Ashley and Other Stories (1897)
Victor Serenus (1898)
Johnny Ludlow. Fifth series (1899)
Johnny Ludlow. Sixth series (1899)

Translations
Les Channing. Traduit de l'Anglais par Mme Abric-Encontre (1864)
Les Filles de Lord Oakburn: Roman traduit de l'anglais par L. Bochet (1876)
La Gloire des Verner: Roman traduit de l'anglais par L. de L'Estrive (1878)
Le Serment de Lady Adelaïde: Roman traduit de l'anglais par Léon Bochet (1878)

www.ingramcontent.com/pod-product-compliance
Lightning Source LLC
Chambersburg PA
CBHW050836180626
46814CB00007B/2482